On the waves
hu

MW01148234

The Scarlet Deep

Patrick Murphy, the immortal leader of Dublin, has been trying to stem the tide of Elixir washing into his territory, but nothing seems to stop the vampire drug. While others in the immortal world work to cure the creeping insanity that Elixir brings, Murphy has been invited to London to join a summit of leaders hoping to discover who is shipping the drug.

Anne O'Dea, Murphy's former lover, retreated from public life over one hundred years ago to help immortals in need... and to heal her own broken heart. Though powerful connections keep her insulated from the violence of vampire politics, even Anne is starting to feel the effects of Elixir in her isolated world. The human blood supply has been tainted, and with Anne's unique needs, even those closest to her might be in danger. Not just from infection, but from Anne's escalating bloodlust.

When Anne and Murphy are both called to London, they're forced to confront a connection as immortal as they are. While they search for a traitor among allies, they must also come to terms with their past. Behind the safe façade of politics, old hungers still burn, even as an ancient power threatens the fate of the Elemental World.

"A work of staggeringly well-written romance, *The Scarlet Deep* saturates the reader in the soul of the story, and gives them a sexy narrative they can really sink their teeth into. Elizabeth Hunter has once again proven she is a literary tempest..."
—Cat Bowen, *Breakfast to Bed Blog*

Praise for the Irin Chronicles

"THE SCRIBE is a perfect marriage of urban fantasy with tinges of romance. Creating a world in which ancient evil battles for turf and the heart, and the innocent are trapped in the crossfire, [Hunter] leads us on a riveting journey through the streets of Old Istanbul and old magic. An awesome ride!"
—Killian McRae, *author of 12.21.12*

"Hunter has created a magnificent world of amazing characters, entangled in a web of deceit, danger, loss, power, politics, and love that will have your heart racing time and time again."
—Sandra Hoover, *Cross My Heart Reviews*

"Complex and emotionally charged… *The Secret* is an amazing finale that showcases all of Hunter's storytelling skills." 4.5 stars
—Jill M. Smith, *RT Magazine*

Praise for the Elemental Mysteries

"A Hidden Fire is saturated with mystery, intrigue, and romance… This book will make my paranormal romance top ten of 2011."
—*Better Read Than Dead*

"Elemental Mysteries turned into one of the best paranormal series I've read this year. It's sharp, elegant, clever, evenly paced without dragging its feet, and at the same time, emotionally intense."
—*Nocturnal Book Reviews*

"An enticing and addictive epic."
—Douglas C. Meeks

The Scarlet Deep

An Elemental World Novel

ELIZABETH HUNTER

The Scarlet Deep
Copyright © 2015
Elizabeth Hunter
ISBN: 9781512268393

Cover artist: Damonza
Editor: Lora Gasway
Editor: Anne Victory
Formatter: Elizabeth Hunter

Elizabeth Hunter
PO Box 8085
Visalia, CA 93290
U.S.A.

For more information about the author or her work, please visit:
ElizabethHunterWrites.com

For my dear friend Sarah

You have been a source of joy, wisdom,
generosity, and enthusiasm for so many years now.
What a year you've had, my friend.
I only wish hugs could cross oceans.

This book is dedicated to the love
of sisters everywhere.

ALSO BY ELIZABETH HUNTER

The Irin Chronicles

The Scribe
The Singer
The Secret

The Elemental Mysteries

A Hidden Fire
This Same Earth
The Force of Wind
A Fall of Water
Lost Letters & Christmas Lights

The Elemental World

Building From Ashes
Waterlocked
Blood and Sand
The Bronze Blade
The Scarlet Deep

The Elemental Legacy

Shadows and Gold

The Cambio Springs Mysteries

Shifting Dreams
Desert Bound

Contemporary Romance

The Genius and the Muse

Water, water, everywhere,
And all the boards did shrink;
Water, water, everywhere,
Nor any drop to drink.

—<u>The Rime of the Ancient Mariner</u>

Prologue

WHEN SHE DREAMED, she dreamed of death and madness. Of the deep and of forgotten things. The moon shone full through the water, and the drifting weeds surrounded her as she stared into the night sky.

The water enveloped her. The pulse of the current took her, and she drifted deeper.

Past the edge of land.

Beyond the silken brush of reeds.

She sank past the touch of moonlight, where the chill of the water crept into her bones and settled her soul.

But the hunger…

The ever-present gnaw in her belly, like the ache of a newborn, stalked her.

In the cradle of darkness, she bit down and drank her own blood.

Chapter One

THE MAN SAT ACROSS from Murphy with desperate, angry eyes. He knew he had no recourse . Nothing he could say to the vampire leader of Dublin would make Patrick Murphy change his mind.

Perfect.

"Andrew," Murphy said, his voice cool, "what did you think was going to happen? Did you think I was going to sit idly by and watch as you tried to maneuver the Blue Delta contract out from under me? That was my contract, Andrew. Just because the Americans will always go with the lowest bidder doesn't make that the way we do business."

"Mr. Murphy—"

"Just Murphy, Andrew." He spread his hands, palms up. "We're not strangers. I thought I knew you better than this. Thought we had respect between us."

He saw Brigid roll her eyes in the corner, but he ignored her. His eyes kept focus on the nervous human across from him.

Garvey wore a work shirt and pants. His clothes and carriage spoke of a man who worked on the water and had since he was a boy. But Murphy also noted that the man's shirt was carefully pressed, even if the pocket was torn. Murphy noted things like that because the measure of a man was often seen in the details.

Garvey was no slob; he had ambition.

Nor was he a threat to Murphy. The man knew about vampires; his father had worked in the docklands before him and knew how things ran. The American contract was Murphy's to turn down. He had a reputation to maintain after all. He needed to make a point with the human, and he wouldn't let a little thing like actual business interests stand in his way.

"I do respect you, Murphy." Garvey's voice said one thing, but his eyes said frustration. The young man had grown up working with his dad and had hustled through the grey areas of the docklands in order to improve his lot. Murphy could respect that. He also knew that Garvey was leaning closer to the darker shades of grey on a few deals lately. "You know my da—"

"Never would have expected Tim's son to pull something like this." Murphy made sure to keep his voice low. He didn't need to project anger. Not anymore. He was aiming for disappointment. "I had people lined up for that contract, Andrew."

He hadn't.

"I had plans for those people."

He didn't.

"And now what do I tell them, Andrew? What do I tell those people who were counting on me?"

Murphy took a deep, considering breath he didn't need. Vampires, after all, had no need to breathe. As long as he had blood and water to draw his elemental strength, he'd last until God and all the saints returned. The breath wasn't for Murphy, the breath was for Andrew Garvey.

He looked down and shuffled some papers on his desk. Papers he'd had his assistant, Angie, bring in a few moments after Andrew Garvey had sat down across from his desk. He lifted up the "Blue Delta Industries" file and paged through it.

You're a bastard, the first paper read.

Murphy didn't let the smile break through his solemn exterior as he perused the papers Angie had typed out at her desk outside his office.

You had no interest in that shipping contract until you heard Blue Delta went to a human first.

He flipped through them one by one, scanning the mostly blank pages as Garvey squirmed across from him.

Pint after work, boss? One of the new lads thinks he can beat you, and I need the money. Declan must have slipped that one in. Declan was full of it. Murphy knew the man lived like a monk and saved like a miser. He didn't need the money. He just wanted to show the new employees what was what.

Andrew Garvey is a nice young man, and his wife just had a baby girl.

Angie was being a touch dramatic, wasn't she? It wasn't as if he was going to kill the human. He just needed to scare him. And maybe remind Garvey why Murphy had been stricter about who did business on his docks the past few years. Despite what Angie thought, this was about more than just a minor human shipping contract.

"I expected courtesy from Tim Garvey's son." Murphy steepled his fingers together and leaned his elbows on his desk.

"I never intended…"

Murphy brought his dark eyes up to lock on Garvey's exasperated gaze, and the man fell silent.

"It's not respectful to bring cargo into my city without knowing what it is, Andrew."

The human's face want from frustrated to downright pale.

"I… There hasn't been any—"

"Don't ever lie to me."

Garvey shut his mouth.

"It's one thing to take a bit that doesn't go on the books." Murphy's voice was barely over a whisper. "We've all shipped a few crates of this and that, haven't we?"

Garvey was trying to smile, but it wasn't working. "Just a few crates, sir. Even my da—"

"But you didn't know what was in those crates, did you? And 'we don't ask questions' isn't an acceptable answer anymore, Andrew. Not for anyone who wants to call me a friend."

4

Murphy had him. Andrew Garvey had gone from confused, to irritated, to angry, to frustrated, and now he was at defeated.

Garvey knew the vampire had laid down the law among those in the know that he would be watching more closely. The drug problem had gone out of control, and one drug in particular had devastated his city only two years before. A drug there was no cure for yet. A drug that killed both humans *and* vampires.

Elixir.

It was supposed to be a cure-all, for mortal and immortal alike. Healing power for humans and a cure for bloodlust all at once.

It wasn't.

"I want to keep my friends in business, Andrew. And I can't do that if they're not open with me."

Garvey leaned forward. "I want to make this right."

Gotcha.

Murphy took another deep breath as Brigid had a suspicious coughing fit in the corner of the room.

"I know you do, lad."

"How do I make this right?"

"The Blue Delta contract—"

"Is yours." The human nodded. "Absolutely. I'll withdraw my bid tomorrow."

"Now, now." Murphy held up a hand. "You already have time and money invested in that. I'm not interested in putting you out of business. I need good people around. Dependable ones."

Garvey nodded enthusiastically. "Absolutely."

"You've a family, don't you, Andrew?"

"Yes, sir." He saw the man grow pale.

Christ, maybe he did need to lay off a bit. He wasn't going after the human's little wife and babies.

Murphy let a smile touch his lips. "I consider my employees my family."

"I know you do, sir." Garvey relaxed a bit.

"I take care of the people who take care of me. And I know you're just as interested—being a family man—in making the city as safe as it can be."

"I am, Murphy."

Murphy let the silence fall between them as he stared at Garvey. He could hear the man's pulse pick up.

It was difficult—very difficult—to not see the man as prey when his heart beat like that. The scent of his fear filled the room. The tang of adrenaline. Murphy glanced back at Brigid to see the younger vampire staring at the back of Garvey's neck with heated eyes.

"*Tóg go bog é,*" he said in a voice only she would hear. *Take it easy.*

Brigid was younger and still struggled with control. He could feel the room heat up from her amnis. While Murphy's elemental affinity was water, Brigid's was fire.

Unstable. Highly dangerous. And excellent for his reputation. It was worth putting up with her temper if it meant having a fire vampire on his payroll.

"No more unquestioned cargo," Murphy said quietly. "It's not a friendly thing to do."

"Sure thing, Murphy."

"And I know you'll be taking a hit," he added. "I'll keep that in mind. I have some contracts I could use a sub for. Local jobs."

The human's face had morphed from scared to grateful. "You'd do that?"

"I told you, Andrew. I take care of my friends."

"Some of these lads—"

"I can send Tom or one of my people around more," Murphy said. "Make sure everyone knows where things stand with you and me. Make sure no one causes trouble. If that would suit you, of course. It's your business, Andrew."

Garvey nodded. "I'd be grateful."

And I'll be grateful for that fat envelope I know you'll have ready.

Murphy picked up the fake file and shuffled a few more papers.

The last in the stack read, *Don't make me poison your tea, Patrick. It won't kill you, but it will give you an awful stomachache you will deserve one hundred percent.*

He let the smile curve the corner of his mouth. Oh, Angie. What a treasure.

Murphy closed the file and stood. "I don't want to keep you any later. Thank you for coming by, Andrew. I know it's after dinner hour with your family."

"It's no problem, Murphy." Garvey stood with him and held out a hand. "Glad we were able to get this cleared up."

Murphy smiled, letting the warmth of it flood the room. He pushed the feeling of security and contentment up the human's arm, knowing that Andrew Garvey would lay his head down in bed tonight knowing that Patrick Murphy was damn near his best friend.

"I know you'll do well with that Blue Delta contract," he said. "Come to me if you have any questions, yes?"

"I will."

"And no more unquestioned loads, yes?" His face grew serious again with just a touch of concern. "We need to know what's coming into our city, don't we? For everyone's safety."

"Yes, sir."

Murphy clasped his other hand around Garvey's and gave it a friendly squeeze. "Good man."

HE tasted the whiskey Brigid poured in two glasses between them.

"You know," she said, "Before I started working for you, I used to think you were serious. And polite."

"I am serious." He lifted one eyebrow. "And Angie taught me manners, so any complaints you'll have to take up with her."

"You, Patrick Murphy, are a fantastic con."

He added more than a dash of water and sipped again, letting the potent taste of the liquor linger on his tongue. Vampire senses were far keener than human, hence the disproportionate amount of water.

"A con?" he asked. "I don't know what you're talking about."

"A confidence man, as the Americans would call it. A grifter. A swindler."

Murphy raised his drink. "I did not swindle young Mr. Garvey out of anything he did not want to give me, Brigid."

"You managed to scare the shite out of Andrew Garvey about taking illegal cigarettes *and* ensure protection payments from him for the foreseeable future. All the while making him feel grateful you were letting him keep a contract you had no intention of pursuing in the first place."

He let the smile grow. "I did do that, didn't I?"

"Admit it, you're a con artist."

Murphy grinned. "Of course I am." He clinked the side of her glass and took another breath, this time to relax. "Impressed?"

"Jesus." Brigid couldn't hold back the smile. "You are a bastard, aren't you?"

"Both literally and figuratively. Does your former priest of a husband know you're taking the Lord's name in vain like that, young lady?"

She couldn't stop the low rumble of laughter. It almost made Murphy sad she'd turned down an alliance with him.

Brigid Connor would have been a perfect romantic partner on paper, but she was hardly his type personally. Most of the time, Brigid looked like a very angry pixie with an acerbic sense of humor, a short temper, and a fondness for hair dye. This month, her dark cap of hair had a distinctly purple cast. The month before, it had been blue.

No, not his type at all, though she made a truly excellent friend and a half-decent drinking partner. She preferred soccer to boxing, but no one was perfect.

"You just can't help yourself, can you? You're the same way with the human girls, though they like to think it's charming. Is everything a con to you?"

"Why shouldn't it be?" He set down his drink and spread his hands. "There are two sides to every job, and the best jobs end with everyone walking away smiling. Just like young Andrew. He'll be more careful of what he allows on his boats, and with my protection behind him, those who want to move things more… discreetly will have greater confidence in his operation. I'm happy. He's happy."

"And you'll get a cut from all of it."

He raised his glass. "Naturally."

"Why did he try it?"

Murphy shrugged. "They always do. The younger humans—the ones who haven't been involved in the quieter aspects of things—will take over for their mam or dad. And they see…" He motioned to the elegant suit his tailor had finished only last week. "This. The suits and the haircut. The manicure and the manners."

"Don't forget the season tickets to the symphony."

He nodded. "Exactly."

Brigid smiled. "How scary could he be? He's a *modern* vampire. Not a monster at all."

He sipped his drink as Brigid continued.

"They push a little, and you let them. They push a little more…"

"It's only to be expected," Murphy said, letting a smile touch his lips. "After all, I'm not a monster."

"Until they push a little too far. Get just a bit over their head. And then you pounce."

A door slammed somewhere in the building and they both fell silent.

"Are you judging me, Brigid?"

She took a deep breath and crossed her arms, staring at him. "No," she finally said. "Everyone has to learn how the real world works eventually. You're hardly the worst teacher out there."

"Now you're just trying to hurt my feelings."

"But you are a right bastard."

Murphy grinned. "And you're still drinking with me."

"I suppose you've lured me in like the others. Does anyone really know you, Patrick Murphy, or do they only see the charm?"

"Ah, Brigid." He resisted the urge to glance at the seascape hanging opposite his desk. The oil painting had captured the sun bouncing off the water of the inlet on Galway Bay. "Don't you know? The charm *is* me."

"Liar."

He shrugged and decided to steer the subject away from introspection. "Want to join me and the boys at the club?"

Brigid finished her glass and stood. "I may drink with you, but I'm not one of your slags. Besides"—she winked at him—"my man is back from London tonight, and I have far better things to do than watch you boys beat each other bloody."

"Such a good girl you are."

"Far better than you could get," she tossed over her shoulder.

"Such a shame you're committing mortal sins with the good Father."

The gun was pointed at his face before he could start laughing.

"Don't make me shoot you again, Murphy."

Declan slipped in as Brigid walked out.

"Hi, Brig. Bye, Brig." Declan turned to him. "What'd you do to piss her off? Ask her if she'd made her confession again?"

"Tell Carwyn I said hello," Murphy shouted after her.

"Oh, you like to live dangerously, boss." Declan picked up a glass and helped himself to a whiskey. "Started without me, did you?"

His second-in-command and second-oldest child had an eager look on his face, far from the somber visage he presented to most of Murphy's crew. To the outside world, Patrick Murphy carried the charm and sophistication in the operation, Declan O'Malley held the razor-sharp mind, and Tom Dargin was the muscle. Only the three of them knew it wasn't as clear-cut as all that.

That was fine. Let the rest of the vampire world underestimate Murphy. He knew many questioned how he'd managed to hold on to Dublin with apparent ease. He was happy to take advantage of his reputation as a playboy. He also knew the quickest way to win a fight was to avoid one in the first place.

At least fights that weren't for his own amusement.

"How much is the pool up to now?"

"High enough."

"And how much did Brigid bet against me?"

"Only a hundred," Declan said. "She seemed a bit halfhearted about it too."

THE SCARLET DEEP

"I suppose someone has to do it, though it hardly seems fair to keep taking her money like this."

THE Buzzcocks were screaming about falling in love when the new lad landed his second punch to Murphy's jaw. He felt his lip split. Tasted the blood as it flooded his mouth. The crowd around the ring shouted as Murphy grinned. He could feel one eye swelling up, and he resisted the urge to laugh.

Yes.

He'd missed this. The pain sent a surge of adrenaline and endorphins through his body. If there was one thing he missed about mortal life, it was this.

Pain. Pleasure. Aches and breaks. When he was boxing, he felt alive.

He always held back against human opponents. The rule with the lads was he couldn't use vampire speed or strength… as much as that was possible. He'd been a vampire for over one hundred sixty years. It was hard to remember what "human strength" felt like.

Too often, immortality was marked by long periods of feeling more and more absent from life. He loved the power he'd attained. Loved the wealth and the influence—and yes, the finer things he'd acquired. But he missed the variety of mortal life. The highs and lows. There was a period of time when he'd felt alive again, but that feeling had left when she did.

A blow to his kidney knocked him back into the moment. Was it time? Had the new lad let down his guard? Murphy danced in the corner, fists up as the music changed and the pounding beat of the Clash filled the basement pub he kept open for his men.

He bounced on his toes, only half listening to Tom cursing him from the corner.

It was a boys' club, he had no problem admitting it. Not that there was any lack of females. Two stared at him from the edge of the ring, eyeing his bloody torso with clear intent.

Human girls. Hmmm. Predictable and yet still entertaining.

Murphy picked up his head and leaned into the lad, landing one quick blow to his right kidney that knocked the wind out of him. The human stumbled back. Then Murphy tapped his jaw, playing a bit, and felt his knuckles split open.

The flash of red ignited the crowd.

Bloodthirsty. Damn, the humans were more bloodthirsty than the vampires.

He abandoned the taps when he saw the two girls' attention waver. They were getting tired of the fight, and Murphy had plans for them.

The lad landed one when his attention was diverted by the girls. Ah, women. At one time, he'd have two or three waiting to feed his appetites after a bout. Sadly, Elixir had changed all that, forcing him and his men to be cautious about where they drank their blood.

That didn't mean humans didn't have their uses.

He flexed his jaw and gave the young man a smile.

"Not bad," he said, spitting out the blood in his mouth. "Tired yet?"

The human was panting. "Can go all night, boss."

"Eh, so could I." Then with one roundhouse punch, Murphy laid him on the canvas. "Don't want to though. I've decided I have other plans."

The crowd erupted, and Tom threw him a towel. Murphy wiped up the blood even as he felt the cuts healing. By the time he reached the edge of the ring, his face was perfect again. He ran a damp hand through the thick black hair his mother had graced him with. He didn't sweat, but as a water vampire, he drew his element to himself as he healed, giving the illusion that he was dripping sweat even if his skin was cool.

"Better go out there," Tom said. "He's a good lad. Don't want him to get down on himself."

"No. He did well. I'd fight him again. Declan should be happy."

"Eh, it's getting harder and harder to find lads to bet against you."

"Is my wallet heavier walking out than walking in?"

Tom smiled his crooked smile. "Always, boss."

"Then you'll hear no complaints from me."

Murphy took a few gulps from the thermos of warm pig's blood that Tom had brought for him, then took another healthy gulp of water to wash it down. He turned and tossed the towel to the boy on the side of the ring, then walked to the center of the canvas and held out a hand for his opponent, who was being helped up by his mates.

"All right there?"

"Jaysus, boss, you've a fist like a hammer," the boy said through smiling, bloody lips. "I guess the rumors were true, eh?"

The two human girls had shoved their way to the ropes, smiling at him with ruby-red lips. He noted their appearance. One blond, one brunette. Alike in height, wearing similar little black dresses and matching smiles for the vampire lord of Dublin.

Lovely. A matched set.

Murphy smiled at the lad and patted his cheek. "What's your name, son?"

"Ronald, sir."

"Well, Ron, you held your own. If I didn't have fangs, I'd be feeling your fists tomorrow, wouldn't I?"

"Thank you, sir."

"Come back and fight again."

The young man nodded happily. "I will, sir."

"And Ronald?"

"Yes, boss?"

Murphy tossed him one more smile before he walked toward the two girls. "You're right. The rumors about me are true."

And with a hearty roar from his lads, Murphy left the club with a heavier wallet and a matched set.

Chapter Two

ANNE O'DEA NODDED, jotting down a few sentences in the small notebook she kept by her easy chair.

"That's very interesting, Alexander. But how did it make you feel?"

"Feel?" His public school accent was clipped with annoyance.

"Yes. Remember, part of this therapy is learning how to rediscover your connection with your emotions."

"I'm not sure I want that." The Englishman glanced at her notebook. "You... don't use names, do you?"

Anne tried not to sigh audibly. It was only Alexander's second visit, and wind vampires were typically paranoid. She shouldn't have been surprised, even if her new patient had been discreetly referred by a mutual acquaintance.

"As I have said, I never use names. And these notes are for my eyes only."

She saw the vampire's eyes narrow. "I wouldn't want my visits here to become known."

Anne let her fangs drop. "I hope you're not threatening me, Alexander. We both know that wouldn't be wise."

The wind vampire shrank back into his seat. "Of course not."

Anne's eyes flicked to a dark stain on the floor near the couch where her clients most often sat. It was only partially covered by a rug. It wouldn't do to let the more… volatile patients forget she was as much a predator as they were. For while the human world might see a quiet, sweet-faced woman in her late twenties with a generous figure and vivid sea-green eyes, her patients would see weakness.

And weakness in her world got you killed quickly.

"Now," she said, resuming her notes. "Let's continue talking about your sire."

He droned on, as typical a case of ennui as she'd ever seen. Alexander didn't seem a bad sort. He treated his human employees fairly, he only killed when necessary, and he mostly kept to himself. His sudden struggle to avoid the sun was likely a symptom of age.

When most of your patients lived hundreds of years, weariness was a common malady. Oh, there were fancier names for it. And narcissism inevitably crept in on many of her kind. But Anne had known for years that their state—immortality—was simply not a natural one. There was a reason most of the planet kicked off after seventy or eighty years. Most of them happily. It took a particular kind of personality to survive forever with mental health intact.

Alexander, she suspected, did not have that kind of verve. He was three hundred years old, from what he said, which likely meant he was closer to her own age, two hundred and some. He had only one child, whom he was estranged from, and more money than friends. Plus he was a wind vampire, which meant he eschewed the roots needed for a long and happy life. In her experience, long-lived wind vampires had either established a very loyal networks of friends or were sociopaths.

Sometimes both.

"Your son," she said. "Tell me about him."

She saw her patient tense, but he didn't make the mistake of letting his hackles rise again. "He has his own life."

"Is he mated? Does he have any children of his own?"

She thought he might not answer for a time.

"He… has a partner. I don't like her."

"Why not?"

"She's an earth vampire."

"Ah."

Anne wasn't surprised. Prejudice based on sex or ethnicity was uncommon in older immortals, who had usually seen too much of the world to be narrow-minded. But prejudice against other elements... that was more expected.

"Do you feel as if she limits him? Has she stifled his nature by asking him to settle?"

"No. And yet he doesn't roam as often as he once did. She has changed him."

"I see." And change was always difficult. Immortals may look young, but Anne knew the truth better than most of her kind.

Vampires were—by and large—very attractive old people. And like most of the elderly, change was difficult.

In the past twenty years, the rapid rate of change in the human world had left many of their kind floundering. Water vampires, with their innate curiosity and adaptability, and earth vampires, who lived "off the grid" and had stronger family ties, tended to be the best adapted to the modern world. Wind vampires, whose roaming nature and tendency toward paranoia was exacerbated by human technology, had a much harder time adjusting.

And fire vampires, the rarest of their kind?

In Anne's opinion, every one of them needed to be in therapy.

"Alexander, I'm going to suggest you try to reconnect with your son. Did you have any kind of falling out? Any arguments?"

"No. We simply went our separate ways. It's the nature of things, and he was well provided for."

"I'm sure he was, but I think reconnecting with him might be beneficial to you both."

His shoulders stiffened. "I don't need him."

"None of us is meant to be alone," she said soothingly. "And your human staff is obviously devoted. But they are mortal. How old is your butler?"

"Eighty?" Alexander shrugged. "Ninety? I'm not sure."

"He's quite elderly then. Is he in good health?" The loss of a long-time servant could push a vampire like her patient over the edge.

"He is. I've considered…" For the first time, the Englishman seemed truly ill at ease. "Do you know anything about Elixir?"

Anne froze. "I know it's very dangerous. And is a death sentence for humans. As a doctor, I would never recommend it."

"He's old anyway. If it could give him a few more years…"

"As I said, I wouldn't advise it. From what I've heard, it's a very horrible death."

"Oh." The Englishman looked put out. "Well, probably not a good idea, I suppose."

"Do you know anyone who has Elixir?"

The man's cagey expression gave her nothing. "I travel. There are ways to acquire what one needs."

"I see."

Damn. She needed to talk to her sister in Belfast, and she'd have to inform Terrance Ramsay in London. She had ways of warning those in leadership without breaking confidentiality, and Elixir wasn't something to be taken lightly.

You should tell Murphy too.

She pushed the thought to the back of her head and wrapped up her session with the patient. She put him on the schedule for six months later, an average span between visits for her vampire clients.

Anne took Alexander's hand at the door to her visiting room. "I do hope you'll consider calling on your son."

The brush of amnis that passed between them wasn't anything the other vampire would remark on. It was friendly and warm. Anne held on for a few moments, "pushing" a sense of well-being toward him along with a strong suggestion that he visit his son.

It wasn't much. Nothing her patient might be able to detect. But Anne had little doubt he'd follow through on her "suggestion."

Vampires could plant far stronger impressions in humans, of course. But the fact that Anne had any influence at all was her most closely guarded secret. The revelation of her "gift" would get her killed immediately, no matter whose daughter she was.

Vampires held fast to the confidence that amnis—the immortal current that connected them to the elements and gave them life—worked as a shield around their mind, protecting it from the manipulation humans were vulnerable to. And for most vampires, it was true.

But Anne had learned early on in her life that she had just enough influence over those around her that she could nudge them into doing her will.

An instant death sentence for her should her secret get out.

She lived quietly. She had strong allies. And she had worked very hard to become a trusted individual to people like her client. After all, being the one entrusted with secrets held its own kind of security.

She walked with Alexander down to the car where his driver was waiting.

"It was good to see you, Anne."

"And you. Safe travels."

Anne watched the lights retreat before she wandered down to her dock overlooking Galway Bay. She sat on the edge overlooking the quiet inlet where grass and rushes rustled in the night breeze. The moon reflected off the water, and the damp salt air soothed her senses. She glanced around to make sure the night birds and the fishes were her only company, then she stripped off her woolen wrap and dove into the sea.

She felt the vast strength of the ocean at her back, holding her body up, surrounding her, embracing her.

Anne never felt quite as lonely in the ocean.

None of us is meant to be alone.

"Áine."

She ignored the memory of his voice on the wind, blaming it on the faint tug of the blood that whispered to her.

After one hundred years of solitude, it was hardly worth looking back.

Or at least that's what she told herself.

HER secretary, Ruth, popped her head in just minutes after Anne arrived at her office the next night.

"Brigid Connor is coming to see you tonight. I told her it was fine, yeah?"

Brigid was one of the few vampires to whom Ruth would give automatic entry. The human woman had been with Anne for over twenty years and had come to remind Anne of the russet-haired Irish terriers Ruth bred. Her wiry red curls were touched with grey, and her face was more lined, but Ruth was cheerful until provoked. Then she could become snappy, even to Anne's immortal clients.

But she had a soft spot for Brigid. The fire vampire had lived with Anne for a month after she'd turned, and the two of them had become confidants. They'd long ago severed their professional relationship. Now they were just friends. Brigid still made the two-and-a-half-hour drive for long weekends when she needed a break from Dublin life or her very intense mate.

"Sure thing," Anne said, already anticipating the visit. "Did she say when?"

"Early, I think. You don't have a client tonight until the Russian at three."

"Excellent."

Anne never used immortal's names in her appointment book. She lived a quiet life and was still under her powerful sire's aegis, but the secrets she knew made her a target. Most of the immortal world left her alone because attacking her or any humans she cared for would be considered too aggressive. Over time, Anne's home had come to be considered neutral territory. So far, all her clients respected this, but she still kept on constant alert.

"You've got free time now. Did you want to feed?" Ruth asked. "You haven't this month."

Anne let out a breath and felt her fangs aching in her gums. She pushed down the thread of unease in her belly and nodded.

"If you don't mind."

Ruth let out a tut and came into the office. "Don't be silly."

"I appreciate this so much."

"Don't be daft, love. Danny and I are happy to have the bit of extra, aren't we?"

Ruth and her husband Dan had become the sole humans Anne drank from now that the threat of Elixir had become a reality. She was old enough that a healthy pint a week should have kept her strong, but Ruth and Dan could only give her one pint a month between the two of them, and Anne had always needed more than the average amount of human blood. Other immortals kept larger household staff, but almost all supplemented with animal blood nowadays. Anne was no exception.

Ruth settled on the couch with Anne next to her, holding out a wrist and chattering about one of her terrier bitches that was about to have puppies. She and Dan had never been able to have children, so the animals had become the focus of all Ruth's maternal leanings.

Well, the terriers and Anne. Though Anne had hired her when Ruth was in her twenties, the woman had always tried to mother her. Amusing, yes, but not unwelcome. Anne was over two hundred years old, but she still enjoyed a bit of mothering from time to time.

"Ready then?"

Ruth smiled and nodded. Anne brushed a hand along the human's forearm, letting the amnis lull her into a light sleep. Both Ruth and Dan preferred it that way, and it made taking the blood slightly less awkward for all.

Anne felt her fangs grow long and she inhaled, taking in the sweet, familiar scent of her friend's blood at the wrist.

"Thank you," she whispered a moment before she bit.

Euphoria.

Anne lost herself in it for the first few swallows. There was nothing like human blood. No other substance on earth carried the taste of pure life to her. It was hardly surprising that newborns and ancients alike craved it. Blood was substance and heat. Air and water. It pulsed with the pounding of the human heart. Filled the arteries and tributaries of the body. Ebb and flow. Beat and brush…

She sank farther and drank.

Her senses heightened and she could hear the lick of water as the tide swelled the bay. A night heron croaked near the shore. The wind raked over the eaves, and the blood slid down her throat, silken heat and lush longing. She ached for more.

More.

Aware she was skating the fine edge of control, Anne closed her eyes and pulled away.

Taking a deep breath, she wrestled her bloodlust under control.

She'd waited too long.

It wasn't working. Human blood once a month was not enough. She hadn't battled her own instincts this way since she'd been a young vampire. There had to be some other solution. She needed to be drinking animal more often or hunting actively. Something to sooth the wild craving in her body.

Anne took another deep breath and returned to Ruth's wrist with a calmer head.

Having blood offered, even if Anne insisted on paying Ruth for it, was still a humbling experience. She needed this. Though she could exist on animal blood alone, only human blood offered the regenerating fifth element immortals needed to feed their bodies and their minds. Animals carried only a hint of it.

Anne had never wondered why the ancients tried to find the elixir of immortal life. A formula that would satisfy bloodlust would ease the aching weakness vampires had for humanity.

It was the great paradox of their lives: superior to humans in every way but desperately in need of them.

Anne felt as if her kind was at a crossroads in their history. As the technological revolution swept the world, it left vampires behind. Because of the amnis that kept them alive, they weren't able to access the technology that was making the world smaller and smaller. The immortal population was never more aware of their weaknesses and never more in need of humans to help them.

And that need fostered a burning resentment toward many who saw humanity as being closer to cattle than equals.

Savoring the last few swallows of live blood, Anne lingered over Ruth's wrist, touching her tongue to her fang to draw a drop of her own blood to heal Ruth before she pulled away and left the woman on the couch. She went to the small refrigerator in Anne's office and grabbed a glass of milk along with a freshly baked cookie.

It was a classic for a reason.

She gave Ruth a few minutes to wake up on her own, jotting down notes in her planner as her secretary's eyes fluttered open.

"Milk and cookie." Anne pointed to the tray on the side table.

"Chocolate chip?"

"Oatmeal raisin."

"Oh, you do love me," Ruth said with a cheerful wink. The woman was as hearty as the fisherfolk she and Anne were both descended from. In a few minutes, she'd be on her way, bustling and bossing with no sign of weakness. Dan was the same.

"So, do you want to join me and Brigid for tea?"

Ruth shook her head. "I've got a mountain of filing to do, along with the correspondence to mail. I'll leave you two. Plus she sounded as if she had business-type things to discuss."

"Oh?"

Brigid was one of Patrick Murphy's security officers. What business did she have that might concern Anne?

LIKE all vampires, Brigid was forced to drive a classic car. Electronics were too pervasive in newer vehicles. It varied with the elements. Earth and wind vampires weren't as reactive. Water vampires were more so. And fire vampires like Brigid were the worst. Brigid's mate, Carwyn, had restored a beauty of an old Triumph coupe for his wife, painted it a glossy black, and taken it to a mechanic that specialized in converting cars for immortals. As a result, the engine purred as Brigid made her way up Anne's road just a few minutes after midnight.

The woman who got out was small, but her stride was anything but delicate. Brigid Connor was one of the toughest women Anne had ever met. She was also a ferociously loyal friend.

"You got away late then?" Anne asked. "Oh! I like the purple. I wish I could do that with my hair. Drive go okay?"

"Fine." Brigid grabbed Anne in a hug. "Good, actually. Nice to stretch my eyes and get away from the lights."

Like many newer immortals, Brigid still had a hard time adjusting to city lights. Vampire eyes were more sensitive and electric lamps in the city could be overwhelming. Wearing sunglasses at night was often a necessity, not a fashion statement.

"So getting away late…"

"Carwyn's fault entirely." Brigid's face immediately softened. "I had to placate the man for leaving him for a few days. You'd think I was going for years the way he pouts."

Anne laughed. "He's adorable."

"And he knows it."

"It's good to see you," Anne said, guiding her inside. "A friendly visit or is something going on?"

Brigid fell back in her usual chair, a smile flirting at the corner of her mouth. "I don't know. Is there?"

"What are you on about?"

Brigid looked out the window to the slip of water that was visible. The moon was waning but still full, and the black water glittered silver in the night.

"I love this place," Brigid said. "I don't know if I ever told you how much it meant to be here after my turning."

"You're always welcome."

"I know." Brigid smiled. "You're so lovely. And this place suits you so well. Such a distinctive part of the world. The water and the land meeting here. So beautiful and isolated…"

Anne was starting to worry. Brigid didn't seem troubled, but why the philosophical rambling? It was hardly her way to make small talk. Usually she loathed it.

"Brigid—"

"Why does Murphy have a painting of your inlet hanging across from his desk?"

Well, shit.

"I always thought it was a bit odd." Brigid's smile had grown now. "He's got such a fantastic view of the river from his office, but his back is to it. Security, I thought at first, but that's not it. He'd hear anyone long before they could sneak up on him. No, he keeps his desk pointed away from the view because it's pointing at the wall where that painting is hanging. And it's not just a seascape, it's *your* inlet. Your view from the dock. It took me a while to figure out why it seemed so familiar, but it finally hit me."

Anne cleared her throat. "Aren't you clever?"

"I really am." The smile had turned into a grin. "He told me once that everyone called him Murphy"—Brigid lowered her voice and wiggled her eyebrows—"'except those who didn't,' which I thought was grossly egotistical of him at the time—check that, I still think it's egotistical. But then it hit me I knew who *did* call him Patrick." She crossed her arms. "Angie calls him Patrick, but then they had a brief fling in the seventies, didn't they? Know who else calls him Patrick?"

"Brigid…"

"You do! And then I thought, 'Why hasn't my dear friend Anne told me about her affair with the luscious Mr. Murphy?' Combine that with a very intriguing painting hanging in his office where he can look at it every night, and it makes me wonder what gossip you've been holding out on. So, my friend who wanted every detail of Carwyn's mad attempts at courtship, tell me the truth." Brigid leaned forward and narrowed her eyes. "Are the rumors true, and does he ever lose control outside the boxing ring?"

She knew it was completely unintentional, but Anne felt as if she'd been punched in the stomach.

"It was… far more than a fling, Brigid."

Some of her turmoil must have finally peeked through, because Brigid lost every hint of frivolity.

THE SCARLET DEEP

"Oh, Anne—"

"It was a long time ago. I… I didn't know about the painting. I used to paint a bit, but I never knew he took one."

Brigid was waving her hands. "No! I'm sorry. You don't have to say anything. I thought it was like Angie, and we tease them both— Shit!" Brigid slapped a hand over her mouth. "Probably shouldn't mention Angie. I'm an arse."

If there was anything Anne couldn't stand, it was a friend feeling uncomfortable in her presence. "Don't be silly. Like I said, it was long ago. We've both had relationships over the years. I know about Angie and… all the others. It's fine."

"I'm an idiot," she said, hanging her head. "So sorry. You're just so quiet about your love life, and I thought I finally had something to tease you with."

"Ah, I'm a nun these days." Anne shrugged. "I can hardly blame you. I had to live vicariously when you and Carwyn got together. Turnabout is fair play, isn't it?"

"No, it's not." Brigid looked up. "Not when it was far more than a fling. I'm sorry."

"It's fine."

"You're going to keep saying that, aren't you?"

Anne huffed out a breath. "If I tell you that most of the rumors are likely true and that he was impressively adventurous for a man of his time, would you stop feeling guilty?"

"Yes, but now I have even more questions."

Anne gave up and laughed. "I love you."

"I know you do. Carwyn worries that one of these days I'll simply stay here, and he'll have to hunt me down and drag me back."

"We'd manage to fight him off if we tried."

ANOTHER hour's conversation left Anne in a troubled state of mind. The worries she'd had at the start of the evening hadn't lessened with her friend's visit; they'd grown worse. Like her hunger.

25

The Elixir problem showed no sign of improving. After the drug had escaped its murky origins in Rome, it had showed up in Ireland and other parts of Europe, but no one knew who was shipping it. Patrick Murphy had tried everything possible to halt its import, but the drug was too easy to transport. Terrance Ramsay in England was having the same problem, and Anne knew she needed to ask her sister some hard questions. Was Belfast having the same issues? Had Mary been hiding it from her?

To humans, Elixir looked like a clear pink liquid that smelled strongly of pomegranate. And yet it acted as a poison to vampires and humans alike. For mortals, there was no cure at all. They wasted away, unable to process any of the vital nutrients their bodies needed to remain healthy. They starved, even on feeding tubes. It was a horrible, painful death.

In vampires, Elixir acted as a cure for the bloodlust that plagued them. The vampire stopped eating. Then drinking. All while remaining in seemingly perfect health. But gradually, he or she went mad from the lack of blood that fed their amnis, the vital energy that kept them alive and connected to their elemental power. Once Elixir invaded their systems, vampires could no longer process the blood they needed to survive. Not even forced feeding was a cure. The only cure—if it could be called one—was a near complete exsanguination of the infected immortal, followed by an infusion of their sire's blood.

For vampires such as Anne, who remained on good terms with her father, not a wholly hopeless proposition. For vampires such as Murphy or her next client, impossible.

The patient Ruth knew as "the Russian" arrived minutes before his appointed time of three a.m. He was a particular sort, and Anne had never known him to be late in all the time he'd been "visiting" her.

He refused to call her his doctor. He refused to consider her anything more than a friend he saw once every six months or so. He always propositioned her, and vodka was always involved.

Psychological practice among vampires necessitated a slightly more individualistic approach.

"Oleg," she said, holding out her arms to embrace the fearsome fire vampire who ruled over most of Russia.

"Anne," he said, pulling her into a heated embrace. "Have you decided to leave these cold shores and warm yourself by my fire?"

"Not tonight, my friend."

Not that it would have been a hardship. Oleg had a handsome, angular face and eyes the color of the grey skies over his home in St. Petersburg. He rarely smiled, but when he did, his teeth were even and his fangs... impressive. His hair was chestnut brown, and he wore a thick beard in defiance of his element.

He also had several houses filled with human and vampire mistresses if rumors were to be believed. Oleg lived more like a czar than the mobster many called him.

"Soon you'll run away with me."

Anne laughed. "We'll see."

He tipped his chin up, and Anne was once again reminded of wind and snow and fire in the night. Oleg was fiercely beautiful, but far from civilized. His human and vampire lineage was drenched in blood. Despite that, he treated her with a gentle respect, and Anne knew their friendship was one of the reasons her home remained safe.

"Come. We'll talk inside out of this cold. I brought a new vodka."

"Oleg—"

"Just a taste, yes? For me. It is a new brand. I want your opinion."

The Russian was one of the most powerful fire vampires in Europe. Brigid, with her fledgling power, would be ash at his feet. Anne wondered whether he'd been able to sense the presence of the young fire vampire when he walked in the house. Probably. Fire vampires had the keenest noses of their kind. She also doubted that an immortal like Oleg considered someone like Brigid Connor to be anything other than amusing. Aside from the ancients, the reclusive scholar and former assassin Giovanni Vecchio would be considered his only rival. And Vecchio wanted as little to do with vampire politics as Anne did.

"There is a fire in you tonight, *lapochka*," Oleg said. "I can sense it."

"Is this the beginning of a very bad pickup line?"

"Perhaps." He smiled slowly. "To have a woman like you at my side? For this, I would offer your sire gold."

"I'm not for sale, but I'll try to be flattered."

"You should be."

"Tell me what's going on with your daughter. Have you spoken with Zara lately?"

An angry stream of Russian was his only response. Anne shook her head and looked for the vodka glasses.

Chapter Three

DECLAN USED HIS HAND to point at the projection on the wall. "We can pick up these three properties for far less than market value, but we'll need to use at least two different shell corporations and space the purchases out over several months."

"Are there any other buyers interested?" Murphy asked.

"Not that I could find. These two are considered prime, but with the economy the way it is, there's no telling when construction will pick up again."

He nodded. The Celtic Tiger had retreated, his country hit as hard as anyone else by the recent economic downturn. What once seemed like a gold mine of development in a revitalized docklands now lingered and crumbled, the city desperate to keep it from devolving more but unsure how to go about doing it. Declan had been careful approaching the human banks who owned the properties he'd determined would have the best long-term market value.

Waterfront property was limited, at the end of the day. And while humans worried about decades of economic activity, an immortal thought about long-term investment.

Very long-term.

"Do it," Murphy said. "We have the cash right now."

Tom finally spoke. "But we don't have any use for 'em right now, either."

"Do we have the means to secure them?"

Tom nodded. "It'll cost though. Always does."

Murphy glanced at Declan, who nodded and said, "I've calculated that into the investment value. Once these two adjacent properties are secure, we can combine security arrangements on them and keep costs down."

Tom grunted. "That'll help. And we do have lads looking for work. Not a bad thing to keep them busy."

"Agreed," Murphy said. "We can use them for storage now. Possibly an off-the-books club."

Most of his businesses were aboveboard, but there was always room for a little fun. And what could be more harmless than a little drinking and gambling with the humans' money? It was going to happen anyway. This way, Murphy could keep an eye on things and make his cut at the same time.

As he'd told Brigid the week before, the best cons walked away with everyone smiling.

"Where's Brigid?" he asked Tom.

"She called last night. Going west for a bit to visit Anne." Tom gave him a loaded look. "Nothing hot going on here, so I told her to go ahead."

"Fine." He ignored the look.

"Brigid's been trying to get Anne to come for a visit, Josie says. Having a hard time understanding why Anne avoids Dublin so much, especially when she loves the symphony and all that," Tom muttered.

Murphy knew exactly how much Anne loved the symphony. It was why he so often sat alone with an empty seat beside him. He disliked anyone sitting in the chair he still considered hers. Josie, Tom's very quiet mate, and Brigid were the only companions he ever let accompany him. And that was only when he was feeling melancholy.

"How is Josie?" he asked, desperate to change the subject.

THE SCARLET DEEP

Tom's ugly mug broke into a smile. "Light of my life, of course. And nagging me about the back flower beds. Something about planting a scent garden, whatever the hell that means."

It wasn't well known—even among Murphy's own people—that Tom Dargin had been mated for over one hundred years. His mate, Josie, was a writer who lived an extremely quiet life. When Tom wasn't working, they both kept to themselves. But Declan, Tom, and Josie were some of the few immortals in Dublin that had known Murphy when he and Anne were together. And Tom and Josie were the only ones who ever brought it up.

"A scent garden," Murphy said, "is one that focuses as much on the fragrance of the flowering plants as the color of the flowers. Lovely things for vampires, since we can't appreciate the color of flowers during the day."

"Yeah, I might have got that, thanks," Tom said, rolling his eyes.

"I have a landscaper I can recommend."

"No need. Josie's designing it herself. Her girl will pick up the flowers, and I'll plant them. But thanks."

"Of course. She going to be all right with you working longer hours when I'm at this summit in London?"

Terrance Ramsay was organizing a summit among the leading immortal shipping powers in the Atlantic. The leader of London was hoping that with enough pooled intelligence they'd be able to figure who was moving Elixir through western Europe and the United States. The problem had been getting enough representatives to attend. There was only so much any of them trusted the others.

"You know Josie won't mind," Tom said. "Besides, she likes me out of the house when she's finishing a book. So tell an old married man. How were those human girls the other night? As featherbrained as they looked?"

"None of your business."

"You thinking I'm just going to drop the Anne thing, are you?

Murphy felt his fangs push in irritation. "When do you ever drop it?"

Tom didn't speak for a long while. Declan was mysteriously quiet. Murphy stood to go.

"Boss—"

"I have no need to talk about Anne O'Dea, Tom."

"You still need her. You think Dec and I can't see it?"

Murphy slammed down the file folder he'd been paging through, and Declan slipped out of the room. He was usually the voice of reason when the three of them argued, so Murphy had a feeling Tom and Declan had talked about this beforehand.

Tom was the oldest, Declan in the middle, and Josie was the youngest now that Jack was gone. But he and his sons had always been more brothers than sire and children, and Tom was one of the few vampires who could speak freely with the immortal lord of Dublin.

"Leave it," Murphy said through clenched teeth.

"It's catchin' up with you."

"I'm fine."

"None of us is able to drink as much human blood as we need, and Elixir isn't going away anytime soon. It's better now that we know the scent of it in humans, but it's still a problem." Tom took a deep breath and leaned forward. "I'm stronger because I'm mated. Brigid—"

"Brigid is mated to one of the oldest vampires in the British Isles. Are you implying that I'm weak?"

"No, if anything, you're the most dangerous I've ever seen you."

"These are dangerous times."

"You're short-tempered. You've been in the ring more often the past couple of months and lost it on some of the lads."

"I'll hunt more."

"And put the Irish deer population at risk? That's not what you need, boss."

Murphy moved toward the door, and Tom put a hand on his arm.

"It's been a hundred years."

"I know that."

"Reach out to her."

He shook of Tom's hand. "Why? So she can ignore me again?"

"Because you came to her so reasonable-like from the beginning, throwing the women in her face like it were her fault, eh?" Tom's face was even stormier than usual. "You may be my sire, Murphy, but you deserved to be tossed on your arse."

"And what's changed so much, hmm? You notice me turning into a monk in the past seventy years?"

"Stop being a stubborn arse," Tom yelled. "You've changed. And she has too. Jaysus, stop acting like a child and talk to her."

"Why are you bringing this up now? Is it because of this bloody summit? I agreed to go, didn't I?"

Tom and Declan had been adamant that Murphy attend. He'd been reluctant but had finally seen the wisdom in pooling resources.

"It's not because of the summit."

Murphy gave him a look.

"Fine. Not *just* because of the summit. But you have to admit you'll likely rip someone's head off at a conference table the way you've been lately. Not only does she level you out, but we need every ally we can get right now. She's Mary Hamilton's sister, and we need that woman's support if we're ever going to get a handle on who is shipping this shite."

"I know all that." Murphy sat down again, his blood cooling. "If I approach Anne O'Dea for any reasons she might interpret as strategic, she will have nothing to do with me, and you know it."

"She's a practical woman."

He shook his head. "She hates me. And her sister does too."

Tom said nothing. Murphy knew there was nothing to say.

Except…

"Tom," Murphy asked, "has Terrance Ramsay invited Mary Hamilton to London for the summit?"

"Yes. She turned him down. Since you're coming, he doesn't really need her to be there, though it would be better to present a united front. That and he wanted to placate the old man."

Murphy pulled an old gold coin from his pocket and flipped it in his fingers. "Anne won't have anything to do with me," he mused. "She's been avoiding me—avoiding us—for seventy years at least."

"Boss—"

"But if I have Terry call her… It might work."

She'd hate him. But she'd have to talk to him. He could probably work with that.

Murphy had never stopped *wanting* her. That would be akin to no longer wanting blood or water. He'd just learned to manage without her.

Tom frowned. "Why would Terrance Ramsay be wanting to call Anne?"

"No, Tom. Have Ramsay call Mary Hamilton. Tell her she's needed at this summit. Just can't do without her oh-so-important perspective. Or better, have Gemma do it."

A smile touched the corner of Tom's mouth. "You conniving bastard. Hamilton won't come herself. She's too antisocial. But if Ramsay insists on it…"

"She'll send someone she trusts."

"And she doesn't trust anyone else as much as she does Anne." Tom crossed his arms and puffed out his barrel chest. "She'll hate you."

"But she'll talk to me." Murphy flipped the coin in the air. It landed heads up. "She'd be forced to."

If there was one thing Patrick Murphy excelled at, it was talking his way around a stubborn adversary.

And there was no one more stubborn than Anne.

TERRANCE Ramsay was amenable to Murphy's plan.

"I knew Hamilton wouldn't come, but Brigid insisted I call her. She turned me down flat. Didn't even let me finish the phone call."

"Call again. You've convinced Jetta to attend?"

"Not quite yet. The Scandinavians have someone involved in this. I'm fairly sure Jetta suspects someone in her organization. If she comes, she might be bringing the suspects with her."

"Jetta and Mary are close. Allies, but rivals too. If you imply Jetta is coming, Mary will send someone. Once Mary sends someone, Jetta will appear."

"Or they both call my bluff and leave me looking like a fool," Terry said, laughing. "Does Hamilton have someone she trusts enough to speak for her?"

"One person, yes."

Terry paused. "You think she'd send Anne?"

Could he be sure? Mary did like to be unpredictable.

"There's no way to be sure," he admitted, "but Mary doesn't trust anyone as much as she trusts Anne."

"And she'd go to a summit like this?"

"She has in the past when the situation has called for it." And in the past, it bothered him. Thought it had divided her loyalties.

Tom was right. He'd been acting like a child. Anne was her own woman and always had been.

"Murphy," Terry said, amusement in his voice. "You sure you want Anne O'Dea at the summit for the good of all vampirekind, or do you have a personal motive?"

Both, but that was hardly Terry's business.

"Just call Mary again," he said. "Tell her you need her there. She'll come or she'll send her sister."

"Fine. But if she hangs up on me again, I'm setting Gemma on you."

Murphy couldn't hold in the laugh. "Fair enough."

TWO nights later, Brigid was back and silently accompanying Murphy to a dinner for some local business organization.

"What is wrong with you?" he muttered, leaning to her ear. "You've been quiet all night."

"I hate these things."

"I know, but Tom's legs are crap and Declan is hopeless when it comes to accessorizing."

He saw her bite back a smile. Murphy would never insist on it, but it did make it easier to have Brigid accompany him on necessary outings like this. If he took a human employee, Brigid would just have to arrange protection anyway. It made sense to have her be his date. Brigid wore a ring, so if anyone asked, Murphy introduced her as his cousin. And to be honest, she made an amusing dinner companion. Usually her commentary on the social elite of Dublin had him in quiet stitches all night, and her brightly colored hair always drew the most amusing attention.

But ever since Brigid had come back from Galway, she'd been… off.

"How was Galway?"

"Fine."

"Or should I ask about Kinvara specifically?"

She paused. "You know Anne and I are close."

"Oh, I do." He leaned down again. "Any interesting topics of conversation?"

If she could have blushed, the look on her face said she would have.

"We talked about painting."

Ah, that damned painting. He knew he should have rid himself of it years ago.

"Finally figured us out, did you?"

Her silence said it all.

"You know, if you were curious, you could have just asked me about our prior relationship."

"Nope. Fairly sure I got a much more detailed story from Anne."

Murphy froze. "How detailed?"

She nodded, a smile touching her lips. "*Impressively* detailed."

"She did not."

"No, but the look on your face speaks volumes." She elbowed him. "Why didn't you tell me? You knew we were friends. I thought *we* were friends."

"It was a long time ago. It's not something I talk about."

"Funny, but she said almost exactly the same thing. I find it curious that it was oh so long ago, and yet both of you are still so touchy about talking about it. You and Angie joke about old stories all the time."

"It's different."

"Oh? How exactly?"

Murphy didn't want to tell her, so he pulled her up and back from their table, making quiet excuses to the host at the back of the room before they left. Brigid was standing out in the cold and he was handing her off to the driver within minutes.

"You're off for the rest of the night," he said. "Go home and bother your husband."

"Someone's feeling tetchy, eh? Not my fault, and you never answered my question." Brigid looked a little irritated.

"And I'm not going to. I'll see you tomorrow. I'm going hunting."

Her face lost all the irritation and turned professional again. "Murphy—"

"I'll be careful."

"Please tell me you're heading out of town or going fishing."

"Fish blood is vile."

"Murphy!"

"You're not my mam, Brigid. You're my employee."

"And you're an asshole." She got into the car, a glare on her face. "I'm calling Tom."

"Fine. At least he doesn't bother me with questions that are none of his bloody business."

Which was completely untrue, but Brigid didn't need to know that.

He was hungry. Murphy hated not being able to hunt as he wished.

He walked toward Merrion Road and headed north, back toward the Grand Canal. He cut through back alleys and skirted humans who were out for a Friday-night stroll. It was early evening still and he made a game of it, stalking a group of humans and getting within a few feet without their seeing him before he melted into the shadows and pursued someone else.

He was almost back to his building when he saw her. Straight dark hair fell down to the middle of her back. Her waist flared out to generous hips that swayed in the formfitting black dress she'd donned that night. Soft, pale arms gestured as she laughed with a friend. Her hair was pinned on the sides to reveal a graceful, plump neck. She held herself proudly, shoulders thrown back as she walked under the canopy of trees that shadowed the path.

He followed them, the dark-haired girl bringing his hunger to a boiling point. She would be luscious. Sweet. He rarely fed from girls who looked like Anne. It was too problematic. But that night, maybe he'd make an exception.

And she would want him. Murphy had little doubt he could seduce the woman, even without the benefit of amnis. She would look on him with lust and desire and welcome him with open arms. He could lose himself in her body. Take her blood. Forget…

As much as he ever forgot.

Or maybe he would ignore her body and simply take her blood. Feed the monster that lived within. Slake the vicious hunger that—even now—stalked him every night.

He drew closer.

The girls were talking about some band they'd gone to see. Raving about the handsome singer and laughing about the boys who'd tried to chat them up at the bar. Good-natured teasing for one girl who'd made a date.

Not the brunette. She belonged to Murphy.

His footsteps were silent. Even if the girls turned, all they'd see was a well-dressed man in his late twenties with a rakish smile and a smooth step. They would blush with pleasure when he passed them. They'd giggle when he dipped his head and greeted them with a charming voice and a wink. Then he could double back and stalk them again, drawing out the pleasure of the hunt until their terror tinged the air.

Murphy paused, waiting in the shadows.

Maybe he would cull the brunette from her friends. Isolate her and—

He spun the moment he caught a hint of movement in his periphery, dodging the fist aimed at his jaw. His attacker moved inhumanly fast, the flurry of blows raining on his midsection forcing him farther into a darkened alley and driving any thoughts of hunting from his mind, for this opponent was his oldest and most fierce.

Murphy whirled and struck, hitting the lantern jaw of his attacker with a solid fist that didn't faze the man. Then Tom caught him in a fierce hug and rained blow after blow into his kidneys as Murphy struggled to breathe.

He was a wall. Even when Murphy wrenched himself from Tom's grasp and jumped away, he kept coming.

Tom landed one more angry blow to Murphy's face before he held up a hand.

"Enough, Tom."

"Fecking hell, Murphy!"

"I'm fine."

"You're not fine."

With a growl, Murphy rammed a fist into the bricks behind Tom and watched in satisfaction as the red clay crumbled beneath his fists. He closed his eyes and let the pain wash over him. It cleared his head, even as the cuts on his face and torso began to close.

"I'm fine," he whispered again.

Tom grabbed him around the neck and pulled him into a fierce hug. "No, boss. You're not fine. You'd have hunted her and bled her dry and hated yourself for it. What's your rule, boss?"

"They have to offer."

"They have to offer. Not like your bloody bastard of a sire. And if you turned into him, you'd kill yourself."

"I'm fine, Tom."

"Come to me and Josie's place. Come over and let her tell you a story, eh? Have a drink. Sleep in one of the guest rooms if you like."

He nodded and tried to straighten his jacket, willing his fangs to recede in his mouth. Willing his mind away from the ever-more-distant scent of prey. He finally regained control, but the jacket was past saving. He tugged it off and draped it over some boxes sitting in the alley. It was torn, but it was still wool. It wouldn't be wasted keeping someone warm, and the boy in him would never be able to throw a coat away.

Tom kept a hold on him as they walked west, heading toward Josie's old Victorian home in Ballsbridge.

"Do you want to talk about what set you off?"

"No."

"Was it Brigid?"

He said nothing, which Tom took as an affirmative.

"I'll talk to the lass," he said. "She didn't know."

"She doesn't need to know. I'll be fine, Tom. It was a moment of weakness."

"She called me, you know. She's a good girl, Brigid. Smart one."

"Yes, a little too smart at times."

"She was just in Galway, yeah? She figure you and Anne out?"

"I don't know how much Anne told her." Just the taste of her name on his tongue made Murphy ill, remembering what he'd planned to do to the girl he'd been following. The girl only bore the most superficial resemblance to Anne, and he'd still been on the verge of…

"I know I need to do something," Murphy said. "I just don't know what."

"I know exactly what you need to do," Tom said cheerfully. "You're gonna take tomorrow night off, get your fancy arse out to Galway, and go talk to your mate."

Chapter Four

THE COUNTRY PUB SAT off the road that led nowhere in particular and was only open for business on weekends most nights unless something notable was happening. Anne didn't care. It still had a decent kitchen, good beer, and a corner booth that no one looked at too closely. Every now and then, when old Mrs. Connelly cast her meaningful looks, she'd sing with whoever was playing in the Friday session. No one remarked on it. No one asked her questions. They gave her a free beer and asked after Ruth and Dan.

And that was that.

Tourists didn't come here, though Anne knew she'd have an easier time blending in if she frequented the bars that were busier. Every now and then when she was particularly lonely, she'd head into Galway to find amusement. But usually a country pub and a cold beer were enough.

That night she sat with a book on the table, letting the sounds of the traditional music wash over her along with the ebb and flow of human conversation. It was lovely and familiar. There was as much Irish as English spoken in this particular pub, and it reminded her of her human years.

Connection with the past is what grounds us in the present.
Forgetting our human nature allows the monster in us to take control.

We must be among the humans without being of them.

Bits of advice she'd parceled out to others over the years now haunted her own thoughts. Her last drink from Ruth had made her wary. She knew it was her unusual amnis that made her hunger more potent, but her "gift" didn't offer any solution.

Mrs. Connelly had set down a dark pint when Anne felt the first tremor of awareness at the back of her neck. She looked up, scanning the corners of the pub for a sign of anything out of the ordinary.

Nothing.

She took a sip of beer. "Thanks, Peg."

"No worries, Anne. A song later?"

"Sure thing. Anyone unusual around tonight?"

The older woman smiled. "Not unless you call the Kinney brothers being here and *bathed* unusual."

"Any bathed Kinney brother is suspicious," Anne said with a wry smile. "I don't recognize them if they don't smell like their sheep."

Mrs. Connelly laughed. "You're not wrong."

The human left, and Anne watched the musicians as they rolled into another song, a more modern one she recognized as an acoustic version of a rock song. Not strictly traditional, but it fit the restless mood that wouldn't leave her alone.

"Anne!" The drummer was waving her over. His wrinkled face broke into a smile as his nimble fingers danced with the tipper, beating out the rhythm on the bodhran. He nodded to the woman with the flute, who caught the drummer's cue and slowed the song, waiting for her to join in.

She left her beer and book in the corner and went to sit next to the drummer, perching on the edge of the chair and leaning forward to sing the lyrics about a pair of brown eyes and a roving man. She rocked with the beat of the guitar and the drum, losing herself in the music for two songs. The music, like the ocean, centered her, made her remember life and not death. Laughter instead of blood. Happiness and not hunger.

Then Anne heard the flute dip low, and the pub quieted when they recognized the melody of the old Gaelic song. They all knew it was a favorite of hers. After a few beats, the music died down and the old woman looked to Anne with a nod.

She raised her voice and let the clear sound of "An Mhaighdean Mhara" fill the dark room. The lonely tale of the fisherman's mermaid bride who left him to return to the sea was a simple old song, one her mother had sung by the evening fire, perhaps wishing she too could abandon the prison of her earthly life and run away to a home beyond the sea.

In the end, Anne supposed she had.

The unexpected melancholy gripped her throat, and a familiar curl of awareness in her blood forced her eyes to a shadowed corner of the pub.

Patrick Murphy stood in the shadows, arms crossed and brown eyes fixed on her.

Her blood surging to life within her, Anne met his gaze and sang on.

Were you born of woman
Or did you come from the earth?
Your eyes speak
Though your lips say naught.

He watched her, the man who'd stolen her heart so long ago, then broken it like the wild, young thing he'd been. He leaned casually against the back wall in his wool slacks and pressed shirt, as if the sight of him wouldn't be enough to break her again. His lush lower lip fell as he stared, and Anne could see the glint of his fangs in the low lights of the pub.

She finished the song, barely controlling the tremor in her throat as she felt her heart pulse twice. His eyes never left her face.

The guitar and fiddle had picked up to a faster tune when she saw him break his stance and start toward the small stage. Anne nodded to a young girl happy to jump in the singer's chair while Anne hurried to the back, forgetting her book in the corner as she grabbed Murphy's arm and dragged him down the hall and toward the kitchen door.

She pushed into the night, Murphy at her heels.

Anne spun. "Patrick, what on earth—"

He silenced her with a furious kiss, spinning her in his arms and pushing her up against the back wall of the pub. His hands dug into the flesh of her hips while his mouth devoured hers, slaking a hundred years' worth of hunger with lips and breath and the bite of fangs against her tongue.

She dug her hands into his hair, pulling him close for one heartbreaking moment before she tugged him away.

Murphy released her mouth only to press his face into her neck, laving his tongue against the hammering pulse in her throat. His arms banded around her waist, pulling her into his powerful frame. She felt him. Every inch of him. The years fell away under his mouth. Her skin came alive. Her amnis left her, rushing toward him, even as his own energy coursed over her skin.

He was a wave crashing over her, pulling her under, and Anne knew she had to step back before she drowned.

"Patrick," she whispered, "stop."

He let out a single shuddering breath against her neck. His fingers dug into her waist one second, and then he stepped back and looked up, avoiding her gaze.

Murphy took two deep breaths before he started in a hoarse voice. "Áine—"

"What are you doing here?"

He let out a string of Gammon curses that let her know he still wasn't entirely under control. Not that she couldn't see that from his fangs and his trousers. But Murphy only let his Traveller show when he was off-kilter.

He finally rubbed two hands over his face, mussing his hair and reminding her of the brash young immortal he'd been once, when she'd toppled head over heels for him and straight into a passionate affair that had lasted nearly thirty years.

By the time he spoke, the flippant tone had returned to his voice. "And how are you this evening, Dr. O'Dea?"

"I was having a fine night until I was interrupted, Mr. Murphy."

"I was going to be much more polite than this."

"You always did get riled when you heard me sing."

"Yes." His voice was rough. "I did. I do."

She waited, but he said nothing.

Finally, he nodded at the pub. "Are they safe? The humans here, I mean."

"I know what you mean."

Murphy had always worried. She knew he checked up on her, but he was usually subtler about it, sending Tom, Josie, or Declan in his stead.

"They don't ask questions," she said. "Sometimes, I need more than my house and Ruth and Dan."

"Come to Dublin then." He let out a wry laugh. "Never mind. You can take care of yourself. You always did."

"You haven't answered my question."

"Noticed that, did you?"

She crossed her arms. "What did you need, Murphy?"

"Many things. And I hate it when you call me Murphy."

"I hate it when you turn up unannounced."

He used to do it often but stopped when she refused to acknowledge him. She hadn't seen him in almost thirty years. He'd left her alone. Left her alone to her life while he played the rogue in Dublin Town.

"This *is* my territory," he said.

Her skin prickled in anger. "Do you think so?"

"You're lovely when you're furious."

Patrick Murphy's smile was as appealing—and as irritating—as the rest of him. And riling her had always made him smile.

"Get to the point," she said.

"Tom forced me to come visit. Said I was getting insufferable."

"You've been insufferable for a hundred years. More than. He's just now catching on?"

"I do miss the bite of your tongue, Dr. O'Dea. Miss a lot about your tongue, in fact."

And she missed his. She'd never had a better lover than Murphy, and she was honest enough to admit it.

"The point, Murphy? It's been thirty years since we've seen each other, and I had no plans to change that. Don't think I missed that little bit of blood you managed to slip me."

Now it was his eyes that were flashing.

"It's not enough," she said. "The bond is fading and we both know it. Don't try to interfere. It's past time this was all history. Now, I'd like to return to my beer and my friends, so—"

"What friends?" he said. "Who in there knows you? Knows you *really*? The bartender? The band? As far as I'm concerned, we never finished our last argument."

She smiled bitterly. "Oh yes. How could I forget that lovely conversation?"

"You've put me off for seventy years, Anne. Wouldn't a psychologist call that avoidance?"

"As I *am* a psychologist, I'd call it steering clear of a toxic relationship."

She tried to ignore the expression on his face. Murphy looked as if she'd punched him. Anne immediately regretted the words, but she couldn't take them back. This was Murphy. If she gave an inch, he'd take more than a mile. He'd take the entire county.

"It doesn't matter," he said, eyes frosting over. "That's not what this is about."

"Then what is it about? Ask your question or your favor or whatever it is you came for and go home."

In the blink of an eye, he was in front of her. His eyes narrowed and he bent close. For a second, she thought he would kiss her again.

He didn't.

"You know," he murmured an inch away from her lips, "I do believe I'll wait for official channels for this."

She felt an uneasy twist in her stomach. "What are you talking about?"

"You'll find out soon enough."

"Fine." She turned and started walking back toward the pub. "Have a safe journey home."

She didn't make it to the door. He grabbed her hand, tugging her back to his chest and wrapping his hand around her waist. She wasn't a small woman, and Murphy was only a little taller than her. She felt his breath on her neck as he bent down and quickly scraped his fangs over the pulse that quickened at his touch.

"Don't. You. Dare."

"I think you forget, Anne O'Dea"—a quick flick of his tongue—"your mate is no *settled* man."

She tried to hold in the shiver, but by the time Anne turned, he was gone.

"ANNE?"

The worried voice broke through her reverie, and Anne looked up. Her patient was a kind, three-hundred-year-old earth vampire from Germany who had lost a mate the year before.

"Elke, I'm so sorry."

The older woman smiled. "You seem quite distracted today, my dear."

"I… am. My apologies. You were talking about your son?"

"I was, but I can talk about you," Elke said. "I'm rather tired of talking about myself."

"Well, that is what you come to therapy for."

"We can reschedule if you'd rather."

"No, no." Anne shook her head and stood to pour herself a cup of tea. "You've come all this way. Tell me about your son."

"Well, Henry's son, to be completely honest. He sired Hans a few years before we met and mated. Oh, we did fight about Hans!" Elke said, smiling again. "He was a problem child. So little restraint. You'd never imagine it now, because he's so very controlled. Almost… cold. That's why I'm worried about him. I don't want him to slip into that distant state and lose his connection to the world."

Henry had been another earth vampire, so she knew any children he sired would be, as well. "Does Hans live near you?"

"Not too far. Bavaria."

Her client chatted about her children for a while longer, and Anne couldn't stop the surge of envy.

What friends? Who in there knows you? Knows you really?

She hated that his words still haunted her. She had friends! She had lots of them.

Okay, she mostly had clients, but she was friendly with them. She had Dan and Ruth. She had Brigid and Josie. Not that she saw them much, but she had them. And once the bond with Murphy had faded, she'd be able to be a real partner for someone again. Someone who didn't drive her crazy and take advantage of her. Someone who respected her. Someone—

"Anne, you're drifting again."

"Dammit, Murphy!" She threw her pen down, the tip digging into the floor where it struck.

Covering her face with one hand, she took measured breaths. She could feel her client watching her from across the room.

"Elke, you're probably right. We should reschedule. I had an unexpected visitor last night, and I am completely distracted."

Elke's mouth had turned up at one corner. "You know, I don't know that I have ever seen you so perturbed. This is a man you're involved with, I presume."

"No. Yes. He's… I'm sorry. This isn't your problem."

"I was mated for two hundred years, my dear. I might be able to offer some advice. Plus, I'm a physician myself. You'd be amazed the things people feel comfortable confiding."

"I knew we got along for a reason," she muttered. "Still… it's not professional for me to do this. You're my patient. You come to me for counsel. I shouldn't."

Elke laughed. "We're not human, Anne. The lines, they are not so clear for us, yes? Tell me about this man. Is he human or vampire?"

"Vampire. We've been mated…" She took a deep breath and noticed the older woman's eyebrows had risen in surprise. "Yes, I was mated. I am mated. We are estranged and have been for many years."

"I'm so very sorry."

"It's fine." She waved a hand. "It's in the past. With enough time, the bond grows weaker. Eventually, it fades."

"How long since you…? If you don't mind my asking."

"It's been around one hundred years since we last exchanged blood."

Elke's eyes grew wide. "And you still feel this connection with him? After all that time? How long were you together?"

"Around thirty years. Isn't that… I'd always heard that it took time, so—"

"Time, yes." Elke's voice turned professional. "The biology isn't strictly clear. It's an emotional connection as much as a physical one, of course. Friends and allies can exchange blood without any serious bonds forming, so we know there is more to it than simply biology. But for most blood bonds, should the couple stop exchanging blood, the connection fades in roughly half the time they were together. So for you—"

"Fifteen years?" Anne asked. "It should have faded after fifteen years? At fifteen years, I still woke up in the morning smelling him next to me."

Elke's mouth opened, but she said nothing.

"Fifteen *years*?" Anne said again.

"Your connection must have been very strong."

"It was," she said roughly.

"May I ask what happened?"

"We had a falling-out."

"It must have been a serious one."

"It was."

> "Why won't you do this for me?"
>
> "How could you even ask?"
>
> "It's not like you haven't done it before, Anne. When it suits you—"
>
> "Not for politics, Patrick! Not for bloody, bloody politics! It's the only thing that matters to you anymore."
>
> "If you loved me…"

Anne cleared her throat. "We parted ways because he asked me to compromise something very important to me. Even years later, when he apologized… Well, he never really apologized. I think he intended to, but he lost his temper. It wasn't pleasant."

"Hot-blooded men," Elke said. "We love them, and yet they drive us mad."

Anne smiled. "From what you've told me, Henry seems like he was a very level-headed partner."

"Of course he was. After two hundred years." Elke smiled. "We didn't start out that way."

"No?"

"Anne dear, anytime you have two strong individuals—and we must be strong to conquer our demons and survive this unnatural life, no? Anytime you have two such people, there will be passion. And with passion comes arguments and fighting. For our kind, we only hope there is no blood."

Anne smiled. "No blood. At least not the violent kind."

"Who left who?"

"I did. He stayed in Dublin and I…"

"Ran away."

Anne's mouth dropped open. "Of course not. I'm originally from here, so when we parted, I decided to return to my home."

"Far enough to keep your distance and yet torment him."

"What was I supposed to do?" Anne asked, somewhat perturbed by Elke's presumption. "Leave the country?"

"I think most of our kind would leave. You could certainly work from anywhere you wished. Even going to England or Scotland would have been farther. But you stayed here. Rather close. That tells me that you didn't want to cut ties as much as you think."

"No. That's ridiculous." Anne sat up straighter. "We have completely separate lives. He's had numerous relationships. I've had relationships. We both…"

Elke leaned forward, her head propped on her hand. "If you weren't *you*, if you were a patient, what would you say to a woman who breaks off a very serious relationship—the most intimate an immortal can have—and yet stays within a day's journey of the one to whom she is bound?"

THE SCARLET DEEP

Anne sat back in her seat. "Well... dammit."

THE trip to Donegal had been scheduled months ago. Twice a year, Anne and her sister would meet at the ruins of the old stone house where both had spent their first years as an immortal. Their sire had cared for Mary there, and Mary had cared for her sister. It was the way of things in their small clan. Should Anne's father ever sire another, that child would be Anne's responsibility to guide through the first few tumultuous years.

So far, she was the youngest. Her father was not a prolific vampire.

Despite both their busy schedules, Anne knew it was important for her and Mary to have these times together. Mary had few people she trusted in Belfast. Unlike Patrick Murphy, who'd come into power with a cadre of trusted advisors at his side, Mary had clawed her way through the bloody wake of a vampire uprising in Belfast two hundred years before. She'd held on to power through intelligence, determination, and a ruthless attitude toward governance that brooked no argument.

But, as Anne often pointed out, that way led toward tyranny.

So Anne met with Mary twice a year and reminded her sister that she had a conscience.

She pulled into the small drive and waved at the caretaker who was already walking back to the smaller house on the edge of the property. Mary's car was in the drive, a luxurious old roadster that she was able to navigate herself. Anne pulled next to it and parked her Mini.

The weather was typically damp. The house in Donegal always smelled of the sea and musk roses in summer. Anne could hear the waves in the distance, washing up the bay, but the night was too dark to see the water through the grove.

The Georgian house that had replaced the stone cottage sat on eighteen carefully landscaped acres. It was big enough to suit their independent natures, but not so big that it wasn't easily taken care of by the groundkeeper and his wife, who lived at the lodge. Over the years, it had come to be what Anne considered her family home.

Following the faint scent of cigarette smoke, Anne rounded the corner to see her sister staring at a bank of blue hydrangeas and sucking on one of those blasted tobacco sticks as she sat on a garden bench that bordered the walk.

Mary had the delicate English beauty that made modern humans think of period films and fine manners. She'd styled her dark brown hair the same since the 1920s because it suited her heart-shaped face. A human would think her a damsel until they looked into her eyes. Then they'd probably run screaming.

"Such a nasty habit," Anne said, sitting next to her and leaning her head on Mary's shoulder.

"Hello," Mary said, reaching over to pat her sister's cheek. "How's my kinder half?"

"Confused."

"Tell your sis, eh?"

"I don't know that I want to."

Mary hated Murphy. Mostly out of rivalry, distrust, and his treatment of Anne. She probably also envied his ease being a male in leadership while she constantly battled human sexism.

"Well, sister, count two of us who don't want to say the things that need to be said." Mary sighed. "Because I've a favor I need to ask that you're going to hate me for."

Anne groaned. "What? Is it a political meeting? Tell me it's not a political—"

"It's business. And politics. More politics, really. You'll really just have to nod and smile and take notes for me."

Anne groaned. "Mary, you know I hate—"

"I can't trust anyone else. I can't leave the city right now, Anne. You know my position is—"

"Far more secure than you think." She gently prodded Mary with her elbow. "You've put a competent team in place, sister. If you continue this level of paranoia, you're going to sabotage yourself."

"Not time for analysis just yet." Mary paused, took another drag on her cigarette. "Do this for me, Annie?"

Anne took a deep breath and drank in the sea air. "You know I will. What is it?"

"I need you to go to London."

"Oh." Anne sat up. "That's not as bad as I thought it would be. Quite welcome, in fact, as long as I have some time to—"

"I need you to go to London with Patrick Murphy."

Anne burst to her feet. "That bloody, conniving bastard!"

Chapter Five

MURPHY WAS GOING THROUGH London security concerns with Brigid when he got the message that Anne had arrived in the building. She'd be staying with Brigid and Carwyn while she was in town for a few weeks, but as she was officially entering his territory, she was following protocol by paying him a visit.

He and Terry had agreed that while Anne would speak for Mary Hamilton, it was best that Ireland as an island speak with a single voice at the summit. Fractured, they were less likely to be taken seriously. Together, they controlled a sizable percentage of the North Atlantic shipping trade.

As such, Anne would need to be briefed on what the current intelligence was on their end, and Murphy hoped that Anne had received a similar briefing from Mary, along with permission to share the information she'd been given. The trust would have to go both ways.

Now, if he only knew how badly he'd blundered in Galway.

He'd intended to drive west and have a rational, friendly conversation with the woman. Bring up the subject of the summit. Show her they could start communicating again. Show her…

Murphy didn't know what he wanted to show her.

Yes, you do.

That he no longer cared for her? He wasn't that self-delusional.

He'd always cared for Anne. But neither was he going to abandon politics and head west like a love-struck newborn. He had too many responsibilities. Further, it irked that she'd left him. It had taken him years to enjoy another lover after finally coming to the conclusion that she was not returning. Then he'd taken dozens in the hopes that she'd fly back to Dublin and bash in his head for betraying her.

Yes, he'd been an idiot. At least he was more discriminating in his affairs now.

Asking her to use her influence on a political rival had been unwise. It had taken a long time for her to trust him with the truth of her gift, and he'd swept away that trust with one reckless request.

He'd learned. He'd grown. He wasn't the brash boy she'd fallen in love with. He'd come to believe in self-control to a fault.

Except when faced with her voice in a dark pub, hearing the haunting notes of the song she sang when she missed her mother. Then he turned into a rabidly jealous, possessive, needy—

"You're going to break your desk if you keep your fingers dug in like that," Brigid muttered. "Poor thing is only marble, after all."

"Shut it, Brigid."

"Can I assume your mate is in the building?"

"Don't call her that. She hates it."

Brigid was silent for a moment. "You know, I would have never put you two together. None of the women you see are anything like Anne."

"In what way?"

"Well…" Brigid put down the file she'd been holding. "You date pretty young things—usually blond—that are in college or just graduated, which just seems like cradle robbing."

"Says the woman married to a thousand-year-old man with a fondness for Hawaiian shirts."

"Carwyn and I both know who the mature one is in our relationship," Brigid said with a sniff worthy of a great-aunt. "Don't change the subject. Your girls are bright, but not *too* bright. And they're always more dazzled by you than you are by them. After a few months of diversion, they're sent off with a kind word and an expensive piece of jewelry, and you never see them again except at cocktail parties or business meetings where everyone is very polite."

"I suppose you're correct." He leaned back in his chair. "How very *un*interesting."

"Anne doesn't wear jewelry."

"Her skin is sensitive. Most jewelry irritates her."

"Is it deliberate?"

"Is what deliberate?"

"Avoiding anyone who even reminds you of her."

Murphy glared at Brigid and rocked forward in his chair. "What do you think?"

"I think—now that I've thought of the two of you together—that she's exactly what you need." Brigid smiled and it lit up the room. "And you're exactly what she needs."

His eyes narrowed. "What does that mean?"

"She's—"

"Murphy?" Angie's voice flowed from the microphone on the voice-activated phone he used.

"Yes?"

"Dr. O'Dea is here to see you."

He took a deep breath and stood, straightening his tie. He'd been a ruffian again when he saw her. He needed to be collected. In control. Polite.

Murphy did everything to remain aloof when Anne walked into his office. But if Woolen Sweater and Leggings Anne had tempted him in the pub, Formally Dressed Anne threatened to bring him to his knees. Her suit was a plum color that made her vivid blue eyes glow. The waist nipped in, highlighting her lush curves in a way that reminded him of the formal dresses she'd once worn.

His cursed mind flashed back to the memory of Anne in a corset. More specifically, Anne coming *out* of a corset. The red lines pressed into her soft flesh where it had bound her body during the night. The groan of release when he unfastened her stays. He'd always sent the maid away for that. He'd release her slowly, kissing the newly revealed skin in the lamplight. Running his tongue under the buttons before the whole contraption fell to the floor.

"Patrick," she said, her voice just breathy enough to make him hope she was as affected as him. "Thank you for welcoming me to your city."

"Anne. Thank you again for coming."

A flash of anger quickly extinguished. Oh, she'd been angrier than that when her sister told her, if he had to guess.

"Of course," she said, her mouth spreading into a true smile when she saw Brigid. "Hi, Brig. You working late tonight?"

"Yeah, I—"

Murphy broke in. "As Brigid is your hostess while you're in the city, she'll be working fewer hours here at the office."

Brigid raised an eyebrow. "I will?"

"Anne is here in Mary Hamilton's stead," Murphy said. "As such, she's to be given the same level of security her sister would be. You'll need to start delegating nightly activities anyway since you'll be going with us to London. Talk to Declan about your schedule."

Brigid nodded. "I have a few people in mind already."

"Excellent." Murphy raised his eyes to Anne and tried to talk through the sudden nerves when he realized she was standing right in front of the painting she'd done that night in Galway. "Anne, I've also considered our… unique situation. I am comfortable stating the nature of our relationship publicly to ensure further security if you would like."

He'd claim her as his mate in public if she wanted. He'd be thrilled, in fact. The strength of that desire surprised him.

"One might speculate," Anne said, "that it would make me a higher-profile target should any threat exist. So no, thank you."

"Please inform me if your wishes change."

"I will."

She was so achingly polite, Murphy thought his fangs might burst through his skin. He wanted to grab her, take her against the glass wall behind him and—

"I won't waste any more of your time tonight," she said. "I understand there is a briefing about the summit in two nights' time with Tom and Declan?"

"There is."

She nodded at him. "I'll see you then. Brigid, I'll see you a bit later, yeah? I'm going to Josie's after this. Call there when you're done?"

"Will do."

And without another word, Anne spun and left him.

Again.

You know what you want, Murphy.

Yes, he did.

He let go of the granite paperweight he'd been holding in one hand, tossing the handful of gravel in the wastebasket beneath his desk. Brigid pretended not to notice as he shuffled files on his desk.

"Brigid?"

"Yes, boss?"

"You know that little network of spies and gossips you have running around Dublin?"

The corner of her mouth lifted. "I have no idea what you're talking about."

"Of course not. I have a message I'd like them to spread, if you please."

"Which is…"

"Patrick Murphy is unavailable. Permanently."

TOM tapped a pencil over the open notebook on the desk of the conference room. "Three issues tonight. Declan, have you and Brigid started on the security protocols for when Murphy will be in London?"

"She's suggested three employees to take her place. One vampire. Two human."

Murphy asked, "Which vampire?"

"Eamon Whitney."

Murphy frowned. "One of Deirdre's clan?"

"Yes."

Earth vampire, then. "I thought he was one of your tech boys."

Declan had been put in charge of the technology division ten years before. Seeing the problems caused by the inability to interact with the modern world, Murphy had chosen to focus on developing technology that vampires *could* use effectively. He refused to have modern advancements completely unavailable to him. It reminded him too much of his life as a human when luxuries had been off-limits.

"He is. But Eamon's also been shadowing Brigid for the past year or so. I've seen some potential there. His observation skills are above average."

"He's new."

"He is," Tom said, flipping through files, "but it looks like the humans she's paired him with for this are experienced men. Castleman and Snyder."

The fact that Snyder was female didn't stop Tom from calling her one of his "men." Murphy approved of the choices, having known both guards for years.

"I'll approve it, but Declan, I want you to be on top of things while we're gone. No disappearing into the labs for a bit, eh?"

Declan nodded. "It might slow down testing on Nocht."

Damn.

"Do what you can," Murphy said. "Security is the priority."

His software companies had spent years developing voice-recognition programs for use in everything from phones to cars to home-security systems. Nocht was their newest program. His hardware divisions focused on building devices and cases for technology out of nonreactive materials that vampires would be able to use.

It was a slow process. Prototypes were destroyed more often than not, and many vampires were resistant to change. But if Murphy had his way, there would be a vampire-friendly mobile device in the next ten years.

And he would make billions.

Declan had always had the sharpest mind, and Murphy had chosen him to lead the division, along with supervising surveillance and intelligence for his overall organization. When Brigid had come on board, it had freed Declan from some of his security duties, but Murphy would always turn to Tom and Declan first.

And Jack...

The pain had not lessened in the years since the revelation of his youngest child's betrayal. It never would. And Murphy doubted if he'd ever sire another.

"Item two," Tom continued. "Security briefing for London. Just how much are we sharing with Mary Hamilton?"

Murphy leaned back and tapped his fingers on his desk. "I don't know yet."

"Because you're not sure how much she's sharing with us?" Tom asked. "Or because we're talking about Anne?"

He pursed his lips. "I don't know that, either."

"Let's keep in mind," Declan said, "that there's very little information we could share with Mary at this point that would put our shipping operations at risk. Our contracts are secure and diverse."

"She doesn't know all our shells," Tom said.

"Does she need to?" Declan asked. "As far as she's concerned, these could be smaller companies—like Garvey's—that we have protection agreements with. There's no need to reveal we actually own them. They just give us information."

Murphy's ears pricked at the name of the young man he'd just made an agreement with. "Andrew Garvey?"

"Yeah, that one. He's your biggest fan now, boss. Making all sorts of inquiries." Declan grinned. "Become a regular docklands Sherlock Holmes, wouldn't you know?"

Murphy wasn't sure he liked that. Garvey was brash, as evidenced by the ambitious swipe he'd made at the contract with those Americans. But brash could also get you killed.

"Why don't you suggest he back off a bit," Murphy said. "He's young. We don't need to deal with a blunder because of his enthusiasm."

Tom gave him a sharp look, but Murphy only shrugged. He liked the young man. And Angie would give him hell if he came to any harm.

"I'll try, boss. But I have to say his activity reports have been gold. He caught an Albanian ship the other day trying to bypass our security check. Had only gone through the humans. Not our people."

"Albanian?"

Declan nodded and Murphy tucked the information away for later use. There had been an increase in traffic from the Balkans and the Black Sea region. It might mean nothing. But Murphy hadn't forgotten that the original company that had produced Elixir was in Bulgaria.

Tom said, "Wonder if Mary's also seeing an increase in traffic from that region."

"Make a note to ask Anne at the meeting."

"We'll need to be open with her," Tom said. "Otherwise, there isn't any use in this summit, boss."

"I know."

"Ease into things with Anne," Declan said with a smile. "It'll make sharing in London easier."

"Has anything with Anne ever been easy?" Murphy asked.

"No," Declan admitted. "But at least it'll be entertaining to see you run ragged again."

"Insolent children," Murphy said. "Both of you."

Joint laughter was the only response he received.

"Third item on the agenda," Tom said, not bothering to wipe the smile from his ugly face. "Josie has to send her regrets for tomorrow evening."

"What?" Murphy frowned. "She's been looking forward to *La Bohème* for months. Is she feeling well? Why—"

Tom held up a hand and pulled out a piece of folded dove-grey paper. "She writes, 'I simply cannot get away tomorrow evening. I do apologize, but it cannot be helped. I should add that when I mentioned my attendance at the opera to Anne earlier this evening—before I knew it was completely and utterly impossible for me to attend—she seemed quite enthusiastic and, dare I say, jealous of my tickets. One might suppose she would be open to an invitation.'" Tom folded the paper and tucked it back in his pocket. "I'm just readin' what she wrote. Don't kill the messenger."

Murphy closed his eyes and tapped a finger against his temple. "Your wife…"

"Meddles. I know," Tom said. "But as she cannot *possibly* get away tomorrow evening, I think you'd better call Anne."

"Maybe I'll give the tickets to Brigid and Anne."

"Brigid hates the opera," Declan said. "But I don't. Can I come?"

Tom and Murphy both spoke at the same time. "No."

MURPHY could admit that he'd cheated by inviting Anne via formal invitation. But if he'd called and asked, she'd have said no.

So, since he'd been an opportunistic bastard and used the excuse of a formal invitation from the leader of Dublin to the representative of Northern Ireland to ask his mate out for a bloody date, Anne was sitting next to him at the blandest concert hall in Europe, halfway through one of her favorite operas.

She'd said nothing to him since he picked her up at Carwyn and Brigid's massive home on the outskirts of town. She slid into the back of his car wearing a cocktail dress in some sort of wrap design and heels that made his fangs drop. The dress was the color of good red wine, the shoes could have been used as weapons, and Murphy couldn't keep his eyes off her.

Murphy didn't follow women's fashion beyond noticing what dates wore and giving the appropriate compliments. Most modern fashions did little to tempt him. Or perhaps it was most modern figures. The majority of his dates were willowy things, lovely in their own way, but they often reminded Murphy of the hollow-cheeked girls he'd grown up with. His sisters and cousins had never had enough to eat.

Anne, on the other hand, was luxury.

Full figured and soft, she embodied everything he'd hungered for as a human and everything he strived for in immortal life.

"You're missing the opera," she whispered.

"Don't care," he murmured. "I have the best view in the hall."

She kept her eyes on the stage, so he didn't know if his words angered or pleased her. Perhaps, if he read the set of her shoulders correctly, a little of both.

He was determined to have her again. She was living her quiet life in the west, but he knew she wanted more. She hadn't retreated back to the place where she'd lived as a human until they'd broken things off. She'd never made any mention of a country life when they lived together. Anne had loved being in the city. Had always hungered for travel.

But then he'd been a fool. And they had fought. And now...

He didn't know what she was hungry for, but he could sense it in his blood. A simmering restlessness that called to him.

Unleash me.

Feed me.

Make me yours again.

Maybe it wasn't a challenge she had intended to give him, but he'd take it up nonetheless. Anne was his mate. He'd done his research after she'd left him, worried that he'd never be whole again with half of himself gone.

Mate bonds were never intended to be taken lightly. That was why so many vampires guarded their blood more closely than gold. To give another immortal your blood tied you to them. To take another's tied them back. They could be bonds of family or friendship. Or passion. Anne and Murphy had shared blood for thirty years. They'd been almost inseparable in that time.

But partnerships—even the closest—did end. With vampires who lived for centuries, it was inevitable. As long as they'd been apart, their mate bond should have faded. That it hadn't told the superstitious part of Murphy they were meant to be. That was why no other relationship had satisfied. No other woman had appealed to him as Anne did.

She was his and he was hers. It was as simple and as complicated as that.

Now he just had to convince her.

"Are you enjoying yourself?" he asked, leaning closer to her. He closed his eyes and allowed his senses to take her in.

She smelled of the ocean and roses. A hint of lilac lingered in her hair from the spring garden at Brigid and Carwyn's home.

"The music is beautiful," Anne said. "It's been years since I've been to the opera."

"We'll have to see what's playing in London while we're there. Go to a proper concert hall."

A hint of a smile. "Such a snob, Patrick. I like this hall. The acoustics are wonderful."

"I'm not a snob. I only know what I like. And acoustics aside, this one looks like a lecture hall. An ugly one."

"It's modern."

"It's ugly."

She put a finger over his lips and he managed to suppress the smile of triumph. Barely.

Too soon, she drew it away again and leaned back in her seat.

Murphy saw one human eyeing Anne from farther down the aisle. He caught the man's eye and let a hint of the predator peek through his urbane exterior. The human looked away quickly and returned his attention to the stage.

"Behave," Anne said.

"Why?"

"I thought you were respectable now."

"I am when I need to be."

The opera flew by when Murphy would have had it drag. He had Anne next to him, dressed like a walking dream and forced to be civil. Sadly, it was over before eleven o'clock, and then they were walking to the car. It was only the beginning of the evening for them. He had meetings before the London strategy session at his office the next night.

"Who will be at the briefing tomorrow night?" Anne asked.

"You and me, obviously. Brigid, Declan, and Tom. Deirdre is going to try to make it, but she wasn't sure."

"Deidre?"

"She's very kindly agreed to make her fearsome presence known in Dublin while we're away to discourage any opportunistic thoughts by others."

Anne smiled. "And what about herself?"

"I'm not worried about Deirdre taking my city. She hates Dublin life."

Anne opened her mouth to respond but then closed it, and they continued to walk toward Iveagh Gardens where Murphy's driver was waiting for them. He might have been running late, per his employer's earlier instructions.

"And you?" Murphy asked. "How are you enjoying Galway?"

"I love it, of course."

"Not too dull?"

Her eyes flashed. "Of course not."

"Have you made it to New York?"

"You know I haven't. One of your little spies would have told you."

She'd always wanted to go to New York, but they'd never gone when they were together, and he hated that. Now air travel made everything easy for humans, but unless you were a vampire who had one of the very rare planes fitted for immortal use, you still had to travel by boat or overland. Murphy could have afforded the plane; he simply didn't see the need when he had so many ships at his disposal.

Anne refused to take any of them.

"Now, now," he chided. "Don't call Josie a spy. She's far more of a meddler than a spy."

She gestured between the two of them, dressed in their formal attire. "Clearly."

"She means well. She's a hopeless romantic, you know? I blame Tom. He's such a sentimental bastard."

For the first time in a hundred years, Murphy had the pleasure of hearing Anne laugh. Full throated and rich, her laughter reached into his chest and pulled something out of him. Desire. Intense satisfaction. He'd loved making her laugh.

I adore you.

He couldn't say it yet. Not yet.

"This was fun," she said, smiling at him, her eyes lit up and laughing. "I'd forgotten what good company you can be when you behave."

"I can be even better company when I *mis*behave."

"Now now," she said. "Let's not do that. We can be... friends, Murphy. We should be friends."

No, we absolutely should not.

"Of course," he said smoothly, lying through his teeth. "We should be. It'll make London much easier. We'll be spending a lot of time together, obviously."

She smiled and picked up the pace as they walked along the cobblestones. Murphy steadied her by grasping her elbow when her heel caught in one, teasing her in a friendly way about wearing proper footwear.

Friends?

Oh, Anne.

Murphy almost felt sorry for her.

Chapter Six

"DON'T DO THIS TO ME."

Brigid crossed her arms over her chest. "You've done it to yourself with the ridiculous comments and always needing to be the center of attention."

"Does our love mean nothing to you?"

The petite vampire shoved her mate toward the door of the library.

"I love you, Carwyn," Anne said. "Don't blame me for Brigid being mean."

"We all love you," Josie added. "But you need to go away now."

Carwyn protested. "I would like it known that I am very useful for girl-talk conversations."

"None of us want to be lectured in wrestling metaphors," Brigid said.

"I have *five*—wait, how many is it again?" He frowned and closed his eyes. "Four. I have *four* daughters. And a mate! I am wise in the ways of women."

He grabbed Brigid before the door closed and laid a scorching kiss on her mouth. When he pulled away, she was laughing.

"Go away, you madman. Go hunt something and run off some energy. You're crazy tonight."

"I'm crazy every night. That's why you love me."

"It's among the many reasons, yes." Brigid slapped his backside when he turned to leave.

"Oh, another please."

"Go!"

All three women were in stitches by the time the door closed.

When Anne was honest with herself, she could admit that she missed the city. As much as she liked her cozy home in Galway, she missed the nightlife and the concerts in Dublin, the museums and history.

And she missed the two women she was drinking with.

"He's mad," Brigid said. "I know. There's no excuse for him."

"He's lovely," Anne said. "If a little loud."

"I'm definitely writing him into a book," Josie added. "A vampire priest who likes Hawaiian shirts? Readers would love it. But do I make him a villain or a hero? I can't decide."

Brigid refilled their glasses of blood-wine and returned to the sofa she'd been sharing with her husband, which was now occupied by a large wolfhound she shoved to the side.

"It gets better every year," Josie said, sipping the wine.

"It does," Brigid said, rubbing the hound between his ears as he cuddled in with a happy groan. "This is the batch Gemma sent last fall. It's so much pleasanter than refrigerated. That winemaker Terry stole from France has made all the difference."

"Agreed," Josie said. "Wait… Terry didn't actually steal him, did he?"

Brigid frowned. "I don't think so."

Anne didn't care where the wine came from. All she knew was that it stemmed the growing hunger in her belly. Her bloodlust had grown worse since she'd arrived in Dublin. She'd had to keep her lips shut during the entire evening with Murphy so he didn't suspect how hungry she was in his presence.

Brigid and Carwyn had supplied her with a case of blood-wine upon her arrival. She was down to two bottles.

The library was Brigid's sanctuary in the large Dublin house. The smaller cottage she and Carwyn had lived in when they first mated had been abandoned in favor of the mansion. After the first year of their marriage, Carwyn's clan had invaded, leaving Brigid and Carwyn with guests or family of one sort or another at almost all times.

Human staff needed to be hired, and the big house had been opened.

Anne knew that marriage to a vampire like Carwyn ap Bryn was something her friend was still becoming accustomed to. Anne had worried about Brigid, but the friendship of Tom Dargin's quiet wife had helped.

Josie Dargin was, without a doubt, the most unusual vampire Anne had ever known. And for a vampire psychologist, that was saying something.

Turned at the edge of a wasting death, Josie still carried an ethereal air that made Anne's head turn to fairy stories and ancient myths. If Brigid looked like an angry pixie, Josie resembled a fae. Her features were too striking to be pretty. Her wide eyes and long nose leaned toward drama, not beauty. She was tall, thin, and claimed her dark hair had never been cut. It often hung wild around her face when she was in a writing daze. For though it was a secret to all but a select few, Josephine Dargin had been a prolific author for over a century.

Using different pen names, she'd written fantastical horror stories since she'd been a human. Gothic romances and macabre fantasies were her favorites, but Josie had tried some of everything. She changed her pen name when it suited her, and none of her publishers over the many years had any idea it was the same woman. A woman who was, in fact, one of the mythical creatures she wrote about.

Anne adored Josie. She had since the moment she'd met her when her friend was still human. But even Anne could admit that Josie was just a bit… different.

She was prone to lingering fugues. Anne had been there when Murphy turned her, knew he'd struggled with the decision, as humans turned during sickness could be unstable in immortality. Tom would have had it no other way. He adored his wife. A more unlikely pair Anne had never met, but they were fiercely devoted and unutterably happy.

"I had a dream the other night," Josie began, pursing her lips and whistling for another of the hounds, who dutifully went and laid his furry head on Josie's lap. "It was a lovely dream, Anne. You and Murphy reunited and you moved back to Dublin. And then you were all mine again, and we could have such lovely dinners."

"It's been one hundred years, Josie. I don't see us reconciling now."

"One hundred years is nothing to us," Josie said with a careless wave. "Has it really been that long? It doesn't seem it. But I suppose the years run together sometimes."

Brigid smiled. "Is this what I have to look forward to? A hundred years passing in a blink?"

"Ask Carwyn," Anne said.

In some ways, it was true. One hundred years away from Murphy hadn't lessened her attraction. Or the way they reacted to each other. It would have been so much easier if it had.

"You and Murphy," Josie continued. "Carwyn and Brig. Me and Tom. Then we'd just have to get Declan paired off and my family would be complete."

"You're such a meddler, Jo. Don't think I didn't know what you were doing with the opera last night."

"Did you have a lovely time?" Her green eyes were alight. "I knew you would. Was it very romantic?"

"It was very awkward."

"Liar. When you and Murphy were together, you were a force of nature," Josie said. "Gorgeous. Just gorgeous."

"You're a hopeless romantic."

Josie balled up a napkin and tossed it at Anne's head. "Of course I am, silly. That's my job."

Brigid said, "I have such a hard time imagining you two together."

"That's because Anne is so quiet now and Murphy is too damn polite," Josie said with a mischievous grin. "In their younger years, they were the wild ones. They heated a room just by walking in."

Anne shook her head. "Josie…"

"It's true. *Oh*"—Josie's head fell back, and she closed her eyes—"the way that man looked at you."

"Still looks at her that way," Brigid muttered.

Anne shook her head. "He does not."

"I'm sure he does," Josie said. "He looked at you as if you were his next breath—well, if he needed to breathe—his last sip of blood. The moon and stars together."

Anne felt her blood begin to surge. "Josie, stop. You're being dramatic."

"I'm glad someone is," Brigid said. "There's so much tension between the two of them things are liable to combust if they don't resolve it."

Josie leaned forward with wide, innocent eyes. "I have several ideas for tension resolution if you'd like to hear them."

"I'm sure you do," Anne said, setting down her wine. "Ladies, I'm here to prepare for the summit. I love spending time with you both, but I will be returning to Galway when this is over. Patrick Murphy is a part of my past, not my future."

"You're not going back to Galway." Josie's eyes drifted as she watched the fire. "No, you're not."

"I am. Don't be—"

"Not." Josie's voice took on a singing tone. "No, you're not not not."

Brigid and Anne exchanged a look.

"Jo?" Anne said, leaning closer.

"Not tonight. Such a sight. What a fright," Josie murmured under her breath.

Brigid looked slightly alarmed, but Anne had become accustomed to Josie's episodes long ago. She was rarely violent and always snapped out of them within a few minutes. The greatest danger was that they left her completely vulnerable, which was why Tom watched over his mate like a hawk.

Anne scooted next to her friend on the settee and laid her cheek on Josie's shoulder, clasping a cold hand in her own. Unlike most vampires,

Josie had never had much control over her amnis, which left her unable to consistently heat her body to a more humanlike temperature. As a water vampire, she remained quite cool.

"Jo-Jo," Anne said in a singsong voice. "Where are you?"

"Hell," Josie said, keeping her voice low. "Fire and rain. Fire and rain and blood in the streets. I'm hungry, and there's so much blood…"

The dog whined on Josie's lap as her rough voice sent a shiver down Anne's spine.

Hungry. So much blood…

"Come back, lovey." Anne stroked her cold cheek. "It doesn't sound very pretty there."

Josie inhaled suddenly, and Anne knew she was back.

"Did I wander?"

Anne nodded, ignoring Brigid's worried gaze. "Just a bit."

"Sorry." Josie took another breath and exhaled slowly. "I want you to be careful in London, Anne."

"Why?" The superstitious part of Anne could never quite dismiss Josie's "feelings."

"Don't know exactly." She squeezed Anne's hand. "Just be careful."

MURPHY'S satellite office in the docklands was well away from the glass-fronted building that housed his public offices. The old warehouse didn't look like much from the outside, but the interior was carefully cleaned and refurbished brick. The industrial braces and ducts hadn't been removed but had been highlighted and worked into the modern furnishings and concealed technology to create an office perfect for immortals. The only windows in the building were high and covered with decorative, solid shutters.

"It's completely secure," Tom said, nudging Anne's shoulder at the conference table, which had been built from reclaimed wooden pallets. "Had a human construction team fit it with the most up-to-date insulation to protect against electronic monitoring, listening devices of all kinds. Murphy ordered the retrofit, but I claimed it as soon as it was finished. I run most of the security out of this office."

Tom's crooked smile had always charmed her.

"Most vampires don't use electronic spying," Anne said.

"The smart ones do," Declan said from across the table. "Or they have their humans use it."

"So I'm to assume you do?" Anne asked, her interest piqued.

Declan looked to Murphy first, but the vampire who'd behaved so rashly in Galway and so politely at the opera only gave a measured nod that reminded Anne her loyalty no longer lay with the three men around her but with a rival who'd openly opposed Murphy at many turns.

She hated her sister a little in that moment.

"We do," Declan said. "It's still very effective. Most immortals are willful Luddites. We use it against them. Our most valuable intelligence usually comes from electronic communications from human employees associated with vampires."

Anne said, "But with a large human staff, don't you run the same—or even increased—risk of exposure?"

"If the left hand doesn't know what the right is doing," Declan said, "the risk is less. Not eliminated, mind you, but—"

"I treat my people well," Murphy said, not looking up from the files he'd been perusing on the table. "A well-fed dog has no need to scavenge." He looked up, focused on Anne. "He'll stay at his master's side through fire."

"Tell me you're not comparing your human employees to dogs," she said.

He shrugged. "Simply an illustration. The fact remains: While temptation is always a threat, humans who are treated well have less inclination to look elsewhere for patronage. As for immortal influence, I make it a point to know who is in my city at all times." His eyes flickered with some dark emotion. "I didn't always, but when I make mistakes, I do not repeat them."

Jack. He was talking about Jack.

And maybe her?

Anne knew it could very well be both. But while her heart was too stubborn to leave him entirely, Anne had also learned her lesson about trusting too easily.

"Brigid is late," she said, remarking on the obvious since she had nothing else to fill the tension-laced air between them.

"She usually is."

As if on cue, a tiny tornado burst through the door. "Sorry! Sorry. Blame this one." She jerked a thumb over her shoulder at the auburn-haired behemoth behind her who was carefully locking the door since they were the last to arrive.

Anne smiled immediately. "Carwyn! I didn't know you were coming."

"Neither did I," Murphy said. "Listen, Carwyn—"

"Sorry to interrupt—wait no. That's a lie," Carwyn said, winking at Anne. "I'm not sorry at all. Don't get your breeches in a bunch, Murphy. Gemma called just before Brig was leaving with the final guest list for the summit. Thought you might want to know who was on the menu in London. I'm not intruding."

"Yes, you are," Brigid said. "I told you I could bring them."

"But then I wouldn't get to see that expression he makes," Carwyn said, nodding toward Murphy. "Like an irritated cat in a necktie. Adorable."

Anne smothered a smile. While she could see the fixed look of annoyance on Murphy's face, she also saw the hint of laughter in his eyes.

It was hard not to love Carwyn. While any immortal leader would chafe at such a powerful and respected vampire living in their territory, Carwyn had a startling lack of personal ambition. He'd been a Catholic priest until only a few years ago, and his devotion to his large extended family had never waned. The fact that he'd mated to one of Murphy's lieutenants had to rankle, but Anne heard it hadn't stopped Murphy from using Carwyn's connections when it suited him.

Gemma, one of their hosts in London, was Carwyn's oldest daughter, and Deirdre, the earth vampire who would be overseeing

Dublin with Tom and Declan in Murphy's absence, was one of his other daughters.

Anne's own sire had the utmost respect for Carwyn, and he didn't like many.

"Do tell," Murphy said, his arm sweeping graciously toward the chairs at the end of the conference table. "I can guess most, but it will be good to review them for Anne's benefit anyway."

"Thank you." She was far from offended by Murphy's assumption of her ignorance. She had made a point to avoid vampire politics as much as possible. She was going as a representative of her sister, but also as a somewhat neutral party since Mary had independent alliances with many of the players in the North Atlantic.

"A quick reminder," Declan said. "For everyone, but especially Anne since she's coming up to speed. This summit is focusing on the shipping and transportation aspect of Elixir. We all know it's shown up in varying degrees across Europe. Terry's aim with this summit is to focus on who is moving the drug, in the hopes that it will reveal who is behind the production. So he only invited those with some kind of shipping interest, particularly in the North Atlantic. As far as we know, infection rates in the North Sea and the Baltic have been the most concentrated."

"Why?"

"We don't know," Declan said. "That's one of the reasons we're going."

"How many were invited?" Anne said.

"Terry didn't tell us," Brigid said. "But we do know seven have accepted, including us. That leaves five foreign-vampire interests outside the British Isles."

"The first fabulous contestant," Carwyn said, leaning back in his seat, "is Jean Desmarais in Marseilles."

"Not a surprise," Tom said. "He and Terry have been doing business for years."

"It'll be good to see Jean," Carwyn said. "Haven't spent much time with him since Rome."

"He's in the Mediterranean, yes?" Anne asked. "Mary mentioned something about cargo from the Eastern Mediterranean as being of some concern when she briefed me."

"It is," Murphy said. "Most of the shipments of Elixir we've intercepted have had origins in the Eastern Mediterranean with final destinations in the north."

"But Mary also mentioned several countries. A Greek ship. A Bulgarian one. Turkish—"

"It would be shortsighted"—Carwyn broke in—"to take human borders or labels into account in that region. The Eastern Mediterranean has some of the oldest shipping interests in the world. Human governments change by the decade sometimes, but the council in Athens has not changed significantly in the past thousand years."

"A thousand years?" Anne said.

Declan said, "Rumors are the Athenians don't even move some years. Literally. They don't *move*. Their court treat them as gods and bring humans for them to feed."

Carwyn shrugged. "Rumors are only that. Rumors. Rome watches Athens with suspicion, and Tripoli does not lower its guard. Don't ever discount the Greeks. They control the Bosphorus, and most of the factions in the Eastern Mediterranean owe them some kind of allegiance, even if it is symbolic."

"Does Jean Desmarais?"

"No. He may have some interests in the Mediterranean," Murphy said, "but the majority of his interests still lie in the Atlantic, and he's a known ally of Terry's. I expect he'll be there for information. I don't think France has been heavily infected."

"He's also Terry's rival," Declan said. "He and Terry have been competing to enter the blood-wine market the past two years."

"Blood-wine is… a whole other issue," Murphy said. "Who's next?"

"Leonor in Spain," Brigid said. "Another ally."

"And another blood-wine competitor," Declan muttered, drawing glares from both Murphy and Tom. "I'm only pointing it out."

Tom said, "Leonor had a challenge a few years back, yes? Got that all straightened out?"

"She has," Anne said. "Mary and Leonor have open communication. I think Leonor's leadership is very solid."

She'd wrested back control of the Iberian Peninsula the same way Mary kept Northern Ireland, ruthlessly and with little conscience.

"Jetta Ommunsdotter will be there," Carwyn said, nodding at Anne. "I believe Mary sending Anne was the decider on that one."

"I can't take credit," Anne said. "Everyone knows Mary and Jetta are friends who hate each other."

Everyone around the table laughed.

"What is it the human girls say?" Brigid asked. "Frenemies?"

"Something along those lines," Declan said. "Good to know even the oldest of us never outgrow those impulses."

"The older I get," Carwyn said, "the more the vampire world resembles a human schoolyard."

"Our party, Terry, Jean, Leonor, and Jetta make five," Murphy said. "None unexpected. So who are the surprises?"

"Two that surprised me," Carwyn said. "Cormac O'Brien is coming and bringing his youngest daughter, Novia."

"New York is coming to the party?" Tom said.

"Cormac doesn't particularly surprise me, but the daughter does," Carwyn said. "When I say young, I mean young. She hasn't been immortal more than five years."

Anne's eyebrows rose of their own volition. "He must be grooming her for something important."

"The O'Briens are a mob," Murphy said. "Half of them are swindlers, and the other half are gamblers."

"Swindlers and gamblers," Anne said. "So that makes them different from you how?"

Brigid snickered, but Murphy only let the corner of his mouth turn up. "I grew up. They never have."

Anne had her doubts about his growing up, but she let them remain silent. This wasn't about her and Murphy, it was about something far more important.

"I can't deny that the O'Briens are clannish and can be a bit... odd," Carwyn said. "But Cormac is the most legitimate of them. He's the youngest of the brothers and trying to take his people in a new direction."

"While fighting with his brothers every step of the way."

"Perhaps this Novia is the new face of the O'Briens," Tom said. "New generation. Less isolated. More political. That might be why he's bringing the girl."

Carwyn nodded. "That's what I suspect. We'll watch and see. Cormac owes me a few favors he doesn't want me to collect. If we can twist any information out of the greedy bastard, I'll count it a win."

"Anyone else?" Anne asked, making notes as fast as her hand could write. It was a mountain of information to take in, and she'd have to translate all of it for Mary before she rested for the day.

"The Dutch."

Anne dropped her pencil. "Really?"

"Really," Brigid said. "Rens Anker has agreed to come."

Even Anne knew that the Dutch, once the powerhouse of world shipping in both the human and vampire worlds, had become isolated in recent decades. The patriarch of the Anker clan had been killed mysteriously, and his two sons had taken over. Rens and Bastiaan Anker had taken their sire's name as their own but had not taken on his public persona. Almost immediately, they'd sold off much of their fleet and focused on domestic issues in the lowlands, most recently scientific and environmental research.

"Gemma's brother has recently mated into the Anker clan. There's a relationship there now. She might have taken advantage of that to lure him to London," Carwyn said.

"The Dutch are unexpected," Murphy said. "But not unwelcome."

He'd been quiet for much of the meeting, so when he spoke, everyone turned to listen.

"They are secretive," he said. "But they've always had the widest connections. Asia. Africa. South America. There's nowhere that they don't have people. Publicly, they've divested from trade. Privately, I've suspected for a while that they're trading in something else."

"Information?" Anne said. "They're building a network of spies?"

"They already have the network," Murphy said. "And they've invested in satellite communications, which is almost unheard of for our kind. Look at vampire history. Only three things really retain value. Gold, blood, and information. The Dutch have plenty of gold. Old Jon Anker saw to that. I think Rens and his brother are trying to corner the market on information."

"That may be," Carwyn said. "But are they coming to London to buy or sell?"

"Or," Anne said, "is it more simple than that? Gold, blood, and information. Elixir has the potential to affect everyone. They could be worried about the blood."

Murphy nodded at her, a smile tipping up the corner of his mouth, and Anne felt a sudden spike of pride for her insight.

Which was quickly killed when she noticed how many notes she'd have to review.

A French playboy.

A Spanish empress.

A Swedish rival.

An American eccentric.

And a Dutch spy.

The conference hadn't started, and Anne was already drowning.

"I HATE you," she told her sister over the speakerphone in her secure wing of Brigid and Carwyn's house.

"No, you don't."

"I do."

"What did Murphy do?"

"Nothing."

Except kiss me in Galway and remind me that I miss him like a lost limb.

Stare at me during the opera as if he'd eat me alive in the most pleasurable way possible.

Show off his intellect, which has always been the most attractive thing about him.

"Patrick Murphy has been a complete gentleman," she said. "Unerringly polite and respectful. *Painfully* welcoming."

Anne heard Mary suck on her cigarette and release a breath. "Hateful man. That would irritate the piss out of me."

She squeezed her eyes shut. "Why did you ask me to do this?"

There was a suspicious pause on the other end of the line.

"To help me, of course."

"And?"

"You need to leave your house more."

"I am happy in Galway."

"No, you aren't."

"I am. I have a nice life. A peaceful life. I help—"

"You, my dear sister, were about to murder a patient or go on a killing spree in the local village."

Anne's mouth dropped. "I was not!"

"I could hear it in your voice."

"I'm a *healer*, Mary."

"Doesn't mean you're not a *vampire*, Anne. You needed a challenge. We all do. And you have been hiding there ever since that man broke your heart. There's something restless in you. Something wrong. I've been sensing it for at least two years."

"So you throw me into a situation where I have to interact with Patrick? That seems... torturous and excessive."

Mary paused. "Torturous?"

Too much.

"Not torturous." She tried to backtrack. "Irritating."

"You didn't say irritating, you said *torturous*. There's a distinct difference."

Anne made an angry fist at the phone. "I hate you."

"So you said." Her sister's voice had taken on a decidedly suspicious tone. "You still have feelings for him."

Anne tugged on the wrap she'd thrown around herself.

"Of course I have feelings," she said calmly. "It's impossible not to have feelings for someone—"

"Don't use the psychologist voice on me."

"I *am* a psychologist, and this is my voice. Therefore—"

"You have *feelings* for him. You've never gotten over that man, have you?"

"Do you have to say 'that man' in that particular tone of voice? It's like you think of him as a disease."

"He is."

"I daresay he's probably improved over the past seventy years."

"He tried to take advantage of you, and then he broke your heart!"

Anne had nothing to say because Mary was correct. In all her sister's struggles to attain power, she'd never once asked Anne to use her influence on a rival. Not even when her own life was at stake. Never had she put her sister in danger or hinted at using Anne's power to her own advantage.

Not once.

"I know he did," Anne said quietly. "It's not like I could forget."

When she had finally told Murphy, years after their mating, the influence she could sometimes effect on other immortals by manipulating amnis, Murphy had assured her of his secrecy. Had sworn the knowledge would be safe with him. And then he'd asked her—not even a year later—to use it on a rival.

Not even a year.

It had been an astounding violation of her trust, and Murphy hadn't even comprehended why she'd been so offended.

Mary had been livid.

"I have never trusted that man," Mary said. "I didn't know you still had feelings for him, and I don't want to—"

"I'll be fine," Anne said. "I can handle it."

"I don't doubt you, but…"

She felt her fangs fall. "The fact that you said 'but' tells me you doubt me entirely."

"Drop it," Mary said abruptly. "Forget the summit. Go home. Or come to Belfast. They can do without me. Without us. I'll write Father and have him explain it to Terrance Ramsay."

"No. I'm staying."

"Why?"

"I don't like the politics. Can't stand all the secrets and intrigue. But this is important. Unless they can find out who's shipping Elixir, they have no chance of eliminating it."

"It's not going to be eliminated," Mary said. "This is all an exercise in futility. Pandora's box is open, and more than one vampire has a death wish. Don't your textbooks say something about that? If there's a market for Elixir, someone will make it. The damn formula is probably on the Internet by now."

Anne threw up her hands. "So why send me at all?"

"I don't like people trying to sneak into my territory," her sister said. "I suppose you're right. Stay, then. Someone is making a power grab, and I won't have others being proactive while I bat away on the defense. Offense is a far better plan. Besides, you said you had shopping to do."

Anne closed her eyes and let her head hit the back of her chair. Trust Mary to change her mind at *least* four times in the space of a single argument.

"What should I share?" Anne asked. "So far, they've been giving me all the information and I've only shared a little."

"I trust you. Share what needs to be shared and no more. You don't have political experience, but you're smarter than most of them and you're perceptive as hell. People tell you things, even without your influence. Use that when you get to London."

"I will."

"And send your notes of the meeting with Robert when he gets there. I'm sending him directly to Carwyn's home. He should be there tomorrow night. Notes in his hand and no one else's."

Robert was Mary's personal courier and the most frightening little human Anne had ever met. He had dead eyes, but he was utterly loyal to her sister.

"Did you translate them yet?"

Anne eyed the stack of paper she had yet to start on. "Not yet. I'll do it when we get off the phone."

"Caution, sister."

"You call it caution, I call it paranoia with disturbing hints of narcissism."

Their sire was old. So old that the language of his human years had died long ago. Only he and his two daughters spoke it anymore, making it the easiest way for them to communicate privately. A keen linguist well versed in early Celtic dialects might be able to decipher some of it, but it would take months of study.

"You'll see Father in London," Mary said.

"I'm sure I will."

"That's the other reason I'm sending you. Terry will want to appease the old man."

Anne pursed her lips. "Should I be offended that I'm the token political daughter here?"

"No," Mary said. "If you were the token political daughter, Father would have mated you to the priest years ago. Don't think he didn't consider it."

"I feel so loved."

"Maybe you don't feel loved enough," Mary said wryly. "That's probably why you're so cross."

Anne banged her head softly against the wall. "Did I mention that I hate you?"

"Not in the past five minutes."

"I do. I really, really do."

Chapter Seven

MURPHY STEPPED INTO HIS OFFICE whistling, only to find an unexpected—though not unwelcome—intrusion.

"Mr. Garvey," he said. "I wasn't expecting you tonight."

Andrew Garvey shoved his hands in his pockets and tried to swallow his obvious nerves. Humans didn't always register their reaction to the predators vampires were, but Garvey was no clueless human. He knew why his pulse sped; he just battled past the urge to run. Murphy had to respect that.

"I, uh, I told Tom I had some news for you, and he wanted me to come to the office with it. Tell you myself."

"Fair enough." Murphy frowned. "Is Tom here?"

"He went out to fetch something. Said he'd be back in a moment."

Murphy motioned to one of the chairs near the couch in his office. "Have a seat then. We'll wait until he comes back."

"Thank you, sir."

He took a seat himself, trying to put the man at ease.

"How's business been? The new contract working out?"

"It is, yeah." Garvey nodded. "Been expanding a bit, even. Don't want to go into debt for it, but I think now's not a bad time to buy with a bunch of lads going out."

"Seems sound."

"Yeah, I hope so." Garvey tapped his finger on his knee. "I just wanted you to know... Tom told me to back off on looking into things for you."

"I'm glad," Murphy said. "These could be dangerous individuals."

"I know. But... this recent thing, I thought you should know." Garvey looked stricken. "Jesus, any decent person would be bothered by it, but especially anyone with a family, yeah?"

He frowned. "I'm afraid I don't know what you're—"

Murphy broke off when the door opened and Tom walked in.

"Evenin', boss. Andrew. Did you tell him anything yet?"

Garvey shook his head. "Was just about to, but—"

"Good. He needs to see." Tom threw a set of photographs onto the coffee table in front of Murphy. "I am rarely tempted to murder, Murphy, but this shit..."

Murphy picked up the photographs and paged through them, wondering what had left his usually calm lieutenant so angry. "What are these?"

He could see the obvious. Young women ranging from early teens to twenties, with hollow cheeks and dead eyes, huddled in what looked like cargo holds. The thing that jumped out at him immediately was their looks.

They were obviously sick, but if you could see past it, all the girls were very attractive. In fact, the cynical thought that leapt to his mind was that the photographs resembled a macabre fashion shoot, only the models were barely clothed in rags.

"Human trafficking?" he asked. There was no way to avoid all of it, but he did his best to eliminate what he could. "Have they been reported to the human authorities?"

"Don't think we want to do that just yet," Tom said. "It's more than that, Murphy."

He folded his hands carefully. "Tell me."

Tom nodded toward Garvey, who started to speak.

"We didn't see the girls. It was the boys on deck that jumped out to some of my lads," Garvey said. "Raised their suspicions right away. They weren't sailors. Didn't look like pros at all. Then one of my lads caught one trying to sneak ashore from a reefer. Cold ship from the Black Sea carrying caviar, of all things. It's an EU country, but the boy trying to sneak ashore had nothing. No papers. Only spoke a little English, and he was desperate to leave. He weren't a regular sailor, Murphy."

Tom nodded. "Once Garvey reported the incident to me, some of the lads and me searched the ship. Thank fuck I took mostly human staff. We found the girls in the hold. More young men up on deck working. I think they used the boys for cheap labor and hid the girls."

Something Tom said jumped out at him. "Why were you glad you took humans?"

Tom pulled out a handkerchief-sized piece of cloth from his pocket and tossed it to Murphy.

He caught it and put it to his nose, almost retching from the sickly-sweet smell of pomegranate.

"That's a piece from one of the boy's shirts."

Elixir.

Murphy said, "Andrew, I'd like you to go now. I need to discuss things with Tom, but I want to thank you for your vigilance. You really must step away though."

"But, Murphy—"

"I insist." Murphy took the human's hand and squeezed. "You'll mind your own business in the harbor, Andrew Garvey. Report anything unusual, but leave the detecting work to others."

Garvey blinked, as if just waking. "Course I will, Mr. Murphy."

"Good man."

Garvey was still frowning and confused when Tom ushered him out. Murphy flipped through the pictures again, looking at the young humans with new eyes.

There were dozens of them.

"Are they all infected?" he asked.

Tom sat in the chair Garvey had vacated. "As far as we can tell, yes."

"Damn." He squeezed his eyes shut. "Damn damn damn."

There was a research base set up in California working on a cure for Elixir, but it hadn't found success. Some of the infected humans they'd treated so far were improving, but none were cured. Whoever had infected these young people had sentenced them to a slow and painful death and sent them to Murphy's city to be unleashed in the vampire population there.

"How many boats?" he wondered aloud.

"There's no way of knowing."

"I need you to get the word out to Mary Hamilton immediately. Belfast needs to be aware we're not just looking for cargo anymore. We're looking for carriers. Call Terry too."

"Already done."

"What have you done with them?" He put down the photos when he came to one of a girl no older than thirteen. "Fecking hell, Tom. What do we do with them? How many are there?"

"Twenty-seven girls and fifteen boys. All from eastern Europe. Right now, I put Angie on getting one of the new warehouses outfitted as a dormitory. We've got doctors checking up on them—ones we trust—but some of them said these kids have weeks or months at most. We're trying to find interpreters. Some of the kids speak a bit of English, so they're helping those that don't."

"We can't let them into human hospitals or the general population. I don't like keeping them captive, but—"

"We have to. We've worked too hard to hide the existing infections from the human hospitals. And it's not as if they can do anything for 'em."

Murphy had gone so far as to set up a private hospital outside the city where most of the human Elixir victims had been treated. But like sanatoriums of old, humans addicted to Elixir truly went there to die.

"We'll secure the warehouse," Tom continued. "Make them as comfortable as possible. A lot of them are in very poor health already. Declan has a call in to Baojia's people in California. He handles the security at the facility there, and we're hoping he'll have some ideas."

"I've heard of him."

"He's also close friends with Lucien Thrax, the doctor working on it. We'll do the best we can."

"Does Brigid know about this?"

"Not yet."

Brigid had lost one of her closest human friends to Elixir, one of the first cases they'd ever seen in Ireland.

"I don't like leaving the city with this hanging over you, Tom."

Tom shook his head. "We'll handle it. You need to go to London, boss. Now more than ever."

IF there was ever a time when Murphy needed to hit something—and hard—it was that night. He'd toured the warehouse not long after Andrew Garvey had left his office, overseeing the preparations from a distance. Elixired humans were more than tempting to vampires. Even the most self-controlled of his lieutenants had confessed to temptation near them. Thus, security for the converted warehouse had to be overseen by his most trusted humans.

They were all angry. Brigid was wrecked. Anne was silent. Every vampire in his organization was on edge. No coincidence then that Carwyn had agreed to enter the ring with Murphy.

Both men stripped off their shirts and tossed them over the railing. There were no humans in the club that night. Murphy had sent them all home early. He'd asked Tom for a bout, only to have the behemoth of an earth vampire volunteer.

"No holding back?" Murphy said. "This should be interesting."

"Are you sure you want that?" Carwyn asked.

"You think I asked Tom for a fight because I wanted easy?"

Murphy bounced on his toes, the water in the room already drawn to his skin, coating it in a fine sheen of what looked like sweat. He flexed his wiry body and eyed Carwyn's bulk.

No way could that giant move fast enough to beat him, but if he got his hands on Murphy, all bets were off. Taking a punch from that bear of a man would put him down.

Carwyn flexed his hands and smiled. "Say when, lad."

"You won't be saying anything, old man."

The first blow caught Carwyn mid-laugh. His jaw snapped back as Murphy punched him full in the mouth.

"Bloody hell," the old earth vampire muttered, flexing his jaw. "They weren't exaggerating."

Anne called from the ropes, "He was a bare-knuckles champion in his human years for a reason, Carwyn."

Puffed up from her words, Murphy almost missed the blur of movement that could have meant his end. He spun and dodged at the last millisecond. Was Carwyn boxing or wrestling?

Did he care?

Fighting at vampire speed meant that all his senses had to be alert. His heart pumped in time with his steps. One-one-two. One-one-two. He had speed, but Carwyn had strength. They flew around the ring faster than human eyes would be able to track.

Murphy released his anger on the other immortal. His rage. His frustration.

The children would die, and there was nothing he could do to stop it.

Another punch, this time to Carwyn's kidney.

He couldn't stem the river of drugs into his city with so many ships and only the slim night hours to properly police them.

Carwyn's fist glanced off Murphy's cheek, splitting it open and releasing a torrent of blood. He felt his fangs drop and cut twin slices on his lower lip.

Murphy had lost a son to this madness, and it had ripped out his heart. He'd almost lost his own mind.

The pain fed the rage until all he felt was the loop of sensation, the quick burning pleasure of anger and ache. Ducking behind his opponent, Murphy landed two vicious blows to Carwyn's kidneys before he dodged away.

But he couldn't avoid the roundhouse punch to the jaw the earth vampire finally landed.

Th-thunk. *Thunk.*

Murphy crashed through the ropes and skidded on the concrete floor outside the ring, shredding his skin as he rolled. Carwyn didn't stop. He followed and crouched to land another blow, but Murphy had already turned away, sending Carwyn's fist cracking into the floor as Murphy leaped on the other man's back, fixing his ropy arms around Carwyn's neck and pulling hard.

He could hear Tom and Declan shouting in the background. Hear Brigid and Anne yelling. He pulled back harder, felt Carwyn's collarbone snap under his arm. Felt his own blood pouring from his eyes and mouth and nose.

Carwyn reached up and patted his arm gently. "I yield, lad."

Murphy gripped tighter.

"There now, Murphy." Carwyn's words were faint because Murphy was cutting off most of his air, but the bigger vampire was utterly patient. "I yield."

Murphy released Carwyn's neck with a gasp, blood clouding his vision as he rolled to the side and spread his arms, his skin knitting together as he stared at the ceiling of the old gymnasium.

"You didn't have to yield." He'd looked. Carwyn wasn't even bleeding. Murphy had barely broken the skin.

Carwyn gave him a small smile. "Feeling better?"

"Not hardly."

Murphy could hear the other vampires approaching, but Carwyn waved them back.

"They call you arrogant," Carwyn said. "And you are. But you took on the responsibility of this town when you were hardly more than a boy. You grabbed the reins from a corrupt leader and wouldn't let go."

"I wanted this city and I took it," Murphy said, still staring at the ceiling. "Don't try to make me a saint."

"I won't. But the fact that this weighs on you as it does everything about your character."

He let out a breath. "I'm so fucking angry."

"You should be."

Murphy finally turned his head to look at him. The old vampire's blue eyes were ancient, the usual joviality stripped bare. Murphy understood why so many were drawn to him. He was as solid as the earth he drew power from. In that moment, Murphy didn't feel like the vampire who led a city and a multinational corporation. He felt like a boy.

"What do I do?" he asked Carwyn.

"You go to London. You let Deirdre and Tom take care of things here," Carwyn said, his blue eyes holding icy rage. "We find out who is doing these terrible things—"

"And we end them," Murphy said, standing and holding his hand out. "I will end them."

"You're not alone."

Glancing at Tom and Declan, at Anne and Brigid, he nodded. "I know."

A knock came at the heavy metal door. Tom and Declan exchanged a look as Murphy grabbed his shirt to wipe the blood away.

"Answer it," he said. "They wouldn't knock if it wasn't an emergency. Not with the mood I left them in."

Murphy caught the words a moment before he flew into the night.

"Garvey… body. Barely recognized… fire."

MURPHY made sure he was fully submerged in the dark river before he screamed his rage. The muddy waters of the Liffey curled around him, threading through his hair and brushing his face. A longing mother, she tried to soothe.

He would not be soothed.

Andrew Garvey's body hadn't been dumped in public. Whoever had killed the observant young man didn't want to attract human attention.

Just Murphy's.

Revenge? Simple frustration that their shipment and boat had been taken? Whoever killed the human had treated him like nothing more than a bug to be squashed. He wasn't a person but an example. If the guard who'd found him burning in the skip behind Murphy's new warehouse hadn't been a water vampire, it was possible there would have been little left to identify Garvey in the end.

Murphy climbed out of the river and walked to his car, snapping at his driver to open the trunk as he approached. Then he peeled off his wet clothes and stuffed them in a bag, toweling off his hair to remove the worst of the damp. He donned a pressed white shirt and wool trousers before he went to examine the body, because Andrew Garvey had pressed his shirt before he met with Murphy, even though the pocket had been torn.

The human's charred body had curled into itself, and the acrid smell of accelerant covered the area, but Murphy could see the single gunshot wound to the back of the head when Brigid turned over the body. At least it appeared that he'd been dead when the fire started.

Murphy stared at the remains of Andrew Garvey in the early-morning hours, wondering how he was going to tell Mrs. Garvey that her husband, the father of her baby girl, was dead. Declan stood next to him while Brigid murmured questions and quiet orders to the guards surrounding the scene. Tom had been dispatched to double-check the security of the warehouse where the Elixir carriers were being held.

"Arsewise, boss," Declan said. "You warned him."

"This is not Andrew Garvey's fault," Murphy said, his eyes never leaving the body. "This was never his fault. He was a good man who was trying to do the right thing. The bastards who did this will die."

Declan shifted. "Murphy—"

"I will kill them myself," he said. "Human or vampire. I don't care who they work for. If you find them, you will hold them for me."

Visions of blood were the only things keeping his rage in check.

"Do we call the Gardai?" Declan asked.

"If we do, we risk them asking questions about the ship we took. Risk coming under suspicion ourselves. We can't do that."

"Whoever did this—"

"Is likely long gone."

Declan said, "I'll do what I can on my end while you're in London. I've already tracked down the ship's manifest and crew, but we both know the names are likely to be fakes."

"Is the reefer secured?"

"It is."

"Tomorrow night you'll go down and try to catch any scent trails left. I want a full investigation."

Brigid came to them. "I don't see an exit wound on the body, which means we might get ballistics."

Murphy caught Anne's scent though she said nothing. She came behind him and slipped a cool hand into his. He wanted her there, but he didn't. It was ugly and reminded him too much of what his mate had to witness before.

"Murphy," Brigid said. "With all this happening, are you sure—"

"You're going to London with Anne and me. Declan knows how to run a murder investigation."

Brigid nodded. "I'll get you the name of my man for ballistics, Dec."

"Thanks," he said before he looked at Murphy. "And the ship?"

"Go through the usual channels. Pay whoever we need to in order to make it disappear."

"Yes, boss."

Declan and Brigid walked away, leaving Murphy alone with the one person in the world he wanted more than any other.

The person who distrusted him the most.

"Patrick, you had no way of knowing—"

"No, that's bollocks, Anne. I should have put a man on him. Should have known they might go after a human in my organization."

"He wasn't in your organization."

"Fuck that. He was. I should have known."

He dropped her hand and walked away from the fire-blackened body and toward his car. There was nothing else he could do that night. He needed to take shelter, and he didn't want to go to any of his homes. Didn't want to face any questions from servants.

His human driver got out and opened the back door for him just as Anne put her hand on his shoulder.

"Patrick, please."

He stopped but didn't turn. "I can't be polite tonight, Áine. Leave me be."

She dropped her hand, and Murphy slid into the car, feeling the first ache in his bones that warned him of the sun.

Where to go?

His old driver, sensing his mood, asked him, "Campsite, sir?"

"Good thinking, Ozzie."

Ozzie made his way out of the city and to the large protected campsite Murphy had set up years ago to appease his human kin. The leader of his clan knew who and what he was. Didn't like it but accepted it. They were too superstitious to give him any problems. Outside of his Traveller clan, his caravan was known only to him and Ozzie, who was a distant kinsman. It wasn't hard to conceal. Not even vampires were more secretive than Travellers.

He noticed the playground had been torn up again when they pulled in. The meadow had been cut, but he could see trash lying about, likely from some other clan passing through. It wasn't surprising.

"Oz."

"I'll take care of it in the morning, sir. Have a word with Old Keenan."

"The rubbish is one thing, but I won't have them selling the children's play set for scrap. Make that clear."

"Yes, sir."

The windowless vardo back in the trees was painted a dusky green to blend in with the forest. It backed onto a small stream so he could hear the water running when he woke. The children did not play near it. There were horseshoes nailed into the trees around it, and mirrors and

94

bits of bone hung from their branches. The old women had planted wild roses around his wagon fifty years ago, but he excused their superstition and chose to enjoy the fragrance instead.

The caravan looked traditional on the outside, but the interior was modern. Ozzie would guard him during the day, but Murphy knew no one would dare bother him. He was safe as houses in the camp.

He undressed and stepped outside to dunk himself in the stream. Braced from the water, he shook off and took refuge in the darkness of the wagon, opening a bottle of blood-wine he kept in reserve. It tasted sour and metallic on his tongue, but beggars could not be choosers, and Ozzie had donated blood to him the week before.

A quiet tap on the door roused him from the stupor he felt creeping closer. It had to be Ozzie, checking to see if he needed anything before dawn. Murphy walked to the door and opened it, clad in nothing more than a woolen blanket wrapped around his hips.

"Oz, I'm…" The words died on his tongue. "What are you doing here?"

Anne said nothing, pushing her way into the vardo and shutting the door behind her. His body, despite his exhaustion, flared to life.

"Did you think I'd forgotten this place?" she asked. "That I could ever forget this place?"

"Yes."

"Well… I didn't."

He stepped closer and leaned in, damning the dawn as he took her mouth. He dropped the blanket and threaded both hands into the windblown hair she'd tried to pull into a loose bun. He tugged at the pins until it flowed down her back, nipped at lips that opened softly for him.

"I told you," he said, his words slurred from exhaustion. "I won't be polite."

She slipped her arms around his waist and maneuvered them closer to the raised bed enclosed by thick curtains. Pushing him back onto the platform, she slipped off her jacket and stepped out of her shoes, climbing into bed beside him and pulling the velvet drape closed.

"You don't have to be polite. Sleep, Patrick. We'll talk in the evening."

And for the first time in one hundred years, Patrick Murphy fell asleep with his body and heart whole, his mate resting her head in the crook of his shoulder, blood of his blood beside him.

Chapter Eight

THE PROBLEM WITH TAKING a younger lover was those stolen moments before they woke. Anne had often wondered whether thirty years' accumulation of moments had led her away from Murphy at the end. For in those quiet moments that age afforded her—when her mind was clear and his body at rest—she could think clearly about the man who'd stolen her heart and captured her soul.

Still waters run deep.

The old saying had no better example than Patrick Murphy. The calm, politic facade he showed the world concealed a depth of passion he revealed to precious few. When he woke, he would consume her.

So in the precious few moments before he colored her world, she paused—leaving her hand resting over his heart—and thought.

Why had she come to him?

It had been automatic. The quick flash of anger had frozen her on the waterfront when he turned her away. By the time she'd processed his rejection, he had been gone. After catching the familiar profile of his driver—for surely that distinctive chin could only belong to one of Murphy's kin—Anne traveled to the one place that had remained his refuge in life and in eternity. And she'd found him.

Now what do you plan to do with him? a tiny voice in her mind nagged.

She had no idea.

Anne was so hungry. For blood. For him. She wanted to bite. Wanted to sink her teeth into his neck, his groin. Bite any hint of gentleness in his hard body and *take*.

"I won't be polite."

A part of her didn't want him to be. Anne knew the urbane, sophisticated vampire lord of Dublin would not wake beside her. She'd sought him in the wild and found him. Her mate, as he admitted, was no settled man. He never had been. He simply knew how to wear the right clothes.

Anne could hear the distant voices of humans outside, smell the roses that grew on the edge of the meadow, and hear the trickling stream that ran behind the old-style wooden caravan. She took a deep breath and calmed her hunger. She let her eyes drift around the wagon as low lights switched on, preparing for the gathering dark.

A vampire vardo, of course. Lightproof. Secure. The curtain surrounding the bed was made of Venetian velvet, the bed beneath them eiderdown layered with silk sheets. Brass fixtures gleamed against mahogany cabinets and shelves.

Only Murphy.

Books and old records sat on the shelves. A few scattered pictures hung on the walls. Peeking into the wagon showed a picture of Murphy's soul. A man who loved his luxuries but valued his people and memories above all else.

She felt him stir. Not his body, but his blood came to life within her.

Anne watched in anticipation. His eyes flew open and his chest rose. Murphy gasped; his first breath upon waking had always reminded Anne of a diver surfacing from the deep. He turned to her with bared fangs and hungry eyes.

Without a word, he was on her.

He framed her face with both hands, crouched over her like a feral thing, leaning down to put his face at the curve of her throat. He drew a deep breath, as if inhaling her into himself along with the night air and the scent of freshwater. He muttered something in Gaelic, his voice rough from day rest. Anne let her head fall back, submitting to the wild in him. His fangs scraped up her throat.

"No blood," she whispered.

He snarled at her but replaced his teeth with sucking kisses and long licks. His hands clutched her hair, and his body pressed into hers.

Anne let out a reluctant groan. Not much had changed about Murphy when he woke.

She drew her knees up and let him rock into the softness of her body, arching back when she felt his arousal. Corded arms banded around her as he drew her closer. She heard her camisole rip at the shoulder.

"Don't bite my clothes," she panted. "I didn't bring a change."

"Then you shouldn't have worn them to sleep."

Anne's jaw ached. Her throat burned. The desire to take his blood—take everything he was offering, was almost overwhelming. He braced himself over her, anger and desire and longing warring in his eyes. It was a hard face. A desperate one.

"Patrick—"

"You're here. You wake before me and you stayed. I told you"—he pressed into the heat between her legs, cocking one knee under her thigh to hold her in place—"I told you I wouldn't be polite."

"I haven't said yes," she said, and he froze. "Yet."

His face softened. The warm brown eyes melted. His fangs didn't fall back, but the corners of his mouth tipped up and he lowered himself, pressing his hard chest into her breasts. She inhaled sharply, the feel of him a drug to her senses.

"Say yes," he whispered, kissing the arch of her cheekbone. "Say yes, my Áine."

His lips traveled over her face, fluttered over the corner of her mouth, her eyes, the tender line of her jaw.

"Say yes."

"I came to talk to you."

"We'll talk after."

"Patrick—"

"Bloody *hell*, Anne." He groaned, rolling to the side and covering his face with an arm. "Why did you come here? Why?"

"I told you, I came to talk."

"Really?" His eyes were fierce when he rolled toward her again. He propped himself up on one elbow and ran a hand up the inside of her leg, his amnis flooding her skin. He paused a few inches above her knee. "And if I keep going? Does your body want to talk as well? Or is it just your damned common sense?"

"You're acting like a spoiled child."

He bared his fangs again; his fingers dug into her inner thigh. "Admit it. You want me. I'm the only one who makes—"

"You're the only one," she said calmly, trying to maintain her composure as her heart cracked open. "I haven't taken a lover in years. You know that. You're the only one I want. The only one I ever really wanted from the night we met."

The desperate light returned to his eyes. "Then why?"

"We are more than our desires, Patrick. And it's not fair for me to bed you—"

"Fuck fair. I want you."

"—when I don't know if it can ever lead to more than sex. I'm not built that way. I can't separate. I've tried. It doesn't work for me the same way it does for you."

He finally pulled away. "Was wondering how long it would take you to bring up the other women."

"I'm not harping." Her face felt like a mask lay over it. "I'm not blaming you. I'm simply stating a fact."

"Then I want to state a fact."

"Fine."

He scooted away from her, leaning his back against the end of the wood-paneled trailer. "We're not friends."

"No, we're not friends."

"And we never will be."

Her heart broke open a little more, and she pulled the sheet to cover herself. "I know that."

"What do you want from me? An apology? You want me to grovel for not turning into a monk because you left me?"

"No, I don't expect an apology."

Of course she wanted him to grovel, though she'd never admit it. She knew it wasn't fair to him. She'd tried to move on as well. She squashed the petty, jealous part of her heart and remained calm.

"Then what do you want?"

"Did you intend to apologize when you came to Galway all those years ago?"

He blinked. "You're bringing that up after seventy years?"

"No, you brought it up when you accosted me at the pub. You said as far as you were concerned, we never finished our last argument. So I'm asking about it. Did you intend to apologize?"

A muscle in his jaw jumped. "Yes."

Yes.

A single word. A single answer that could have changed everything. Anne forced herself to remain calm.

"But you didn't, Patrick. You threw all your conquests in my face and told me it was my fault that you'd fucked them. That you hated me."

"I didn't…" He cleared his throat. "I didn't hate you."

"You said you did."

He scrubbed both hands over his face and took a deep breath. "I said a lot of things then. I didn't mean them."

"Then why did you say them?"

"Because you drove me mad!" He tore at his hair. "You stood there, so calm. Not a spot of care on your face. Like I was nothing to you."

Still schooling her features, she asked, "How could you think that?"

"You had so many walls, Anne. You let me in, but never completely."

Anne felt it like a physical blow.

"I told you everything," he continued. "Every twisted story. Every dirty secret. And there were times when it was as if I didn't know you. Who were you as a human? Why did your father turn you? When did you decide to become a healer? I don't even know your mother's name, just that you still mourn her."

"I don't like to talk about my past," she said. "I never have. I barely talk to Mary—"

"But I'm not your sister. I'm your *mate*."

"You never told me this bothered you," she said, her anger piqued. "Of all the arguments we had, not once did you bring it up."

"Of course I didn't. I hated that you had so much power over me. And you were a sphinx."

"It wasn't intentional."

"Of course it wasn't." He took a calming breath and sat up straighter. "And then I fucked up. Is that what you want to hear?" He bent down, inches from her face. "*I fucked up*. I was wrong. I let ambition get the best of me. I never should have asked you to use your ability like that. I broke your trust. Is that what you wanted to hear?"

She felt small and mean in the face of his brutal honesty. "Yes."

"There." He sat back, crossing his arms over his chest. "I said it. I fucked up. But you did too."

She sat up, still clutching the sheet to her body. "How is this my fault?"

"Because you left!"

"You let me."

He said nothing. A trickle of blood ran from the corner of his lip where he'd broken the skin. Before her eyes, it healed.

"You…" She struggled to speak. "You came into my life and you took it over. You took everything, Patrick."

"I loved you. I would have given you anything. You were my world."

"And I loved you too. But it consumed me. You were in every moment. Every thought. I loved you to madness. If I put up subconscious walls, it was probably because I feared losing myself in you. You were… so passionate. So charismatic. The universe whirled around Patrick Murphy, and I was in your orbit. We all were. You wanted your sire dead for turning you against your will, and within five years, he was gone and you took everything he owned. No one. Said. Anything. You wanted Dublin; you took it."

"Anne—"

"You didn't win. You conquered. We were all along for the ride. And then you asked me…"

His proud face was stricken. "I didn't think then. Didn't think what danger that could put you in. I was young. I didn't know—"

"My father was going to kill you," she said quietly. "When he discovered I told you, he was going to kill you. I *begged*… Mary did too. We begged for your life."

He blinked. "Mary did?"

"And then months later, you did exactly what Father had warned me about."

His head fell into his hands. "Áine, I'm sorry. How many times do you need to hear? I'm sorry."

"What was I to think, Patrick? The very thing he'd warned me about happened. I ran. I couldn't hurt you, but I didn't trust you anymore."

An edge of dark laughter touched his voice. "It's a miracle the old man hasn't killed me in my sleep."

"He wouldn't do that to me. You're still my mate."

Murphy shook his head. "Why?"

"What?"

"Haven't you ever wondered why? You and me." He waved a hand between them. "This isn't normal. Our bond should have died decades ago. And it didn't. Don't you wonder why?"

She pulled the sheet up to her shoulders. "I don't—"

"I've thought about it. So many nights. When no woman would satisfy me. When no one was clever enough. No one could make me laugh or touch my heart. And we both know I tried, don't we?"

Anne felt her fangs drop, this time in anger. "If you're trying to prove some kind of point—"

"I tried to forget you, Anne. Not because I didn't love you, but because I loved you *so damn much*. It didn't matter. None of it mattered."

She tipped her chin up. "You did without me in the end. Dublin is yours. Your fortune is made. No rival opposes you. Isn't that better? You did it on your own. No one can take that victory from you."

The smooth facade was gone. Murphy's face was as open as a boy's.

ELIZABETH HUNTER

"But I didn't want to do it on my own. I never did."

"Patrick—"

"I had Tom and Dec and Josie. I had Jack… at least I did then. But mostly, I had you. I never wanted to rule without you."

Anne shook her head, her heart broken open, her walls demolished by his words.

"We're *meant*, Anne. You know we are. We were so good together." He crawled to her, drawing the silken sheet away. "We were young and stupid. Or at least I was. I'm not anymore."

Anne shook her head, but he stopped her, cupping her cheeks between hands that had never grown soft. His knuckles still carried the scars of his human life. No matter what suit he wore, Murphy had fighter's hands. His thumb rubbed softly against her cheek. He brushed away an errant strand of dark hair that had fallen into her eyes.

"Let me prove it to you."

"Patrick—"

"I want you back, Anne O'Dea."

Her mouth dropped. Her heart beat once. "Just like that?"

"Exactly like that. Is that enough honesty for the famous vampire therapist? I want you to tell me your stories. I want you to hold me accountable for my arrogance. I want to prove that we belong together. That we can be better now."

"I have a life in the west."

"You have a shadow of a life. We both do. I say all the right things and charm all the right people, but I've been dancing around life for seventy years. I became exactly the man I thought you would want. I wore the right things and listened to the correct music. Business and politics became my life. I am so fecking polite I bore myself. And I don't have you anyway."

She shook her head. "I never wanted you to be anyone but yourself."

"I realized that thirty years ago, but by then proper manners were a habit."

The corner of her mouth turned up. He tilted her chin up and forced her eyes to his laughing gaze.

"There's my sweet girl," he whispered. "So beautiful. You were the heart of me. The best part. Is it any wonder I went a little mad when I lost you?"

It was the "going mad" part she was worried about.

"I don't know if I can do this again, Patrick."

"Give us a chance. We're going to London. I need you there. Give me a chance to prove we can be better than we were. There's no one better for me than you."

The other corner of her mouth quirked up. "Oh, I know. But what do I get out of it?"

He pressed forward, taunting her lips with his own. "Drop the sheet and let me show you." His tongue darted out, teasing her lower lip. "I'm still your mate, Anne. It's my duty to meet your needs."

She turned her head so his lips only brushed the corner of her mouth. "And who's meeting yours?"

Petty. Jealous. Small. She'd turned him away. What did she expect?

He pressed small kisses along her cheek, nibbling his way to her ear while she tried to remain calm.

"No one but you anymore. I'm done pretending."

"Really?" She knew better than anyone what kind of appetites Patrick Murphy had.

"Ask Brigid," he said, playing with her earlobe like it was his fascinating new toy. "The word went out as soon as you arrived in town. You still smell so good. Have you been up to Donegal? You smell like the roses there. I swear it's in your skin."

"Mary and I…" She let him nudge her head to the side. "We met there before I came here."

"You were angry, weren't you?" He chuckled. "When she told you what she wanted."

"I assume this was all some scheme of yours."

"Of course it was. It's a good plan, you have to admit." His hand was light on her skin. Touching her softly on her shoulder. Her waist. Her hip and thigh. "I do value your input, and we need your sister's cooperation if we're going to present a united front in London."

Somehow, Murphy had managed to wrap himself around her without Anne even realizing it. His leg was propped behind her back, pressing her slightly forward. One hand played with her hair while the other played with the silken sheet over her knees. Her thighs. Her—

"You know, I never agreed to this plan of yours." She tried to lean away, but dammit, his arm was suddenly on that side too. How had the irritating man managed to wrap her completely up? Had he suddenly grown five arms to trap her on his bed?

He blinked innocently. "What? You don't want to give this a chance? We'll be in London anyway. Spending time together. There are already various social functions we'll be forced to attend."

She narrowed her eyes at him. "Murphy—"

He kissed her. Hard. "Don't call me Murphy. If you still want to go back to Galway by the time Terry and Gemma's summit is over, then go." His voice was deceptively casual. "I'm certainly not going to kidnap you. I'm just warning you that while we're in London, I'll be doing everything in my power to show you what excellent partners we'd be."

"Partners?"

He kissed her neck. "Lovers. Mates. Companions in eternity. Husband and wife, if you'd still like. Bound before God and all the saints." He lifted his head. "And so fecking much more than friends."

It was a good thing she was a vampire, because he'd stolen the last breath from her lungs.

"Are you trying to make me fall in love with you, Mr. Murphy?"

"Of course I am, Dr. O'Dea."

In the pain of their separation and his anger after, Anne had forgotten how he could delight her. His charm. His play. His wit.

"I'll think about it," she said. "While we're in London."

"Good."

His hands slid down her back, playing along the edge of her silk camisole, teasing the skin at the small of her back. Then without warning, they dipped down to her ample backside and gave it a good, hard squeeze.

"Patrick!"

"Just checking it was still there, love." He laid a smacking kiss over her collarbone before she shoved him away. "I always did prefer a filly with an ample rump."

"Rude man! I'm a vampire." She refused to laugh at his impertinence. "My bottom has not changed in the past seventy years."

He did nothing but laugh and fall back into the pillows lining the bed alcove. His face was alight with amusement. His eyes teasing. His mouth spread into a smile. Dark hair fell into his eyes and dusted his chest, trailing down in a tempting pattern that pointed toward the part of his anatomy she was very decidedly ignoring. Murphy was naked as the day he was born. And God help her, she never could resist him when he was laughing.

His eyes stayed locked on her. "How do you like my caravan?"

"It's beautiful. I love it, though I'll admit"—her eyes darted around—"it scares me a bit. I feel very exposed, even without windows. My house in Galway has rooms underground."

He banged a fist against the wall, which thudded in a very un-wood-like manner. "Think of it as a large vault on wheels. No one's getting in. Even if they could find this place."

"You opened up your sire's land."

"Just for my people. They invite others occasionally, but for the most part, it's still the same clan. It's good for the children to have a safe place. The local school has a special program for them."

"Do they follow it?"

He shrugged. "Sometimes. Some of them do. I won't force them, Anne."

"I know. You shouldn't. The choice is there if they want it."

He said nothing. His mother's people had always been a sore spot. She'd run away with a settled Irishman, then left him and gone back to her clan, her infant son in tow. Murphy's people considered him a bastard of a sort, neither fully Traveller or fully settled. But at the end of the day, they'd been the only family he had, and they were fiercely loyal in their way.

"Your driver. Is he related to James?"

He nodded. "His great-nephew. He's a good man."

"I thought he looked familiar." James had been their driver before the First World War. "They still protect you."

The light in his eyes flickered. "They fear me. But they like the benefits of calling me their own, don't they? They're good at keeping secrets anyway."

She crawled over, lying down next to him, crossing her arms and nudging his shoulder with her own. "You are a good man, Patrick Murphy. Probably better than they deserve."

He was having none of it. He snuck an arm under her waist and tumbled her into his chest.

"Don't fool yourself, love." Dark brown eyes narrowed with intent. "I'm not a good man at all. You said it yourself. I don't win. I conquer."

Chapter Nine

London

THE TWITTERING HUMAN FLUTTERED her hands like a panicking goose. "But... but Mr. Murphy—"

"That will be fine." He checked off a room on the notebook he had absconded with. "That one will not. Dr. O'Dea will require the suite next to mine. Our security team will flank either side."

"Mr. Murphy, I must insist—"

"Are any of the other attendees staying in this location?" He gave her a cool glare, railroading her objections with a look. Their London assistant might have been competent, but she was not Angie. Nor was this Dublin. He needed to establish his authority over the Irish contingent immediately, or they would have to move house.

"None of the other parties are staying here, no." She tucked a wild curl of greying hair behind her ear. Gemma's personal secretary had assigned this human as liaison for both him and Anne, but so far, she was not holding up under the pressure. "And three rooms have already been provided for your security team. There's no need to—"

"Two will suffice." He held the diagram up and pointed to it like a primary teacher. "I will be here. Dr. O'Dea will be in this room. Are these rooms adjoining?"

"I—yes, but they're designed for your security so they would be able to—"

"Is this room as well-appointed as the master suite?"

"Well, of course not!"

"Then that will be your task before Dr. O'Dea arrives… what was your name?"

"Judith."

He softened his face into his most charming smile, and the human's eyes dilated. "Judith. You've been so lovely. But I will need you to take care of this personally. Please make sure Dr. O'Dea's room has every luxury. If that is not possible, you will switch her to the master suite and I will take the adjoining room. Our security teams will flank us in these rooms. They don't need a third room because I really don't want them sleeping all that much, do I?"

Judith blinked. "Well, I suppose—"

"Now, as for Ms. Connor's room, I assume she is located in the family quarters?"

Terry and Gemma's townhouse in Mayfair was really more of a complex. Over the years, they had discreetly bought most of the property surrounding their communal garden, expanding their own home, connecting the basements, and creating a secure and private oasis they could call their own. While the family resided under the main house, luxurious guest quarters were available. Murphy and Anne, being some of Terry's closest allies, had decided to stay in Mayfair for convenience. Carwyn and Brigid resided with the family, and since Brigid was attached to Murphy, it made sense.

Judith stiffened. "Ms. Connor and Carwyn's room is in the family wing. I am not allowed to discuss details."

"Of course not. But if you could inform Ms. Connor of where Dr. O'Dea and I will be located, I would appreciate that. She is my chief of security while we are in town, and I know she'll want to coordinate with our human teams before dawn."

"Of... of course, Mr. Murphy."

He handed the diagram of rooms back to her and tucked the pencil behind her ear. "Did you have any questions for me, Judith?"

"I..." She was back to fluttering. "Just... so many. I'll need to rearrange your luggage and restock the kitchens. How many cases of blood-wine will each room need now? How much food? How much fresh blood? I'm afraid I had all this sorted, I'd made notes of everyone's preferences, and now you've—"

"Ah, ah." He patted her shoulder. "You'll get everything taken care of. I have confidence. If you could see to Dr. O'Dea's room first, please. Her luggage has already been moved."

Judith seemed to give up at that point, nodding along. "Of course, Mr. Murphy."

"Now, please."

She straightened and sped off in the direction of the new rooms.

Poor Judith.

But honestly, she'd put Anne in a suite down a completely different hallway. How was Murphy supposed to convince Anne to give him a chance when she was that far away? Yes, adjoining rooms were a necessity.

He felt her approaching before he turned.

"Anne," he murmured, brushing a kiss along her arched cheekbone. "Did you find a drink?"

"I did. Gemma said her secretary has taken care of settling us." She accepted his affection cautiously but maintained her distance. "Is my room ready?"

Her color was high. She'd just fed, but her eyes still held the shine of hunger.

Murphy frowned. That didn't seem right.

"I'm afraid I had to rearrange things a bit," he said. "Are you well?"

She smiled. "Of course. Just how high-handed were you?"

"Very. But now your room is adjacent to mine as I wanted. Anne, are you sure you—"

"Really, Patrick"—she brushed past him—"I hope you don't sent Terry and Gemma's household into nervous fits. I remember how particular you can be with the servants."

He followed cautiously. "My tastes are specific. If they're not willing to accommodate them, we'll find other lodging."

She turned and her careful mask was in place again. Murphy hated her careful mask. She stopped and brushed her fingers along the knot of his tie. Then she ran a hand over his shoulder. "This is a very nice suit."

"I'm glad you like it. I bought it on my last trip here. Do you have plans to shop while we're in town?"

"Yes. I need formal clothing. Things are more casual in Galway, aren't they?"

"You always look beautiful. Do you need funds? This is a professional expense, after all. And you're part of my entourage for this trip."

She smiled up at him. "I am the official representative of the Ulster territories and the personal representative of Mary Hamilton. My sister can pay for my clothes, Mr. Murphy."

He put a finger under her chin and tilted her head up. "I only wanted to offer."

"You're very presumptuous. You do know that, don't you?"

"It may have been mentioned once or twice."

She didn't pull away, so he brushed his lips over hers, nibbling on the full lower lip he adored. In seconds, it was his hunger that was spiking.

"Sadly, our rooms are not ready yet," he said. "Otherwise, I'd steal you away for a private conference before our meeting tonight."

"A private conference? Is that necessary?"

"Very necessary, Dr. O'Dea." He spoke against her lips, teasing her mouth with fleeting touches and heated breaths. "It's imperative that Ireland be of a single mind during this summit." Murphy slid a hand around her waist, ignoring the rush of servants and security that bustled through the hallway. He pulled her closer, pressing his body into hers.

"A single mind?" Her eyes were clouded and her fangs had fallen.

"Indeed. Coordination is key. We'll need to work very, very closely throughout any negotiations. Proper discourse is vital."

"Discourse? I'm not sure the discourse you're interested in is proper at all."

The corner of his mouth lifted. "Nonsense. I am a consummate professional in all things."

"You consummate professionally? That's fascinating. And possibly illegal. You'll have to check the local regulations."

He'd managed to back her into the wall, but Anne wasn't trying to escape. Bloody hell, he'd missed playing with her like this. He almost growled when the fluttery human cleared her throat behind him.

"Ahem. Mr. Murphy?"

Anne was biting her lip to hold in a laugh while he cursed under his breath.

"Yes, Judith?"

"Mr. Ramsay has requested that you join him for a drink in the billiards room of the main house when you're able."

He frowned. "I have to travel for a meeting later tonight," he told Anne. "I should meet with Terry before it gets too late."

She nodded. "Fill me in later? I believe Gemma has a shop or two she said would open for us. I don't want to delay choosing a wardrobe. I'm sure everything will need to be tailored."

Murphy ran a hand just under her ribs and down her waist, spreading his fingers over the full curve of her hip. "Buy some suits like the one you first wore to Dublin. You looked stunning in it."

"I'll see what I can do."

"In red."

"Bossy."

"And appropriate dresses. Or inappropriate ones. Either will do. I want to take you out while we're here."

The hunger touched her eyes again, so he stole a kiss before he turned to Judith.

"Judith, this is Dr. O'Dea. Please see to her needs while I am meeting with Mr. Ramsay."

The human almost curtsied. "As you wish, Mr. Murphy."

"Presumptuous," Anne called. "Very presumptuous, Patrick."

TERRY handed him a full glass of blood-wine when he entered the room. "What's your game?"

Murphy looked around the room. It was a proper billiards room with three tables and a long wall of racks, balls, and the various accoutrement needed to play any billiard game one could think of. Noting the almost imperceptible layer of dust on the large snooker table, he made his choice.

"Snooker."

Terry raised an eyebrow but told the servant standing in the corner, "Set it up, then leave."

Murphy sipped the wine and waited for his host to speak.

"How are your rooms?"

"Sufficient. Thank you."

"Let Gemma's people know if there's anything you need. They're far more efficient than my crew."

"I will." He took another sip of the wine, noting with satisfaction that the copper bite of the blood hadn't oxidized as it usually did in attempts to preserve it. "This is very good."

"Is it?" Terry drank from his own glass. "Christ, I miss beer."

Murphy let out a sharp laugh. "You don't need to drink it on my account."

"Gem'd have my head if I didn't. I'm a winemaker now, she says. Need to be selling the product."

"I'm no snitch, Ramsay."

"Thank Christ." He walked over and set his glass on the bar in the corner, pulling a dark bottle from the fridge below. "It's not bad stuff."

"It's not. In fact, it's quite good."

"And it gets better every year. I'm just bloody sick of the stuff, no pun intended."

"You've solved the preservation problems?"

He shrugged and walked to the wall of sticks. "So my winemaker tells me. Bloody Frenchman. Opinionated as hell, but worth his weight. A bottle of what you're drinking will sell for five hundred pounds."

Patrick almost spit it out and grabbed a bottle of beer. "So much?"

Terry turned and smiled wickedly. "And we'll make more than that, my friend."

Murphy walked over and chose his cue stick. "Vampires will pay."

"They will." Terry motioned toward the carefully set table. "Guests first."

Murphy walked around the table, scoping out the angles and noting the minute imperfections of the baize, the age of the cushions, and the weight of the stick in his hand. He chalked the tip of his cue and leaned over to break the pyramid of red balls.

"So, Ramsay. I can assume this isn't just a friendly game."

"Friendly game. Serious conversation." Terry set his beer down and lined up the cue at an angle Murphy knew would fail while setting him up for his first pot. Excellent. "I've always liked you, Murphy, even though you picked my worst game."

He suppressed the smile. "Is that so?"

"Don't act like you didn't know. You spotted that before you walked through the door. That's part of the reason I like you."

Terry missed the shot, leaving Murphy to pot a red and a colored ball before he gave his host another chance to strike.

Murphy finished his wine and went to grab a bottle of porter. "So you like me because I can beat you at snooker?"

"No, I like you because you're like me, Murphy." Terry straightened and grinned a crooked smile. "You and I are a couple of old criminals. You just wear a suit better than me, mate."

He clinked the neck of his beer against Murphy's and leaned against the wood-paneled wall.

"So..." Murphy leaned over and lined up another shot. Then another. "What did you want to discuss outside the presence of the respectable vampires, Ramsay?"

"Straight talk. Who do you think is shipping it?"

Murphy shook his head. "I can't see it yet. Someone in the Mediterranean. Whoever is behind this is smart. They're using a mix. Human and immortal lines. Smugglers and legitimate shippers. Black Sea. Mediterranean. There have even been ships that've stopped in North Africa."

Terry asked, "Could it be Rome after all? Deciding to pick up where Livia left off?"

"I don't think so. Emil Conti is too conservative."

"The Libyans?"

Murphy shook his head. "Also too conservative. And their human governments have been unstable of late. They're keeping their ambitions at home."

"The Turks?"

"It's not the Turks." Murphy lined up another red. "Istanbul is the only shipping location we've seen any mention of, and that's controlled by Athens."

Murphy blinked and missed the shot.

Fuck him. That was it. Click.

"It's the Greeks," he said, stepping away from the table. "Athens is shipping it."

Terry gave him a withering look. "Athens? Why?"

"I'm not sure of that part yet."

"But you're sure it's them?"

He was. And… he wasn't. What was their motivation? They had to have a reason to poison their own blood supply. There were too many variables. Too many angles he couldn't yet see.

Terry said, "The Greeks don't have the money to finance this. They make a fortune in the Bosphorus, but they spend it faster than they make it from what I hear."

"They don't have the cash." He stepped up to take another shot. "But they could have an investor. They have the infrastructure and the connections to organize it."

"I don't agree."

"Fine. But you are wrong." A red. A color. The balls around the table were potted in quick succession. "This game, Ramsay, it's all about thinking ahead. Don't think of the shot you're taking, think of the next angle. The next pot. The ball after that."

"Vampires aren't as predictable as cue balls."

"They are and they aren't." He sank another red. "Why are you charging five hundred pounds for a bottle of blood-wine when I can hunt for free? Let's be honest, blood always tastes better fresh from the neck. So why five hundred a bottle?"

"Because the market supports it. The blood supply is uncertain right now because of Elixir. And most vampires have more money than scruples."

"You're absolutely right." Murphy finished the game without Terry ever stepping up to the table again. "So from one old criminal to another, let's follow the money, shall we?"

Terry asked, "Who benefits from an uncertain blood supply?"

Murphy set down his cue stick and swallowed the last of his beer. "You do."

Terry let a slow smile spread over his face. "I suppose I do. But I'm not the only one."

No, Terry wasn't the only one who might benefit from Elixir continuing to spread.

But he was the easiest one to spy on.

THE Cockleshell Pub in Gravesend was one swift storm away from drifting down the river in pieces. But the strange old floating pub was still the best place to get in touch with the one water vampire too elusive for anyone to find unless he wanted to be found. It was also closed to humans at this time of night. From the outside, the place looked abandoned.

But Murphy knew there was a strange brotherhood of water vampires who chose the pub as their unofficial office, and Anne's sire was the oldest among them.

Murphy ignored the curious look from the vampire who opened the door. He slipped inside, enjoying the smell of the river even if he didn't appreciate the stink of old piss and stale beer inside the pub. He took a booth in the corner and waited for someone to approach him.

After a few moments, the barman approached. "Don't get many from your end of town. What'll ya have?"

"What are you serving?"

The one-eyed publican gave him a grim smile. "A fancy Irishman. How about that?"

Murphy didn't respond.

"We've got fresh if you like," the old man said. "Girls in back for those wanting a tup along with a meal. They're clean. Preserved human. Cow and pig. That's all, mate."

"Not serving blood-wine yet?"

The old one swore. "Not likely."

"I'll have the pig's blood."

"Heated or cold?"

"Cold."

"As ya like."

The barman slipped away, as silent as any of their kind, but Murphy waited. He knew the old man would find him. Hell, he'd probably been tracking Murphy's every move since his boat landed at the docks.

He heard a door slam in back and a few murmuring voices. A clear glass of thick red blood was set before him, not that Murphy had any intention of drinking it. But it would have been rude not to order. There was a quick female cry from the back. Pleasure or pain, he couldn't tell, but it was none of his business, so he ignored it and waited.

The old man appeared from one moment to the next, sitting across from him in the booth. Murphy had never understood how the wiry old man could move so silently.

"Good evening, Tywyll."

The canny old waterman sniffed but said nothing. He looked at the barman, who immediately brought over a brown earthenware mug of what smelled like preserved cow's blood. He drank slowly, wiping away the smear of red that colored his top lip with the back of his sleeve.

"Someone told me you wanted to kill me," Murphy said.

"That was some time ago."

"Good to know."

"Don't know as I've changed my mind on it though."

Murphy said nothing. It was best to school your reactions around the old man.

"Ye've brought my lass to visit me," Tywyll said. "So maybe I'll thank ye instead of kill ye. Fer now."

"Fair enough," Murphy said. "So you know, I'm trying to make things right with her."

"Is that so?"

"Yes."

"She's a soft heart and a hard head, my Annie. She won't trust ye."

"I'm working on that," he said through gritted teeth.

Tywyll gave him a raspy chuckle. "Such a pair of bastards we are. I did like ye, Murphy, until ye made my girl sad. I don't like seeing my girls sad."

Murphy had always wondered why Tywyll had turned Anne. It was unheard of for him to leave England in the past century, but he must have roamed at one point. Mary was his oldest known child, but she was English. What had drawn him to Anne?

"I'm doing everything I can to make her happy, but it will take time for her to trust me again. At least she's speaking to me though. If there's one thing your daughter has taught me, it's patience."

"And is she well?"

It was an odd question about a vampire, but it niggled at something Murphy had noticed in the hallway earlier.

"Why wouldn't she be?"

"My Mary might have mentioned concerns."

He paused. It was always best to measure your words with a vampire as ancient as Tywyll. "If there's something wrong with Anne, I need to know."

Tywyll sipped his blood, staring at him. He tried not to react.

"Mary didn't say exactly," the old man finally said. "My Annie, she's different."

From the light in his eyes and his near-silent voice, Murphy knew the old man was talking about Anne's ability to push her will onto other immortals.

"I know," Murphy said.

"I know you know."

Another long silence descended between them.

"I would never—"

"Don't say never when ye already have," Tywyll said.

"And I learned a hard lesson. I'd never expose her. Never try to take advantage. Never again."

Tywyll waited for a silent vampire to pass across the room. When Murphy looked over his shoulder, he realized that all but two of the others had left the pub. Afraid of the old man? Eager to remain anonymous? If Tywyll didn't care about their presence, neither did Murphy.

"She was always so hungry," the old man said. "Never wanted for food as a mortal—it was the one thing her bastard of a stepfather did for her—but once she turned…" He shook his head. "That first year, Mary thought she'd have to leave her to the day once or twice. Her hunger burned."

"In all the time we were together, she never had a problem with bloodlust."

"She grew up. Managed to control it. But she's always had a rougher time of it. She needs to drink more. I think whatever curious thing her amnis does, it uses more energy. So she needs to feed it." Tywyll nudged a bowl of peanuts left on the scarred table. "Not food. She has little appetite for her body. But blood? She's always needed more."

And human supplies were at risk. Murphy wondered just how many humans Anne trusted to drink from in Galway. Only Ruth? Murphy's control had been riding a razor-thin edge, and he had an entire household of servants to feed him. If Anne had been trying to exist on little to no human blood or only on animal…

"Bollocks."

Tywyll nodded. "Ye need to watch her."

"Is she dangerous?"

"Possibly. Though it goes against her nature."

"I'll watch her." And try to feed her. If Anne would take his blood, it would help. Tom had been right in Dublin. Mated vampires needed less blood, particularly if they were mated to another element. He and Anne were both born to water, but any exchange would help.

"Now, we've got family business out of the way, young Murphy. Tell me about this meeting that Ramsay is hosting about this drug nastiness. Who will be on my river?"

"Besides his and mine? Six foreigners. All water vampires except the Americans."

Tywyll took a drink. "But they're watermen, nonetheless. The Americans, I mean."

"You're familiar with the O'Briens?"

He chuckled. "There's no one on the river I don't know, lad. I know the O'Briens. Don't particularly like them. No manners, that lot. I suppose that's to be expected with the sire they had."

"Jean Desmarais from France is already here, I believe. Jetta from Scandinavia—"

"Ah, now *that's* a woman. I do like that Jetta."

Murphy tried not to cringe at the blatant appreciation in Tywyll's eyes. Apparently the tiny waterman preferred the statuesque, frightening type.

He cleared his throat. "Yes, well… She'll be arriving tomorrow night. Along with Leonor from Spain—"

"Watch that one."

"And Rens Anker from the Netherlands."

Tywyll's eyes took on a calculating gleam. "One of the Anker boys, eh?"

"Know them?"

"Know they're trying to put me out of business in the information trade, not that they will. At least not around these parts."

"I was wondering about that."

Tywyll looked up sharply. "That's not all yer wondering about, is it?"

Murphy paused but decided that Tywyll's loyalty to family was likely greater than to whoever happened to be running London in the current century. And since Murphy considered Anne family, he might just qualify.

"Ramsay," Murphy said, almost silently. "Is he involved in this business?"

"In the drug business?"

"Yes."

"Not likely. He's an up-front bastard. He took London and killed anyone who'd been involved in the coupe against his sire. Kidnapped his own bloody wife and didn't make a secret of it. Subterfuge"—Tywyll pronounced the word carefully—"is not his style."

"Fair enough. I had to ask. He'll make a fortune in this mess with his blood-wine business."

"Ah, interesting that." Tywyll nodded. "But he's keen. I imagine he'd probably mint coin no matter what."

Murphy paused. "That was my main concern. We're in his house. His wife is kin to a friend. I didn't want him to be involved, so I had to ask."

"Smart of ye. I have no loyalty to Ramsay, though he's aligned himself to a family I respect."

"Carwyn's?"

Tywyll nodded. "His new young mate is working for ye?"

"Yes."

"Then yer a lucky bastard. And that makes me glad my Annie is in Dublin."

From the tone of his voice, Tywyll obviously didn't like Anne being isolated in Galway. Perhaps he might have an ally in Anne's sire after all.

Murphy said, "I'll do my best to keep her in Dublin."

"She thinks she needs solitude, but she doesn't."

"What does she need?"

"Love," Tywyll said without pause. "Trust. And to be needed. It surprised me none that she became a healer, for she has the finest heart of any woman I've known, including her mother. It's a strong heart. A survivor's heart. Honor that heart. Respect the woman, Patrick Murphy, and you'll find a treasure greater than any fortune ye could earn or vengeance ye could take."

Chapter Ten

SHE'D HAD A FULL BOTTLE of blood-wine before she'd gone shopping with Gemma and another when she returned, yet Anne was still hungry. Her hunger was getting worse, and she didn't know what she was going to do. In an unfamiliar city, feeding from random humans was too dangerous. Terry and Gemma had blood donors on staff, but feeding over the norm would be cause for scrutiny. Still, she could ignore the burn in her throat when she was swimming.

Terry had installed a magnificent salt-water pool in the basement of the Mayfair house. Anne took the length of it in long strokes, stretching her body and soaking up the energy she drew from the water. She'd missed swimming in Dublin. Neither Brigid nor Carwyn particularly cared for water. Murphy had a pool, but she'd never wanted to ask. And the river... well, she was too accustomed to the ocean. At home she greeted every night with a long swim in the bay before she set foot in her office.

Anne had grown up by the sea. As a human, she'd loved it and feared it in equal measure. It was the fierce mistress that had taken her father, and the harsh master that drove her stepfather. Her mother had spent most of her time by the shore, looking out in hope and dread and love and longing.

Tywyll had loved her mother. Fallen in love with her voice as she sang in the night. Had raged over the tearful girl who told him the same sea her mother sang to had claimed her.

Accident or suicide?

Anne had never known.

The awareness of Murphy brushed away the melancholy thoughts. She didn't need to surface to know he watched her. She could feel it.

She kept swimming.

Lap after lap, she swam. Sometimes using a formal stroke, sometimes slipping underwater like a seal, turning and twisting as the depths held her. When she finally surfaced, he was still there, lounging in a three-piece suit and watching her with an enigmatic smile.

"Could you swim as a human?"

Anne found herself coming up with clever retorts to avoid his question and was reminded of his anger in the caravan. He'd complained that she never shared her past. He was right. She didn't like dwelling on it, but she had to admit that avoiding it was something she would never advise a patient.

"Anne?" His voice was laced with concern.

"Sorry. Having a moment of inconvenient self-revelation."

Murphy smiled. "Take your time."

If he could change, she would have to as well.

"No, I couldn't swim. Would have made it much harder for Liam O'Dea to kill me, wouldn't it?"

A dark flash of anger at the mention of her long-dead stepfather. "You told me he killed you, but you never told me why."

"Clearly he didn't like me."

When Murphy said nothing, Anne knew her glib reply wouldn't satisfy him this time. When he was younger, she'd been able to distract Murphy from uncomfortable questions about her past. But he was no longer a young immortal. He watched her with calm expectation.

"Liam O'Dea married my mother when I was a child, but he never liked me. Barely liked his own children when my mother birthed them. The more I grew, the more he hated me."

"But you kept his name?"

"It was my father's name as well," Anne said. "My da was Liam's cousin, a big, strong, jovial man everyone loved." Anne forced a smile to her face. "Nobody much loved Liam."

"Do you look like your father?"

She nodded. "Everyone mourned Da when his boat was lost, especially my mother. She never truly recovered. She married Liam to provide for us, because she was young and pretty and that was what women did then."

"And she had more children?"

"I had four younger brothers and sisters." This was why she didn't speak of the past. The pain in her chest was excruciating. "My mother walked into the sea when the youngest was only a few months old. Severe postpartum depression, I believe. Or an accident? She loved the sea, but she couldn't swim. And we had those horrible long skirts then..." Anne shook her head. "I was nearing twenty, mourning, and desperate to leave Liam's house, but no one wanted me."

"I find that inconceivable," Murphy said. "You're intelligent. A beautiful woman. You've always been a hard worker—"

"But I was very desperate and very adamant about taking four children with me." Her smile was sad. "Not the most attractive prospect. Then Liam suggested *strongly* that I marry him. And not even the priest objected. I knew... I tried to run away. That did not go well."

She let her silence speak. Anne felt wrung out.

Inconvenient self-revelation, indeed.

"I'd finish him myself if I could," Murphy growled.

"No need," Anne said blithely. "Father took care of him long ago. He'd been watching us for some time. I didn't know who or what he was. I thought he was a tramp who liked my mother's songs and wandered down at the shore by our cottage at night."

"Do you think he loved her?"

"In a way." She couldn't stop the smile. "She was a very delicate woman. She inspired that instinct in men."

"Is that why you're so blasted independent?" Humor laced his voice. "So you're not like your mother?"

"Probably."

Anne said nothing else.

"Your father said you're to come visit him as soon as you can." As if sensing her emotional exhaustion, Murphy's voice was pitched deliberately lighter. "And be prepared to sing a song or two at the pub."

"Ah." She dove under and surfaced, wiping the cobwebs of memory away and brushing her wet hair back as she climbed the steps. "I'd wondered if that's where you were going tonight."

"Did he say something?"

"No. I just knew you would."

Murphy watched her with intent. "I don't like to avoid people when I know we have a disagreement."

"Unlike me," she said, picking up a towel and pressing her long hair to dry it. "The queen of avoidance."

"I didn't say that. Come here." He crooked a finger at her, still slouched in the lounge chair.

Anne walked over but didn't get too close. "I'm dripping. And I don't want to get your suit wet."

"I don't care." He hooked a finger in the towel wrapped round her waist. "Hello, what have we here?"

He parted the towel and let it drop, running both hands down her sides.

Confession had stripped her bare. "Murphy—"

"Quiet. I'm enjoying the view." He put both hands on her hips and spread his legs, bringing her between his knees. "Lovely."

"It's a very black, very practical bathing suit. Hardly worth admiring."

"Is that so? Perhaps you should get rid of it then."

"Shameless man." Hunger struck again, but she swallowed the burn. "I went shopping earlier today. I'll be professionally wardrobed by Thursday evening."

"Until then, I think it best for you to remain naked in our suite. It's the only acceptable option, I'm afraid."

"*Our* suite? I thought the very efficient Judith told me the room was mine."

"You can't expect me to sleep in a queen bed, can you? You wound me, Anne. You know how sensitive I am."

"Oh yes, *sensitive* is the first word that comes to mind."

His hands intoxicated her. Murphy had barely moved them, but she was seduced. His thumbs stroked over her bathing suit. His fingertips pressed into her flesh. Not hard, just sure enough to remind her how strong his hands could be. What they could do to her skin. Her body.

Cunning vampire.

"Anne…" He leaned closer and drew a deep breath. "What are you thinking about?"

"You, of course."

His grip tightened. "You test my patience."

"I'm trying to be very honest. You know I want you. That has never been the issue. I just don't know if I trust you yet."

He leaned his head against her belly, and she stroked her hands through his hair. "What do I do?"

"Give me time," she whispered. "You were the debonair playboy of Dublin up until a few weeks ago. Romancing human girls and roaming the town. And I was living a very boring, very separate life in Galway. Give me some time to believe you when you say you want me back."

"I've always wanted you back."

"No, Patrick, don't lie." She pulled his head back until he met her eyes. "There was a time you hated me."

His brown eyes never wavered. "Only because you took away the thing I wanted most."

That was… accurate. Murphy could be very possessive with the things he considered his. And he had most definitely considered Anne "his."

"I left you. You never thought I'd do that."

"No, I didn't," he murmured. "I took you for granted, didn't I? I apologize for that. I'm a smarter man now."

"Maybe that's why I'm wary. You seduced me when you were young and reckless. But now? You could conquer me completely if I let my guard down. I'd have no chance."

"Does that scare you?"

"Yes."

His eyes softened. "Don't be scared."

"I'm too smart not to be. I know myself too well."

He sat back with a sigh. "This is the peril of loving a psychologist, isn't it?"

Anne smiled. "That and the bad sex jokes."

He perked up. "There are bad sex jokes?"

"So many bad sex jokes. Thousands of them."

"That'll give me something to look forward to then."

"MURPHY."

He leaned closer as they waited for the formal arrival of Jetta Ommunsdotter in Terry and Gemma's drawing room. "Yes, love?"

"What do a condom and a coffin have in common?"

"I'm shocked that I don't know. What do a condom and a coffin have in common?"

"They both hold stiffs. But one is coming and one is going."

The corner of his mouth turned up. "I want to ask what kind of clients you've been seeing, but I'm afraid to ask."

"Vampires. Despicable creatures. The necrophilia jokes almost write themselves."

He smothered his laugh with a hard cough as Anne calmly sipped her glass of blood-wine.

Jetta arrived with a full retinue of what Anne privately thought of as her "Viking marauders." No, not all of them were that old, but they were—both male and female—very tall, very handsome, and very serious. Every now and then, one of the Viking marauders would smile, but not often.

Anne stepped forward. "Jetta."

"Anne!" Jetta smiled and reached out to grip her hand in a hard but friendly shake. "It's very good to see you. How is Mary?"

"Doing very well, but very busy. I was happy to come as her representative this trip."

Jetta spoke in completely unaccented English. She sounded more American than many American vampires. Her eyes were a frosty blue, and her dark blond hair was cut in stylish layers around her face. She wore an elegant pantsuit as businesslike as it was feminine. Despite her height and fierce expression, she was a friendly sort and defaulted to cool detachment instead of rage when she was displeased. Overall, Anne knew Jetta would be one of the easiest political players to spend time with during this summit.

"It is always pleasant to see you." Jetta turned to Murphy. "And you, Murphy. I see Ireland is well represented in London."

"It took long enough."

Jetta smiled. "A republican till the end."

Anne closed her eyes. "And that's one more debate that we don't need for this trip."

Gemma and Terry interrupted to show Jetta to the wine and make sure her entourage was settled.

Anne tapped a fingernail on her wineglass. "Why is she here?"

"Jetta?"

"Yes."

"Her trading interests are extensive."

"But most have to do with energy and fossil fuels, don't they?"

"She's already transitioning. Deepwater drilling won't always be as profitable as it is now."

"Alternative energies?"

"Something about deepwater-wave energy conversion. Her research is very hush-hush, but the rumors are promising."

"So she's forward thinking."

"Jetta?" Murphy raised an eyebrow. "Always."

"She must be concerned about the blood supply too."

"Undoubtedly. We've had the devil's time finding out how much Elixir has encroached in Scandinavia. Traditionally they've had far more open borders than we have, so it could be quite extensive. But it's geographically big, and many of her people are what the Americans would call 'off the grid.' Even the water vampires tend to live in more isolated locations. Their immortal population isn't as condensed, and that may have shielded them from infection."

Anne surveyed the Viking marauders. "Her people don't look any weaker." Anne looked up at his continued silence. "What?"

Murphy glanced at her glass of blood-wine. "Appearances can be deceiving."

She schooled her expression to remain placid. "What does that mean? Do you think there's something wrong with Jetta's people?"

Redirection didn't work.

"How many glasses of blood-wine tonight, Anne?"

"None of your business. You like your whiskey; I like my wine."

"You know that's not what I'm talking about."

Anne's eyes searched the room. "I believe Gemma is calling me over. Excuse me, Murphy."

"Anne!" He bent to her ear and whispered, "If you would take my vein—"

"I refuse to discuss this here." She put a hand to his chest and felt the hard thump of his heartbeat twice. "I'll speak with you later. Right now, I believe Gemma wants me to meet someone."

She left him without another look and walked toward Gemma, who was standing near a boyish-looking vampire with tousled brown hair.

"Anne!" Gemma said. "Have you met my youngest brother, Daniel? He does this constantly, appearing out of nowhere."

"I can transform into a bat," the young man said in mock solemnity. "Didn't Father teach you that trick, Gem?"

Gemma grinned and pinched his arm. "You're terrible. Daniel lives near The Lakes, but he mostly rambles all over the place and climbs mountains. I had no idea he was going to be here."

"It's very nice to meet you," Anne said.

"Gemma has mentioned you before. You live in Galway?"

"Galway County, yes. Almost into Clare, actually."

"I love Clare. I haven't climbed the cliffs in too long."

"The cliffs? Of Moher?"

He grinned. "Yes, those."

Anne laughed. "Are you allowed to climb those?"

"Probably not the parts I like." He winked. "Luckily you can get away with a lot in the dark."

"Well…" Anne had to smile at his cheek. "Welcome to the summit."

"Oh no." Daniel held up both hands. "I have absolutely no interest in politics. I simply wanted to catch up with Father and Brigid. I haven't seen them in ages."

As if on cue, something landed on Daniel's back, causing him to stumble forward with an "oof." A bright purple head appeared over Daniel's shoulder.

"You're here!" Brigid said with a grin, clutching Daniel's shoulders as he held her up. "We didn't know you'd be here."

"Brigid"—Gemma broke in—"do try to avoid destroying any antiques."

"Relax, Gem," Daniel said. "And I didn't know myself until Tavish mentioned it last week. How've you been, Mum?"

Brigid scowled. "Please stop calling me that."

Large hands plucked Brigid off Daniel's back as Carwyn joined the family reunion in Gemma's front room.

"Good to see you," he said, tucking Brigid under his arm and giving Daniel's shoulders a back-slapping hug. "And you should absolutely call her Mum. Don't be fooled. She loves it. She's very sentimental—ow, stop pinching me!"

"He's older than me, cradle robber," Brigid said. "Don't encourage him. The two of you are terrible."

Anne heard Murphy come behind her and slip an arm around her waist.

"Then he's learned from the best," Murphy said, smiling at Carwyn. "Hello, Daniel. How are you?"

Daniel's smile fell. "Murphy." His eyes dropped to the arm around Anne's waist. "Well, I see you've moved on from Emma, but don't you always?"

Anne's smile froze, even as Murphy's fingers dug into her waist.

"That was a long time ago, Dan. She was just a human."

"Typical." Daniel's lip curled. "And she was 'just a human' to you. She was my friend."

Carwyn stepped between the two vampires. "Gentlemen," he said, keeping his voice low, "this is neither the time nor the place. Daniel, Murphy is an invited guest. Do not bring shame on your sister's hospitality."

"It's fine, *tad*. I'm leaving."

Brigid said, "Daniel—"

"I've my own place in town," Daniel said, dropping a kiss on her cheek. "I'll be around. Anne…" Daniel turned, and his warm eyes almost caused her heart to thump. "It was truly lovely to meet you. I've heard so much from Gemma. I'll look forward to seeing you again."

"Thank you, Daniel. You too."

Murphy's fingers dug in again, and she felt her fangs drop. His possessiveness did not sit well with her, especially in a formal setting such as this. He was marking his territory like a neighborhood dog. She peeled his fingers away the moment Daniel was out of sight.

"Pardon me," she said. "I have a message for Jetta that Mary wanted me to pass along."

Chapter Eleven

MURPHY'S FANGS THROBBED as he watched her walk away. Gemma and Carwyn were silent. Brigid was glaring.

"What?" he asked them, sipping his drink.

"What was that?" Brigid said.

"I'm not going to explain myself to you lot."

Carwyn craned his neck around to shoot a pointed look at Anne's retreating figure. "Maybe you should. Just to practice."

"Daniel is very young and has a limited perspective on something that happened thirty years ago," Murphy said.

"Just a human?" Brigid asked.

"I do not view humans as viable long-term romantic partners," Murphy said. "I never have."

Brigid frowned. "That's true. You didn't proposition me until after I'd turned. I'd forgotten that."

Murphy glanced at Carwyn uneasily, Gemma's warning about not breaking antiques in the back of his mind.

"Don't mind me," Carwyn said with a grin, throwing his arm around Brigid's shoulders. "I won."

Brigid elbowed him. "Stop."

"It's true though. Murphy's still chasing his woman." Carwyn looked over his shoulder again. "Not very successfully."

Murphy narrowed his eyes. Anne was talking with a very tall Swede who looked like an underwear model. Really, the Scandinavians needed to stop turning humans solely for their looks. It was very bad policy. The man's hair was almost to his waist. Ridiculous. How could that not be a detriment in a fight?

"As amusing as all of you are," Gemma said, "I need to go make sure that Jetta's people are settled and find out who will be attending the meeting tomorrow night. Excuse me."

"Gemma, can you introduce me to…" Brigid pulled out a piece of paper. "Gunnar Jarlson? He's their security chief, and Roger wanted me to grab him when he got here."

"Of course."

Murphy watched the women walk toward the Scandinavian vampires, Carwyn at his side. Then Gemma was introducing Brigid to the tall blond talking to Anne.

"His name is Gunnar?" Murphy asked.

Carwyn nodded. "Security chief. Quite good from what Terry's man says. Been working with Jetta for thirty or forty years. They might be related."

"They *all* look related."

"Ha!" Carwyn shook his head. "They're an impressive sight, for sure. Tall, blond, and immortal."

"Viking vampire assassins," Murphy said, barely stifling a sneer. "Sounds like the subject of a bad romance novel."

"I disagree," Carwyn said. "That sounds like a rather excellent romance novel. You realize that when they raided Ireland many of the women ran after them, don't you? I think it's something about the hair."

"Shut up, Carwyn."

"I am the one with the adoring mate. Just pointing that out."

"Adoring?" Murphy glanced at his fierce young enforcer. "Oh yes, the fawning must be quite tiresome. I don't know how you put up with it."

"It's difficult, but I manage."

THE meeting the following night was as tedious as Murphy had expected, though he might have simply been in a foul mood because Anne had locked him out of her room. He'd never been able to catch up with her at the party, and by the time dawn rolled around, she was firmly ensconced in her suite, while Murphy was forced to his own very cold—if admittedly comfortable—bed.

Evening started with a knock on his door from one of Brigid's men, who needed to confirm his itinerary, then a quick drink from the refrigerated store of cow's blood—still vile—and a shower and change of suit.

He needed to swim. Murphy hadn't touched the water in days, and the pool Terry had was salt. He needed freshwater. Needed a good dousing in the river or a lake nearby. Perhaps it would take the edge off when he spent night after night wearing his civilized face without the relief of beating anyone up.

"Boss?"

He heard Brigid calling from the entryway. She was the only one with the code to his room.

"I'm in the bedroom, Brigid. Be out in a moment."

"Roger confirmed your itinerary. Since there are no changes, the same security team will be with you as there was last night. Anne's people are the same too."

He paused. "Did she confirm that she was going to the meeting?"

"Of course."

Excellent. He'd be able to corner her in the car.

"She did have another meeting with Jetta earlier though. So she'll be meeting you and me there. Carter and Lands will be going with her. Roger is also sending two of his men."

He curled his lip. "Fine."

"Boss?"

"Yes, Brigid."

"About Anne…"

Murphy stepped out of the bedroom, still adjusting his tie. "Yes?"

Brigid took a deep breath. "Is there something wrong with her?"

"What do you think?"

"I think I remember the look I've seen on her lately."

"What look?"

"The hungry one. The one that says she's thinking about her next fix."

This was one of the reasons he put up with Carwyn in his city. Brigid's skills of observation were uncanny.

"I've thought the same," he said. "I'm watching her. Apparently, this is something her sister was aware of. Her sire too."

"She's having issues with bloodlust?"

"I think so."

Brigid looked flummoxed.

"But why? I know she doesn't like animal blood, but I'm much younger than she is, and I've been able to—"

"Everyone's different, Brig. We all have our own appetites." He trusted Brigid, but only Anne had the right to tell her friend of her more unusual needs. "I'll keep an eye on her."

"I will too."

"You're a good friend."

"I know." She eyed him from head to toe. "Looking sharp, boss."

"Thank you. Now, let's go wrangle information out of Vikings, shall we?"

TWO hours later, it was Anne who finally broke through the doublespeak that Jetta's team had perfected.

"I don't know about you," Anne said, interrupting Jetta's secretary, "but while the illegal weapons trade is troubling, that's not something the human authorities can't handle. Aren't we here to talk about Elixir?"

"But the weapons are coming in through Russia," the man said. Murphy couldn't remember his name.

"But Russia is not attending the summit, are they?" Anne leaned forward. "I'm not a politician. You're going to have to spell it out for me."

The man exchanged a look with Jetta, who nodded.

"We know that the Dutch have a special relationship with the Russians," he said. "If they expect us to share information about the Elixir trade, then we want a halt to the weapons. Our human governments have very strict weapons policies and part of our responsibility is supporting that."

Rens Anker had been silent throughout the meeting. The quiet man had arrived shortly after Jetta the night before, but with far less fanfare. If Murphy hadn't known what Rens looked like, he never would have guessed the tall, academic Dutchman was anyone other than an assistant. He was thin in a way that led Murphy to believe he'd not been wealthy in human life. His angular face and dark hair should have made him stand out among all the Norsemen at Terry and Gemma's house, but he somehow managed to blend into the woodwork.

It was a pleasant enough face. Kind, even.

But his eyes were wary.

Anker smoothed his tie down the front of his shirt. "The Russians will do what the Russians will do. To think that my brother or I have any kind of influence over them would be false."

"So they do not use your satellites?" Jetta's secretary—who Murphy was beginning to believe was her attack dog—pointed out.

"I didn't say they don't use our satellites," Rens said. "Nor will I confirm it. I would do neither, as discretion"—he pointedly looked at Jetta—"is very much part of what my clients pay me for. There are many, many organizations, both human and immortal, who are valued clients. But that does not make their business mine."

"What is your business, Rens?" Murphy asked quietly. "Your shipping interests have shrunk every year. Why are you here?"

"Mr. Murphy, I believe—as I'm sure we all do—that the stability of the human blood supply is a problem that knows no borders." He spread his hands. "And thus I am here to offer what I can to stabilize it."

And not answer questions.

"What exactly are you offering?" Murphy asked.

"Information. When I deem it useful."

A few quiet sounds of frustration were scattered around the room.

"And who are you to decide what is or isn't useful?" Jetta asked. "The Russians—"

"The Russians have their own problems, such as weapons proliferation," Rens said. "And the lovely Dr. O'Dea is correct; this is a problem the human authorities can deal with. Elixir is not. And that—I am sad to say—has been as much a problem in our small country as it has been in any of yours. Possibly worse."

Gemma asked, "What is your current status?"

"Our immortal population is very concentrated in our city centers. Many of the clubs and underground bars our donors frequent have been infested. We're facing a real problem if we can't find a cure. Hundreds of humans have been contaminated. The human authorities are baffled because we can't hide all the deaths. This is the problem we are facing. Now, what problems are your countries facing?"

Anne slid Murphy a note.

So the spy offers information first?

He quickly responded. *By doing so, he controls the direction of the conversation and puts all of us in obligation to him. Anker has laid out the parameters of what he is willing to share and avoided questions. Never underestimate him or his brother.*

Understood.

Terry was the next to speak, looking to Gemma, who nodded before he began. "It's no surprise to anyone that we've been hit in the UK. The North Sea and the Baltic countries seem to have been the first affected by this, which is why I wanted to speak to everyone at this table first. We'll talk to France and Spain tomorrow. The Americans will be here later in the week. In Britain, I can confirm over three hundred human infections, mostly centered around three clubs here in London—and we've had thirteen vampire infections."

Anne asked, "The status of the immortals infected?"

"Eight have living sires," Gemma said. "We've sent them to their sires with the instructions we received from Katya Grigorieva's lab in California. That's all we can do."

"And the humans?" Murphy asked.

"Isolated those who belonged to us," Gemma said. "But we can't keep everyone prisoner, especially if they're not aware of our true natures. We've watched them. Our doctors don't think it's transferable, even by bodily fluids. We've tracked those in the general population, and so far, none of them have spread the infection to anyone else. Elixir needs to be taken directly for infection to occur."

Murphy saw Rens taking notes and Jetta exchanging meaningful glances with her secretary.

"We are not as concentrated," Jetta's secretary said, "but we have seen infection as well. Five immortals and one hundred twenty-three humans. Also centered around two nightclubs in Stockholm, both owned and frequented by immortals. We've taken care of the infection in a similar manner. I am curious about our Irish friends."

All eyes turned to Anne and Murphy.

"As most of you know," Murphy began, "Ireland had some of the first confirmed cases of both human and vampire Elixir poisoning. It was Brigid Connor, my security chief here, who detected the pattern among the missing, and Carwyn ap Bryn, her mate, who was involved in the Battle of Rome where Livia was killed, who finally gave us the answers about what was infecting our population. Unfortunately, because we were not aware of the drug, we had some of the highest rates of infection at first. There have been humans and vampires affected, many of whom are now dead. After the initial surge, I laid down very specific rules about feeding that those in my territories have been following for over two years now."

Murphy heard a few muffled laughs around the room.

Jetta raised an eyebrow. "What? You told your people not to feed from humans in clubs, and they obeyed you?"

"Yes."

His one-word answer seemed to shock the room into silence.

"Because of that," he continued, "we've had far lower rates of vampire infection in that time, though we've had similar numbers regarding human infection."

"Why Dublin?" Rens Anker asked.

"It's a good question." Murphy turned to Anne. "Dr. O'Dea?"

Anne said, "As most of you know, Dublin has become a magnet for university-aged humans under immortal aegis. There are students from all over the world in the city because it is well controlled and considered quite safe for both humans and vampires. We believe Dublin may have been targeted because of this. There was also a doctor in Dublin, Ioan ap Carwyn, working with the original researcher who uncovered the Elixir manuscript. Ioan was doing research that made him a target. And though he was killed, some of Livia's allies, the ones who killed Ioan, stayed in Dublin. We believe they were the ones who received the initial shipments."

"What happened to them?" Rens asked.

"They're dead," Murphy said, the pain of Jack's betrayal still a sharp lance in his chest.

He felt Anne's hand reach for his under the table.

"So." Terry quickly changed the subject. "Kids get infected in Dublin, go home for holidays or when they graduate. Just another way to spread Elixir."

"Are the humans that stupid?" Jetta asked. "I realize they're mortal, but—"

"Don't forget," Anne said. "Elixir is a drug, even though it doesn't give a typical 'high' and doesn't present as one initially. Effects and timing vary from person to person, but almost all humans who take it feel wonderful and healthy at first. It improves their looks. If young people get their hands on it, they will want more."

Jetta said, "That seems like a madness of its own kind. Isn't it simple enough to smell them? Don't those who have taken Elixir smell of pomegranates?"

"They do," Murphy said. "But the scent can be masked, and both the smell and taste are intoxicating to our kind. Vampires who drink from an infected human want more. They're not always able to think rationally."

"Especially if they're young and their sires are living," Brigid said quietly in the corner behind Murphy. "The risk is considered a thrill."

Murphy continued, "And whoever is behind this continues to innovate. We're currently holding a group of infected humans that was shipped into Dublin recently. They are quite far advanced in the infection, but that may be as much a consequence of the smuggling as the Elixir. It appears the idea was to seed them into the local immortal population. The humans were told they were going to be domestic servants. We don't know who shipped them from the Black Sea or where they were ultimately intended to go."

"Damn Russians…," Jetta muttered.

"The Russians don't control every port on the Black Sea," Rens Anker said.

"They control many of them."

"That investigation is ongoing." Murphy tried to get the meeting back on track. "From the beginning, I've found the best way of controlling the spread of this drug has been to offer information among my people as freely and as quickly as possible. Secrecy only leads to more infection."

Rens said, "You don't worry about creating a panic?"

"What could I tell them that wouldn't be worse whispered in shadows?" Murphy asked. "By sharing what I know, they feel free to come to me if they suspect any of their humans or employees are infected. They're more alert to smuggling. More aware in their own business dealings. Secrecy will only lead to misinformation and create greater panic, not less."

Jetta and her secretary were exchanging more pointed looks.

"Anne," Jetta said, "Northern Ireland has also seen infection, yes?"

"It has. It's a small population—also mainly urban—but there have been cases. Over fifty humans infected. Only three vampires."

Jetta's eyes lit. "And how did Mary deal with the vampires?"

Anne paused, clearly not expecting the question. "She killed them. Then she forbade her people from feeding outside their household staff. There have been no vampire infections since."

"Effective," Rens said.

"Yes, it was." Anne shifted her attention to the Dutchman. "Mr. Anker, I notice that you have not shared your rate of infection with the rest of us. Would you mind?" She held up her pencil. "For note-taking purposes, of course."

A reluctant smile crossed the man's lip. "Of course. We have had two hundred forty-three human infections and twenty-six vampire infections. Most of those vampires have living sires. We also contacted Katya's people about how to treat them. They are being taken care of."

It was an alarming rate for such a small country. Murphy had to admit Rens's participation in the summit wasn't such a mystery anymore. Almost two dozen immortals infected? It was disproportionally high.

"And the infected humans?" Anne asked.

Rens shrugged slowly. "The humans? Most were nothing. Club kids. That sort of thing. Not attached to anyone in particular. They left Amsterdam one way or another. We don't need the human authorities beginning an investigation."

Anne's pencil froze on her page.

Note to Tom and Declan, Murphy thought. *Restrict travel to the Netherlands for humans under Irish aegis.*

Chapter Twelve

AFTER THAT EXCHANGE, the meeting wrapped up quickly. Jetta and her entourage were still settling in. Rens and his small staff drifted back to… wherever they were staying. No one seemed to know. Murphy followed Anne into the crisp spring evening.

"What are you doing the rest of the night?" Murphy asked. "Would you join me for a drink?"

Her cheeks were pale and her eyes bright again. "I think I'll go for a swim," she said. "Then maybe read a bit. I'll need to transcribe the evening notes for Mary as well."

He frowned. "You already took them."

"But I need to translate."

He nodded. "Ah yes. Tywyll's mystery language."

"You don't forget much, do you, Mr. Murphy?"

"Your secrets are safe with me, Dr. O'Dea."

She nodded and turned. "Good to know."

"Go for a swim with me?" he asked. "I was heading down to the river."

Anne cringed. "Surely not, Patrick. The water is filthy."

"Far cleaner than it used to be," he said with a smile. "I was planning to go upriver. The saltwater irritates my skin."

Water vampires always tended toward either freshwater or salt, with the vast majority preferring the ocean. But for Murphy, freshwater was his home. Springs and lakes. Rivers and creeks. Any bit of it would do. The ocean was fine… but it wasn't the same.

"No, find a pool or a lake or something. The river is…" She shuddered.

"I hope you don't share your feelings with your sire."

"I don't. Though he's as cross about the pollution as any environmentalist. I'll be fine. Enjoy your swim."

She turned to walk toward her driver.

"Anne, wait." Murphy caught up with her and put a hand on her arm. "Why are you cross with me?"

"The posturing last night was a bit much, don't you think?"

"Oh, I don't know. Did you enjoy flirting with Daniel and that Viking? Were you trying to make me jealous?"

Her mouth twisted in a bitter smile. "Yes, you horse's ass, because every conversation I have is a reaction to you. Egotistical much, Murphy?"

"Don't call me Murphy!" He leaned down and spoke in her ear. "And talk to whoever you like, but don't shut me out when I'm trying to resolve something. Your door was locked long before dawn. I thought we were giving this a go."

"Just because you decided something doesn't mean I agreed to it." She jerked away, her movements sharp and brittle.

He narrowed his eyes and watched her walk down the dark street, passing her driver, whom she waved away with a gloved hand.

Murphy followed at a distance.

She was angry, yes, but Anne was usually far more mild-tempered, even when she was furious with him. Her steps were long, eating up the cobblestones for two blocks past Terry's offices, then she turned right onto a larger street. Murphy continued to follow, watching any humans who came too close.

None did. Most humans subconsciously sensed a predator, and Anne was the picture of predatory that night. Her dark, fitted coat swept shapely calves covered in leather boots. Her hair was pulled back into a sleek chignon at the nape of her neck. Gradually her steps slowed toward calculation. Her movements became smoother. Her breath evened out to the rhythm of her steps, and her body transformed into a singular deadly tool.

So *that's* why she was cross. She needed to hunt.

Problematic. Especially as close to the edge as she appeared to be.

Murphy could close his eyes and see her face. Watch the cold light that would slide behind her eyes and the flush that would plump her lips. He'd watched her hunt in the past. He knew her tricks and her lures.

She slid behind groups of humans, matching her pace to theirs, following at a distance until they turned or ducked into a restaurant or pub. The hour was late and most were heading home, jumping into taxis or ducking into underground stations for the train.

Anne started following a group of young men who were joking and walking at a leisurely pace. They must have lived nearby, for the three young men turned off the main road and away from the flickering lights and traffic toward a residential area bordering a small park. Murphy hurried to catch up with them before he lost sight of Anne.

Except when he turned the corner, she was no longer there.

Nor were the humans.

His heart began to thump.

"Anne?"

He turned and walked into the small park, only to trip over the legs of one of the boys.

Dammit. She'd always been fast.

"Anne, stop," Murphy said, his voice calm and quiet. "Whatever you're doing, stop right now."

A rustling behind him. Murphy dragged the boy out from behind the bush and crouched down to look, but there were no marks on him. He appeared to be sleeping. The park was only a small triangle of shrubs and trees, with three paths that all led to a fountain in the middle. If she was in the park, there weren't many places to hide.

"Anne?" He stood and opened his senses, searching for her with his amnis. "Áine, love, don't do this. You'll be very angry with yourself tomorrow."

He closed his eyes when he felt her behind him. Her cool lips touched the nape of his neck.

"Go home," she whispered. "*Leave.*"

The push of her amnis flooded him, but he was prepared for it.

"No," he said, focusing on his concern for his mate and not on the nearly irresistible compulsion to flee. "I don't think I will."

He spun and tried to trap her, but she'd already jumped back.

Her lips had curled back, and she bared her fangs. "I told you to leave!"

"No."

The last thing he wanted to do was hurt her. Anne wasn't much of a fighter. She could defend herself when necessary, but she depended on her ability to push vampires to her will more than she used brute strength. Murphy reached for the water trickling from the fountain, dashing it into her eyes and hoping it was enough to jolt his mate out of her bloodlust.

She reared back with a short gasp, the cold water snapping her back to herself. Murphy held himself very still, watching her as reason returned to her eyes and the predatory edge softened, even if it didn't quite leave.

"Patrick?"

"Are you back?"

Anne looked around, saw the boy on the grass. "Dammit!" she said, running back into the shadows. She emerged with another young man thrown over her shoulder. "Quick," she said. "Grab the other one. They're sleeping, but it won't be for long."

"Wanted them awake and frightened when you fed from them?"

"Lecture me later. Help me now."

He gathered the other human and propped him on the bench next to his friend. Then Anne dragged the first boy on the grass over to the same bench and sat him on the ground next to his friends. The boys were already blinking awake as Anne bent down and patted their cheeks.

"Lads," she said. "Are you all right?"

The one on the ground blinked awake first. " Oi. What the—"

"Little too much at the pub, eh?" Murphy said, putting on his most fatherly voice, though the young men only looked a few years younger than him. "Do you live close by? Need us to call someone for you?"

All three were awake and looking around.

"Oi, Jazz, where is she?"

"What are you talking 'bout?"

"The girl. Lush." He shook his head as Murphy and Anne stepped farther back into the shadows. "Don't remember exactly."

Murphy put his arm around Anne's shoulders and said, "If you're close to home, we'll be going. You boys all right?"

"Yeah, mate. Thanks for that." The boy on the ground stood. "Sorry. Yeah, we're just around the corner. I'll get them home. Weird night."

"Have a good evening and stay safe."

"Will do, mate. Thanks."

Murphy herded Anne toward the iron gate and back toward their drivers, his hand gripping her upper arm. "Well, Anne love, why don't we grab that drink after all?" he whispered. "Then you can explain to me back in *our room* how you got this bloody close to the edge."

"Patrick, I just need to feed. I'm f—"

"I don't like being lied to, so why don't you stop before you start?"

Now that concern was wearing off, he was angry. Blazingly angry. And, he had to admit, more than a little scared.

Anne was one of the most self-controlled vampires he'd ever met. What was happening to her?

ANNE'S hunger was burning her from the inside out. She felt as if she could crawl out of her own skin. Hot then cold. Her throat burned, but her stomach threatened nausea. Murphy almost dragged her back to the car. He opened the door and shoved her in the backseat, then he crawled in behind her and barked at the driver.

"Ozzie!"

"Yes, boss."

"When was the last time you gave blood?"

"Eh… two weeks ago."

Murphy snapped. "Your arm. Now."

Without a word, the driver rolled up his sleeve and stuck his arm over the backseat. Murphy hauled Anne into his lap despite her protests.

"Two weeks is too soon," Anne said.

"Have you seen the man? He's built like an ox. Drink."

The scent of Ozzie's wrist caused her fangs to ache. They hadn't retracted since the park. She was too hungry.

"Drink, dammit! You've been taking nothing but blood-wine since we've been here, for fuck knows what reason. That's not a full meal. It was never intended to be. Drink, Anne."

"I've been drinking animal blood…" She turned her face away. "It's like nothing. It only makes me hungrier."

"This comes to an end tonight. You will stop starving yourself."

She could hear the fear behind his anger, but she still resisted. "Murphy, I'm too close. Get me a bag."

"I don't have a bag. I'll hold you. Drink."

"Too close."

"Drink!"

Murphy shoved Ozzie's wrist in her face, and Anne lost control. She struck without a hint of finesse. She felt the human flinch, but he didn't jerk away. Murphy held her neck, palm against her throat, gently stroking the nape with his thumb as she reveled in the feeding. The human's blood was like swallowing warm silk. It wrapped around Anne, her amnis awakening.

For the first time in weeks, her mind was clear. Her senses on alert. Her heart beat. Her blood moved. She felt Murphy's body beneath her, felt him begin to respond to her energy, to the scent of blood spiking the air.

"Enough," he finally said, his voice rough as he pulled her back with his gentle grip.

Anne forced herself to let go. Ozzie withdrew his arm, and Murphy leaned forward, capturing Anne's lips with his own, tongue licking at the hot blood that still stained her lips. She groaned into his mouth, even as he banged a fist on the front seat. Anne heard the divider going up and Murphy pushed her back, curling his body over hers in the car, caging her in while the engine rumbled.

Anne reached up and gripped his hair, pulling him closer as she parted her thighs, eager for the heavy weight of his body over hers.

"Anne," he gasped, pulling away. "We need to get back."

"No." She was still hungry. "I want you."

He groaned and kissed her again, his tongue curling around her fangs, stroking down each slick length as she shuddered beneath him. His hands tugged at her coat and she arched up, wishing they were alone, wishing the car…

"Oh bollocks," she blinked back to reason. "We're in a car."

Murphy dragged his fangs across the hypersensitive skin of her throat. His hand was gripping her thigh where he'd torn the stocking away to reach her bare flesh.

"I know," he panted. "Don't worry, the windows are blacked out."

"And I just fed from the driver."

"He'll be fine. You didn't take too much."

He was still breathing against her neck, and each warm breath sent a shiver of excitement through her system. She was primed for him. Aching for it. There was no way he'd be able to ignore her acute arousal. She didn't want him to.

"Murphy—"

A low stream of curses cut her off as Murphy took a deep breath and pulled away from her. "We can't do this now."

"What?"

"We should head back." He shifted to the side and knocked on the partition while Anne attempted to straighten her clothes.

The driver called back, "Yes, boss?"

"You good to drive, Oz?"

"I'll be fine. We're not going far, and I already drank some juice."

"Good man. Get us home."

"Is Dr. O'Dea feeling better?"

Anne wanted to dissolve into the seat. "I'm feeling much better, Ozzie. I appreciate your assistance."

"Anytime, miss."

"Get us back to Terry's," Murphy said as he straightened his tie.

"Yes, boss."

They drove in silence as Anne tried not to think of her earlier actions. She had no excuse. She'd known she was on the edge, and she went out into town. If Murphy hadn't followed her…

"Thank you," she said quietly. "I was not in control of myself earlier. I would have regretted that. I appreciate your intervention."

"No more than you did for me countless times, Anne."

"Still. I thank you."

"At least I could finally be useful."

She blinked. "What does that mean?"

He pulled his lip back and she watched as he deliberately retracted his fangs. "Nothing. I'm out of sorts. Could use a swim is all."

"Why did you say that?" She knew he wanted her to drop it, but she was too disturbed by his statement. "'Finally useful?' What does that mean?"

"Anne—"

"When did I ever imply that I had no use for you, Patrick?"

He slammed his hand down on the door, and she could hear the leather rip. "You didn't have to. You're one of the most bloody self-contained women I know. I'm just glad that for once you needed my help instead of me needing yours. I realize that's probably very childish or regressive…" He waved a hand. "Fine. I have never claimed to be modern. Now, let's get you back to Carwyn and Brigid's room. I know they have extra space."

Her mouth dropped. "Are you kicking me out of my room. *My* room? I don't think so, Murphy."

"I fecking hate when you call me Murphy, and you know it!" he roared as they stopped in traffic. "You need immortal blood, Anne. You need blood from someone we trust, because you won't take it from me, and it's the only thing I can think of that might keep you going until we figure out what the hell is going on. Your sister is too far away. It could take days to track down your sire, and you need something now. So you're going to ask Brigid or Carwyn, or I will."

She crossed her arms and stared forward. Anne knew what he was thinking. Her body had become so malnourished that the best course would be to take blood from another immortal with richer amnis than even human blood held. Her sire would be ideal, but any blood drawn from a vampire would work. The problem was it created a tie, even between friends. No vampire wanted to create that link with an immortal they didn't trust.

"Patrick, you know why I shouldn't take yours."

"Because you want our bloody mate bond to die," he bit out. "I understand perfectly well, Anne. That's been made clear. I'll leave you with Carwyn and Brigid. I'm sure some arrangement can be made to move your things closer to them while we're in town."

"No, that's not… It's not what I was thinking."

Murphy had said he would wait. He'd said he'd learned patience. Was he giving up so quickly?

Without a word, he reached over and took her hand. She clutched it with both her own.

"I don't want the bond to die," Anne said. "I just need to be able to trust my own heart. You claim I didn't need you, but you know that's not true. It would be so easy to lose myself in you."

They said nothing for a long time, and Anne watched the lights of the city zip by. The car windows were dark, but she could see a few people still stumbling home after a night out. Friends laughing. Couples holding hands. She could feel the tentative brush of Murphy's amnis against her palm where he held her hand securely.

"Would it be so terrible to lose yourself in me?" he murmured as they neared the house. "Was it so awful before?"

"It wasn't awful at all. Just consuming. This is me, Patrick. When I love, I love completely. I know this about me. You do the same."

"You say I consumed you, but I never saw it that way." His thumb stroked along the inside of her wrist. "You were my anchor."

"Patrick—"

"Take your time. Keep your distance if you need to, Anne." He took a carefully measured breath and released it. "God knows, I've made more than my share of mistakes. I've waited a hundred years for you to start speaking to me again. I'll wait longer. Just don't cut me out completely, and don't hurt yourself because you don't want to ask for help."

Patrick Murphy had taken her heart, held it, and nurtured it. Then he'd dropped it, crushed it, and left her behind. Yet she'd never turned away from him. Not completely. And he'd never forgotten her.

Are you trying to make me fall in love with you, Mr. Murphy?

Of course I am, Dr. O'Dea.

Didn't he know?

She'd never stopped.

He held her hand all the way home, but Anne couldn't say another word.

Chapter Thirteen

CARWYN ANSWERED THEIR KNOCK with uncharacteristic churlishness.

"What?" The heavy door swung open, and his mood dissolved as soon as he saw her face. "Anne? What's wrong?"

"May we come in?" she asked.

Carwyn frowned. "Murphy?"

"A few moments would be greatly appreciated, Father."

He waved them in and shut the door. "You've got to stop with the father business. It bothers Brigid."

"Sorry," Murphy said, feeling moderately regretful. "It's habit."

"I understand." He walked down the hall and led them into a library where Anne noticed a sleeping Brigid curled on the couch.

"Carwyn." She halted. "I'm so sorry. I had no idea we were so close to dawn."

"It's fine." He tucked a blanket around his mate. "Since we mated, she'll sometimes wake when I'm still conscious. It's very random. I'd put her to bed"—Carwyn poured two glasses of whiskey for them—"but she hates waking when I'm not there. She'll be fine. Sit. You've a look about you, Anne. What's wrong?"

"Is it so obvious?"

Murphy pulled her down to a couch and sat close to her.

Carwyn frowned. "Only obvious to someone who knows you well. What is it?"

Murphy said nothing, leaving Anne to decide how much she wanted to share. She trusted Carwyn completely, but…

"I have a condition," Anne said. "I've had it for years. It's nothing damaging, but I've always needed to feed more. I haven't had a problem since I was a newborn, but with the feeding restrictions in place, I've been… limited. Animal blood doesn't seem to suffice."

The old vampire leaned forward, immediately alert. "You're struggling with bloodlust?"

"Yes."

"How often?"

"Do I struggle with my control?" *Every night.*

"No," he said. "How often are you feeding?"

"Once a month with live blood. Animal and blood-wine between. But those don't seem to be enough."

"That's surprising. And you've had problems recently?"

Murphy took Anne's hand in his. "She took three humans in a park tonight. Was on the verge of tearing their throats out before I found her."

Carwyn's eyes widened, but he remained silent.

"Before the feeding restrictions," Anne said, "I would feed twice a week. I never had a problem."

"Twice a week at your age?"

She nodded. "As I said, I've always needed more. I can't share why."

"Hmm." Carwyn scratched the heavy stubble of his beard. Unlike Murphy, he preferred to wear facial hair even though it took ages for vampire hair to grow. Combined with his size, deep auburn hair, and roughly handsome face, it gave the old earth vampire a wild and dangerous look. But as there were few who'd challenge him anyway, Anne suspected he kept the beard for his own pleasure. There was little to no artifice around Carwyn ap Bryn.

"The simple solution is that you need to be feeding more," Carwyn said. "Your body is healthy, but your amnis must be starved if you're having trouble controlling bloodlust at your age. Your mind was accustomed to a certain level of human blood, and then you cut it off. You essentially put your amnis on a diet your mind wasn't prepared for."

"But why isn't animal blood enough? You drink nothing but animal blood."

"That is what I have drunk for most of the past thousand years. And I hunt. Wild animals, not domestic. Elder vampires will tell you domestic blood does not have enough of the fifth element to feed our energy." He glanced at Murphy. "And I'm mated, Anne. That *has* made a difference. Brigid does not keep to a strict animal diet. She drinks from our household staff. Taking her blood has made me far stronger."

"What are you suggesting?"

Was Carwyn going to suggest she renew her mating bond with Murphy just to regain her health?

That wasn't going to happen. If and when she took his blood, Anne didn't want it to be for health reasons or out of desperation. Murphy deserved better than to be the option of last resort.

Carwyn said, "You need to drink living blood to set your system to rights. A lot of it."

Murphy said nothing, but she could almost hear his "I told you so" in her mind. She knew Carwyn was probably thinking the same thing.

"Anne hasn't asked, so I will," Murphy said, speaking quickly. "Would you or Brigid give her some blood? She would prefer not to drink mine, and I believe she needs an infusion of amnis. Even more than just drinking from humans. You're the only two vampires in Dublin that we can ask."

"I agree about the blood," Carwyn said. "I was going to suggest Tywyll, but I know he's often hard to track down, and I think you need blood immediately. I can sense the... I'll call it an imbalance. Your hunger is obvious to others, which presents as a weakness we cannot afford in foreign territory. I do offer, my friend. If you have need."

"I don't want to ask." Anne blinked back tears and tried to ignore the simmering anger from Murphy.

"You're not asking; I'm offering. After all you've given of your time and friendship for Brigid and me? You know either of us would be happy to help you in any way we can. Will you take it, please?"

She nodded, and Carwyn rose to his feet.

"Let me get you a glass. That will make things more comfortable for both of us."

"Thank you."

As soon as Carwyn left the room, Anne turned to Murphy. "Patrick—"

"I'm going to go." His jaw was clenched. "I can accept the necessity of this, but don't ask me—"

"I wasn't going to," she said. "Thank you for understanding."

"I don't understand," he said, his voice low. "I'm sitting next to you, and yet you won't… I need to leave."

Anne put her hand on his arm. "Patrick, I'm not doing this to hurt you."

"What then?" His jaw tensed. "To test me?"

"It's not a test. I just… I want—"

"What?" he snapped, rousing Brigid from her sleep.

The small woman leapt to her feet, twin pools of flame in her palms, glaring at Murphy with clouded eyes and bared fangs.

"Brigid"—Anne leaped between Murphy and her friend—"it's just us. We're fighting is all. There's no danger."

"Anne, get back!" Murphy tried to shove her to the side, but Anne was unmoved, even as she felt Murphy wrap her in a layer of water drawn from the moisture in the air. The young vampire snarled as footsteps came pounding down the hall.

"Hello, my lovely girl," Carwyn said, sliding his arms around Brigid from behind. He curled his body over her, putting his cheek to hers and wrapping both arms around her waist, his eyes fixed on the fire in her hands. "Calm, love. You're among friends."

Anne was about to call on the water in the air to douse the flames, but Brigid sank into her mate, her body softening as he drew her heat into his body. The flames disappeared as the fire vampire drew a deep breath. Anne relaxed. She glanced over her shoulder at Murphy, whose fangs were down; he looked ready to lunge toward the tiny woman. She put a hand on his arm and he fell back.

"What's going on?" Brigid said, her voice hoarse. "Why's Anne and Murphy here?"

"Anne's not feeling well, my love."

"I told you that last night." Brigid nuzzled into his neck. "Something all wrong with her amnis. 'S obvious."

"I'm so glad you shared your concerns with me," Anne said sharply.

"So's you can brush 'em off? D'you kill anyone yet?" She slurred her words, still drowsy. "Told Murphy... So damn stubborn 'bout asking for help."

Carwyn hid his face in Brigid's neck to hide his smile.

"I love you too, Brigid. Carwyn has offered me some of his blood to help with my... condition. With his age, it's probably the strongest."

That seemed to snap Brigid more awake. "What the hell you need my mate's blood for when yours is standing behind you?"

Carwyn's mouth dropped open. "Well... ah, Brigid. Anne and Murphy—"

"Are mated. And they love each other. It's bloody obvious."

Anne felt Murphy tense again.

Brigid rubbed her eyes. "Bollocks. I'm too tired to be polite. Ignore me, Anne. Or don't." She held out her arm. "Here now, you're like my sister. Take mine. I won't react well to you taking Carwyn's. And taking mine won't drive Murphy as crazy. We all know that if your amnis is weak, drinking my blood will be like putting your mouth on a lightning bolt. There, everyone happy?"

Murphy growled, but Carwyn stepped away from Brigid and held up a hand. "Here now, lad. Let's leave them. I've a few ideas about the meeting tomorrow night I wanted to run by you. Join me in Terry's library?"

Anne felt Murphy shift behind her, then he bent down and dragged his cheek over hers. She felt the edge of one of his fangs scrape against her neck, and then he was gone. Carwyn followed him as Brigid sat on the couch again and pulled up her arm.

Anne sat down next to her, knowing that she needed the blood and just as reluctant about taking it. "Brigid, do you really think—"

"That he's in love with you? As if it wasn't obvious with that territorial display. I've never seen him possessive around a woman. Ever. This test you have running for him is almost cruel, Anne."

Anne's mouth dropped open. "I was going to ask about the lightning-bolt thing actually. And it's not a test for him. It's a test for myself."

"Neither of you need to be tested."

She tried to remain calm. "I realize that Patrick is your friend, but I'm afraid you weren't there when we ended our relationship. It wasn't pleasant. If you were there, you'd understand my reservations."

"Everyone fights, Anne."

"Nearly thirty years after we separated, he drove out to Galway in one of his fancy motorcars, accompanied by three human women who were fawning all over him, and showed up at my house without warning while I was hosting a dinner party. Then he proceeded to ask me why he was forced to invite humans to his bed when he had a mate who should be 'seeing to his needs.'"

Brigid's mouth dropped. "Okay, that's bad."

"Then he accused me of leaving him for one of my dinner guests. A guest who happened to be married. I had met his new wife that same evening."

Brigid winced. "Murphy created a *scene*. He never does that. He hates scenes with a passion."

"I suspect he does now. But at that time? He could be a proper bastard, Brigid. I'm glad to say he's grown, but he was horrid to me. To my sister. To my friends. You're welcome to ask Josie if you like. She was the one who finally put a stop to it. Tom is the one who knocked sense into him."

Brigid grumbled, "I think I want to change my vote."

"Don't judge him for who he was seventy years ago," Anne said. "In his defense, the war was an awful time for everyone. And he *has* changed. I can see that. He tried to show me before, but I wasn't willing to listen."

"Are you ready to take his blood?"

"No. I don't want it to be because of my health."

Brigid held out her arm. "Then we should do this."

"I don't want to have to take your blood either."

"So *bloody* independent—no pun intended." Brigid rubbed her eyes. "How many times did you have to help me my first year? It's not like you never shoved a wrist in my face to keep me from biting a human. Let someone else help you for a change."

"Brigid…" Anne closed her eyes and fingered the remnants of her stockings where they were torn at the thighs. "I feel like such a ninny."

"You are one, but mostly about Murphy."

"Will you stop?"

"You said yourself that he's changed."

"And you think he's possessive now?" Anne shook her head. "You didn't know him before. I have a life. Is it so hard to understand that I don't want to lose myself again?"

"Why not?" Brigid asked. "Look at Carwyn. You think I don't feel lost in that crazy man sometimes? His love is… enormous. Baffling. I feel like he takes over every part of me." Brigid's smile was halting. "But by some miracle, he'd tell you the same thing. That's why it works."

"And if you lost it?" Anne pulled her legs up to her chest. "Have you ever asked yourself what you'd do?"

"I *have* lost love," Brigid said. "You know that more than anyone. I know the worst that can happen, because it killed me. But if I spent every moment of eternity wondering about what *might* happen, I'd meet the dawn tomorrow. There are no guarantees. Not even from those who love you the most."

"Patrick and I—"

"One hundred *years*, Anne. You separated one hundred years ago, and you've found your way back to each other. Grab on to happiness when it's given to you and fight for it."

"Brigid—"

"*Fight for it.*" Brigid's expression was fierce. "Even if it means you're fighting him. If Carwyn broke my trust, I'd break his head! We'd fight.

We'd yell. I'd burn things up. *Mostly* by accident. And then he'd apologize and I'd apologize and we'd make it work again. Love is messy, but it's worth it. It's worth fighting for. Don't you believe that?"

"Of course I do."

"Really?" Brigid's look said she doubted her.

"I…" She couldn't finish a thought.

Anne counseled other immortals to allow emotion in their lives. Admonished them to find love and trust. But when it was her own heart at stake?

So much harder.

"Drink." Brigid held out her arm. "Maybe then things will be clearer."

Chapter Fourteen

"I HAVE MY SUSPICIONS ABOUT Leonor and the Russians," Carwyn said. "She and Oleg have a history."

Murphy almost snapped the cue stick in two, he was gripping it so tightly. "Oleg has a history with the majority of the female vampire lords in Europe. The man has a type and it usually involves breasts, political savvy, and massive ego. It's not the Russians."

"How do you know?" Carwyn asked. "I'd never thought about it before, but when Jetta brought it up, it made sense. And we all know they're cagey bastards."

Murphy didn't know. It was instinct. Or—as Tom more correctly surmised—a meeting of a multitude of facts in his mind. It was the same way he knew an opponent might come from the left instead of the right. It wasn't their feet, but the lean of their hips and the angle of their eyes. The flinch in a shoulder. A minute lift of elbow or a clenched hand. Murphy couldn't quantify it. Boxing or politics. He made decisions based on a hundred tiny pieces of knowledge that coalesced into assurance.

"The Russians are not behind this," he said again. "I think it's Athens."

Carwyn frowned. "The Greeks? They might be involved peripherally, but they wouldn't get their hands dirty. Impossible."

Murphy missed potting a red ball and stepped away from the table, letting out a frustrated breath. "Because we're all so familiar with the impossible, yes? Carwyn, we're mythical creatures who feed on blood and live for hundreds or thousands of years. Do you really believe Athens masterminding this plot is too far-fetched?"

"They're lazy."

"They invented democracy. Give them a little credit for original thought."

"They're also cash poor. Their court is bloated."

"But they have the connections." He tapped his stick on the ground, grateful for the distraction of politics. "There's something. There's a thread I'm not seeing. I need to think about it more. Elixir is touching water in the Black Sea. With this shipment of infected humans, I'm almost positive that's the source. But the Greeks wouldn't be shipping from the Black Sea."

"Because…" Carwyn pointed his cue stick at Murphy. "It's not the Greeks,"

He potted three balls in a row before he miscalculated a cushion shot.

"You're much better at this game than Terry is."

"I've been playing longer."

"It is the Greeks. I just can't see the connection. Yet. Who runs the Russian ports in the Black Sea?"

Carwyn shrugged. "It will be one of Oleg's children. He only trusts his children to run things."

"It's a good thing he has so many of them."

"Unusual for a fire vampire."

"But smart for anyone who wants to hold Russia." Murphy frowned. "What element was Oleg sired from?"

Fire vampires could be sired from any element, and their offspring would be sired back to it. Murphy wondered what particular animal Oleg's children were.

"There are contradictory rumors, but I know for a fact that Oleg's sire was an earth vampire. And a very nasty individual."

"Really?" That didn't fit with what Murphy had imagined. Earth vampires were solid leaders, but not as politically motivated. Or as scheming. "No, the Greeks wouldn't work with an earth vampire."

Carwyn laughed. "I do enjoy how the facts don't seem to matter when they don't fit your narrative."

"Because I know I'm right." Murphy stepped back to the snooker table. "If something doesn't fit, then there's something I'm not seeing. Yet."

"No one ever accused you of lacking confidence."

He took four shots, racking up points while Carwyn watched silently.

"You've distracted me admirably, Father. My thanks."

"You're welcome." Carwyn leaned against the paneled wall. "In case you were wondering, she is worth it."

"I know she is."

"Anne's loyalty is absolute. That's why she's so cautious giving it."

"I know that as well." He took another drink. "We met when I was quite young. I was… careless with her. I will not be again."

Carwyn nodded and began putting the room to rights. Dawn wasn't far off. "Give her the night. Let her get her equilibrium back. She's not been thinking clearly, I imagine."

"But does that work for or against me?"

Carwyn laughed. "I cannot tell you that, my friend. But I imagine Brigid is in your corner."

"Brigid is a good friend."

His smile softened. "She is. My mate is a woman of extraordinary character. Don't think I didn't try to convince her to leave Dublin. But she's loyal, just like Anne."

"Then I suppose we're both lucky bastards, aren't we?"

MURPHY didn't see Anne until the meeting the next night with Jetta, Rens, and the British vampires. Jean Desmarais from Marseilles and

Leonor from Spain had arrived just before dawn the night before, and both were now meeting with the larger group.

"Leonor." Terry was starting to lose patience. "Everything we've uncovered so far says that Elixir is coming out of the Eastern Mediterranean and is pointed at the North Sea. It has to be coming through Gibraltar."

"You have no evidence of that," the Spanish leader said, nonchalant. "I came here in good faith. I had no idea I was going to be immediately accused by those I considered allies."

Leonor was a dark-haired water vampire who claimed to be of Spanish royal descent. Though royal blood certainly wasn't an unusual claim made by immortals, Murphy suspected Leonor was an aristocrat in truth. She appeared as a handsome woman in her midforties to humans, though Murphy suspected she'd been closer to thirty in mortal years. But she wore her age well and had always—as long as Murphy had known her—had immaculate style. More importantly, she was a dependable immortal leader in the notoriously unstable path between Europe and Africa. Her shipping interests and joint economic investment with Tripoli had been vital in stabilizing the region.

And she was more than respected. She was feared. Leonor had no consort and was allegedly very choosy regarding lovers lest one challenge her authority.

Shortsighted, in Murphy's opinion. In his experience, leaders with a trusted consort were far more powerful and less vulnerable to takeover.

"No one is accusing you of anything, Leonor," Murphy said. "We're simply asking you what you've heard."

"Most likely the same that you have," she said. "Do you realize how many freighters pass through the strait in even a single day?"

"But surely there is some gossip," Jetta said. "You must have made inquiries."

She shrugged. "This drug has not been seen in our cities. It is not a priority for us. A few isolated cases of humans in Majorca, but that is all."

Murphy glanced at Anne, who passed him a note.

She's lying. There've been more cases than that, and she knows it.

Murphy nodded. Terry and Leonor were allies, but Terry and Gemma had been attacked in Spanish territory at one point, and that had damaged the relationship. Further, Terry and Leonor had become rivals in the race to push blood-wine to market. Their host was being too aggressive.

"Jean," Murphy interrupted before Terry could speak again. "I'd like to know what the status in France is. I know Rome has been surprisingly isolated from infection. What about Marseilles?"

Jean smiled, knowing exactly what Murphy was doing.

"Of course," he said. "We've not seen as great an effect as your territories, but it has been increasing."

Jean Desmarais had arrived in London shortly before Leonor and was staying at his own property in Kensington with a sizable entourage. Far from the refined stereotype of the European businessman, Jean's face still bore signs of his human life on the water. Though, like Murphy, he knew how to clean up for company.

He and Terry had done business for years and were known allies, though Murphy had heard rumors the relationship had been strained by the blood-wine business. Some rumors even implied that the blood-wine preservation technique that Terry and Gemma had perfected was first developed by Jean.

If an ally had swiped proprietary information from one of Murphy's businesses, he would have been livid. But so far, Jean appeared to be as amenable and friendly as always.

He'd arrived for the meeting with only two guards and an attractive human assistant carrying his electronics. Jean had always been a likable sort, though he used his affability and friendships to hide a ruthless business acumen. France was no easy country to govern within, having some of the most divided immortal population in Europe. Jean ruled Marseilles and most of the southern coast, but the vampires in Paris detested the dapper Frenchman, whom they saw as an upstart.

"Nice has had a few cases"—Jean was still speaking—"Marseilles has had more. I'm very fortunate that only two of my own people have been infected, and both of them have living sires, but it is an increasing concern. There are rumors that Paris is heavily infected, and I have limited travel there for those under my aegis. Even I must admit there are more rumors swirling at this point than facts. I've held off on speaking publicly until I came to the summit. And"—he looked at Leonor—"I also must admit an extreme curiosity about information from Gibraltar. You have to know more than you are sharing, Leonor."

"If you want to know what is happening in the strait," Leonor said waspishly, "ask your friend Rens. He has plenty of his little spies in the city."

Rens spread his hands. "My father had a historic relationship with immortals in Gibraltar. Surely you don't expect us to cut ties with our friends because he is no longer living?"

"Friends? Is that what you call your informants?"

Rens said nothing but gave Leonor an enigmatic smile.

"I think we're all curious, Leonor," Gemma said calmly. "Curious, not suspicious. If everyone would endeavor to be civil, please."

"You need a new shipping dispatcher in London," Jean said with a smile. "Then you would have all the information about Leonor's ports that you need. But perhaps that's not a very civil suggestion."

Murphy raised an eyebrow and watched Terry glare at Jean. Perhaps the Frenchman wasn't as indifferent about the loss of his winemaker as Terry and Gemma thought.

"It's quite clear from the information we have pooled that the source is somewhere in the Eastern Mediterranean," Jetta said, getting the conversation back on track. "But it is the North Sea and the Baltic countries that have been more heavily infected. No one suspects you of producing or shipping this drug, Leonor. We are simply curious what you have heard. Your territories do lie between the apparent source and the territories most affected. Though your own country seems safe for now, if this is not stemmed, it will affect us all."

Anne spoke up. "What about Suez? Does anyone have any information from the Libyans?"

Rens said, "I may have something I can share by the end of this week. I've made inquiries because I anticipated this question."

"What about America?" Anne asked, glancing at her notes. "Is there anything new?"

"New York is coming tomorrow night," Jean said. "Have there been cases of infection in the New World?"

"Other than the outbreak in California, none that I'm aware of," Gemma said.

"Ah yes," Jetta said. "The large outbreak in Ernesto's territory that was tied to the *Russians*, was it not?"

"It's not the Russians," Murphy said.

"You don't know that," Jetta said. "None of us do. Elixir is affecting all the countries we know of along the Baltic Sea except for Russia. How could this be if Oleg is not involved?"

He sensed Anne's tension increase at the mention of the Russians and made a note to ask her about it later.

Jean said, "Just because Oleg has not publicly acknowledged Elixir infection does not mean it does not exist. We all know he is cautious about what information leaves his country."

"Jean," Murphy said. "The rumors you mentioned, what have you heard?"

"In France? A little of everything," Jean said. "Some say that whoever is producing it has perfected Livia's formula and it is no longer lethal. Some say that Livia never died in Rome at all and she is still producing it in Bulgaria."

"Livia is most assuredly dead, but Bulgaria *would* fit with the shipping history," Terry said. "It's Eastern Mediterranean. Have we checked into that?"

"Bulgaria is run by a Greek figurehead," Jean said. "We all know how difficult it is to get reliable information from that part of the world."

"Oh really?" Murphy said, looking at Carwyn at one end of the table. "A *Greek* figurehead? How interesting."

"Not really," Jean said. "Most of those smaller territories have allegiance to Athens in some way, either by political marriage or economic tie. It's mostly symbolic. You know the Greeks; they're archaic."

"And we're not?" Terry said.

Murphy said, "Speak for yourself, old man."

Friendly laughter spread through the room, leaving the air a little lighter than it had been moments before. Murphy was happy to have broken the tension, if only for a while. Terry announced a half-hour break for everyone to conference with their people.

Murphy was having a hard time reconciling Leonor's past cooperation with her attitude at the table earlier. She was usually more agreeable. Perhaps there were other factors in play. He'd have to talk with Brigid and see what the chatter among the security teams had been. Often the greater intelligence came from those who observed, not those who spoke.

"Did you get your notes transcribed for Mary last night?" he asked Anne quietly. "I saw her courier here at dusk."

"I did. I told him not to come back until the end of the week though. If Mary wants more current reports, she can call."

"How are you feeling?" He tried to keep his tone light even as he whispered.

"Fine."

"I'm coming to hate that word."

"Truly." She gave him a small smile. "I do mean it this time. My head is much clearer, and I fed at dusk from one of Carwyn and Brigid's staff."

"Good." He flipped through the notes he'd taken during the meeting. "Have you... Did you decide what you wanted to do about your quarters? Shall I send one of our people over with your things?"

He'd heard her early in the night, getting ready in her rooms. But he also knew she's rested at Brigid and Carwyn's suite during the day.

"My things are fine where they are," she said quietly.

"Thank you."

"You don't need to thank me," she said. "You've shown... great patience, Murphy. I didn't know you had such restraint."

His hands froze. "I told you I'd mastered my more impulsive instincts."

"I believe you."

"But do you trust me?"

She said nothing, and Murphy looked up. For the first time, there was something else in her eyes besides caution. Regret? Had she already decided against him?

"Anne—"

"I need to apologize to you," she said. "I realize that now. But not here."

"No." His heart thumped once. "Not here."

IF anything could make the tedium of political maneuvering even slower than normal, it was the knowledge that Anne wanted to speak to him. Wanted to apologize? For what?

Murphy tried to focus on the other parties as each one gave their most self-serving pitch about why it was important for the others to share information before they did. Two hours in, he was ready to murder them all. He'd have the fallout from across Europe to deal with, but he was almost to the point that he didn't care.

As if sensing the level of subdued violence in the room, Gemma decided to adjourn the meeting early, giving the excuse of needing to speak with Leonor about a shipment of wine grapes. Every other party fled after that, though Murphy and Terry had been trapped by Brigid and Roger, who were concerned that they still had no idea where Rens Anker and his people were staying in the city.

He left Terry to deal with reassuring them and made it back to the Mayfair house, only to find Anne absent from their suite.

"Judith!" he called to the human secretary, who still jumped every time he appeared.

"Yes, Mr. Murphy?" She was fiddling with her hair again. "Did you need something, sir? Can I transcribe your notes from the meeting? Did you need to make any calls?"

"No. I mean yes, but not right now." He shoved his notes at her. "You can have these. I'll schedule a call later. Right now, I need to find

Dr. O'Dea. Where is she?" If she'd left the house, he might go on a rampage.

"I believe I saw Dr. O'Dea heading toward the pool room, Mr. Murphy. Will that be all?"

He waved her away and stalked down the hall, following the scent of saltwater. The pool beneath Terry and Gemma's home resembled one of the old Roman baths at Aquae Sulis. Marble lined the walls and columns rose around the perimeter of the large rectangular pool. It was only one of the pools in the home. A smaller one had been built in the family wing. This one was for guests, and Anne swam nearly every night.

He reached the double doors, opened them, and checked for any other company. A human attendant stood near the opposite set of doors, holding towels and looking at a mobile phone while Anne swam laps.

"Leave," he told the young woman, nodding at the door behind her. "And lock that."

She glanced at Anne, then at him. He saw a light flush color her cheeks. "Yes, Mr. Murphy."

"See that we're not disturbed."

"Yes, sir."

He locked the double doors and dragged a heavy lounge chair to the edge of the pool, watching as she flipped and turned under the water.

Patient? He could be patient. But patience was wearing thin.

Anne surfaced at the far end of the pool and turned. "Murphy?"

"Our meetings are finished for the evening, Dr. O'Dea."

"Are they? That's good to know."

She sat on the steps and faced him across the length of the water, then took the elastic band from her hair and dipped the length in the water to smooth it away from her face. He saw the nerves in her eyes, but he couldn't comprehend why.

"Did you want a swim?" she asked. "You never got yours last night. I know it's salt, but—"

"You said you needed to apologize to me. For what?"

She paused and he wished she'd come closer, but she remained at the far end. Their words echoed off the marble walls.

THE SCARLET DEEP

Anne rose from the water and he watched it pour off her, fine rivulets running down her shapely shoulders and over her breasts. The water caressed the curve of her waist and her thighs as she walked up the marble steps and out of the pool. She made no attempt to cover herself as she walked toward him.

"I asked Brigid last night what she would do if she lost Carwyn's love. If he ever betrayed her or broke her trust."

His heart was beating, the sluggish flow of blood beginning to pulse in his veins.

"I imagine her response bordered on violent."

"Oh yes."

She kept walking toward him, and his body rose in greeting, his arousal pressing against the fine wool trousers he'd donned for the evening. He sat perfectly still and watched his mate.

"I wanted to laugh at her," Anne said. "But then I realized what she really meant was that she would fight for him. For their relationship."

"Yes."

"She asked me if I thought love was worth fighting for."

His voice came out in a low rumble. "And what did you say?"

"I said I did. But then I realized I hadn't done that. When the time came that our relationship was challenged, I didn't fight for us."

A new wave of guilt slapped him. "Anne, it wasn't your—"

"I was hurt. I was shocked. And I didn't fight."

The look on her face tore him apart.

"I was the one in the wrong," he said. "I know that. I knew it then; I was too proud. I deserved to lose you."

"But I have to admit my part, Patrick. I walked away to nurse my wounds. I am sorry for that."

His palms clenched into fists. He rested them on the edge of the chair where he still sat, trying to remain calm as she approached.

"I accept your apology," he said. "Do you accept mine?"

"Yes." She paused, closed her eyes, and said, "I forgave you years ago."

"Open your eyes, Anne. I need to see them."

171

She opened them, and Murphy saw everything he'd missed in her. The strong heart. The stubborn will. Tenderness. Passion. *Love.*

Anne might not have admitted her feelings yet, but he could read the love in her eyes.

"Why didn't you come to me?" he asked.

She choked out a laugh. "Why did it take you a hundred years to apologize?"

"So we're both stubborn. We knew this already." His eyes locked with hers. "What now then?"

"I don't know exactly, but I want the past to be past."

Her eyes were lit again, this time in sensual hunger. He reached up and loosened the tie he was wearing, pulling it away from his neck. Her eyes fell to his hands as they worked the silk that concealed his throat.

"There is one more issue we need to discuss."

"Oh?"

"You've been starving yourself. I'm still quite angry about that."

Her eyes didn't stray from the fingers at his throat. "You're the one who laid down the feeding restrictions."

"And I was the one person you could have come to when you started having trouble."

"I know."

"But you didn't." He pulled the tie off and let it fall to the ground. Then he started unbuttoning his collar.

Her breath came in soft pants, and she took two steps toward him. He could sense her body readying for him. Her breasts swelled. Her lips flushed. Her fangs were long in her mouth.

"Patrick—"

"You've starved yourself instead of drinking from your mate," he said, parting his shirt at the collar, sitting like an offering before her. "I do not approve of this."

"It's not your—"

"It is my place, and *only* my place. Bite *me*," he said, spreading his arms wide. "Drink *me*. Take what you need."

Take everything.

He sat, braced for her rejection. His tipped his chin up, arrogance warring with supplication. The water in the room drew to his skin as he waited for her response.

He didn't wait long.

Anne leapt on him like a wild thing, tugging his hair back at the nape, baring his neck to her mouth as she licked and sucked the skin there. He gripped her hips, bracing his legs to keep balance in the chair as she sat astride him. Her legs draped over his, and his hand dug into the flesh of her thighs. Murphy's back arched when she struck.

And then… bliss.

Life.

His mate drew the blood from his vein, and he felt his amnis enter her, swimming in her blood as he groaned. His head fell back, resting on the edge of the chair. His legs spread farther apart, welcoming her body with his own. He felt her draw back.

"Not yet. Take more," he said roughly.

"Yes." She pulled the top of her bathing suit off, and Murphy's eyes fell to her breasts. Her belly. The delicate blue veins like rivers below her milk-white skin. She leaned forward again, bringing his neck back to her mouth as she bit the other side of his neck.

"I want these off." He tugged at the bottom of her swimsuit.

She released his neck, his blood red on her lips. "I'm sorry about your suit."

He gave her a dark laugh. "I'm not."

She reached down and tore open his fly. Murphy grabbed her hands when he heard the cloth rip, bringing them up to his mouth, nipping her fingers as he rose to his feet, holding her body against his.

"Now now. That wasn't necessary. Show a little patience, love."

She smiled and licked her lips. "I'm done being patient."

"Good. So am I." He walked her to one of the columns that lined the pool, then he set her down and knelt before her, sliding the rest of her bathing suit off until she stood bare. His hands ran from her waist, down her thighs, teasing the sensitive backs of her knees before he leaned in and nipped at them.

She watched him, her hair a wild tangle surrounding her face and her eyes savage with hunger. Murphy licked up her legs, letting his fangs scrape along her skin, raising dark red lines but not breaking the skin.

He'd forgotten nothing about her body. The freckle on the inside of her thigh. The rosy birthmark behind her left knee. The way her flesh molded to his hands and mouth and teeth. He paused to suck harder at her hip, delighting in the flush of red that welled under his mouth.

"Patrick," she panted. "I need—"

"Shhh," he whispered, softly kissing the inside of her thighs, the dark hair at the juncture of her legs, then her belly, her breasts. He kissed up her body as he rose until both hands framed her face. He pressed urgent kisses against her mouth until she opened for him. Then Murphy tasted his blood on her tongue and lost the last shred of control.

He groaned and reached down, yanking his trousers open with one hand as he clutched Anne's hair with the other.

"I can't... wait—"

"Then don't."

"Take me?"

"*Yes*." She sucked in a quick breath as he entered her in a long, slow thrust. Her arms came around his shoulders as he hiked her up against the column, pressing deeper into her body. Murphy lifted Anne with both hands, holding her close.

"Anne," he groaned, resting his face against her neck, kissing her collarbone and the rise of her breasts. "You feel..."

"Consumed." Her voice was barely over a whisper. "You consume me."

I adore you.

He couldn't say it; he was beyond speaking. Murphy could feel his blood pulsing through her body even as he moved in her. The combination was intoxicating. Body, blood, amnis. His mate. She had claimed him in the most elemental way. In every way.

They said nothing as the room filled with the sound of their breathing and the smell of their blood. Both their bodies dripped with water as their amnis swirled over them, building in the space between and filling the void that loss had hollowed out so many years before.

Anne gasped as her swollen flesh tightened around him, and Murphy let himself go, taking her body roughly as his control snapped. He heard a crack from the marble and pulled back just as he came, crushing her body to his chest as he buried his face in her neck. Anne's nails dug into his neck, and she pulled his hair as she groaned again, the small aftershocks of her pleasure wringing the last from Murphy.

He held her, breathing in her scent, reveling in her possession as he walked them to the edge of the pool.

"Patrick?"

I adore you.

I love you.

You are mine.

You have always been mine.

He thought she knew it, but he couldn't say it. Not yet.

Soon.

Murphy smiled a second before he tipped them in, laughing as she squealed.

Chapter Fifteen

"THERE WERE TWO SISTERS, a blonde and a redhead. The redhead tells her sister, 'Guess what, I slept with a Brazilian.' The blonde says, 'You slag! How many is a Brazilian?'"

Murphy buried his face in the tangle of Anne's damp hair and laughed.

"That's very bad."

"I have worse ones."

"I'll remember."

They were stretched out on one of the lounge chairs next to the pool, both wearing nothing but skin. Anne was replete. Murphy lay at her side, one hand running up and down her back as he tried to untangle her hair with the other. He smoothed it away from her face, only to twist it around a finger or tuck it behind her ear. He was toying with her absently, his heart beating a slow rhythm in his chest.

"I think we ruined your suit," she said, looking at the sad scraps of grey wool that were scattered over the limestone deck.

"It was a noble sacrifice."

"It was a nice suit."

"I have others. Feel free to ruin them all."

She lifted her chin and propped it on his chest. "You won."

Murphy raised an eyebrow at her. "I'm fairly sure we both did. At least four times for you and twice on my side."

"You really counted, didn't you?"

"Yes, I did."

Anne pinched his waist. "That's not what I'm talking about."

"It should be."

"Patrick—"

"Can we not?" He lifted both hands and framed her face, brushing his thumbs across her cheeks. "Allow me to explore my sensitive side as I ask you to wait on the postcoital analysis, Dr. O'Dea. I know we have things to talk about. I know not everything is resolved."

She said, "I wasn't going to analyze—"

"Yes, you were." He kissed her forehead. "And Anne, it's fine. I'm not asking you to be someone else. You'll analyze. I'll be contrary for the sake of disrupting your analysis."

"All I want to—"

He put a finger over her lips, and she resisted the urge to bite it. Barely.

"For now, I'm asking you to wait. I want… No, I *need* you to give me this night. Give me a day of sleeping next to you. Give me a night waking up with you in my bed. Let me make love to you again. Let me do all that without thinking of every consequence."

Anne thought for a moment and then asked, "Why?"

Murphy frowned. "I work hard to maintain that devil-may-care attitude I show the world because it's useful. But from one night to the next, I do not make a single move without considering how it will affect my children, my city, and all those under my aegis. I deliberate every angle. I debate every eventuality. For once—with you—let me… enjoy."

Lying on his chest, the weight of water in the air covering them like a soft blanket, she found it all too easy to give in. "Yes."

"Yes?"

Anne nodded.

"Thank you," he murmured, exploring her face with his lips, teasing kisses across her eyes and down her cheek. "You smell lovely when you smell of me."

She stretched against him, pressing her curves along the hard ridges and angles of his body. It was purely a side benefit of the man he was, but Murphy had an exceptional form and she enjoyed showing her appreciation.

His body was naturally lean, but the fighting he'd done during his human years had shaped his arms and torso with an extra layer of muscle. Most vampires of his age were thinner, nothing like the sculpted humans Anne saw in modern advertisements. Murphy was the perfect balance, a man who had worked with his body in human life, but not for vanity.

And his blood…

Her lover tasted of the woods and sweet water. His blood hummed within her, his amnis mingling with her own. When she drank of him, she smelled campfires and pine.

"I missed you," she whispered against his shoulder. "So much, Patrick."

He paused. "I missed you too."

Silence fell between them, and it was so laden with unspoken truths that Anne could feel them like a weight upon her body.

Murphy held her against him, one arm wrapped tightly around her waist and the other hand petting and stroking her body, as if reassuring himself that she was real.

Anne held still in his arms. Moving might break the fragile bubble they'd constructed.

They both stirred when they heard human voices in the hall.

"So"—he reached down and patted her backside—"more swimming or shall we turn in for the day?"

Murphy's voice had taken on a deliberately lighter tone that Anne forced herself to imitate.

"And by turning in you mean—"

"You tell me horrible sex jokes and I punish you in creative ways? Yes, that's exactly what I had in mind."

She bit back a laugh. "I'm not sure that's what I meant, actually."

"Yes, it was." He slapped her backside, rubbing it slowly when she jumped.

"Patrick!"

"Bloody hell, woman, keep your voice down—you'll embarrass the servants."

Then Murphy threw a thick towel over Anne as she laughed, and strode out of the pool room wearing nothing but the skin he'd been born in.

THE following night, their meetings dragged. Anne couldn't keep her mind off Murphy's rough commands when she woke him with her mouth and fangs. He'd roused with a gasp, only to drag her up the bed, taking her mouth with his, nipping at her tongue before he pushed her away and let her continue to pleasure him. He lay back and closed his eyes; the slow stream of curses that dropped from his lips was thanks enough in Anne's mind.

Now he was covered in more of his Savile Row armor, as she thought of it, taking tidy notes in a leather-bound journal and scrutinizing the newest additions from the Americas.

Anne had never met Cormac O'Brien, but she'd heard of him. He appeared to be in his midthirties. He wore a full beard and a pocket watch that made Anne wonder if he still reminisced fondly over the late nineteenth century. The rest of his clothes seemed designed to distract. His glasses were likely an affectation—she'd never met an eye problem that immortality didn't cure—but they suited him. His waistcoat was blood-red velvet, and he wore a worn tweed jacket over it. Dark plaid trousers and black motorcycle boots rounded out the look. It was as far from coordinated as Anne could imagine, but somehow O'Brien made it work.

His daughter, Novia, had taken the O'Brien name when she turned, though she was clearly of African-American descent. Her hair curled around her face in a mass of reddish-brown corkscrews, highlighting her light brown skin and vivid green eyes the same shade as her sire's. Novia listened with rapt attention to every detail, took furious notes, and said nothing, often glancing at O'Brien for cues. She was young but sharp.

The Americans hadn't contributed much to the conversation about Elixir, though Cormac had offered a few bits of intelligence about ships he'd encountered in the Baltic Sea. Mostly, despite Cormac's brash appearance, he listened.

Neither Cormac nor his daughter were what Anne had expected, and she wondered if Murphy even considered them allies. She'd have to talk with him later.

"Later."

It had been his whispered promise before he'd left to bathe and dress for the night. A single word drenched in sensual possibilities that had Anne's blood leaping to life within her. She saw Murphy's knuckles whiten as he gripped his pencil. His eyes turned to her.

"You need to stop," he said under his breath, clearly distracted by her arousal.

Anne took a deep breath and thought about translating notes. About Ruth and Dan's litter of Irish terrier puppies. About Brigid's latest whim to dye her hair midnight blue. Anything but what Murphy's eyes told her he wanted to do later in the safe confines of their suite.

Having forced her thoughts back to those talking, she heard Jetta mention the Russians another time.

"The fact that suspicious ships have been spotted in the Baltic and yet no reports have come out of Russia regarding Elixir makes me suspicious about the Russian's involvement. I know you've spent time building a trade relationship with Oleg, Terry, but if we're talking about someone who has access to the Black Sea or the Eastern Mediterranean *and* the capability of shipping something like this that targets political powers in the North Atlantic, we can't ignore him. It would be foolish."

"I'm not saying we ignore them," Terry said. "I'm simply saying that trying to determine Oleg's motivations is damn near impossible. So far, the status quo has been profitable for him. Why would he change that?"

Anne froze. They were talking about Russia. Again. They were talking about Oleg.

Oleg and the Black Sea.

Murphy leaned toward her and spoke quietly in Gaelic. "What is it? You had the same reaction the other day when someone mentioned Russia."

"I... Murphy, I can't say."

She hadn't anticipated this. There was information she *could* share, but it would break every rule of confidentiality she'd ever lived by as a healer.

"What do you mean, you can't say?" He sounded annoyed. "Is it Mary? Because we've been nothing but open with her about—"

"It's not Mary. It's..." How could she explain without revealing that Oleg was a patient? Not that he considered himself a patient, but in Anne's mind, he was. "I can't say, Patrick."

He still looked confused, verging toward angry.

Anne looked at him with pleading eyes. "Do you understand? *I can't say.*"

He must have understood enough, because he leaned back and muttered, "Fecking hell."

"I didn't anticipate this. I don't... know any of the players here except through Mary, and I didn't anticipate—"

"Clearly."

Murphy tapped a pen on his knee for a few moments until there was a pause in the flow of the meeting. Then he stood up and said, "If our associates would excuse Dr. O'Dea and me for a moment, it would be appreciated."

"Of course," Gemma said. "Your secretary can take notes."

He put a hand on her shoulder and led her out of the room and to a deserted office down the hall. Anne realized, to her surprise, that he was angry.

"You're angry with me?"

He said nothing until he closed the door.

"Tell me."

"I told you I can't."

Murphy gritted his teeth. "We're not with the others now, Anne. Tell me why you keep reacting to the Russians. This is important."

"I know it is. And I still cannot tell you."

"Because of Mary?"

"No."

"Because of a patient?"

She said nothing.

"We don't have the luxury of confidentiality here, Anne. We need every piece of information we can get."

Anne's mouth dropped. "The *luxury* of confidentiality?"

"We're all revealing uncomfortable truths. And we're doing it to save lives. This isn't a game."

"I know it's not a game!"

"Then stop playing and tell me what you know about Russia!"

"I will not."

He was furious.

"You and Mary agreed—"

"This is not about Mary. This is about your asking me to violate my own principles. *Again.*"

His jaw tensed, but he didn't back down. "For the greater good, Anne. This isn't about me."

"You know who I am and what I do. And I will remind you that I was not the one who wanted to attend this summit, Patrick. It was you who dragged me along. My sister who forced me to come. This wasn't my idea."

"You didn't put up much of a fight either, did you? You wanted to come," he said. "Your little life in the west was driving you mad, and you jumped at the chance to do something other than listen to sob stories from vampires with more money than sense."

Anne felt as if he'd slapped her. "*Póg mo thóin.*"

"Already did, love. And you *liked* it."

She saw his eye twitch as soon as the words left his mouth.

"Anne, I'm—"

"No."

She shoved him to the side, but he refused to budge. Then Anne put her hand on his neck and *pushed*.

"Move."

Blinking, he stepped to the side long enough for her to unlock the door and slip into the hallway.

"Bloody fecking woman…" He muttered behind her. "Anne!"

Anne dodged the security guard, only to run into Gemma in the hall. "Anne, did you—"

"I need to leave, Gemma."

Gemma glanced over Anne's shoulder, and she must have seen Murphy stalking down the hall.

"Go," she said. "I'll call him back to the meeting. One of you has to attend."

"Thank you." She rushed out of the house, one of Murphy's men following her, and jumped into the back of Ozzie's car.

"Take me back," she said.

"Are we waiting for Murphy, miss?"

"No."

She was stupid. So, so stupid.

He would break her. Again. And she was the one who let him.

SHE found Carwyn visiting with Daniel in a drawing room at the Mayfair house.

"Anne!" He smiled and rose to his feet. "Daniel and I were just discussing his plans to visit Clare. He's thinking next fall, but I wasn't sure… And you don't want to talk about rock climbing, do you?"

She managed a smile. "Not really."

"Excuse us," Carwyn said to Daniel. "I believe Dr. O'Dea and I have business to discuss in the library."

"Of course," Daniel said with a smile. "But Anne, when you have a chance, I would love to talk with you about my trip. If you'd like."

"Yes, of course," Anne said. "Carwyn... I'll meet you in the library?"

"I'll walk with you now." He gave his son a hearty embrace and slapped his back, whispering something in his ear before he escorted her to a wood-paneled room surrounded on all sides by bookcases bursting at the seams.

Anne asked the computer attendant to leave them and took a seat on a settee close to the fireplace.

"How are you feeling?" Carwyn asked.

"Much better physically, thanks to your wife."

"I know she was happy to offer. We both feel indebted to you, Anne, for helping Brigid with so many of her demons."

"That's what I do."

"It is." Carwyn sat in a sofa across from her. "It is what you do. What I did for so many years as well."

"We help people." Anne frowned. "Or you did."

"I hope I still do. What can I help you with?"

She took a deep breath and decided to ignore the fight with Murphy for the moment and focus on the greater problem. "How did you balance what was told to you in confidence and the realities of our life?"

Carwyn nodded slowly. "I was wondering whether this would be an issue. It doesn't surprise me that it has become one."

"I know things—things told to me in sessions—and... they're pertinent. They would add information, possibly vital information—to the discussion."

"You cannot share them," he said quietly.

Anne leaned forward. "I told myself that. Before I came here, I drew a line, and I knew... It seemed so simple."

Carwyn's face took on the weight of a thousand years. "Oh no, my dear. It is never simple. Bearing another's secrets, holding their trust, is a precious burden. But it is never simple."

"Faced with the prospect of others being hurt because of this knowledge or sharing it and violating the trust of a patient, I confess I do not know what to do."

"Is Murphy aware of this?"

"He is now. I don't think either he or Mary thought through the consequences of sending me here in a political position. The negotiating I've done for Mary in the past has been smaller scale. Business related. But now... I'm hearing things and realizing that I know things that could have a bearing on this summit."

Carwyn stared into the fire. "It's possible that Murphy didn't think through the consequences of bringing you here because he was so eager to have you join him, but I very much doubt that Mary wasn't aware of the position she was putting you in."

Anne froze. "Why do you say that?"

"You don't really think she approves of what you do, do you?" Carwyn's voice was kind, but his eyes were piercing when he looked at her. "I have much respect for your sister, but she is ruthless, Anne. She wants you at her side. Or at Murphy's. This strange independent space you've occupied between them has never sat well with her."

"You think she put me in this position intentionally?"

"I do."

"You think she wants me to choose?"

"Yes."

Anne took a deep breath and realized she wasn't as surprised as she would have expected. Forcing Anne to declare political allegiance and abandon her assumed neutrality was just so... Mary.

"I love my sister, Carwyn, but sometimes I want to strangle her."

He burst into laughter. "Family is the most infuriating and rewarding of problems, isn't it?"

"She hates Murphy. And yet she sends me to him, practically throws me into his arms."

"Oh..." Carwyn's eyes twinkled. "I don't think you were averse to the toss, were you?"

"Shut up, Father Brat. Oh, he made me so angry earlier." Anne shook her head. "That man drives me mad. He'll come in and apologize profusely."

"And you'll forgive him."

"Yes, and then he'll do it all over again. Do I really want my life to be that?"

"Everyone's life is like that," Carwyn said, smiling. "Life is one long series of making mistakes and seeking grace. What makes you and Murphy special?"

She sighed and closed her eyes. "Do you really think Mary wants me to choose between them?"

"Yes and no. I don't think she has any desire to lose you as a sister. But if you chose to put yourself under Murphy's aegis, she wouldn't object."

"Put myself under Murphy's aegis…" She must have made a face, because he laughed.

"Everyone has to be under someone's aegis, unless you want to rule," he said. "The fact that you're not has grated on her. Mary doesn't hate Murphy. Well… she does and she doesn't. She likes him for you. Do you know why?"

"Honestly no."

"*Because* he drives you mad. Because he throws you out of your comfort zone. He makes you live, Anne. And that's why Mary likes him, not for himself, but for you. That man adores you. I don't know if you even see the way he looks at you. I do. Brigid does."

"And that excuses hurtful words?"

"Absolutely not," he growled. "But you need to let him apologize if he comes to you."

"Carwyn—"

"You gave me a piece of advice once. You told me to leave Brigid. It went against every instinct in me to do it, but you were right. She needed the time on her own. So I'll return the favor now with a few words of advice from a very old man who loves a very difficult woman."

"She'd say the same about you, you know."

"Please," he said with a wink. "I'm a lamb. But Murphy—"

"Is an arse."

"That he is."

"So I should leave him?"

"No." He leaned forward and took her hand. "I'm going to tell you to stay. No matter what. Rail at him when he crosses the lines. Bite back when he pushes too far. Mostly, tell him when he hurts you. Because I can guarantee there is no greater punishment for that man than hurting the woman he loves. He loves you, Anne, but he expects you to leave."

Because she had before. He'd hurt her, and she had left.

Anne sighed. "How can we be so old and still so bloody clueless about love?"

"Speak for yourself; I am an expert."

She heard a tap on the door a moment before Brigid poked her head in.

"I heard you were gabbing in here. Anything I can join in?"

Anne smiled at her friend. "Did you know your mate was an expert at love?"

The sound of Brigid's laughter drove the last of the shadows from Anne's mood.

She had some difficult decisions to make, but first…

Anne needed to write a letter to a Russian.

Chapter Sixteen

MURPHY RUSHED OUT THE DOOR as soon as the meeting adjourned. He was almost to his car when he heard the Dutchman's voice.

"Mr. Murphy?"

He turned, pasting a polite facade over his frustration. "Mr. Anker."

"Please, if you would call me Rens."

"Then you must call me Murphy."

"Of course."

He paused long enough that Murphy started to wonder what his purpose was.

"I wonder if you might share a drink with me," Rens said. "I have... a theory I would like to discuss in private."

Murphy might have wanted to apologize to Anne, but he knew it needed to wait. A meeting with one of the primary intelligence peddlers in Europe could not.

"Of course." He plastered on his most charming smile. "Walk with me. There's a club nearby that has late hours."

"Excellent."

He walked down the mostly deserted sidewalk, enjoying the smell of rain in the air. Puddles reflected the streetlights, and damp filled the air. He took a deep breath and drew the water into his lungs.

"I am also attuned to freshwater," Rens said, "more than salt."

"We're some of the few, then."

"And yet my brother loves the sea." Rens shrugged. "I love the canals and the rivers. He loves the sea."

"A good balance."

"It is."

Murphy said, "My sire was of the ocean. And I was not. Some things cannot be predicted, can they?"

"No. I have watched you this past week, Murphy. Watched you as you observed the others. You are everyone's friend, I think. And yet you take everything in and only speak when you must."

Murphy disliked being scrutinized. "You're very observant. Of course, I suppose it pays to be."

"You are correct. I think… you are a man who sees many angles, not all of them visible."

Murphy shrugged. "I do my job, same as the rest of us."

"My sire called Livia of Rome '*de spinnekop.*' The spider. I believe—even after her death—her web still entangles."

Murphy paused at the corner and watched low clouds move across the sky.

"The spider? I hadn't heard that one before."

"Come," Rens said, putting on his own charming smile. "We need beer."

"HOW much do you know about Livia?" Rens asked when they were sitting in a secluded booth with dark pints of porter between them.

"I know she was the mate of Andreas, son of Kato. I know she supported Giovanni Vecchio's son, Lorenzo, as he hunted the original formula for the Elixir of Life. I know she succeeded in making it, only to have Vecchio kill her in a massive explosion outside Rome."

"And yet," Rens said, "Elixir still lives." He held up three fingers. "Three original strands in the spider's web. Production. Distribution. Advertising."

"Production was in Bulgaria. Distribution, no one knows exactly. And Livia was the advertising. Is that what you're getting at?"

"Livia was trying to sell it as a legitimate cure for bloodlust. It was not."

Murphy had never truly understood the need to "cure" bloodlust. He enjoyed drinking blood. He enjoyed hunting. Enjoyed the taste and the heat of it. But since experiencing Anne's more extreme hunger, he had changed his mind. If there was a true cure for her thirst, Murphy knew he would pay a fortune to obtain it, and he wouldn't be the only one.

"But she was found out," Murphy said. "Vecchio and his mate discovered the side effects for humans, and vampires and exposed her. Exposed the drug."

"And one strand of her web—the legitimate one—is torn," Rens said. "There are two others remaining. Production and distribution. And there is no need to seek approval for either of those. Livia produced the drug in Bulgaria using her cosmetics factories. But she needed blood from all four elements to even begin. Substantial amounts of blood from all four."

"She was a water vampire," Murphy said.

"And she had both earth and wind vampires under her aegis. Livia only lacked the last."

"No fire," Murphy said. "She was a known antagonist of fire vampires. Rumor has it she tried to convince Andreas to kill his son when he was sired to fire."

Rens smiled. "Considering that same son killed her in the end, it could be argued that she exhibited foresight. But that didn't solve the problem of obtaining a substantial donation of blood from a fire vampire for the initial production."

"Who was it? Do you know? Was he or she killed in the battle in Rome?"

"He wasn't killed. He walked out before the battle even started. Livia was paranoid about information dissemination. When her fire donor discovered the side effects of Elixir, he abandoned her. He wanted no part in it."

"Who was it?" Murphy asked.

"Oleg."

He sat up. "The Russian?"

Rens nodded.

"Oleg Sokolov had knowledge of the Elixir—"

"And I believe he was also an investor. He would have demanded some kind of financial stake. That is his way."

Murphy let out a breath. "No wonder Jetta is so suspicious of the Russians."

Rens waved a hand. "Jetta has never liked Oleg. He once tried to seduce her. That never goes well."

"She's a very direct woman."

"That she is. But back to Livia. There were cases of Elixir found— some by Jean Desmarais and an associate—but others went missing. The formula was out. Rumors abounded."

"You think Oleg took over after Livia? That he's behind all this?"

"Do you?"

"No."

"I don't either." Rens sipped his beer. "But I cannot tell you why."

Murphy leaned over the table. "What do you know, Rens?"

"Know?" The vampire shrugged. "Nothing. Suspect? Many things."

"Such as?"

"I believe Oleg took the missing cases."

"To do what? You said he wanted nothing to do with Livia. From what I know about him, he would have no interest in this drug."

"But those cases were still *his blood*. And Oleg does not share his blood lightly. He had one mate—many years ago—and it was a nightmare, from what I've heard. He probably killed her. I imagine he only donated the blood because he thought he could make a substantial amount of money from the investment."

Murphy said, "But then Livia's scheme fell apart, and he discovered the truth."

"Indeed," Rens said. "He might not have done anything with it, but he would want the remainder of the Elixir under his control. In his mind, that drug was his."

"That makes sense," Murphy said. "What about distributors? Could any of them have had stock in transit that Vecchio and his allies were unaware of? Livia's shipping interests were taken over by the new leadership in Rome."

"Conti is not involved in this," Rens said. "And neither were her previous distributors."

"Why not?" The answer occurred to Murphy before Rens had a chance to answer. "Of course. It's moving over water."

"If Livia's sales pitch had been successful," Rens said, "then she would have no need to conceal the distribution of Elixir. She would have moved it by truck, along with her cosmetics. Possibly to the same vendors, even. But her sales pitch failed. So now whoever is making this must move it covertly."

"And make it covertly."

"But the ingredients are particular. Some of them are only grown commercially in southeastern Europe. That was the reason she chose Bulgaria."

Murphy said, "Bulgaria pays some kind of tribute to Athens, doesn't it?"

Rens shrugged. "In that part of the world, everyone pays some kind of tribute to Athens. It is… symbolic. They have little power."

"What did Livia think of the council?"

"They were rivals, of course. But not only rivals."

"Explain."

Rens cocked his head. "Livia was mated to an ancient. She still saw the court at Athens as the most legitimate in Europe. She wouldn't have worked in Bulgaria without their approval."

"But Bulgaria isn't on the Mediterranean."

"No," Rens said. "It has ports on the Black Sea—"

"And we come back to the Russians."

"Yes." Rens paused to drink his beer. "But I do not think the Russians are behind this."

"Neither do I." Murphy frowned. "But why not? Oleg had access to the initial production. Probably some investment in it. He has the money to fund it. Little to no scruples. And he would be able to move it out of the region without question. So why don't I think he is behind all this?"

Rens's eyes were calculating. "How much do you know about Oleg?"

"Personally? Not much. We've only met once."

"You should ask your woman," Rens said. "She knows more."

Murphy froze. "Do you think so?"

"I'd gamble she knows the Russian better than most, not that either one would admit it."

What was the Dutchman trying to say? Murphy schooled his features carefully, taking a long drink of his beer. It was bitter, and not only because of the hops.

"I'll ask." Murphy glanced at the clock on the wall. It was getting close to dawn, and he still needed to resolve things with Anne. "Will you be at the meeting on Friday?"

"I will. I look forward to annoying Leonor some more." Rens sipped his own beer, his long ascetic face a careful mask, though Murphy could have sworn he saw laughter in the vampire's eyes. "She only plays ignorant for Jean's sake, you know?"

"No, I don't."

"Those two… they should really fuck and be done with it. They've been at each other's throats for fifty years."

Murphy rose to leave. "I think I'll head back to Mayfair. Can my driver take you anywhere?"

"No thank you." An enigmatic smile touched his lips. "Make sure to ask about Oleg. I believe your woman would have an… interesting perspective on the Russian."

"I will." Murphy walked to the hostess and gave her his driver's number. Ozzie would need a few minutes to pull the car around.

"And Murphy?"

"Hmm?" He walked back to the booth.

"We also must be honest about who will profit from this epidemic."

"You're talking about blood-wine," Murphy said. "Do you think Terry, Jean, or Leonor could be behind this?"

"The Elixir? No. But who is producing this and who is smuggling it are not necessarily the same. Terry, Jean, and Leonor are all competent smugglers. It's how they made their money."

Murphy mouth lifted in the corner. "We all have a bit of pirate blood, Rens."

"Yes, but not many of us have the climate for grapes or the expertise to make blood-wine. The process is a closely guarded secret. There are tests running right now in both France and England. It is believed that blood preserved by this method cannot carry the Elixir's taint. If that is true, blood-wine may be the most profitable venture in our history."

"So Terry, Jean, and Leonor don't have much incentive to find who's really behind this."

"Perhaps. Perhaps not. No matter what happens, we both know this drug will not go away."

"Then why do we bother with this, Rens?"

He was genuinely curious what the vampire would say, because Murphy had asked himself the same question too many times to count.

"Because this—what is happening right now—it isn't about a drug. It's about power. About one of our own kind seeking to control us all. Seeking to destroy our world and profit from the deaths of our children." For the first time, Rens showed a hint of passion. "I have no patience for this spider's web."

MURPHY'S mind was exhausted by the time he returned to Terry and Gemma's house, but he couldn't delay resolving things with Anne. He'd been an arse when confronted by the fact that there were things in her life that he couldn't be a part of. It was one more reminder that they had many steps to take before their relationship could maintain a steady course.

He sought her out in the pool, but she wasn't there. The servants said she had been to the family wing but had left hours before. He walked into his suite, ready to leave his jacket and return to searching for her, only to see Anne sitting at the desk, calmly transcribing notes by lamplight.

"Anne—"

"Can I borrow your notes from the rest of the meeting? I'd like to review them before I start the rest of the translation."

"I'm sorry."

She turned, a smile teasing the corner of her mouth. "Is your handwriting that messy?"

He dropped his jacket on the armchair near the entryway. "You know that's not what I'm talking about."

She took a deep breath. "I know."

"I am sorry."

"For what?"

Murphy frowned. "For earlier. I know I spoke in anger."

"Why do you think I left, Patrick?"

"Oh no." He unknotted his tie and paced the room. "You're not going to use your analyst voice on me. That won't be happening."

"Fine." She rose and walked to him. "I understand you're sorry, but I want you to understand what you said that pissed me right the feck off. Is that nonanalyst enough for you?"

The moment she got in his face, his blood began to move. "Yes."

"Do you like it when I'm angry?"

"Not exactly. I like it when you're not calm."

She stepped back. "Why?"

He grabbed her wrist to keep her from moving away. "Because that's when I know you're feeling things. I was angry that you had knowledge about something to do with Russia—don't think I forgot about it—and you weren't sharing with me."

"I can't share it with you. You have to understand that."

"I do." He closed his eyes. "I thought I did. You weren't a psychologist when we were together. I didn't expect to feel resentment. I'll learn to deal with it. I know you'll always have your secrets, Anne."

"They're not *my* secrets, Patrick. That's the point. And that's not why I walked out."

He frowned. "Then why?"

"You diminished what I do. You treated my practice—my whole life— as something less than yours. Just because I'm not running a city doesn't mean what I do isn't important."

"I know that."

"But that's not what you said. You called it a 'little life.' Said that I listened to sob stories. The work I do is important. And if you think that I'm going to give it up because we're trying to—"

"But don't you see, Anne?" The dread pierced his chest when he realized the full ramifications of their reunion for her. He didn't want to say the words. He wanted to forget them. Wanted to enthrall her so completely that she would never even think of leaving him again.

But he couldn't do that. Not if he wanted her to stay.

"You'll have to give it up," he said, still holding her wrist in his hand. "Because if you return to me—if you're known as my consort, my mate— no one will confide in you. You will have entered the political arena. You will be a player, whether you like it or not."

The pain jabbed deep as she pulled her arm away. Her face was bleak.

"No."

"It might already be too late."

And he might not have thought about it in his enthusiasm to reconcile, but her sister would have. Mary would have known this would happen.

Fecking Mary.

"Why are you saying this?" Anne asked. "Do you want me to leave?"

"Of course not!"

"Then why would you—"

"I wish we could have stayed in last night for a bit longer." The smile was bitter on his face. "That we could have enjoyed… Do you think I like this? Like admitting you'll probably choose your life over a life with me?" He could hear the brittleness of his own voice. Hear the automatic coolness that tainted the edges of it. "I want you. But I don't want to have you under any false pretenses, Anne. I will not be giving up my position in Dublin. I have too many depending on me. I will not abandon them."

"But you want me to abandon my patients?"

"I don't want it. I'm simply predicting what will happen. If you are with me, you won't be seen as politically neutral."

She kept walking away from him until she reached the edge of the bed. Her knees hit the back of it and she sat slowly.

"I help people, Patrick."

"I know you do."

"There aren't many… Some of my clients only confide in me. There's no one else they trust."

"Like Oleg?"

Her eyes burned. "I will not talk about Oleg."

"But you admit he's a patient."

"He's a friend. That's all you need to know."

Murphy stepped closer. "Not a patient? Is there something you're not telling me?"

"Will you stop?" She groaned. "Why do you like fighting so much?"

"I'm not fighting about it. Any and all relationship you had with him is over, as far as I'm concerned."

She jumped to her feet. "You asshole!"

"I'm just curious. We've both had our romantic entanglements. What's admitting to one more?"

"Oh, thank you so much for bringing that up again."

"Are you jealous?"

Her lip curled. "No."

"Liar."

He'd kept files on all her lovers. There hadn't been many. Just enough to drive him mad with jealousy. He knew it was hypocritical, and he didn't care. He hadn't known about Oleg.

"And you're not jealous?" She rose to face him. "Of something that never even existed?"

"Why are you lying about it?"

"Damn you!" she yelled. "Why do you have the right to accuse me of anything? Countless women lay in your bed, and I said nothing. Because you weren't mine anymore."

"I was always yours," he said, grabbing her around the waist. "Always. Do you understand me? None of them shared my bed. No one but you has ever done that. And I know I was a bastard. But you made me so angry. You could leave me right now, and I could do nothing to stop you. And I *hate* that."

He was barely holding on to control. The urge to take her, bite her, claim her, was thick in his blood. His fangs had dropped. Hers had too. He wanted her bite again. Wanted to sink his own teeth into her flesh.

"You're pushing me away and holding on to me, all at the same time," she said.

"I know," he said. "I'm a bastard who has no claim over you, and it doesn't matter because I want you. I want to keep you. I want to bite you. I want to make love to you every night. I want to have you to confide in. I want to make you laugh. Mostly I want to be your world again. Because the last time I felt alive was when I was inside you."

Anne whispered, "You realize that's highly dysfunctional, don't you?"

"Yes, and I don't care."

He could feel the tug of dawn coming. Anne was still alert, but he was fading. Damn it. It was later that he'd realized. He wanted to make up with her and spend the moments before dawn in her arms, but that clearly wasn't going to happen. He tugged off his jacket and headed toward the adjoining room. He secured the lock, then went to check the entrance to the master suite, leaving the door between them open.

"I'm sorry," Murphy said. "I'll stay next door tonight. Just don't... please don't leave the suite. Stay here. I don't have enough security in the other parts of the house."

"Patrick..."

"What?"

"Stay," she said with a sigh. "You can stay."

He turned. "You'll share my bed?"

She nodded even though her eyes were troubled. "Yes."

198

It felt like the memory of the sun on his skin. A blessing. A reprieve. Grace.

Murphy walked to her, peeling off his shirt and unhooking his belt. He wrapped his arms around her waist, pressed his face into her neck, and felt her arms come around his shoulders.

"Thank you."

"I'll stay. I know we haven't settled everything, but until we do, I promise I'll stay. I won't walk away again."

He urged her down to the bed and spent the last moments before day took him kissing Anne. It was a languid joining of mouths and hands. She threaded their fingers together as he tasted her. He hooked his thigh over her legs.

"We're still dressed," she murmured against his mouth.

"I'm fine."

"No, you always wake up uncomfortable if you sleep in your clothes." She sat up, his practical mate, and helped him divest himself of the rest of his suit, then he watched her drape his clothes over the chair by the bed.

"Your turn," he said, watching her with heavy-lidded eyes.

She slowly stripped out of her dress and walked toward him. He could tell she enjoyed his eyes on her. She slid under the silk duvet and lay her head on the pillows.

"It feels so domestic to sleep with you," she said. "I've missed that."

"I have too."

He pulled her to his chest and wrapped an arm around her waist, hoping but not trusting she'd stay there until dusk.

"Áine," he murmured.

"Yes."

"I know I'm an arse. But I do love you."

"PATRICK."

His head swam. He always became aware a few moments before he actually woke. It was as if his brain switched on, even if his body hadn't yet followed.

He heard the voices from underwater.

Good fighter. Decided to keep him.

Scrappy.

More trouble than he's worth.

Will they come back?

They think he's dead.

…can make him loyal?

He'll have to be…

The voices became clearer.

"Patrick!"

Did he want it?

Doesn't matter.

Doesn't matter.

Doesn't matter.

It mattered.

"Patrick, wake up."

He opened his eyes and surfaced, gasping for breath. Every night like the last. Alive. He was alive despite the pain. Despite the burning in his lungs. A miracle? A curse?

A hand patted his face. Not hard like Tom. It was someone…

"Patrick."

Anne?

"A chuisle mo chroí."

He was the pulse of her heart. She told him so…

No.

She'd left him and he died again. Every night he died when he woke.

"It's early for him, Carwyn. I'm trying, but—"

"I'm awake," he said, his voice like gravel against a ship's hull. "What's wrong?"

He blinked and sat up.

THE SCARLET DEEP

"Carwyn is at the door. We need to wake up and get dressed. Something terrible has happened."

He wiped a hand across his face and finally looked at Anne. She was truly there. Awake and with him. Again. Murphy knew it wasn't a dream, because she was dressed.

"What's going on?"

"It's Rens Anker. Someone burned his house to the ground yesterday. And there was an attack on the O'Briens, as well."

"*What?*"

"There's no sign of Rens or any of his people. The house was completely destroyed. They think he's dead."

Chapter Seventeen

RENS WAS DEFINITELY DEAD. No vampire could survive a fire while resting. Anne and Murphy stood across the street from the inconspicuous house in Chelsea where firefighters sorted through rubble.

Murphy said, "This must have been the reason the Dutchman was so cagey about where his people were staying."

"You think he knew he was in danger?"

"He's an information merchant. His kind are always in danger."

"Has Terry called his brother yet?"

"Carwyn can wake long enough to be lucid during daylight. He was informed the minute the fire was reported, and he sent a call to Amsterdam. I imagine a representative will be here tonight."

"This is not good."

"No." Murphy shook his head. "This makes Terry look very, very bad."

"Even though Rens refused his protection? Not even Brigid knew where he was staying."

Suddenly Murphy leaned forward, craning his neck to look at the streetlights above them, and Anne saw him frown.

"What? What are you thinking?"

"Does Terry have a computer technician on staff? Or a contact in law enforcement?"

"I'm not sure. Probably."

"Street cameras. London has a ridiculous number of traffic cams, and it looks like some may be pointing to the house. If Terry can access those and find out who started the fire, it might help him when Amsterdam gets here."

"Good idea."

Murphy tapped on the divider, and Ozzie pulled the car back into traffic. One of the benefits, Anne thought, of being nocturnal was distinctly lighter traffic. In a city like London, that benefit was priceless.

"What's the news about the O'Briens?" she asked.

"Cormac is properly mental. Someone tried to kill Novia, but her human guard stopped him, though he was badly wounded in the attack. It was a human. Middle of the day. Cormac was roused during the commotion, and the attacker cut off part of his arm before Cormac managed to kill him."

"Damn," Anne said.

"What?"

"Cormac killed him. There's no way to question him if he's dead."

Murphy smiled. "It would have been better if he'd been taken alive, but the man had a sword in the middle of the day, and half of Cormac's left arm is gone. I think he was keener to eliminate the threat than think about who was behind it."

"Do you think someone took offense at not being invited?"

Murphy raised an eyebrow. "Is it time for us to talk rationally about Oleg?"

"I can't talk about Oleg."

He took a deep breath. "I can admit that my conversation with Rens last night—"

"You had a conversation with Rens?"

"Yes, and he implied that there was something more between you and Oleg than I realized."

"I can't tell you, Patrick."

His jaw clenched again, and Anne knew he was biting his tongue.

"If it puts your mind at ease on a personal level, know that the only relationship I am invested in—the only serious one for many years—is ours. I don't want to know details of your time during our separation, and I certainly don't expect to share mine with you. Can you leave it at that?"

She could tell Murphy wanted to ask more, but he simply nodded and took her hand.

It wasn't as if she didn't know he'd been keeping an eye on her. They lived in a small country. But the situation with Oleg was another matter entirely. She'd made it clear to Tom years ago that while Murphy might dig into her personal life, she expected him to stay out of her professional one. Being too visible put her at risk.

Anne didn't fear Oleg... exactly. But she had a healthy respect for any fire vampire, and most certainly one who had managed to hold on to the vast Russian territories for over two hundred years. She'd sent out a letter last night with one of Terry's couriers, but she'd decided that until she heard from Oleg it was too large a risk to reveal anything about his family situation. Not only would she be violating her own principles, but she ran the risk of alienating a powerful vampire she tentatively considered a friend.

"We should get back," Murphy said. "Talk to Terry and look into the camera angle. If we manage to salvage anything from this summit at this point, it will be a miracle."

ANNE tried to watch silently as Terry berated his chief of security, but it was difficult. She wondered if Murphy could be as cruel.

"Not my style," he said almost silently, as if reading her mind.

"What?"

"Terry and I have very different governing styles. I generally find a subtler approach to be more effective."

"Roger is quite brave to speak up when he's in this mood though, isn't he?"

"That would be why Roger is bleeding," Brigid said.

Murphy said, "That would also be why Roger is his first lieutenant. Do you think Tom and I have never gone a few bloody rounds, Brigid?"

Anne nodded behind Murphy's back. Some of Murphy and Tom's fights had been epic.

"He's not actually going to cut off part of his arm since Cormac was injured that way, is he?"

Murphy pursed his lips. "No. Probably not, anyway."

Brigid was looking over the shoulder of a young human with a laptop. It was one of Declan's pair of "hands" that he'd sent from Dublin.

"What's that?" Brigid asked, pointing to the screen. "Can you zoom in?"

The human tensed. "It will short out if you get too close. See what the screen just did? I just managed to get into their system, and I don't want to have to start all over. Please stand back, Ms. Connor."

"But there was something—"

"It's not like the telly," the young man said through gritted teeth. "Do you understand the concept of camera resolution? There are only so many—"

"Freddie." Carwyn wandered over and patted the young man's arm before Brigid started steaming. "Just do the best you can."

Murphy looked away from Terry and Roger. "Lad, move to that table. There's better light. Let us know when you have something."

"Yes, Mr. Murphy."

"And Brigid?"

"Yes, boss?"

"Take a deep breath and tell me what the story is before the O'Briens arrive."

Just as Brigid began to summarize, Anne saw Gemma motion to her from the doorway. Anne touched Murphy's hand and nodded toward the door. He smiled and pressed a quick kiss to her palm before she left, then turned back to Brigid and Carwyn.

Anne walked to the doorway, where Gemma was watching Terry and Roger.

"A courier from your sister will be arriving in a few minutes," Gemma said. "Will he need accommodations?"

"No, but thank you." Anne glanced at Terry and his lieutenant. "Will poor Roger survive?"

Gemma pursed her lips. "Terry's angry, but Roger is his best man. This was, sadly, unavoidable. We cannot protect those who don't want to be protected. Rens refused our security, as did Cormac. The O'Briens can bluster, but that's all they'll do. Bastiaan Anker, on the other hand, is a total mystery."

Anne tried not to wince. If Bastiaan Anker was as protective of his sibling as Mary was of her, there would be hell to pay.

"And the others?" she asked. "Have we heard from Jean and Leonor? What about Jetta?"

"All accounted for. There is enough of a French community here in London that Jean uses their resources when he'd in town. Jetta's chief of security has worked very closely with us while they've been here, as has Leonor's."

"Do you think the summit can continue?"

Gemma paused. "I honestly don't know."

"Do you think stopping it was the goal?"

Gemma shook her head. "Then why not target Terry or me? Or the meeting locations? There are any number of ways to halt meetings, if that's all that was wanted. Killing Rens was a drastic step. He must have known something the killer didn't want to get out."

Anne couldn't help but think about Murphy's meeting with Rens the night before. They'd spoken of Oleg. Could the Russian have been watching? Did he know? Anne didn't even know if her knowledge of Oleg was pertinent to the discussion about shipping. Who wanted to quiet Rens Anker so much that they would kill him and risk the wrath of his powerful clan?

A butler came in and announced Robert's arrival.

Mary's messenger squinted as if the low light in the hallway was simply too much for him. Anne had finished her notes for Mary after Murphy had fallen asleep the night before. She handed over her packet and took the one he held out for her.

"Robert, much has happened during the day. Please see one of Brigid Connor's people for a briefing before you go. I want Mary informed."

"Yes, Dr. O'Dea."

"How is everything in Belfast?"

"Your sister is well and healthy."

"That will be fine." The little man gave her the shivers. "You're dismissed."

"Yes, madam."

Gemma watched him walk away. "He's quite something, isn't he?"

"I do not like him, but he's absolutely loyal to Mary. I don't know the details, and I don't want to."

"Like most things in politics, it's probably more palatable that you don't."

"Gemma?"

The Englishwoman was watching Terry intently. "Hmm?"

"What is it like? Being consort to a leader like Terry?"

Gemma turned to her. "I never wanted to be so visible, to be honest. But I found that there were many things I could accomplish more effectively in a leadership role. It was a political arrangement from the beginning, Anne. So I'm not sure if there is much wisdom I can offer you if you're seriously considering Murphy."

"Would you be happier if Terry gave up the city? Lived a quieter life?"

Gemma looked surprised. "Of course not. That wouldn't be him. Or me. Not anymore." She cocked her head, still watching her mate. "I've grown into a different person with Terry. I like myself more for it."

"So it's worth it?"

"Oh yes." Her eyes heated. "I would fight to the death for that man."

"Madam." An older butler approached Gemma.

"Yes, Adams?"

"The O'Briens have arrived."

"Which ones?"

"Mister Cormac O'Brien and Miss Novia O'Brien."

"Thank you, Adams. Please escort them to the library and fetch them in… five minutes, please."

Anne nodded to Terry. "Do you think he's finished?"

"He will be."

Gemma walked over and touched Terry's shoulder. The vampire spun, baring his teeth. Gemma grabbed the front of his jacket and yanked him down, pressing her mouth to his. Anne saw a trickle of blood fall down Terry's chin. Roger, his jacket mussed and his lip bloody, looked relieved.

Anne could feel Murphy's eyes on her. She walked over and sat next to him.

"If I lose my temper like that, will you bring me to my senses by kissing me?"

"No," she said. "You throw too fast a punch. I might have Carwyn do it for me."

Carwyn asked, "Do I have to kiss him?"

"Only if you want to."

"I'll have to think it over." Carwyn sniffed. "He's not my type at all."

Brigid barked a laugh from the table where she was still hovering over the young man on the computer. Then she yelped and pointed to the computer. "There!"

"Yes, I see it. Give me a moment…" The young man's fingers flew over the keyboard. "And… there. That's the best I'll be able to do. These cameras are not designed for night surveillance."

Cormac and Novia were announced. The vampire stalked in, his sleeve hanging half-empty and a thunderous expression on his face. Novia's face was unreadable.

"Ramsay!"

Gemma held up both hands. "Cormac, don't start. You are the one who refused our protection. There's only so much we can do—"

"Why the hell did this happen? I'm here less than a week! My daughter, Ramsay. My only daughter!"

"Who is fine," Novia said quietly. "Lamar did his job. The guy never even touched me." She looked around, her eyes landing on Carwyn. "Thank you so much. The doctor you sent saved his life. The ones at the hospital said he'd be dead if he hadn't gotten blood so quickly."

"I'm glad I could help," Carwyn said. "Gladder to hear that he'll recover. He sounds like a good man."

Anne said, "Cormac, how are you feeling? Your arm—"

"It'll grow back." He tossed up his sleeve. "Eventually. At least it's my left one."

"But Rens?" Novia asked. "Is he really... dead?"

"It appears so," Murphy said. "Anne and I went by the house, and I don't believe he could have survived that fire. Brigid, do you have the surveillance footage?"

"I do." She twirled her finger, and the young man spun the computer around to face the room. "Roger's people are trying to track down the private footage that might have caught your house, Cormac, but Rens and his people were staying on a relatively major road, so we were able to see the footage from the traffic cameras."

"Clever," Cormac muttered.

"As you can see," Brigid continued, "Rens and his people entered an hour or so before dawn. The sun comes up. Traffic and all that..."

"Is there access in the back?" Cormac asked.

"A small garden, but no alley and no cameras. Matthew, slow it down a bit." Brigid leaned over but didn't touch the screen. "There. Point it out for them. The older woman."

"Oh, I see her. She looks like a housekeeper or something," Novia said.

"It's the only human we see coming or going," Brigid said. "That in itself is notable. This house, for instance, has security and servants exiting and entering throughout the day. But in the Anker house, we see no one but this old woman. A few minutes after she leaves..." Brigid waited for the recording to catch up. "The smoke is visible from the upstairs windows first, but it's soon everywhere. An accelerant was used throughout the house. There were secured rooms in the basement, but they were gutted. There was no chance for the firefighters to save it. They focused on keeping the houses on either side from burning."

Terry walked to Cormac. "I know your first instinct is to take your daughter and leave. Christ knows, I'd want to. And if you do that, I'll understand, but I hope you don't. Someone wanted you gone. *That's* why they went after your girl. I want you both to be safe. Will you let my people coordinate with yours? Add some local lads?"

Cormac said nothing until Novia nudged him. "Fine," he growled. "We'll stay. For now. Consider this my happy mood—I had a big breakfast."

"The question is," Anne said, "what did both you and Rens know that made you targets for whoever is doing this?"

"Beats me," Cormac said. "I'd never even met the man before I came here. His clan's not welcome in my city."

"Why not?"

Cormac looked at her as if she were an idiot. "Because I don't want spies stirring up trouble and selling my information to the highest bidder? Who are you, anyway? You're not Mary Hamilton, so why are you here?"

Murphy snarled. "Watch your tone, O'Brien. She's Mary's sister and my mate. Show some respect."

Anne spun, her mouth open. "You presumptuous man. I can speak for myself."

Murphy shrugged, and Brigid stifled a laugh.

"It's true," Murphy said. Then he smiled at Cormac. "She doesn't always like me, but she's still my mate. So watch your bloody mouth, O'Brien."

"Fine."

Anne decided to ignore Murphy. "Did you determine anything about your attacker before you killed him?"

"He tasted Spanish."

"Dad," Novia protested, "don't be prejudiced."

"What?" Cormac said. "He did. Or maybe he smelled like Spanish food. I don't know."

Anne thought Novia resembled a frustrated teenager dealing with a clueless parent. "He's only saying that because when we went to visit Lamar, he said the guy was speaking Spanish during their fight. Like *Spain*-Spanish."

"Was he sure?" Anne asked. "Accents can be difficult to determine."

"Pretty sure," Novia said. "Lamar's my bodyguard, but he's also my translator. He speaks like four or five languages. Used to work at the UN. If he said the guy was speaking Spanish, then he was speaking Spanish."

"Interesting," Murphy muttered.

Terry's face was grim. "Where's Leonor?"

ANNE was in the second car that drove to Leonor's house later that night. She didn't know what she'd been expecting from the Spanish regent, but the ultra-modern penthouse on the Isle of Dogs was certainly not it.

"This is where she lives?" Anne asked Murphy as they pulled up to the glittering high-rise.

"I think she owns the building," Murphy said. "Very good investment. I own property here too."

The neighborhood was mainly industrial, but Anne could see signs of gentrification.

"Interesting."

"What's interesting is the fact that none of Leonor's humans are answering their phones," Murphy said. "I don't like this."

"But she checked in earlier?"

"She did."

Anne settled back and tried not to worry. She liked Leonor, who had always been a reliable ally for her sister, Mary. But first the Spanish vampire had been cagey about sharing information with others in the meeting, and then Cormac and Novia had been attacked by a Spanish-speaking assassin. It didn't look good.

"Terry's angry," Murphy said, "but this is too easy. She's too obvious a suspect."

"He and Gemma were attacked in her territory a year and a half ago. She's a competitor in the blood-wine business—"

"She's also one of their grape suppliers."

"True. But she does know more than she's letting on about Elixir. Maybe she's just being cautious, but maybe not. We don't know, Patrick."

He shook his head. "Nothing this complicated is this neat. I think she's being set up."

"By whom?"

"Whoever is actually behind this."

"Someone who knows she's been acting suspicious?"

"Yes."

"Then," Anne admitted, "whoever attacked Novia and Cormac— whoever murdered Rens—is someone at the summit."

Chapter Eighteen

MURPHY STOOD BEHIND TERRY when he knocked on the door. Four humans flanked them, and Roger stood on his left. Gemma and Anne were waiting in the lobby with four other guards, watching for anyone who might try to exit.

"Leonor," Terry said, his voice low. "Come out."

Murphy said, "We just want to talk, Leonor."

He heard her voice coming from the other room. "Send your men away. I'll meet with you and Terry. That's all."

"Murphy, me and six of your men?" Terry asked. "Not a chance."

"You know how many people I have with me," she said. "I'll send all but Gasper out. Your men wait with mine in the lobby."

Murphy murmured, "Do it. She's too smart to come at us directly like this, and we need to talk to her."

"Fine." Terry nodded at Roger, who backed up and stood against the opposite wall with his men while Leonor's door cracked open. Three men and two women walked out. They stood across from Terry's men, watching with narrowed eyes. Only a sharp command from inside the penthouse caused them to move. One by one, the soldiers walked down the hall and exited the stairwell.

Murphy was the first in the door. He decided to turn on the charm since Terry was sadly lacking in anything that resembled it.

"Leonor," Murphy said, switching on a lamp that bathed the dark room in a soft light. "For the record, darling, I don't think you had anything to do with this."

"Some son of a bitch is trying to make it look like I did." Leonor was spitting mad, stalking the length of the loft-style room, its wall of glass overlooking the city lights south of the Thames. Murphy noted that the vampire was dressed casually. She had donned worn denim jeans and a skintight black shirt that showed an impressive figure normally hidden behind business attire.

A handsome young man lounged behind her in similar dress, watching them silently with coal-black eyes. Gasper was Leonor's lieutenant, a water vampire nearly as old as his mistress, and—according to rumors—her occasional lover. He watched them like the shrewd soldier he'd been in his human life.

There had been no official meetings scheduled for the night, and Leonor looked very much like someone who had planned to enjoy the abundant nightlife of the city. She didn't look like someone who had been expecting to be the suspect in a murder.

"You're angry," Terry said.

A violent stream of Spanish almost blew back his hair. Gasper said something under his breath, and Leonor glared at him. Murphy saw her take a breath before she turned to them.

"I am angry. Terry, you know how much respect I have for both you and Gemma, but from the beginning, something about this summit bothered me. I couldn't say what it was exactly, but I'm sure you knew I was withholding information. I did not trust Rens Anker, but I am not a fool to provoke his brother's wrath."

"Why didn't you say something privately?" Murphy asked. "It was quite obvious you weren't cooperating. It puts the rest of us in an odd position, Leonor. You look guilty."

Leonor frowned at him as if she'd just noticed Murphy was there. "Why are you here?"

Murphy shrugged carelessly. "I was bored. I also happen to think you didn't kill Rens or attack the O'Briens. If you want me to send Cormac, I'd be happy to fetch him."

Leonor curled her lip. "The American is beneath my notice. I have no interest in him or his child."

"So why did a Spanish-speaking assassin go after Novia O'Brien?" Terry asked.

"Because Spaniards are excellent killers?" Gasper said, his voice low. "We don't control every human of Spanish blood in England, Mr. Ramsay. That's your job, isn't it?"

Murphy broke in before Terry erupted. "Clearly, someone who wanted to kill Rens and get rid of Cormac has noted Leonor's antagonistic behavior and decided to take advantage."

"So you do think Rens was killed by someone at the summit?" Leonor asked.

"Yes."

Terry growled, "Who?"

"Who benefits from my mistress's trouble?" Gasper asked. "Terry is the most obvious, of course."

"Why?" Terry asked.

"The wine," Leonor said. "I'm expanding my operation into South America." She smiled at Terry. "Surprise."

Terry waved his hand and went to sit across from Gasper. "Gemma told me you would make that jump months ago. I know about the land in Chile."

Leonor narrowed her eyes but offered nothing else.

Murphy followed Terry's example, leaving Leonor standing. After a few moments of the three men staring up at her, she relented and perched on a barstool.

"Also, I... *acquired* a new winemaker last year."

Terry laughed and asked, "Did Jean lose another one?"

"He treats his people like horse dung and expects them to be grateful. It was easy to tempt the young human away. This winemaker studied under your man, Terry. The others aren't nearly as good."

"They know how to make it," Gasper said, "but Jean will be making the vampire version of box wine. At least for a long time. He won't be able to compete."

Murphy listened silently, taking everything in.

"Ramsay," he said when Leonor and Gasper had finished. "I know we weren't scheduled to have a meeting tonight, but don't you think we should call one?"

"Why?"

"I want to see all of us in one room," Murphy said. "I can't decide who to believe." His eyes went to Leonor. "Are you going to share information now that Rens is conveniently gone?"

More Spanish curses assaulted him, and Gasper rose to his feet.

"Relax," Murphy said. "I told you I didn't think you killed anyone. This time." He rose to his feet and buttoned his jacket. "Get everyone in the same room. Let's see what shakes out when we all have to look at each other. I'm going to relieve Gemma and Anne. Hopefully none of your goons have killed each other yet. If they damage my woman, I'll be annoyed."

MOSTLY what happened when everyone was in the same room was a whole lot of glaring.

Murphy had ordered one of his people to find a giant map. He and Anne spread it out in the conference room they'd been meeting in and weighted down the corners with whatever they could find. Murphy walked around the room, tossing colored markers to each of the vampire leaders in turn.

"Now," he said, smoothing his tie as they watched him. "The humans are gone. We've all given up our entourages—thank you, Gemma—so what we're going to do now is cut through the massive piles of rubbish that everyone has been peddling while we've been here."

"Who gave you permission to speak, Murphy?" Jetta asked. "This is Terry's summit."

"I suppose that's true," Terry said, "But I'm fucking pissed off at all of you, so I decided I'd let him talk."

"And with that gracious introduction," Murphy continued, "I'll proceed. I've given you all colored markers. We're going to put our notes on this map so we can all see what we're dealing with. No double-talk. No posturing. People are dead and injured tonight, and someone in this room is responsible for it." Murphy purposefully didn't watch their reactions. He'd asked Anne to do that before the meeting. "I'll start."

He put a dot representing every ship he knew that had landed in Dublin with questionable cargo or crew, and a corresponding dot at the cargo's point of origin, connecting the two. After he was finished, Anne did the same thing while he watched the participants.

Jetta looked annoyed. She clearly had something to say but was biting her tongue while glaring at Leonor.

Jean looked amused. He watched everyone's reactions as more information went onto the schoolroom map, even catching Murphy's eye and winking as Terry started to add his notes.

Leonor sat stiffly, aware that many suspected her of Rens's murder.

Cormac glared at Leonor. But then, he glared at everyone. Novia wasn't with him, and he was the only one Terry had allowed to keep a security guard in the room. But then, he was the only one currently missing half an arm.

Anne passed him a note. *When will the Dutch be here?*

Murphy shrugged. "We're letting Carwyn deal with them," he murmured. "That's what he and Brigid are doing tonight with Roger."

"That's good. He's probably the least likely to be killed."

"He does have his uses."

"Be nice."

"I can be very, very nice." He took her hand under the table. "I was hoping to have time with you tonight."

"I was too." She didn't look at him, but he could see the smile touch her lips. "It's all right, Patrick. I'm not going anywhere."

"I'm counting on it."

As more and more information went on the map, everyone began to see the pattern that Murphy had only suspected before.

Almost every ship that had carried Elixir had originated in the Black Sea. Most of the crews were either Eastern European or Turkish. And the vast majority of the Elixir and human carriers had ended up in the North Sea or the Baltic regions.

Cormac O'Brien was the last to stand and walk toward the map.

"I don't have much to add here," he said. "North America isn't even on here. But the points of origin I can…" He cocked his head and marked down a few dates before he paused. He put a finger on the Black Sea and didn't move.

"Cormac?" Anne asked.

"Fucking hell," he murmured. "That's why."

Murphy leaned forward. "O'Brien, if you've got—"

"Fucking *hell*." The American spun and glared at Jetta, then at Leonor and Jean. "One of you killed the Dutchman. Which one did she get to? What did she offer?"

Anne stood. "Cormac, who are you talking—"

"That Albanian bitch." His pointing finger swung around the room. "That Albanian bitch got to one of you. I wondered what the hell she had planned, but I never thought one of you would cave." He threw down his marker. "I'm gone. Novia and I are gone. Call me when she's dead."

Albanian? Murphy stopped him before he stormed out. "Who the hell are you talking about?"

"Zara," he spit out, scribbling something in a small notebook that he put in his pocket. "That's why someone tried to kill my daughter. Well, fuck you all. I'm not staying here to get caught in her web."

De spinnekop.

Rens had called Livia "the spider."

"O'Brien," Terry yelled, "tell me what's going on."

Cormac looked over Murphy's shoulder at the rest of the room. "Forget it."

If he hadn't been such an accomplished pickpocket in life, he would have missed the pass from the American. He let Cormac go and turned back to the room.

"Fuck off then," Terry said, throwing a disgusted look at Cormac's back. "Bloody American."

"It appears," Murphy said, "we might be missing an Albanian connection."

"Albania?" Jetta said. "None of the ships have come from Albania."

"What is he talking about?" Jean asked. "Is the American unbalanced?"

"I don't know any Albanians," Leonor said. "It's not important. Who is running Albania? Athens, yes?"

"Saying Athens actually runs anything is being generous," Jetta said.

While the rest of them started shouting over each other, trying to figure out who Cormac was talking about, Murphy slipped the piece of paper from his suit pocket.

King's Cross Station, 4am.

He slipped the paper back in his pocket and absently noted that Anne had fallen silent at his side.

MURPHY wandered around King's Cross for ten minutes before he managed to find Cormac O'Brien, who was smoking a pipe and leaning against one of the arches. The station wasn't open, but there were still a few humans around. Murphy drew the fog closer, concealing them from curious eyes.

"King's Cross?" he asked.

Cormac frowned. "That is a really cool trick with the fog. And my girl insisted we stay here. Platform 9 3/4 and all that. She made her bodyguard take pictures."

"Platform what?"

Cormac lifted an eyebrow. "Don't you read?"

"Not as much as I'd like." Murphy took out a thin cigar and lit it. "Tell me about this Zara."

"Sorry about the theatrics earlier. Not that I wasn't genuinely pissed, but I don't trust anyone in there."

"But you're meeting with me?"

Cormac blew out a stream of smoke. "I don't think she has anything you'd be interested in buying."

"Who is Zara?"

"A crazy Albanian water-vampire bitch."

"I gathered as much," Murphy said, trying not to snap at the man. "I've never heard of her."

"She likes to keep it that way."

"Why do you think she has anything to do with Elixir?"

"Because of the ports. Samsun. Poti. Varda. Athens doesn't acknowledge it, but Zara's been quietly running Istanbul for the past two years. That means nearly every ship that's been carrying Elixir is leaving one of her ports and passing through the Bosphorus."

Murphy's instincts started humming. "Athens has controlled the Bosphorus for a thousand years."

"More specifically, Laskaris does."

There was the Greek connection. Athens might not be on the Black Sea, but they controlled it. Though Istanbul had changed hands in the human realm, in the vampire world, it had remained under Greek control.

"And Laskaris," Cormac said, naming one of the oldest on the Athenian council, "is Zara's current plaything. She hooked up with him after she broke with Oleg. She'd been overseeing the ports on his side until then."

"The Russian? Were they lovers? I thought only his children ran his ports. You said she was a water vampire."

"Yeah, I don't know what they were," Cormac said. "She hates him, that's for sure."

More of those disparate puzzle pieces fell into place. "So she broke with Oleg and took up with Laskaris?"

"Trust me, there's no romance involved. Istanbul belongs to Laskaris. He's the most active member of the council, but that's not really saying much. He's lazy as hell. Zara saw an opportunity to stick it to Oleg when she hooked up with him. She runs the strait for him and strokes his ego, and he lets her do what she wants while remaining under the radar. Rumor is Istanbul has been raising the tariffs through the Bosphorus over the past year or so. If they're going up, it's because of Zara."

Because no one shipped anything—including oil—from the Black Sea without passing through the narrow seventeen-mile strait that connected the Black Sea to the rest of the world. And any freighter owned by an immortal paid a heavy tax.

It was one of the sole means of support the Greeks had managed to retain control over. If their court weren't so bloated, it would have been enough. Sadly, the Athenians were more interested in luxury than economy.

Cormac continued, his empty sleeve waving as if he'd forgotten half his left arm was gone. "Oleg has been working on his Baltic ports for a few years now, but he still needs the Black Sea. Not enough of his oil pipelines going to the Baltic yet."

"Most of the Elixir has been moving toward the North Sea and up to the Baltic."

"I'd be willing to bet if you managed to nail down the vampires running those territories—which, let's be honest, most of them are puppets for Oleg anyway—you'd see even higher numbers of Elixir infection than what you've seen in the Netherlands and Scandinavia."

"She's choking Oleg. Crippling the Baltic territories and forcing him to use the Black Sea," Murphy said.

"That's what I think."

"And she's using the Greeks to do it. Are they the ones producing Elixir, then?"

Cormac took another drag on his pipe before he spoke. "Probably. They've been trying to remain relevant for years now. They're greedy. And they don't like Russians. Laskaris, especially, would be happy to fuck with Oleg. And if Athens makes money in the process? All the better. They're hemorrhaging Euros right now."

"But what are they thinking?" Murphy said. "This Zara is poisoning the blood supply all over the world. She's destabilizing Oleg. I've never even heard of this woman. Does she think she's going to be able to control Oleg's territories? That's madness."

"I told you she's nuts," Cormac said. "This is Zara. She hasn't thought that far ahead."

"Do you think she's in London and we missed her?"

Cormac shook his head. "She likes to fuck with people from a distance. But I bet my other arm she's got someone in that meeting on her payroll. She's found out what they want and she's using them to be her eyes and ears. My guess is Jetta, because she hates the Russians so much, but I could be wrong. Rens probably had information on her, which is why he's dust. And when she found out I was here, she sent someone after my daughter."

The immortal's devotion to the girl almost made Murphy like him.

Almost.

"How do you know all this?"

"Because Zara approached me and offered to kill all my brothers if I'd let her ship into New Jersey no questions asked."

Even Murphy knew that was a mistake. The O'Briens fought like cats and dogs amongst themselves, but *only* amongst themselves. They were like his mother's people. They could fight with each other and still be fiercely loyal against outsiders.

"You said no."

He shook his head. "Not even the Albanian bosses in my city want to deal with Zara. And they're considered so crazy the *Russians* want nothing to do with them."

"Is your entire city made up of criminals, O'Brien?"

The other vampire grinned. "It keeps things interesting."

"Clearly. So Zara made you curious after she approached you."

"Yep. I did some digging with the aforementioned criminal elements in my city. She doesn't like attention, but she's got a reputation. I'm surprised you haven't heard of her."

"Don't think we keep similar company, O'Brien, because we don't."

"Please." He spit a fleck of tobacco from his lip. "I know you like to come across as a prissy bastard, but you're as much of a criminal as me, Murphy. You just have a prettier accent."

"I won't disagree with you."

"Fuck you," Cormac growled. "I better leave before I actually start liking your pansy ass. Take it easy, Irish. And send a card when the crazy bitch is dead."

Murphy leaned against a pillar and drew the fog closer as he watched Cormac walk into the night.

It *was* the Greeks. He'd been right all along, but to truly understand what was going on, he needed to know about the Russian. Zara hated Oleg so much that she'd poison their world to hurt him. That kind of hate was more than a lovers' quarrel, and he bet Anne knew the details.

She likes to fuck with people from a distance.

If O'Brien was right, then Murphy couldn't do much about Zara. At least not yet. But there was someone he could hurt. Whoever had killed Rens and attacked Cormac was in the city. One of the vampires at Terry's summit had double-crossed them.

And that individual was fair game.

Chapter Nineteen

ANNE WAITED FOR MURPHY in their room, but he arrived barely in time to escape the sun before he collapsed into bed. She'd have to wait until the next night before she found out what Cormac had told him.

Hopefully the American had somehow come across the knowledge that Anne hadn't been able to reveal. She knew that her knowledge of Oleg and Zara's relationship could help sort through the mystery and possibly help catch whoever killed Rens, but she still hadn't heard from her patient.

She couldn't reveal Oleg's history without his permission. It could be the death of her.

There was a tap on her door shortly after dawn.

"Yes?" she asked at the door.

Judith's voice came from the other side. "Dr. O'Dea, I have a message here from your sire. Shall I slip it under the door?"

"Yes, thank you, Judith."

A small slip of paper was pushed through, and Anne picked it up as the human's footsteps retreated. She could hear the guards pacing outside, so she took the note and went back to the bed to open it. Her father had written in his old language.

Annie—
An old friend wants to see you. Meet me at the pub tomorrow at ten.
—T

An old friend? Of hers? Of her father's? Anne had long ago ceased to expect any kind of clarity from him unless he was sitting in front of her. Still, if her father was hosting this old friend, Anne knew she'd be safe. The question was, would Murphy insist on going along?

With the last of his consciousness, the vampire in question pulled her against his body and wrapped both arms around her, burrowing into her hair and pushing one of his legs between her own, effectively trapping her on the bed.

Would he insist on going? Anne was guessing yes.

SHE woke gradually, coming to awareness with the comfort of Murphy wrapped around her. She could feel the easy ebb and flow of their amnis, like soft breaths exchanged between lovers. Though he hadn't yet bitten her, his blood had flooded Anne's system, and their bond had snapped into place as if the hundred years that had parted them had been no more than the blink of an eye.

We're meant, Anne. You know we are. We were so good together. We were young and stupid. Or at least I was. I'm not anymore.

His actions the night before had proven his words true. While others had railed and ranted, Murphy had remained calm. In the face of a situation that would have spurred panic and violence in him when he was young, he'd proposed conversation and clarity.

And while he was still presumptuous, Anne found that she couldn't fault him for it when he told the truth.

She *was* his mate.

Sometimes she didn't like him much. Sometimes he pushed her buttons a little too far.

But oh, how she loved him.

The only remaining question was, did she want him more than the life she'd established? More than her patients? More than her home?

Who in there knows you? Knows you really?

No one.

But Murphy did. Josie did. Brigid and Carwyn did.

She still cared for her immortal patients. But… she didn't care for them *more* than she loved the man beside her.

Patrick Murphy had grown into a responsible leader. Respected. Admired for qualities beyond his bravado or brute strength. He'd done all that on his own, and she found herself fiercely proud of him.

He'd broken her trust, and she'd abandoned him. They had both made mistakes. Maybe Murphy's were more obvious, but she wasn't perfect either.

Part of her wished she had fought harder for him, but part of her also realized that losing her might have been the thing that drove him to become the man he was. He could still be rash. He still fought his temper and his demons, as she did. But he had also learned care and patience. He had taken control of a city and made it a thriving, safe place. He sacrificed for his people.

Anne had loved the man he'd been, but she loved and *admired* the man he'd become.

She opened her eyes and twisted so that she was facing him. His skin was cool to the touch, as hers was. She took a deliberate breath and let her amnis run faster, heating her body to warm them both. It was a little thing, but she liked the idea of Murphy waking to warmth. She knew there had been many human years when that hadn't been the case.

Anne hummed a low tune as she brushed the hair out of his eyes and smoothed it back from his forehead. She closed her eyes and let herself revel in the feel of his blood waking within her.

Such powerful amnis.

Much was made of the strength of older immortals, and it was true that they had far more control. But the vigor of youth couldn't be forgotten. She felt Murphy's leg twitch against hers, and his amnis, which had been washing gently over her as he rested, rushed back to his body as he began to wake.

She whispered the words to a song he loved as he woke. Murphy sucked in a deep breath as he always did when the sun set, but instead of sitting up or rolling over, he stayed exactly where he was, watching her with lidded eyes as she sang him awake.

The wonder in his eyes put to rest any lingering doubts that had plagued her.

She belonged with him.

"What were you thinking about?" he asked. "Before I woke. What made you sing that song?"

"I knew you loved it."

"I do."

Anne smiled. "That's all. I know you love that song, so I sang it for you."

"And what thing can I do for you, Anne Margaret O'Dea"—gentle fingers began to play at the small of her back—"to repay you for the gift of that song? I may have fine houses and a fleet of ships, but I don't think I own its equal."

She smiled. "There is one thing."

"Please," he said. "Tell me how I can repay you."

She put her cheek against his chest and closed her eyes.

"Do you know of a fine wild man," she whispered, "with dark hair and brown eyes who might love me? I lost one long ago. I ran away, but I could never go far enough to forget the sound of his voice."

His voice was rough. "Anne—"

"Do you know of one who might have me? For I'm lonely, and I'm needing him back."

Murphy said nothing but pulled back and tipped her chin up so her eyes met his. All his gentle amusement had fled, and his gaze held the longing of the young immortal she'd met so long ago.

Angry and cocksure, he'd been. Passionate and impulsive.

Vulnerable.

Age had shaped him and molded him, but in that moment, he was as unguarded as she'd ever seen him.

"Truly, Áine?"

"*A chuisle mo chroí,*" she said. "Pulse of my heart, Patrick. Your blood runs with mine. I don't want to live without you anymore. Don't make me —"

He stopped her mouth with a hungry kiss. His arms banded around her, and she could feel the length of his fangs against her skin as he rolled her under his body. He was hard against her soft. Her head began to spin with his energy as he kissed her over and over again. He was already naked, and he quickly stripped the nightclothes she had donned.

Anne was painfully, instantly aroused. She tilted her head back, baring her neck. "Please…"

She didn't have to ask twice. His fangs pierced her skin as he entered her. Pleasure and pain and a dizzying swell of energy. Her legs came up and pressed against his hips, holding him closer.

It wasn't close enough.

He drank, pulling hard against her neck as the first wave of pleasure crested and swept over her. She felt him inside. Her body. Her blood. There was no truer joining than this.

Were you born of woman
Or did you come from the earth?

He didn't come from the earth but from the water. From the springs deep within and the waters that fed the land. And when she closed her eyes, she saw them—the river against the sea—and it was a beauty she understood with trembling awe. They were more than two in that moment. They were the blood of creation.

Her mate licked the wound closed and began a gentle rhythm that seemed to go on for hours. Murphy didn't rush. Didn't race. He savored her with every stroke and every kiss.

"Patrick—"

"You feel amazing," he murmured. "You taste even better. I feel you everywhere, Anne. I love you so much."

"I love you too." She closed her eyes. "But right now, I'm wishing you hadn't learned patience so well."

He smiled and bent to press a hard kiss against her lips. "Are you ready for me to be impatient?"

"Yes, please."

He laughed as he picked up a faster rhythm, bracing over her and staring into her eyes. Anne pulled him down to her kiss, teasing the small of his back as her feet stroked his legs and the back of his knees. Any of the sensitive spots she remembered. She felt the wave crest between them, and she rode it, throwing her head back as he struck again, biting the curve where her neck met her shoulder as she came hard.

Anne felt him groan deep in his chest as he followed her, licking her skin where his fangs had pierced it, kissing her as the last tremors of pleasure shook them both. Then he rolled to the side and gathered her close. Anne threw her arm over his chest and let the afterglow of amnis light them from within.

She was in him now, as he was in her.

"You love me?" he murmured.

"Silly man, of course I do. When have I ever not loved you?"

He paused and reached for her hand, knitting their fingers together. "But do you trust me, Anne O'Dea?"

She paused. "Do I trust you?"

"I hope you do." He brushed a strand of hair back from her forehead. "For I plan to love you more than myself. Plan to depend on you to tell me when I'm being an arse. Plan to love you better every night, until you can't imagine your life without me. That way I'll trap you, love. And you'll never leave me again."

She thought her heart might burst with love for him.

"Are you trying to make me fall in love with you, Mr. Murphy?"

He smiled a cheeky grin. "I take nothing for granted, Dr. O'Dea."

IF Anne were a wind vampire, she'd have been flying when she arrived at the Cockleshell Pub later that night. Not even the smell of piss and old fish could dampen her mood.

"Did you really think I was going to let you go by yourself?" Murphy asked, her hand gripped firmly in his.

He'd become her shadow, even more affectionate than he'd been before and twice as watchful.

"I'm going to start calling you a limpet if this continues, Patrick."

"Give me a few years," he grumbled, his eyes sweeping the waterfront. "I'll calm down. It'll be better when we're home."

"We haven't talked about that yet," she said. "Home."

"One thing at a time. Your father didn't give any indication who this was?"

"An old friend was all he said. Could be an old friend of mine. Or his. Or a new friend who's actually old in years. It's Da. I have no idea."

"That's helpful."

Brigid and Carwyn had stayed behind to deal with the representatives from Amsterdam, but four of Murphy's men and two of Terry's accompanied them. They walked behind them, but not far. Anne had protested that guards were unnecessary, but Murphy and Terry had overruled her.

Murphy's paranoia seemed prescient when several large vampires stepped out of the shadows. Anne didn't recognize any of them, and her fangs dropped.

"Anne O'Dea?" one said, his thick Russian accent stumbling over her name.

"Who's asking?" Murphy said. "And where's Tywyll?"

The large vampire wore a heavy beard, his hair hanging into his eyes. Anne thought he resembled a very bad-tempered bear.

"I don't answer you, Englishman," he said. "Are you Anne O'Dea of Galway?"

Anne rose on her tiptoes to see over Murphy's shoulder as their guards moved closer.

"I'm Anne. Are you Russian?"

"Don't talk to them," Murphy said. "I don't know what's going on —"

"You'll come with us," the bearlike vampire said, stepping forward and moving to grab Anne.

Murphy's fist hit his face faster than Anne could see. In a flurry of blows, the large immortal was on the ground and Murphy was kicking him.

"Patrick!"

Their guards moved forward, blocking the other vampire's compatriots and pulling Anne back to the edge of the road. With a loud snarl, the foreign vampires lunged forward, teeth bared and weapons out. One carried a long dagger, but the rest pulled handguns.

Guns couldn't kill a vampire unless the bullet severed the spine at the base of the neck, but they were still an efficient means of stopping one. Bullets hurt, and the guns these Russians took out looked like they could take down an elephant.

With no idea who was trying to grab her, Anne went immediately into defensive mode. She elbowed one vampire who managed to get too close before one of Terry's men belted him with a cricket bat. The solid swing sent the vampire flying toward the riverbank, over Murphy and the surly Russian.

The bearded vampire had rallied and was tumbling over the ground, trying to get a grip on Murphy, who dodged in with another kick every time the man made a move to stand. Two of Murphy's men, one human and one vampire, blocked Anne from the fight as the others pulled out weapons to face the foreigners.

"You don't touch her," Murphy growled, pulling the Russian's hair back and punching him in the throat with three quick jabs guaranteed to crush the vampire's windpipe. "Do you understand that?"

Anne could see that two of the foreign vampires had one of Murphy's guards by the neck. She heard someone cock a gun.

"No!" she yelled, frightened that the situation was escalating past the point of salvage.

Just as she was about to push calm into the ruckus, she saw the water at the edge of the riverbank rise.

"Stop," a low voice said. "Ye're bleedin' eejits. All of ye."

The slap of water came suddenly when two waves rose from the river and grabbed Murphy, the bearded Russian vampire, and most of the guards, pulling them into the river and submersing them with a resounding smack.

In a second, everything was silent.

Tywyll stepped from the shadows with Oleg at his side.

Anne heard Oleg cursing low in Russian. "That boy. Always wanting to travel, and these things keep happening. I cannot travel with him."

"I'll just keep 'em down there while we talk." Tywyll nodded toward the black water before he turned to Anne. "There's my girl! How're things, lamb?"

Anne pushed past her guards. "Da, could you let Patrick out of the river, please?"

Her sire's eyes twinkled. "Was young Murphy in that ruckus? Oi, the lad. He needs to stay out of trouble, eh?"

"The big bearded one tried to grab for me. What did you expect him to do?" She looked at her friend. "Hello, Oleg."

"Apologies for Misha. He is a good boy, but young. Not so bright yet. He will learn."

"Well, he won't be able to talk for a bit after Patrick's fists. Da?"

With a swish and a slap, Murphy was spit out of the river, dripping and glaring at Tywyll.

"Tywyll," he spat. "So very nice to see you again."

"You too, lad! See you've made things right with my girl."

"Indeed." He stood and did his best to straighten a sopping wet suit. He snapped at one of the guards who had covered Anne, and the man turned and trotted back to the car. "Campbell will get me some dry clothes in a moment." His attention turned to the Russian fire vampire towering over Tywyll. "Oleg Sokolov."

"Patrick Murphy."

"This is how you meet friends, Sokolov?" The water behind Murphy stirred with his anger.

Oleg, to his credit, raised his hands immediately. "I take responsibility for the boy. Misha is young and quite stupid. Very loyal, but stupid."

"He tried to grab Anne."

Oleg shook his head. "Did you punish him for me, Irishman?"

"He won't be talking for a while."

The Russian shrugged. "Good. This is good. I can see you are a man who appreciates protocol." He gave a shallow bow. "Anne O'Dea, I come in the company of your sire to speak with you. I hope I will be welcome. If I am not, I ask that you allow my guards and me to depart with no offense on either side."

Anne caught Murphy's eye and nodded. This was better than she'd expected. She'd been hoping, at the most, for a phone call from Oleg. Talking with him in person would be much better.

One of Terry's men asked, "Mr. Tywyll, sir, does Mr. Ramsay know about this one?" He nodded toward Oleg.

Tywyll's chin tipped up. "I don't recognize ye, so I'll assume yer new, boy. This ain't London here." He gestured to the broad expanse of water behind the old floating pub and Tywyll's flat barge. "This is the river. And the river's my own and none other. Yer master knows that better'n anyone."

Murphy put a hand up to stop Terry's man before he could speak again. "It'll be fine, Cooper. I'll explain it to Ramsay."

"Yes sir, Mr. Murphy."

The first guard returned from the car carrying a garment bag. Murphy took it and went to Anne. She put her hand on his cold cheek and gave him a quick kiss.

"Enjoy your swim, *mo chuisle*?"

"Refreshing," he muttered. "I'll change and meet you inside. Stay with your father, yes?"

"Of course." She glanced at Oleg, who was watching them with a curious expression on his face. "He's a friend, Patrick."

"Let's hope so." He tucked a strand of her hair behind her ear. "Stay with your father until I get back."

"I'm not helpless."

"I know you're not."

Anne felt the cool slide of the steel against her skin as Murphy passed a dagger to her before he slipped away.

She took a deep breath and turned. "Oleg," she said, walking toward her sire and the Russian. "It's so good to see you. Thank you for coming, even though I doubt this pub serves any of your vodka."

Oleg smiled. "An inauspicious beginning, my friend, but we will survive, no? Come talk with me. Your father assures me we will have privacy."

"We will." They turned toward the pub, and Anne noticed the still-churning water. "Da, are you just going to leave them down there?"

Tywyll shrugged. "They're vampires, girl. They'll be fine."

Chapter Twenty

BY THE TIME MURPHY RETURNED to the Cockleshell Pub, Tywyll, Oleg, and Anne were the only inhabitants. The two guards not currently submerged in the river were standing by the door. He slipped inside, grateful that the low lights of the pub masked the less than hygienic condition of the place.

Oleg and Anne were speaking in a booth while Tywyll watched from a distance. They were speaking low enough that Murphy couldn't hear them, but judging from their body language, Anne was trying to convince Oleg of something the Russian wasn't very happy about.

He sat down next to Tywyll.

"When did he approach you?"

"Just last night. Anne sent him a message, and he wanted to talk in person. I've had dealings with him in the past. I trust him as much as I trust any fire vampire."

"They're the least dangerous to our kind."

"Oleg is dangerous to everyone," Tywyll said, watching Murphy from the corner of his eye. "You're a smart lad and a good fighter. But Oleg? Steam. Any water you sent against him would be nothing."

Murphy watched his mate and the Russian.

Oleg leaned forward, listening intently, but he made no move to touch her, nor was his body language aggressive. If Murphy had come upon them as human, he'd assume the two were colleagues of some kind, which confirmed what he had suspected after his flair of jealousy had calmed. Oleg was one of Anne's patients.

So the Russian saw a shrink? That might explain why Oleg was considered one of the more well-adjusted despots in their world.

He was shaking his head, pulling back, but Anne caught his hand and placed her palm on the back of it.

Was she pushing?

Murphy wanted to scream no, but he didn't want to give her away either. If Oleg even suspected Anne of using any mental manipulation on him, she'd be dead. Murphy tried to reassure himself that Anne would never push a patient to reveal their secrets to others; she told him she only used it to reinforce suggestions for their mental health.

Murphy still waited breathlessly until Oleg's face softened just a hint and he began nodding. His face was grim, but he was nodding and he'd taken Anne's hand and held it affectionately.

And if Murphy had the inclination to be jealous, he *would* have been jealous of that look. Because for a short moment, he saw the buried longing on the Russian's face. He did want Anne. He also knew he couldn't have her.

Anne turned her eyes to him and nodded silently. Murphy walked over and slid into the booth next to his mate as Oleg released Anne's hand.

"Oleg," he said. "I hope—"

"I offer my felicitations on your reunion, Patrick Murphy. Anne is a good woman and a powerful vampire. She will make a wise and excellent consort for you."

Murphy slid his hand to Anne's and clasped it. "Thank you, Oleg."

"It is only because of my respect for her judgment that I will share this information with you. I trust Anne will share it only with those for whom that information is necessary. I trust your *mate* to make that determination."

Anne said, "You honor me with your trust, Oleg."

The Russian's eyes glinted. "I know a good friend when I have one. Should… certain things come to light, I expect you will be a friend then, as well."

"I understand your motives, Oleg."

"As few do." Oleg looked at Murphy. "Anne shared with me that the American tells you Zara is behind the shipments of Elixir coming out of the Black Sea."

"He implied that she's running Istanbul and the Bosphorus."

"The American is correct. I have been forced to contend with her for two years now. There is no need to detail how successful that has been. Zara hates me. Most sincerely. Luring Laskaris into an affair was a very effective revenge. I had no quarrel with the sleepy Greek until Zara started whispering in his ear."

"Oleg, surely a lover's quarrel—"

"She was not his lover, Patrick," Anne said. She looked at Oleg. "Please?"

Oleg growled, "Zara is my daughter."

Murphy blinked. "All reports I've been able to find since I talked to O'Brien say she is a water vampire."

"She is a water vampire."

"But you're sired from earth—"

"Did you know I had a mate once?" Oleg said, eyes falling to their clasped hands. "I envy you, Patrick Murphy. For my mate was not as yours is. She was quite insane."

"Oleg," Anne said, "I don't think you need to talk about Luana. We really only need to know about Zara."

"Zara is a water vampire," he said, "because my mate, Luana, was a water vampire. Though it is rare, when two vampires exchange blood— and Luana and I exchanged *much* blood—a vampire's child may be sired to their mate's element. This is why many people misunderstand our relationship, which I have done nothing to clarify. Zara was a favorite of Luana's when she was human. Luana asked me to sire her plaything."

Oleg shrugged. "It was not the wisest decision. But then, many of my decisions with Luana were not wise."

"So Zara is your daughter, but she is a water vampire," Murphy said, ignoring the truly twisted dynamic that made a vampire sire a child to be a lover or "plaything" for their own mate.

Oleg raised the pint of lager he'd been drinking. "A stroke of luck, I thought at first. My mate is happy her favorite is of her own element. Zara is very powerful. And after some time, I thought she could run my ports on the Black Sea. The council in Athens is entirely water vampires. They have always preferred working with their own kind. I thought Zara would be an excellent intermediary." He took a long swallow of the beer, then shoved it to the side with a curled lip. "Why is there no good vodka? I do not understand England."

Anne reached in her handbag and drew out a narrow bottle of very high-end vodka she must have swiped from one of Terry's cars. "I found reinforcements," she said. "Just in case."

"No no," the Russian demurred. "The beer is fine."

"Oleg, you hate beer."

He paused. "I do hate beer." He let loose a stream of Russian that sounded very complimentary as he opened the bottle and went to the bar to help himself to three glasses. Murphy had no idea how to speak Russian. He wondered if Anne did.

"Beautiful woman," Oleg finally said as he poured for them all. "You are a treasure, Anne O'Dea. Irishman, I would steal her from you if I did not see so much happiness in her eyes."

Oleg raised his glass and offered some toast Murphy assumed was the equivalent of *sláinte* in Russian. Then he and Anne followed Oleg's lead and sipped the vodka, which was decent, though Murphy had never been a fan of the liquor.

"So yes," the Russian continued. "Zara was a good choice to run my ports in the south. Luana was often with her there. They were happy—as much as Luana was ever happy. It was peaceful... mostly. But then I hear rumors. I ignore them. Zara makes me too much money. And then more rumors. Even after Luana died, I ignored many of the rumors because it was easier. Zara was effective. And I did not have to deal with her if she was in the south."

"What happened two years ago?" Murphy asked.

"I discovered Zara had stolen the remaining Elixir from me," Oleg said. "There were pallets Livia had hidden. The Roman thought the rest of us were stupid." Oleg shrugged. "Maybe the others were, because they are dead. I am not. I watched Livia carefully. After I discovered what this… poison did to humans, I wanted nothing to do with it. Madness, I thought. What do we have to gain from poisoning the humans? Would the mortals kill all their cattle? Salt their own fields? It was then I realized that Livia was as insane as my mate had been. I left her in Rome when Vecchio arrived. Then I instructed my people to steal the remaining Elixir and secure it in one of my warehouses in Moscow."

"Why the hell didn't you destroy it?" Murphy asked.

"Do you know how to destroy Elixir?" Oleg asked. "Please tell me. Do I burn it and risk putting it into the atmosphere? Do I dilute it? I didn't know enough about it to safely destroy it, so I secured it—I thought —and figured that I would destroy it when I discovered how." He shrugged. "I didn't think anyone would steal it because *who would be enough of an idiot to want to take a poison?*"

Anne said, "You forgot that Zara likes to manipulate people for fun."

"See?" Oleg tapped his temple. "This is why I should have seduced you fifty years ago, *lapochka*. You would keep me from forgetting things like this. Yes, Zara likes to… twist people. Manipulate them. She finds it amusing, like Luana did."

Murphy asked, "Was she involved with the initial theft?"

"Not directly. She was a lover to one of my lieutenants in Moscow. He is the one she convinced to help steal the Elixir. He is dead now. Unfortunately, Zara still had the Elixir. By the time I discover my man's betrayal, Zara had already become the Greek's lover. I cannot openly oppose Laskaris, or he will cut off my access to the Bosphorus. Zara will not return to St. Petersburg to face punishment from me, of course. So I cut her off. I close all her accounts and tell her she is no longer under my aegis and must leave my home in Sevastopol."

Murphy asked, "And her settlement?"

No sire, even the most evil, would release a child from their aegis without a financial settlement. It wasn't a matter of the worthiness of the child, but the resources of the sire. To release a vampire without providing for their independence would be seen as an embarrassment to anyone, but especially a vampire like Oleg, who had vast wealth.

"Her settlement is generous, of course," Oleg said with an evil smile. "Millions in gold waiting for her in a chest in my home. All she has to do is come retrieve it."

Murphy had to admire the vampire. No immortal could find fault with his cunning. Zara had been provided for, but not without facing discipline from her sire. And Murphy knew firsthand that no vampire would interfere with a sire's discipline of their offspring.

"But she refused to come to you," he said. "And she went to Laskaris."

"I'm sure the old Greek finds her very exciting. And she has made him much money, some of which I'm sure she has probably put into producing more Elixir."

"Are you sure?"

"I am sure of very little with Zara. If she is producing it, Athens is not ignorant."

Murphy said, "Laskaris may know about it and not care. Athens will see this as an opportunity to raise their profile. To be a world power again, which they've been wanting for some time. Libya looks poised to become a major power again with Inaya's rise to power. That would leave Athens as the oldest and most static player in the Old World. They won't like that."

"But Zara isn't in London?" Anne asked. "You're sure of it?"

"I'm positive."

"So who is she using in London?"

Oleg shook his head. "I have no idea about this, my friend. She likes money, and she'll be careful with Laskaris, at least for some time. So look for some financial incentive. Whoever is helping her will be wealthy, or be convinced that Zara can make him wealthy."

"Him?" Murphy asked.

Oleg shrugged again. "Or her. Zara will use anyone. But the motivation will be financial, I'm certain."

Anne asked, "Who makes money from Rens being dead?"

Tywyll piped up from across the room, "I do. But I didn't kill him."

Murphy shook his head. "Rens wasn't likely killed for money, but because of what he knew." He looked at Oleg. "Did Anker know about Zara?"

"The Dutchman? Probably. If he was interested to look, there are plenty of people who might talk. It wasn't a secret, though Zara does not like to gain attention. She prefers to work behind the scenes."

Who, of the remaining summit attendees, was poised to make money as Zara continued to spread Elixir? Murphy thought. Jetta? The Scandinavian was the least likely. Most of her financial investments were energy related. Leonor and Jean were the only two left, and both would make money from Elixir infection because both produced blood-wine.

As did Terry.

"Do you know where Zara is?" asked Anne.

"Yes and no. I don't think she leaves Greek territory often, because she'd be fair game. Laskaris hasn't officially declared her under his aegis, because that would make him accountable for her actions. But she's not under mine, either. As long as she stays near Athens, she'll be protected. But other than that, I have no idea. There are many places she could be hiding in comfort. They have so many islands it's ridiculous. They've long been a haven for those looking to disappear."

"But Athens is protecting her?" Now that Murphy's anger had a focus, it began to burn brighter. "This drug she's been producing and shipping has killed hundreds. Possibly thousands now. Vampires. Mortals. She's poisoned them, sent others out. Whoever was shipping into Ireland for her has killed humans and vampires under my aegis. Most recently, a good man whose only fault was being curious and wanting to help me."

"Tell me"—Oleg leaned forward—"are you prepared to go to war with Athens, Irishman?"

Murphy had to bite back a growl because he knew he wasn't. He didn't have the resources to attack Athens, though he'd certainly do what he could to harm them in business.

"You know I'm not," he bit out. "But you could."

"I could." Oleg nodded. "And I might. I haven't decided yet."

"Murphy." Anne squeezed his hand. "Oleg has asked that—in exchange for him being so open about his daughter—that we leave Zara to him."

"And let her get away with poisoning our kind and tainting the blood supply?" Murphy was steps away from livid. The water drew to him, dampening his clothes where he sat. Anne held his hand firmly.

"Zara will not be ignored," Anne said. "Not anymore."

Oleg said, "Find the one responsible for the deaths in London. Take your vengeance on those working with her. But Zara is my blood. Leave her to me."

"Then get your blood under control, Russian."

The booth heated immediately, though Oleg's expression didn't flinch. Murphy felt the steam rise on his skin where the Russian's fire met his water. Tywyll muttered something across the room, and the heat died back slightly.

"Out of respect for her"—Oleg nodded at Anne—"you live. But do not speak of things you know nothing about. And pray you do not meet me without your mate, for I do not tolerate disrespect. I have nothing more to say to you."

The Russian stood and left the booth.

"Move!" Anne said, pushing him. "Let me out."

Reluctantly, Murphy slid out of her way and Anne ran to the door. She grabbed Oleg's hand before he could leave the pub.

"Oleg, please—"

He said something in Russian.

"I know," Anne said. "But he has lost people who looked to him for protection. You of all vampires understand this."

"Fine." Oleg sent a withering look toward Murphy, who leaned against the side of the bench with his arms crossed over his chest. "He is rash, *lapochka*. You should teach him wisdom."

She smiled. "Because I've been so successful with you?"

Oleg put his hand on Anne's cheek, cupping it. Murphy stood up straighter, but Tywyll caught his eye, shaking his head deliberately.

Murphy gritted his teeth and stayed put.

"You have taught me more than you know, Anne O'Dea."

"Oleg—"

"But I must bid you farewell now."

Anne froze. "I'm not going to see you again, am I?"

A wicked smile curled the corner of Oleg's lip. "Will you run away with me tonight?"

Anne sighed. "The answer is still no."

"Then no, my friend, you will not."

The Russian bent down carefully, kissing her cheeks before he straightened. He said something quietly in Russian. Anne nodded. Then Oleg nodded to Tywyll and walked out the door.

WHEN Murphy, Anne, and Tywyll made their way outside, all the previously drowned guards were standing mutely by the riverbank, their faces written with embarrassment. Murphy went to stand in front of them, his hands hanging loosely in his pockets.

"The Russians all leave?"

"Yes, boss."

"Took off in a boat," another said. "High-end. Headed away from the city."

Murphy said nothing. Oleg would have arranged his departure with Tywyll. If the old vampire was satisfied, he wouldn't complain.

That still left four men standing dripping wet and shamefaced by the river.

"I'd say I was angry, but it's Tywyll."

One of the men coughed up a piece of sea grass and a spurt of river water that must have lodged in his throat.

"Come on then, lads," Murphy said, nodding toward the cars. "Back to Mayfair. We'll all pretend this didn't happen"—he glared at Tywyll, who only laughed—"and none of us will speak of it again."

"Yes, boss."

"But don't even think you're riding in the front car," he added. "And you're cleaning the second one when we get back."

One of his men said, "But boss—"

"I always carry a change of clothes," Murphy said, straightening his tie. "None of you did. There's a lesson about preparation there. Think about it while you clean the cars."

Anne slipped her hand in his and tugged him toward the car where Ozzie was waiting while Murphy began to chew over the information Oleg had given them.

Jetta.

Leonor.

Jean.

Ramsay.

He slid into Terry's car with Anne at his side. At the end of the night, it was really only Terry that Murphy trusted.

He'd dismissed Jetta earlier because she had no financial incentive to spread Elixir and her territories were harder hit. But Jetta didn't count the Russian as a friend, and Zara might use that to persuade Jetta to help her cross her sire. Oleg and Jetta were rivals when it came to their energy interests. They coordinated when they had to, but both were heavily invested in petroleum and gas.

Leonor and Jean would both make money off blood-wine, even with Jean producing a lower-end product. If Elixir spread far enough, everyone would be drinking it. Leonor might have come across as innocent the night before, or she might have covered herself well because she had known she'd be a suspect. After all, Jean didn't have a history of ambition outside France, and few would call him violent unless someone had personally offended him. He was mainly proprietary about his people—

His *people*.

"Anne," Murphy asked, "where did Terry get his winemaker?"

"His winemaker?" Anne frowned. "I believe Brigid said he hired him away from Jean Desmarais."

"That's what I thought I remembered."

Leonor's comments the night before came back to him.

I acquired a new winemaker last year.

He treats his people like horse-dung and expects them to be grateful.

It was easy to tempt the young one away.

Jean had lost two of his employees to Terry and Leonor. One after the other. Two employees who were poised to become some of the most valuable people in his organization.

Murphy banged on the front divider, and Ozzie rolled down the window.

"Yes, boss?"

"Turn around. Go back to the pub."

Anne looked confused. "Patrick?"

"I know who's helping Zara, and we're going to need your father's help."

Chapter Twenty-one

ANNE WATCHED MURPHY standing at the front of Tywyll's barge as it moved across the river. The night was clouded, and no moon shone in the sky. A boon, her father had said. The red-sailed barge would be nearly invisible in the night, which was just how the old waterman liked it.

When Tywyll had told them the French vampire was keeping a reefer ship at Tilbury, on the north shore of the Thames, Murphy was quick to ask for passage across the river.

One call to Terry, and Carwyn and Brigid were sent to help.

"Why does it always end up being a ship?" Brigid groused on Anne's left. "Every time, a ship."

"We were out in the desert in California," Carwyn added, standing on her other side.

"That was one time. Every other time? Ship. Bloody water vampires."

"You're the one who wanted to work for one, love."

"I'm going to end up drowned again. Or blown up. Possibly both."

"It's not like you can die from it."

"If you put a Taser on me again, so help me…"

Brigid kept complaining while Carwyn laughed quietly at his mate. Anne ignored them both and leaned forward, wishing she had more comfortable clothes like Brigid wore. She hadn't expected to be doing any heroics, and the wool slacks and delicate blouse she was wearing would surely be ruined on whatever greasy old freighter Jean traveled in.

Fine, it probably wasn't greasy. Jean loved his luxuries. Any ship Jean Desmarais traveled in was likely to be as well equipped as a yacht. But Anne still wished she had practical clothing.

"This isn't going to end well," Brigid said.

Anne said, "Jean's not even on the ship, Brig. Terry's gone to his house in Kensington to speak to him. All Murphy and I have to do is take a look at his freighter. I don't know why he sent you two."

"Better to be cautious," Carwyn said. "How sure is Murphy that—"

"Ask Patrick," Anne said, nodding toward her mate. "He's the one convinced it's Jean."

Anne wasn't as sure, to be honest. It wasn't just that she liked Jean, it was that it seemed ludicrous that anyone would kill one immortal, severely injure another, and alienate established allies over losing two employees.

It's not losing two employees, Anne. It's the knowledge those employees had.

Murphy did have a point. Terry's blood-wine had taken a giant leap forward when he'd hired Jean's winemaker. And if Leonor had hired his other man... It was a form of industrial espionage. Hardly unexpected in the vampire world, but still costly. Added to the financial loss was the loss of face. The Frenchman was constantly battling immortal factions in Paris and Lyon. He had little stability in his home country. Terry's underhanded dealings had damaged their relationship, possibly far more than Terry or Gemma had realized.

"Patrick?" she called softly.

He turned and held out his hand. Anne went to him, leaving Carwyn and Brigid sitting near the mast where Tywyll and a young human piloted the ship.

"What is it?" he said, pulling her closer when the cool breeze gusted over the river. "Are you cold?"

"No, of course not. Why does Jean travel in a reefer?"

"He doesn't. At least, not officially. I imagine Terry has no idea this boat is docked in the port."

But her father knew. Of *course* her father knew. Not that he considered it a priority to share information unless someone asked very nicely and followed the question up with gold.

"Do we know how many he might have on board?"

"No, but your father says there are more human guards than anything else."

She sighed. "This seems like a waste of time. Shouldn't we go back to town and help Terry? The Dutch—"

A low rumble sounded from his throat. "Terry knows exactly what to do with Jean if he is the one behind this."

"Rens's brother—"

"If Jean is the one coordinating Elixir shipping in the North Atlantic, Ireland has the first claim. We lost the first vampires and the first humans to Elixir death. Jean Desmarais is mine. The Dutch can take their revenge elsewhere."

Anne stood silent. She knew it wasn't merely vengeance that urged her mate on. It was standing, as well. Ireland had been hit first, and she had the first blood claim. If Jean Desmarais was guilty, the night was going to turn very, very bloody.

DOCKS, in Anne's experience, were never truly quiet. They bustled at all times of night, though she'd become a stranger to them in her time away from Murphy. From the great steam vessels he'd inherited from his sire to the modern oil-fed tankers, he owned some of them all. And though he'd been born on land, the ocean had become his second home.

Jean Desmarais's ship was a midsized reefer, a refrigerated ship ostensibly used to ship luxury foodstuffs like caviar and cheese. Whether it was carrying anything else was the question Murphy wanted to answer.

"Go by the water, lad," Tywyll said, coiling a length of rope around one arm as his young human assistant held the boat steady in the evening chop. "Too many blasted humans on the docks."

"As I don't have anyone here on my payroll, I'd have to agree," Murphy said. "I'll swim over and see what the situation is. Give you the signal if you can approach."

Murphy stripped off his shirt and toed off his shoes before slipping into the black water with deadly grace. Within moments, she saw him at the side of the vessel. With a silent surge, the water beneath him pressed up, lifting Murphy to the lower deck before it sank back into sea. He disappeared for a moment, and Anne knew he was scouting the deck of the ship.

After only a few minutes, he was back, waving to them. Tywyll steered the barge closer, and the young man took a length of rope and tossed it to Murphy, who quickly tied the length to the railing. Brigid was the first to cross, followed by Carwyn scrambling across the rope with unexpected speed. Anne was just about to cross before her father pulled her aside.

"Be careful."

"We're just looking around, Da."

Tywyll's eyes narrowed. "I don't like this. The boat's too quiet-like."

"You worry."

"Aye, about my girls." Tywyll nodded toward the boat. "You and the lad. Yer good, then?"

She nodded.

"And he makes ye happy."

"He does."

Her sire nodded. "He's grown, but he's still got a temper. Mind you, temper ain't a bad trait to have for a long life. Keeps you moving when things look dim. A bit of hot blood never hurt a vampire as long as he knows how to rein it."

"Are we done, Da? I think they're waiting for me."

Tywyll sniffed. "I'm yer da. They can wait."

"Tywyll—"

"I'll wait for ye here. Don't like these big ships none. Don't be long."

MURPHY grabbed her hands and helped her onto the deck. She was barefoot, having left her useless heels back on the barge.

"What's the story?" she asked as they climbed the stairway to the upper deck.

Carwyn said, "Murphy put the deck crew to sleep."

"The bridge?" Brigid asked.

"We haven't gone there yet." Carwyn looked far up at the row of black windows overlooking the deck. The ship had been painted a gleaming white with red trim. The massive superstructure with the bridge on top towered over the now-empty deck.

"Why don't you two check the bridge?" Brigid said. "See if you can find Jean's office. Anne and I will go belowdecks and look around."

Murphy narrowed his eyes. "I don't know—"

"Feck's sake," Brigid said. "Anne's better than either of you at keeping me from burning the place up. You good with going below, Anne?"

Anne paused and thought about it. Brigid would be more than enough protection from anyone who might be a danger to her. They would just have to stick together. And Anne could keep her friend from igniting in the close quarters even better than Carwyn could. Murphy would be able to, as well, but he was also the only one who might be able to decipher any clues that Jean or his people had left behind.

"I agree with Brigid," Anne said. "Murphy, you've got to search the offices. The paperwork won't make sense to any of the rest of us. You'll know what to look for."

Carwyn slapped Murphy's bare shoulder. "I'm with you, then. As soon as we clear the bridge, I'll follow them down."

Murphy gave a swift nod and pressed a quick kiss to Anne's mouth.

"Be careful," he said before he walked behind the bridge and began to climb silently.

Anne and Brigid approached a sealed door.

"Do you know anything about boats?" Brigid asked.

Anne smiled. "It's been a while since I've been on one of these monsters, but I think I can stumble through."

Chapter Twenty-two

MURPHY FORCED HIMSELF TO REMEMBER that Anne was an imminently capable vampire who was paired with one of his fiercest soldiers. His worry must have shown on his face though, because Carwyn slapped him on his shoulder.

"If you're wondering if it gets easier, it doesn't."

"Thank you. That's reassuring."

"She's not a fierce woman like my Brigid. It's not her nature. But Anne is smart. They'll be fine."

There were a few muttered curses when they entered the bridge, but the three humans working were no match for their speed or their amnis.

Murphy grabbed one of the human's mobile phones, pleased that the man had a watertight, shatterproof—and thus fairly vampire proof—case covering it. He gingerly put it on the table and grabbed a pencil, hoping the phone wasn't password protected.

He was in luck.

The screen came to life with the slide of the pencil eraser. Murphy put it on speaker and immediately called Ozzie.

"Yeah, boss?"

"Have you heard from Terry's people? Have they found Jean?"

"The house in Kensington was empty 'cept for a few humans. I ain't heard more than that. I imagine they're still looking. If he's disappeared, that don't look good."

"No," he muttered, "it most certainly does not. Oz, I'll keep this phone close. Call when you hear anything."

"Will do."

If Jean had abandoned the house in Kensington, he could be coming back to the ship. Or he could have other properties in London that Terry didn't know about. Terry and Jean had been doing business for over one hundred years. He likely had a hundred bolt-holes and backup plans.

Carwyn was looking around, oddly quiet.

"Thoughts, Father?"

The other vampire didn't rise to the bait. "Hmm?"

"You're very quiet over there."

"Eh, well…" He shook his head. "It's Jean."

"What about Jean?" Murphy was searching through the ship's log, but nothing looked out of place. He needed to find Jean's quarters or his office.

"He helped us in Rome."

Murphy stopped and waited for Carwyn to finish his thoughts.

Carwyn continued. "Jean… helped break my best friend out of prison. Helped to keep Beatrice sane. I don't just consider this man an ally. He is a friend."

And suddenly, Terry sending Carwyn to help Murphy and Anne wasn't such a mystery. He hadn't done it for Murphy. He'd done it to keep Carwyn away from the ugliness of tracking a friend.

Murphy said, "Sometimes, people do things you wouldn't expect when money is involved."

"He doesn't need money," Carwyn said bitterly. "If he did this, it was because his pride was wounded. Is pride so precious? Is it worth killing over? Worth betraying friends?"

"I betrayed the woman I loved because of pride," Murphy admitted. "I broke her trust. I might have lost her forever, if she weren't so forgiving. Pride is… seductive. Addictive. And a harder habit to break than any drug. So yes, Jean might think Terry and Leonor's slights were worth killing over."

"He *saw* what this did to Lucien," Carwyn said. "And he ships this poison anyway? He has no excuse."

"Carwyn—"

"If he did this, I never knew him," Carwyn said, an edge of steel cutting through his sadness. "If he could lie like this…"

"Come on," Murphy said. "Let's look for proof before we condemn him."

Carwyn nodded, but Murphy knew in his gut that he was right.

Oleg's daughter Zara might have been pulling the strings, but Jean Desmarais had willingly become her puppet.

Chapter Twenty-three

ANNE AND BRIGID WERE CHECKING the holds. Unfortunately, Jean's ship had been fitted with many compartments, not just one larger hold. Some were refrigerated. Some were not. They came across only a skeleton crew of humans that Brigid subdued—mostly with amnis—and stuffed in one of the rooms. If the tiny woman had to rough up a few of the more aggressive crew members, that was hardly Brigid's fault.

"How many more, do you think?" Brigid asked as they climbed down to the third deck.

"I don't have any kind of map," Anne said. "So we'll have to check door-to-door, deck by deck, if we want to search everywhere."

Brigid huffed. "If you were going to transport Elixir, where would you store it?"

Anne laughed. "That's a joke, right? Pallets can be stored—" She broke off when she heard a thumping sound coming from below.

Brigid and Anne both looked down.

"No voices," Anne said after a few silent moments.

"There's no way to keep our steps silent on this bloody boat." Brigid started toward the stairs. "Follow me. Stay behind."

Brigid was about half her size, but Anne didn't argue. She was well aware she wasn't a fighter. She followed Brigid down the stairs and opened the door to the lower deck.

"Keys," Anne said, coming to an abrupt stop and tugging on Brigid's arm. "The crewman who tried to shoot us was wearing keys, but none of the doors so far have been locked."

"Let's go back," Brigid said, climbing two decks up. "If we delay, that might confuse whoever is down there. Confused prey is better than expectant prey."

PILED in one of the equipment rooms under the deckhouse, most of the humans were still sleeping when they returned. A few were waking and confused, so Anne put them under again. Her mental influence with humans was particularly strong.

"Found them," Brigid said, raising a crowded ring of keys.

"Now we'll see what they're trying to hide," Anne said, walking out of the storage room quickly.

There had been something in the crew that had spiked her hunger, even though she'd fed before they met with Oleg at the Cockleshell. She shouldn't be feeling hungry. She hadn't in days. The infusion of Brigid's blood, combined with what she'd taken from Murphy, had put an end to the bloodlust that had plagued her.

But Murphy had taken her blood earlier that evening, and she wondered if she was feeling the effects.

"Anne?" Brigid waited for her in the hallway.

"I'm coming. Sorry."

THE scuffling came from behind a locked door. No voices. But definitely footsteps. It was the only sound in the low-lit passage, despite the doors that stretched into darkness.

"This fecking door…" Brigid had been trying each key without success, but there could easily have been forty on the ring. Anne leaned against the opposite wall, watching her and keeping an eye out for anyone approaching. She wondered how long it would take Carwyn and Murphy to check the bridge.

"Shall I try?" she asked Brigid. "Just to give your hands a rest."

In truth, Anne was worried that Brigid was so irritated she'd break the key off in her hand if she ever managed to turn one.

"No, I'll calm down." Brigid took a deep breath just as there was a creaking down the hall.

Anne turned her head.

It sounded like a door, but she didn't hear footsteps except those coming from the locked room. Freighters were noisy places, and she couldn't swear that it wasn't the normal swell and shift of the metal on the water.

"Anne, stay here," Brigid said, looking over her shoulder

"I'm just going to look. I can see that door cracked open. It's probably just the shifting of the boat."

"Do you think it could be another door to this room?"

Anne looked at the door that had cracked open. "Different number. I doubt they'd be connected. The ones on the deck above weren't. It's probably nothing."

"Stay in the hall where I can see you."

"Yes, mam."

She walked down the passageway, hands braced on either side, enjoying the cool dampness of the air. When she got to the door, she pushed it farther open and peered into the dim compartment.

Anne saw a low light she hadn't noticed when they walked past, but she thought the door must have been closed.

"Do you see anything?" Brigid asked.

"There's a light, but no one that I can see. No footsteps." She angled her head in, trying to get a better look. "The door probably opened when the ship—" The freighter tilted again, and the light illuminated a tiny figure huddled in the corner.

"Anne, what is it?"

"There's a child."

"No!"

Anne heard Brigid's shout a second after she ran into the room, then the door slammed behind her, and Brigid's voice was muffled by steel. Anne turned, expecting a threat, but there was only a slip of a man—hardly more than a teenager—staring at her as he leaned up against the door.

"It locks automatically," he said in a heavy Eastern European accent. "You're one of them. You can help us."

The relief of a mortal opponent fled when she saw the glassy sheen of the man's eyes. Then the figure at Anne's feet threw off the blanket that had been covering it, and a gust of sweet pomegranate permeated the room. Anne's fangs dropped with a piercing rush. Her throat burned. Her gut twisted in acute hunger. Desperate, *raging* hunger, as if she hadn't fed in months.

Oh, Jesus, no. Anne bit back a growl.

"Please," the young man said desperately, holding out both arms, which were littered with angry red bites. "Please, you have to bite us. It's been too long."

"Please," came a small voice from the ground.

The girl clutching her leg couldn't have been more than fifteen or sixteen, but her skin was wan and her hair dull. Bites marked her neck and back where Anne could see the skin.

"Please," she said again. "It is the only thing that helps."

Anne could hear Brigid banging on the door and screaming, but she knew it would take time to open the door. She was caught in the throes of bloodlust, trapped with Elixired humans.

Chapter Twenty-four

IT WAS ALL THERE IN BLACK-AND-WHITE. Jean had been coordinating the shipping for months, at first straightening out the mess of distribution that Zara had entangled herself in since she started shipping the drug, then expanding the operation, moving ships to lesser-known ports that would be lightly regulated by immortal interests.

Jean, being the organized smuggler that he was, had notes in the ledger on every load, along with abbreviations for what Murphy suspected were human carriers.

It was horrifying.

So many more than Murphy had expected. Dozens of ships had left Varna and Bourgas with cargo. Carriers had left from Constanța and Samsun. They had landed in dozens of ports all over the Mediterranean and in the North Sea, showing heavy traffic in the Baltic states. They had not, apparently, been able to dock in Russia.

Carwyn was reading over his shoulder.

"He is dead," the old vampire said. "If you or Terry do not finish him, then I will."

"We need to take this to Terry."

He felt Brigid's scream before he heard it. The heat rushing toward the room was near overwhelming. He lifted a veil of water to the door a second before she burst in. She sizzled as her burning skin ran through the mist, but it seemed to cool her down.

"Brigid, what in hell—"

"Anne is in a locked room with two Elixired humans!"

Murphy's stomach dropped to his feet. "No."

He ran out of the room and down endless flights of stairs, following Brigid's newest scent trail, the burning-hawthorn smell drawing him toward his mate.

He ran, desperate for her.

No.

He skidded past a sealed door and slowed, walking back to it with careful steps. He listened. He opened his amnis and felt for her, drawing the water to his body as he searched.

There.

He was trying to wrench the door open when he heard Brigid and Carwyn make it to him.

"Help me, Father." He put his shoulder into it, but not even immortal strength was budging the locked door. "You can break through this," Murphy said. "I can feel her on the other side."

"Anne!" Brigid yelled. "We're coming for you!"

ANNE heard her friend on the other side of the door, heard her mate and her friend, desperately trying to reach her. She closed her eyes and kept pushing the humans back, but they were relentless. Anne didn't want to hurt them. Or herself.

"Please," the girl said. "It hurts. But when the monsters bite us, it is better. They've been gone and we haven't slept in so long."

The boy said, "The water doesn't satisfy our thirst anymore."

There were empty cans of food and bottles of water scattered in the corner. How had Zara and Jean drugged them? With the water bottles? Had they boarded the ship infected? Anne focused on the questions racing through her mind and not on the seductive pull of their blood.

"Please," the girl said again, reaching for her.

Anne grabbed for both their hands, then she pushed her amnis toward them and both humans fell to the ground, forced into a deep sleep.

But their blood still called her, teasing her senses and promising satisfaction she knew was a lie.

"Murphy," she whispered. "Please."

Anne didn't know how much longer she could hold out. Her stomach ached, but she could live with that. Her fangs throbbed, but she'd felt worse.

The haze that had started to fall over her mind, however…

If she lost control of her senses, she didn't know what she'd do.

She closed her eyes and drew the water in the air around her, bolstering her resistance to the sweet blood the humans had begged her to take from them.

Her mind swam. And Murphy's shouts grew farther and farther away.

"ANNE!" he yelled, his voice hoarse from it. He kicked the door and felt his foot break with the impact.

Brigid had started trying keys again, desperately flipping from one to the next as Carwyn muttered under his breath and looked around at the ship.

"We have to get in there," Murphy said.

Unfortunately, Jean's freighter was spotless, and well-maintained ships didn't tend to break apart.

Carwyn braced his hands on the door, and Murphy felt the metal tremble, but it held together. Not even the thousand-year-old earth vampire could break the door apart.

Cursing Jean Desmarais, Murphy pressed his hands to the metal again, wishing he could control metal instead of water. What could water do to save his mate? Right now? Nothing.

"Fecking boats," Brigid said, blood-tinged tears streaming down her face. "Hold on, Anne. Don't give in."

Murphy spun at Carwyn. "Are you telling me that in all your time on earth, you've never had to break through a ship's door? Or any other kind of metal? Tell me how to get in there, Carwyn!"

Carwyn glanced at Brigid, and Murphy caught the look.

"What is it?"

"Gio could do it. But he's much older than Brigid."

"What are you talking about?" Brigid asked, standing up and brushing hair out of her eyes. "What can Gio do that I can't?"

"Melt the door without killing everyone around you."

"What?"

"Melt the door?" Murphy asked. "Is that even possible?"

"Yes."

Brigid shook her head. "I don't know if I could melt the door without bringing down the ship. My control…"

Murphy's mind spun. "Then don't melt it. Just heat it. If I can cool it fast enough, it'll be brittle. Then Carwyn—"

"You think I might be able to crack it?" Carwyn glared. "That's well and good, but what if Brigid loses control? I told you, she can't—"

"I can!" Brigid broke in.

Murphy could see the stark terror on Carwyn's face.

"Brigid, no."

"I can do it," she said, pressing a hard kiss to his mouth. "I know I can. Now stand back."

Murphy pulled Carwyn away from the door as Brigid stripped her loose shirt and jeans off, leaving her in a thin undershirt and pants. Her pale body glowed in the darkness as she began to gather energy. Her amnis sparked and jumped. Murphy could feel it. Could feel the rigid tension in the immortal behind him.

Brigid's hands were hovering over the door as she yelled. "Anne, stand back!"

The flames came from her palms, red and gold with a swirl of other colors, like a fire opal brought to life. The air filled with the smell of burned hawthorn as the air belowdecks was sucked into the fire. Murphy saw Brigid struggle for control.

A harsh stream of curses came from Carwyn's mouth, but he didn't try to stop her.

"Murphy," Carwyn said from behind him, "step away, lad."

He was transfixed. Murphy had never seen Brigid work with fire. Not like this. It was as if the flames danced along her skin.

"It's beautiful," he murmured.

"Stand back."

The fire centered, focused. It was too hot. The air belowdecks was gone, pulled into the dance of Brigid's flame.

Carwyn shoved him to the side and walked toward his mate, waiting a few meters away.

Murphy tried to yell at him to stop, but couldn't pull enough air to talk. The door was cherry red, but Brigid wasn't stopping. Her face was peaceful, adoring the fire that curled and licked at her skin.

She would burn them all.

No, she couldn't. His heart lay beyond the barrier of that door. Murphy shook his head and reached out with his amnis, trying to dampen the flames, but the water in the air had fled, eaten by the fire. Murphy fell to his knees and felt the metal beneath him tremble and shake. It was enough to break Brigid's concentration, and she turned to look at her mate. Reason returned to her and the fire died back.

Carwyn said nothing, only opened his arms as Brigid ran to him. Murphy heard a swift pop, and the damp sea air rushed back into the vacuum of the corridor. He shook his head, lifting his arms and calling the water to him as he never had before.

He felt for it, and the sea rushed to him, almost suffocating him. It hissed along Brigid and Carwyn's skin and coated his own before he sent it out, directing the damp air to the door, which was still glowing red. It gave a giant whoosh as the corridor filled with steam. The water condensed on the cooling metal around him and he pushed it again, a whipping cycle of steam and water lashing against the door blocking him from Anne.

Carwyn touched his shoulder and pulled him away. "My turn."

Chapter Twenty-five

FIRE AND RAIN. FIRE AND RAIN and blood in the streets. I'm hungry and there's so much blood…

Josie's singsong words echoed in her mind.

Fire and rain. Rain and fire.

Blood.

So much blood.

The humans were huddled against her as the small metal room turned to hell.

She heard nothing but the roar of blood in their veins. She felt nothing but the press of their bodies, begging for her bite.

Anne swam in the heat, surrendering to the pull of death. She cried when the blood slid down her throat, but she kept drinking.

More.

She wanted more.

She drank and drank, but the blood tasted of death. She spat it out of her mouth, but then she bit again.

So much blood.

Her mind went black.

In her dreams, the metal screamed in protest as the ship rocked beneath her. The humans rolled, lifeless in the hold of the great ship, their throats torn by her fangs. Their blood painted her skin and coated her tongue. She smoothed the hot red over her face, painting her body with death.

"Anne!"

She curled to the side, hiding from his voice. She could feel the poison seeping into her. She had to hide.

Urgent hands lifted her, tried to open her eyes.

"Anne, let us—"

She lashed out, baring her teeth even as the room came into focus. She felt cool, watery air wash over her, and her eyes rolled back. Hands caught her before she hit the floor.

"Áine." He cradled her body, but she tried to roll away.

Dirty. The dirty blood was everywhere.

"Anne?" he said again, desperate for her.

Her heart bled. She loved him so much. The sobs tore from her throat, and she pushed him with her mind.

Away. Safe.

"Anne, stop!"

"Why does he keep letting her go?"

"Don't ask, love. Murphy, let Brigid—"

"*Stay away!*" Anne screamed.

The fog cleared from her mind as the damp air coated her body. She felt the blood coating her face. The sickly sweet smell made her stomach roil. She bent over, retching in the corner of the hold, streams of blood pouring from her mouth. She vomited the blackness from her belly, but she could still feel it leaching into her veins, infecting her amnis.

"Let me help her," Brigid said. "Don't you see? She's bitten them, Murphy. She's afraid of infecting you."

There was a roar of rage, and Anne felt her mate's amnis surge to life in her blood. She clung to the clean, bright thread of his energy.

"Anne"—Brigid had a hand at her back—"we need to get you to your father."

Her father.

"Da?" she choked out on a sob.

"Let me help you. My mother's alive, remember? I'll be fine as long as my mother is alive. You can touch me."

"Anne." Murphy's tortured voice came to her, but she pushed him away again.

"Can't," she gasped. "Don't touch me, Patrick. You can't touch me."

She stumbled out of the ruins of the ship and let Brigid pull her up the stairs. She felt the sea around her as soon as she stepped onto the deck. Without another word, she ran to it, stripping from her bloody clothes and leaping into the ocean.

The sea claimed her.

WHEN Anne dreamed, she dreamed of death and madness. Of the deep and of forgotten things. The moon shone full through the water, and the drifting weeds surrounded her as she stared into the night sky. She heard her father's voice, singing Coleridge's poem:

> *Water, water, every where,*
> *And all the boards did shrink;*
> *Water, water, every where,*
> *Nor any drop to drink.*

The water enveloped her. The pulse of the current took her and she drifted deeper.

Past the edge of land.

Beyond the silken brush of reeds.

> *About, about, in reel and rout*
> *The death-fires danced at night;*
> *The water, like a witch's oils,*
> *Burnt green, and blue and white.*

She sank past the touch of moonlight, where the chill of the water crept into her bones and settled her soul.

HE found her in the darkness.

He pressed his hand to hers, though she tried to pull away.

Murphy wrapped his arms around her and lifted her to the surface where moonlight touched her face and bathed her in its cool glow.

MURPHY swam Anne back to the red-sailed barge and lifted her as he would a child. He handed her to her father, who carried her past her friends and belowdecks, where he tucked her under a woolen blanket.

"Sleep, lass," Tywyll's rasping voice commanded. "Ye've had a long night, and we've some longer ones ahead."

"Keep Murphy away. His sire is dead. If I infected him—"

"I'll give ye tonight, but I won't keep a man from his woman, even if she is my daughter. He loves ye, Annie. I won't drive him mad from yer fear. He won't be biting you, I can promise ye that."

"Da, you need to bleed me. Bleed me. Please. Get the dirty blood out."

Tywyll walked over and met her eyes. His face was grim. "I know. We'll start tomorrow night. It's too close to dawn now."

"Did I kill them?"

"Ah, lamb, I saw their bodies." He brushed the damp hair back from her forehead. "They were skin and bones. Ye hastened it is all. The one who killed them was the one who gave them that poison."

"I tore their throats out."

"From what young Brigid said, ye weren't in yer right mind."

"It was Jean."

"It were definitely his boat. At least it was you who found them, not yer man. Like you said, he's not got a sire living." He pressed a kiss to her forehead. "Rest now. I've got to get you lot to shelter. We won't leave the river before dawn."

Chapter Twenty-six

MURPHY WOKE IN A SQUAT HOUSE by the riverbank, the smell of water in his nose and the ache of Anne's absence in his chest. Anne had refused to rest beside him, worried that she could somehow infect him with the blood she'd taken from the humans the night before. Tywyll had guided them upriver before dawn, hiding them in a secluded cottage before he disappeared for the day.

He could feel her.

It was only her blood in him that gave him rest; he could feel her amnis alive within him. When Carwyn had torn into the compartment the night before, it had been the only thing that told him she was alive, though her face was painted red with blood and her body lay limp on the floor. He could feel her now, a quiet hum in his chest.

He wanted to find her. Hold her. His arms ached with the desire to keep her safe.

Someone tapped at the heavy wooden door.

He rose and wrapped a sheet around his waist. He unlocked the door and cracked it open.

"Where is Anne?" he asked Brigid.

"And good evening to you too. She's in her room. Resting. Doesn't want to see anyone as yet. Tywyll showed up at dusk. They're talking about when to start the process."

"The process" being Anne's complete exsanguination, followed by a new infusion of her sire's blood. She would be like a newborn again, though with a shorter time to adapt to vampire life, hopefully. It had worked on most of the vampires who had tried it, though the process itself carried risks. Some vampires who were too far gone into madness didn't wake. Anne was not out of danger yet, though the fact that her sire was already with her was promising.

His mate couldn't die. He wouldn't allow his mind to consider it.

A night's forced rest had done nothing to quell his rage. Jean Desmarais would pay for his crimes against the immortal world, including Anne's pain.

"What's the story from Terry?"

Brigid was silent.

"They still haven't found Jean?"

"Terry found him. But Jean is claiming that Leonor is trying to frame him. Leonor, of course, is denying it, but some of her people are backing him up. Terry's holding both of them at his old offices in the Temple, but it's a mess. He has both the Spanish and French delegations under guard until he can sort things out. It's a political nightmare."

"Utter rubbish." He turned and picked up his still-damp trousers from the night before, then put them on. "Did you and Carwyn go back to recover the ledger?"

"We did."

"Send it with Ozzie. Have him and Carwyn meet me in the Temple. Does Carwyn know where Terry's offices are?"

"Yes." She put her hands on her hips. "And where are you going then?"

"I'm not waiting to get my hands on Jean. I'm taking the river."

"You should stay with Anne."

"I won't face her again without Jean's blood on my hands."

"She wouldn't want it, and you know that."

"*I want it*," he snarled. "Stay with Anne. Do not leave her side until I return. Carwyn can go with me. He saw the ledger and the humans on the ship. No one will doubt his word against Jean's."

Murphy walked out of the cottage without another word, then dived into the river from the secluded dock where Tywyll had dropped them off the night before. He felt the river move around him, muddy and alive. Stretching his senses, he swam upriver, dodging boats and fishes with equal speed until he was swimming in the murkier water of the city. He passed under the glowing lights of Blackfriars Bridge and searched the north shore of the river, looking for Temple Pier. Ignoring the surprised looks from humans boarding a dinner cruise, the shirtless man in dripping wool trousers cut through the Middle Temple Gardens, shaking off the river water as he walked barefoot through the park and into the narrow streets of the Temple.

The front of Terry's offices looked like one of the many barrister's offices in the neighborhood. Only a few knew they sank far beneath the street, providing river access for the vampire lord of London along with being the setting for many of his more infamous exploits. At one point, Terrance Ramsay had held the entire vampire population of London captive under the embankment for night after night as he questioned and executed anyone involved in the death of his beloved sire.

Now the old offices were mainly used for storage, construction...

And very quiet interrogations.

Roger stood just inside the door, but there were no other guards or security.

"Mr. Murphy—"

"It was the Frenchman," he interrupted. "Where is he?"

Roger froze. "Are you sure?"

"As I'm standing."

"Bloody hell of a mess, Murphy."

"Where is he?"

"Downstairs, but Terry—"

"Carwyn and Ozzie will be here within an hour. Send them down. They have the ledger."

Murphy had no intention of waiting for the ledger. He followed his nose down a set of stone stairs, the air growing damp against his skin.

Terry was pacing when Murphy entered the room at the foot of the stairs. Two figures were chained to the wall, both with hoods over their heads. Gemma sat opposite her mate, watching him and the prisoners in turn.

Ah, manacles. They never really went out of style.

"Murphy." Gemma spotted him. "What are you doing h—"

"It was Jean." Murphy walked to the chained vampire, picked up a Taser from the edge of a table, and placed it under the vampire's neck, taking pleasure in watching Jean's body jolt and shudder when he pressed the button. The Taser shorted out, and the water in the air rushed to him as his amnis went haywire, but Murphy drew it to his body, greedy for its elemental power.

He leaned in, not knowing if Jean could hear him or not. "I found your ledger, you greedy bastard."

Terry was fuming. He pulled Murphy from Jean. "You come to my dungeon and—"

"He was keeping drugged humans on his boat, Terry. Anne bit one."

Gemma gasped. "She's infected?"

The rage fell from Terry's face. "Murphy, will she—"

"She's with her father now." He turned and kneed Jean in the balls just to take the edge off some of his anger. "I have questions for this one. But you can let Leonor go, unless she'd like to participate."

Terry walked grim faced to the other prisoner and pulled the hood off Leonor's head.

"Reparations," Terry said immediately. "I did not lay a hand on you. You know I had no choice. But reparations are yours. What do you want, Leonor?"

A furious stream of Spanish met his ears, but Murphy ignored Leonor's enraged shouting. That was for Terry and Gemma to resolve.

He pulled the hood from Jean's head and dropped it to the ground. The vampire was just regaining consciousness. Murphy reached up, grabbed Jean's pinky finger, and yanked, pulling the digit from the screaming vampire's hand without warning.

"You crazy bastard!" Jean yelled.

"Cormac isn't here, but you took his left arm at the elbow," Murphy said calmly. "That leaves four more fingers, a hand, and two bones in your forearm before I start dealing anything you haven't served yourself."

The vampire's pale face grew paler as his blood rushed to the wound to begin healing it. "You're insane."

"No, I'm livid," Murphy said. "It's quite different, Jean. Shall we list your other kills? Let's name them, starting with Rens and working backward."

Jean's eyes were glassy, but he said, "Murphy, I don't know what you think you know, but—"

"Rens Anker, vampire. Andrew Garvey, human. Victoria Mansfield, vampire. Sarah Leeds, human. Jason Stanton, human."

Murphy continued, naming off every human and vampire name he could remember who had lost their lives to Elixir.

"Paul Mason, human. Dory Mason, human. Alexander Mason, vampire." He took out the knife he'd strapped to his ankle and began to cut Jean's shirt from his body, carefully slicing the crisp cotton away, leaving the vampire's chest bare. The water was drawn to him, but Murphy pulled it back, fierce with rage.

"Anabeth Vargas, human. Destiny Renner, human." The names tumbled from his mouth. Murphy hadn't even realized he remembered so many victims. It was as if they whispered to him as he stood over their murderer.

Dillon McCaffrey.

Cristina Leon.

Otto Smith.

"Emily Neely," he said, naming the first known victim of Elixir poisoning. Brigid's friend. A girl raised under his protection.

The first child who had wasted away.

The first parents who had lost their trust in him.

The first funeral, but not the last.

"Murphy, I have not done this to your people," Jean said. "I swear it. Whoever killed Rens—"

"We found your ship, Jean. Found the humans. You should know better than to think you could hide anything from the old man."

"I don't know what you're talking about," Jean said. "My boat is moored—"

"We know you're working with Zara. Arranging her shipments for her."

"Murphy, this is madness! The assassin was Spanish! The housekeeper, Portuguese. Clearly, Leonor is behind this. Even her own people—"

"Shut your bloody mouth!" Murphy took a deep breath and said quietly, "I found your ledger."

Jean fell silent.

"I recognize your writing, Jean. I watched you take notes in meetings. Signed contracts written with your own hand. A hundred letters of correspondence…" He stepped closer and leaned to Jean's ear. "You condemned yourself, old friend. As you condemned a thousand others. Including. My. Mate."

Defeat flickered behind Jean's eyes.

"Murphy," Terry said, "it's not that I don't trust you, but I need to see that ledger."

"Carwyn is bringing it in."

For the first time, Murphy saw something other than pompous rage cross Jean's face.

"How does it feel?" he asked. "Betraying a friend like that? Turning your back on those of your race with honor?"

Jean's lip curled, and he looked at Terry. "You speak of *honor*? Was it honor when he stole my human from me? That the Spanish bitch did, as well?"

"If you treated your people better than cattle, they wouldn't have been tempted," Terry said. "And nothing I did can excuse poisoning humans and vampires as you have."

"Admit it," Murphy said, dragging the tip of his knife across Jean's abdomen. "We both know you're not going to live much longer."

Jean's face went slack. "The Elixir was Zara. I never produced it."

"But you shipped it, didn't you?" Murphy said, gripping Jean's chin. "Zara knows how to run a port, but she doesn't know how to smuggle, does she? She doesn't know what ports to use. What people to contact. That was all you, Jean."

"I never meant to hurt Anne."

"You pathetic bastard." Murphy spat the words at him, hating that his mate's name even crossed the traitor's lips. "What did Zara promise you?"

Jean said nothing, so Murphy reached up and twisted off another finger as the vampire started screaming again.

Murphy turned to Terry. "Soundproof?"

"Very."

"Good."

Leonor was watching Murphy's interrogation intently.

"I have no quarrel with you," he said.

She nodded regally. "Nor I you, Patrick Murphy. I am in your debt for revealing the truth of this deception." The Spanish leader looked down her nose at both Gemma and Terry. "I have nothing to say to you."

Gemma said, "You'd have done the same thing to us if the situation were reversed."

"No," Leonor said, "I would have done worse."

Murphy turned back to Jean, who was limp in his shackles. "What did she promise you, Jean?"

"Spain."

"*Madre de dios,*" Leonor swore. "This Zara promised you *my territory?*"

"The whole point was to frame you," Jean said, clearly understanding that survival was no longer an option. "I would step in and take over the Iberian Peninsula, giving Zara control over Gibraltar and a direct route to North Africa."

"Between the Bosphorus and Gibraltar, she would control the entire Mediterranean," Terry said. "Everything except the Suez."

Jean laughed bitterly. "Oh, she has plans for that too. Why do you think Rens is dead?"

"Why?"

"Why not? She likes power. Laskaris wants to take control of Athens from his brothers and sisters, and she wants to help him. Elixir was their opportunity. If she can screw her sire in the process, all the better."

"All this"—Gemma stepped forward, nudging Murphy to the side—"because we bested you in business?"

"You cheated me out of billions, Gemma!"

"It's *money*," she said. "We're immortal. We can always make more *money*. We lose fortunes and find them in the space of a single human lifetime. Money is a game, Jean. But I treated you as an ally. A friend. I welcomed you into my home. I celebrated with your children." Gemma bared her teeth and yelled, "What have you done, you fool?"

Gemma drew a dagger from her pocket and stabbed him in the heart. "That is for poisoning Anne."

She turned and walked back to Terry, who enfolded her in a hard embrace.

"Tell me more about Zara," Murphy said. "Who else is she working with?"

Jean shook his head, and Murphy reached up, tearing off another finger.

"What do you want?" the Frenchman screamed. "I don't know, damn you! There's someone in Germany, but I don't know who. She supplied the Russians in California. She has plans for North Africa. She hates Oleg and thinks she has some way of toppling him."

"And what does she plan to do with Russia?" Leonor asked from the corner.

"Nothing!" Jean let out a sobbing laugh. "Don't you understand? Zara loves chaos. She would topple Russia, sit back, watch Oleg's lieutenants fight for it, and laugh."

Terry said, "And this is who you align yourself with?"

"I *thought* I was dealing with Athens."

"But you weren't?"

"They told me…" He grew quiet until Murphy reached up and ripped off another finger. "*They told me they had fixed it,*" he screamed. "They told me it was safe."

"But even after it became obvious it wasn't," Murphy hissed, "you still kept shipping it."

"She would have killed me if I stopped."

Murphy bent down and looked into the dead man's eyes. "Who is in charge? Is it Laskaris and the Athenians? Or is it this Zara?"

"I don't know anymore." Jean's head rolled to the side. "Please, Gemma," he begged her, "will you speak for my children?"

"Jean," she said, shaking her head. "I don't—"

"How many years did I shelter Rene?" he asked. "When your man threw him out of England, I welcomed him. Me. I am a friend to your brothers. I do not ask for myself. I ask you to intervene for my children. They had no part in this."

Gemma glanced at Murphy.

"Jean, I… I'll see what I can do."

He smiled through bloody lips. "*Merci, ma chérie.*"

The vampire begging for his children undid Murphy, and the taste of blood grew sour in his mouth.

She wouldn't want this.

Anne would have been disgusted by this. Murphy's rage seeped out with his enemy's blood, falling to the stone floor and trickling toward the river.

"I will find everything," he said, stepping close to Jean. "And if any of your children are involved, I will kill them myself."

"She's making it in Bulgaria. Laskaris knows; he doesn't care. He thinks they can control the spread of Elixir. He thinks that this will subdue humanity. The humans will exist to serve us or die painful deaths."

"Dear God," Gemma breathed out.

"Exactly," Jean said. "Laskaris thinks he is a god. And like any god, he wants to rule."

"And Zara?" Murphy asked.

"She controls him? He controls her? I thought I knew, but I don't know anything anymore." He met Murphy's eyes. "Kill me. Take revenge for your people and your mate. I would do the same. But kill me before the priest comes. Tell him... *je suis désolé.*"

Murphy stared into the eyes of Jean Desmarais and realized the vampire was already dead.

And he had someone to return to.

He reached up and twisted Jean's neck to the side, sickened by the quick snap and slump of the vampire's body. Then he grabbed Gemma's dagger from Jean's heart and finished him with a quick slice across the back of his neck, severing his spine and leaving his corpse shackled to the wall.

Without a word, Murphy left Gemma, Terry, and Leonor, tracking the sound of the water as it lapped against the sides of the underground tunnel nearby. He followed the gentle noise and the scent farther into the black passage, knowing instinctively that even though the darkness became deeper the water would lead him back to her. And when Murphy found the river, he dove in and let it wash him clean.

Chapter Twenty-seven

SHE WATCHED HIM WAKE. And for the first time in her memory, her mate did not wake with a gasp, but with a whisper.

"Áine?"

"I'm here."

He released the breath he must have been holding. "Thank you for not kicking me out."

"I would have if I'd been conscious. I'm not hungry at all, but I'm sleeping so much earlier."

It had been six nights since Murphy had returned to the cottage by the river. Six nights since Jean's blood had been spilled. The word had gone out to both of the Frenchman's victims that justice had been meted out, though the Dutch were making noises about seizing Desmarais property in Marseilles, much to the consternation of Paris, which was already claiming territorial rights. Murphy, having killed Jean Desmarais, had the right to claim his territory, but Anne knew her mate had no interest in splitting his interests by claiming part of France.

Gemma was doing what she could to protect Jean's children, but none were old enough or strong enough to hold their sire's city. They would have to seek protection elsewhere.

More importantly, word was spreading aggressively about any ships coming from Greek-controlled ports on the Black Sea. Inspections were increased. Elixir was seized.

Sadly, so were more human carriers.

But among the infected humans, there had been found a few anomalies whose health had not been infected. Humans who showed no sign of sickness and were eating regularly. Among the victims, the vampires fighting Elixir had found a thin thread of hope.

Murphy rolled over and put an arm around Anne's waist, nuzzling his face into her neck. "If I promise not to bite you, will you let me stay?"

Anne tried not to tense, but she was terrified of infecting him.

"Murphy, your sire is dead."

"I know."

"If I infected you—"

"I have three living children," he murmured. "It's not as quick, but treatment from offspring's blood has also proven effective. And it's about time that lot proved their usefulness. But it doesn't matter, because I'm not going to bite you while you're infected. You're going to the doctor Gemma found. He's going to perform the procedure, your father will give you new blood, and you will be fine."

Anne knew nothing was guaranteed, but she didn't protest. She needed to believe she would live as much as he did.

"Do I smell wrong?" she asked.

"You smell *good*," he groaned, licking her neck.

"Don't!"

"I won't." He kissed her neck and pressed his body against hers. "I understand the lure of it though."

"I hate that it works," she said softly. "For the past few nights, I've woken feeling wonderful. No burn in my throat. No hunger. The relief, Patrick... I can't describe it. If it wouldn't make me go mad—"

"Hunger I can handle. Your losing your mind, I cannot."

"I'm sorry," she whispered. "I wish I'd been stronger."

His arm tensed. "I will not have you blaming yourself."

"You wouldn't have bitten them."

"I don't know what I would have done, and neither do you. I wasn't there. I have not struggled with bloodlust my entire life. I wasn't faced with the prospect of two addicted humans begging for my bite while I was locked with them in a small room."

"You would have been stronger."

"Perhaps I should blame myself," Murphy said, turning her to face him. He held her chin between his fingers, forcing her to meet his eyes. "Perhaps if I'd paid better attention to you, I would have known you were struggling. I would have looked past my own bloody ego, and I would have fed my mate. Should I blame myself for denying you my vein?"

"Of course not!"

"This was Jean's fault," he said. "Not yours. Not mine. Jean's."

"And Zara's."

Murphy paused. "Is she as unbalanced as everyone says?"

"I only know from what Oleg has said, but you heard him at the pub. From everything I have heard, I would likely diagnose Zara with severe antisocial personality disorder with narcissistic tendencies. Though obviously I have not examined her, nor do I have any plans to do so."

He smiled.

"What?"

"I love your clinical voice," he said. "Have I told you that? It makes me want to provoke you and make you lose your temper."

"And you *like* that?" Men, she decided, were a mystery.

"I do." He pulled her across his chest while his hands went down to cup her bottom.

"Making sure my bottom is still there?"

"Yes." He gave it a gentle pat. "Do you want to know my favorite part of your being a vampire?"

"Eternal youth?"

"No."

"No worrying about suntans?"

"No, I'd say we worry more about the sun than the average human."

"Good point. Is it..." She lifted her head, resting her chin on his chest. "Having a partner in immortality? A lover to walk through this endless night at your side? A mate who adores you?"

He kissed her forehead. "Those are all very, very important, my love. But my favorite part"—he gave her backside a squeeze—"is that while you might swim a thousand miles... this beautiful arse will never get any smaller."

Anne burst into laughter, surprised and delighted that her mate—a proud, strong, sometimes-vicious vampire—was still more than a bit of a scoundrel.

And she loved him for it.

HER arms and legs were strapped down, and the lines running from her arteries, though the taps, as she jokingly called them, had not been pulled. Murphy was on one side and her father was on the other in the cold white room.

Murphy curled his lip as he looked around. "Wasn't there a better place to do this?"

Gemma's physician raised an eyebrow. "Did you want to pour ten pints of infected blood down the sink in a five-star hotel? Where did you think we were going to exsanguinate her?"

She squeezed his hand. "It's fine, Patrick."

"It's a morgue, Anne."

Tywyll sniffed. "She ain't gonna die. What're ye worried about?"

"I'm fine."

He looked over his shoulder at Carwyn. "You're sure?"

"Lucien sent very detailed notes. As long as the doctor and Tywyll follow his instructions, everything should be all right."

"And the donor blood is ready?"

"They're standing by. She won't wake until tomorrow night anyway."

Murphy smoothed a hand over her forehead. He'd already insisted on a hospital bed instead of the usual metal table. Then he'd replaced the institutional sheets with a higher thread count and put a down pillow behind her back.

"Patrick?"

He frowned. "Hmm? Are you comfortable enough? Shall I get you—"

"I'm fine. Kiss me."

She could see his fussing for what it was. Even though they had a plan, even though the human doctor was present along with her sire, he was still worried. He'd been the one to reassure her the night before, now it was her turn.

She grabbed the end of his tie and pulled him down for a soft kiss. "I'm going to go to sleep, *a chuisle*. Just for a bit. And then my father will give me his blood and I'll sleep some more. Then I'm going to wake up, and I expect you to be there."

"I will be."

"I also expect chocolate. And possibly a bottle of very good wine."

A small smile broke through his anxious mask. "So noted, Dr. O'Dea."

"Shall I keep making demands, Mr. Murphy?"

"Not unless you want to embarrass your poor da."

The human doctor and Carwyn both laughed, and her father squeezed her hand.

"Let's get on with it, then," he said. "And lad? Be prepared for her. I'm older than the first time I sired her."

"What does that mean?"

Carwyn patted Murphy's shoulder. "Older sire, stronger amnis. It means she'll truly be kicking your arse this time around."

Murphy locked his eyes with hers. "I'm counting on it."

"Do it," she said.

Anne felt the soothing brush of her father's amnis on one side, her mate's on the other, then the almost imperceptible tug of her blood leaving her body. Her amnis spiked, rushing over her skin until her sire and mate calmed her. Anne's mind clouded as the minutes passed. There was a clock ticking on the wall. An odd hum coming from the next room. Soft voices and whispered questions surrounded her.

Seconds dragged into minutes dragged into…

A shallow breath soughed through her lips.

Was death so quiet when he came for her again?

She thought she heard an old lullaby her mother had sung when she was a babe. But when she listened closer, she realized it wasn't her mother, but her sire. Tywyll's reedy voice surrounded her as she sank into the deep, his energy a gentle blanket over her.

Anne closed her eyes and died.

"NO!"

"Step back," Carwyn told him, pulling at his shoulders. "Murphy, you're going to break the bed."

She was gone. *Gone*. Her amnis, the glowing life within him, had gone dark. Her face was slack, her skin almost translucent.

For long minutes, he'd felt it fading, but he'd held onto it, held onto the thread until…

Gone.

"Anne!" He clutched at Carwyn's arm as the other vampire forced him to a chair and away from her body. "Let me go!"

"She's not gone." Carwyn brushed a hand over Murphy's hair as the pain exploded within him.

It hurt.

Physically. Mentally. Murphy's heart ached with the lack of her. The sound that came from him was a groan of rage and pain and loss. A dying sound wrenched from the depths of his soul. Carwyn held him by the shoulders, the vampire's ancient bulk the only thing holding him back.

The human physician removed the lines running from Anne's thighs, arms, and neck.

"It's done. I cannot remove any more."

"Tywyll?" Carwyn asked. "Do you have her?"

The old vampire leaned over his daughter, ripping open his wrist with his own fangs, holding her limp body in his arms as he tilted her head back and forced her mouth open.

Thick red blood dripped into her mouth, but Anne's lips did not move.

Murphy felt the gathering rage. "Carwyn…"

"Hold, lad."

Each second was an eternity. Anne's father stroked her neck, working the blood into her system, forcing more down her throat even as Murphy saw the color draining from his face. Carwyn snapped at the doctor, who opened the ice chest he'd brought with him and tossed Carwyn a bag of human blood.

He handed it to Tywyll, still keeping a wary hand on Murphy. "Drink."

Tywyll bit into the cold plastic with a grimace, but he did not move his wrist from Anne's mouth. He kept ripping open the wound to feed her again.

After a dark eternity of minutes, Murphy felt it.

The first creeping tendrils of energy snaked from her body toward her sire. Her neck arched imperceptibly, and her mouth fell open as bright fangs grew in her mouth.

A snarling noise came from her throat, and she latched onto Tywyll's wrist, biting hard into the old man, who wrapped an arm around her back and smiled.

"There's my girl," he said, brushing the hair back from her forehead. "There's my Annie girl."

Murphy let out the breath he'd been holding, and his shoulders slumped.

She was back.

ANNE woke with a burn in her throat. She felt Murphy at her side, helping her to sit, holding a glass to her lips.

Ambrosia.

She gulped down the first glass, then the second. Fresh blood. Cool, but still pulsing with life.

Three glasses.

Four.

"Keep going," he murmured, stroking her back. "There's plenty more, love."

Anne felt some spill over her lip. "Murphy?"

He kissed her chin, lapping up the spilled blood and kissing her stained mouth quickly before he pulled away.

"I'm here."

She felt her fangs lengthen and ache. She wanted to bite. Wanted to suck. Wanted to sink her teeth into his neck. His chest.

Anne pulled him closer, throwing her leg over his.

Murphy chuckled. "Someone woke hungry. Take a break now. You can drink the rest at a slower pace."

"Want you," she rasped. "Need…"

"What do you need, love?"

"*Bite.*" A wave of her amnis spiked outward.

"Well, that hasn't changed. Careful now," he murmured. "Your influence is a lot stronger than it used to be."

Murphy pulled her closer, letting his amnis meet hers. A wave of his desire and longing. He was as naked as she was. His body had been the one warming hers in the darkness. His arms had been her armor.

"Murphy?" Her voice came out high and needy. She pressed a hand to her belly. "Please."

"Shhhh," he murmured, drawing her head toward his neck. "I was worried. You were out for two nights, not one."

She scraped her fangs along his neck, drawing a thick red line that made his back arch.

"Bite me now," he commanded, pressing her mouth to his neck.

She bit, and the rich taste of his blood only stoked the fire growing in her. She pushed him back, sliding her body down his until she could feel the hard length of his arousal pressing against her.

"Yes," he hissed. "Now. Take me."

She slid down, hungry for him to fill her as she drank from his vein. Murphy wrapped strong arms around her and rocked, pressing a hand to the small of her back to control her movements, gripping her hip as she began to come.

Their loving went on for hours, but her hunger was not sated. Anne hungered for and feared his bite, still uncertain that her blood was clean.

"No," she said, pressing him back when he kissed her throat.

"Anne—"

"Wait for me," she begged him. "Make sure it's safe. I couldn't bear it if I hurt you, Patrick." Her emotions ran wild, and the tears slipped down her face. "Please."

He kissed her, sliding his tongue against hers in a luxurious caress.

"I'll wait," he said against her lips. "For you, I'd wait an eternity."

Epilogue

Six months later

MURPHY STRODE THROUGH THE OFFICE, ignoring Angie, who was asking him to sign papers about… something.

Something far less interesting than what he held in his hands.

"Patrick, you have got to stop and—"

She almost ran into him when he came to a halt in the hallway. He spun and grabbed her hand, kissing the back of it before he lifted it high.

"This is fecking brilliant!"

Angie's mouth dropped open, and he pressed a quick kiss to her forehead. His smile was laughter and wickedness all at once.

"And we're going to make a fortune."

"Patrick, the Reedley papers. They're ready for you to review before the final signatures."

He waved a hand toward his office as his eyes went back to his new toy. "Fine. Just… set them on my desk and I'll— Wait! No." He did a small dance in the hallway. "E-mail them to me, Ang." He held up the electronic tablet in his hand. "I have a PDF reader."

"Oh," she groaned. "You're going to be as bad as the young people now. Christ help us if you get a mobile phone."

"That's next!"

Murphy kept walking. He had to show Anne.

He took the stairs two at a time down to street level and walked the few blocks to her office, glad that he'd had the foresight to buy the small building. It was close enough to easily secure, but far enough that her immortal clients still felt comfortable visiting.

Part of what he'd predicted had come to pass. Anne didn't have as many immortal clients since she'd publicly taken her place as his consort. But there were still plenty of vampires who trusted her. Many who were not active in politics didn't care if her offices were in Galway or Dublin. And her human patients cared even less.

He tucked the precious tablet under his arm and whistled as he walked down the sidewalk, glancing at the clock—a digital clock!—on the front of the screen to check the time. It was late, and he was hoping to catch her between clients. Or, if he was very lucky, she'd be done for the night and he could tempt her home.

He'd heard the good-natured teasing among his men, but he ignored it. Murphy wasn't a regular at the club these days, though he made a point to come in every now and then to keep everyone on their toes.

What could he say? Home had become infinitely more interesting once Dr. O'Dea had taken up residence.

He pushed through the door and spotted Anne's very efficient assistant, Holly, holding up a finger, which meant his mate was with a patient.

"What's that you have there, Mr. Murphy?" the girl asked in a subdued voice.

Murphy smiled and held it up. "First prototype of a new device."

"Oh, how clever." Holly's eyes lit up. "How does it work, then? You don't break it at all?"

"Not so far." He pulled a chair over and began showing the girl the different features, including the case made out of a new type of nonconductive polymer.

She humored him. The young woman was the daughter of one of his software engineers and had recently graduated from Trinity. No doubt

Holly had something far more sophisticated at home, with a much sleeker case. Murphy didn't care.

It *worked*.

"That's brilliant, sir. I have to admit, I can use the keyboard regular, but I do prefer the voice software you gave me. It's very convenient."

"What do you like the best?"

Nothing like a little market research to pass the time. He might send Declan around to question the girl more. The Nocht software had been in testing for four months within their organization. Combined with the tablet, Murphy and Declan were hoping that it would give vampires a smooth platform for running most home computer programs, security systems, and mobile applications. It wasn't perfect—far from it—but it was a start.

"What time did her patient get here?"

"Oh, I don't know if she's strictly a patient. Dr. O'Dea said you had a meeting with her and her husband later tonight. I think they might be getting acquainted is all. She asked not to be disturbed."

As if on cue, the door opened, and two laughing women exited. One was human, clearly pregnant from both her scent and her appearance. She had curling red hair that looked right at home in Ireland, though she spoke with an American accent.

"Murphy!" Anne said with a smile. "Are you finished with work?"

He held up the tablet. "It works."

She clapped her hands together, grinning as she held out her hands. "Show me!"

Murphy hid it behind his back even as he bent to kiss her cheek. "You have a guest, love."

"Sorry, yes." Anne didn't look sorry; she looked happy. "I'm a very bad politician."

"But an excellent hostess," the American said, holding out her hand. "You must be Patrick Murphy. Thank you so much for meeting with us. I'm Natalie Ellis, Baojia's wife."

He took her hand and shook it. "My apologies. I didn't expect to meet you until later this evening."

ELIZABETH HUNTER

"I have to thank Anne for indulging me. Our oldest son is two, and he is not the best about going to sleep away from home. Combine that with jet lag…" She rolled her eyes. "My husband is attempting bedtime while I make myself scarce. If Jacob sees me, all bets are off. I called Anne, hoping to find someone to hang out with at this time of night."

He put an arm around his mate, who promptly swiped the tablet.

Murphy laughed and said, "I hope your accommodations are comfortable."

"They are, thank you. Carwyn and Brigid are awesome hosts. And Brigid's Aunt Sinead has Jake completely charmed. We might end up stealing her and taking her back to California."

It was unusual for vampires to have families, but not unheard of, especially if they took human mates. It wasn't biologically possible for immortals to breed, but modern technology had proved helpful in some areas.

Murphy's nosiness about the arrangement grew from pure curiosity. Baojia's deadly reputation had crossed oceans. It was hard to imagine the vicious killer coaxing a small child to bed. Murphy wondered if Baojia had remaining blood relatives or whether his children's biological father was anonymous.

None of his business really, though it did make him grateful that his mate was already immortal.

There were no tests for Elixir in the bloodstream, but Anne's appetite was as voracious as a newborn. While that caused its own set of problems, especially since blood restrictions were still in place, it did reassure them that the transfusion from her sire had been effective. If Elixir had still been in her system, a lack of hunger would have been the first symptom.

"I don't suppose," Murphy said, "that you can tell me why Baojia requested a visit?"

Natalie opened her mouth, then closed it. "I think I need to leave that to him. I try not to poke my nose into official business *too* much. I can say I think it'll be welcome news. I tagged along because I've never been to Ireland. Well, and my husband has a hard time letting me out of his sight while I'm gestating."

Anne blinked. "I suppose he would."

"Is your family Irish?" Murphy asked. She certainly looked it with her red hair and smattering of freckles.

"My dad was, but a long way back. I'm from Northern California."

"It's a beautiful part of America." He reached over and grabbed the tablet from Anne. "My toy."

"Greedy."

"Declan made one for you too."

Natalie leaned over. "That's really a working tablet?"

"It's a prototype," Murphy said. "But it's looking very promising."

"My husband will be green with envy." Natalie paused. "You won't be able to tell, because he'll be making this face." She held her expression perfectly still, with a slight frown between her eyebrows. "But he will be."

Murphy smiled and decided that a vampire who could charm the witty Ms. Ellis was probably a vampire he would enjoy knowing.

"Holly, can you close up the office and call Ozzie?" Anne asked her assistant. "We'll be heading out."

They waited on the sidewalk in the misty Dublin air until Ozzie's familiar profile came into view behind the wheel of the black sedan. He pulled to the curb, and Murphy helped both ladies into the car, taking special care with Natalie, who was more than a little off-balance with her pregnancy.

"When are you due?" he asked. "With... the child?"

"This little pipsqueak is six months along," Natalie said, patting her belly. "So she'll be born in early spring. Then this will be it. We've got fang-related plans after that."

Anne asked, "When the children are young?"

Natalie sighed. "That's the somewhat constant source of debate in our household, but I doubt you want to hear about that."

Anne promptly changed the subject. "We've heard good things from California. Lucien seems to have encouraging areas of research."

Natalie nodded. "The blood samples taken from those humans in Gibraltar got him really excited. Something about vaccines and antibodies?"

Murphy and Anne exchanged a glance. A vaccine sounded promising.

While various pharmaceutical companies around the world were quietly researching a cure for Elixir in vampires, Lucien Thrax was the only vampire to Murphy's knowledge who was targeting a cure for humans. Baojia, whom Murphy would be meeting with later that night, was chief of security for his research facility. Thrax's reasoning was that if the Elixir could be cured in humans, then the vampire infection problem would take care of itself. Cured humans meant a safer blood supply.

Of course, that still left the problem of detecting infected blood.

But if humans were vaccinated, initial infection might not even occur.

They were heading out to Carwyn and Brigid's home well after any traffic clogged the roads, so they arrived in quick order. Pulling up to Carwyn's grand estate made Murphy wonder if Anne found their smaller home lacking.

"Why are you frowning?" she asked, slipping her hand into his.

"Do you want a larger home?"

"No, why?"

"I just wondered."

"I like your place now that you've made room for my things in the closet."

It still grated. Maybe he'd buy them a new place just so she could have her own closet. His had been so perfectly organized...

Anne asked him, "Do you have any desire for children?"

"I don't. Not the mortal variety that requires nappies, anyway. You?"

"I raised four brothers and sisters when my mother died. That was more than enough for me."

"I can't blame you for that. Come," he said, tugging her hand. "Let's go meet the assassin with the toddler."

As it happened, they met both the assassin *and* the toddler once Carwyn's butler had let them in. The vampire was pacing in the downstairs hallway, a tiny, dark-haired boy clinging to his chest. Baojia was of medium height and build, though Murphy could detect the quick energy of a lethal predator even as the immortal held the vulnerable child.

Then the assassin spun toward them, and Murphy realized the vampire was even more dangerous than he'd expected. He had never seen eyes that cold. This was why whatever law governed their unnatural life had decided that his race could not breed. While Murphy was dangerous, he suspected nothing was deadlier than this creature protecting his young.

The man's eyes turned toward his mate and softened just enough to lower the tension in the hallway.

"I tried," Baojia said, voice low. "There were five stories, three songs, and two glasses of water. He refuses to go to sleep."

Natalie winced when the small child's head popped up. The baby turned and held out his arms.

"Mama!"

"Wide awake." Natalie sighed, taking the baby. "I blame the father and uncle who wake him up at all hours to play."

"You know the solution to this," Baojia said, crossing his arms over his chest.

"I don't like it when you do that. It's not natural."

"Neither is traveling in a giant plane across the ocean, my love. Please." He walked to Natalie, cupping her cheek with his hand and kissing her mouth. "*Please.*"

"Okay…" Natalie held out the little boy, whose cap of dark hair was mussed and who rubbed his eyes stubbornly. "Night, baby." She kissed his cheek as the child started to fuss.

"Come here, little man," Baojia said, brushing a hand over the top of his son's head and down his back, resting his palm under his pale green T-shirt. "You're going to feel much better right about… now."

In seconds, the child was snoring.

Anne laughed. "You used amnis!"

Natalie shook her head. "That still feels like cheating."

A true smile spread across Baojia's solemn face. "But it's so *quiet*."

"Here," Natalie said, "give him to me. I'll put him to bed while you guys talk."

She took the small child, and Murphy looked away while the pair exchanged a tender kiss and a few quiet words.

Assassin and human might have been an unlikely pairing, but Murphy could feel the connection between them. It was like a banked fire, its heat no less intense for its quiet.

Anne took Murphy's hand and led him into the drawing room off the entryway where a fire had already been lit. Winter was approaching, and the chill in the old house reminded Murphy why he preferred modern construction. He was just pouring drinks for Anne and himself when Baojia entered. The man paused, then extended a shallow bow.

"I apologize for my informality earlier. I am Chen Baojia, lieutenant of Katya Grigorieva of San Francisco. I thank you for your invitation and welcome to both me and my family."

Murphy could appreciate this formal side of the soldier. He returned the bow and said, "You are welcome. I'm pleased to make your acquaintance. Terry speaks very highly of you."

Baojia said nothing, but he nodded toward Anne and took the seat across from her. "Thank you, also, for welcoming my wife. Though she has little trouble making friends, I am glad you were able to meet with her earlier."

"Natalie is a very interesting woman," Anne said. "I enjoyed our visit."

"Not that I don't enjoy conversation," Murphy said, "but can I ask why you are here?"

"Of course. And thank you. I am not overly fond of political small talk." Baojia took a thin folder from his jacket, no larger than the size of a billfold. He placed the leather folder on the table between them and opened it, revealing what looked like a testing kit of some kind. There was small meter with a needle-sharp prong at the base, an empty tube, and three small bottles of different colored liquids with droppers in them.

"Is that a testing kit?" Anne said.

"Yes."

"For blood sugar?"

"That's where we got the idea," Baojia said. "But it doesn't test sugar. It tests for Elixir."

Murphy froze. "How?"

"Lucien has isolated the protein in human blood that he believes Elixir attacks and mutates. This testing kit targets that protein. The testing fluid with tainted blood will turn bright blue if any mutated protein is detected."

"And how accurate is this?"

They knew that humans who'd taken Elixir smelled like pomegranate, but a smell-test was hardly the most accurate, even among vampires.

"Preliminary results are promising."

Anne said, "I hear a 'but…'"

Baojia smiled. "But we're hoping you can help with that."

"How's that?"

"As a country, Ireland has the highest number of Elixir cases we've seen among our allies. While our testing in California has been productive, we simply don't have the necessary sample size to test it further."

Murphy took a moment, taking a sip of his whiskey while inside he was leaping with much the same excitement as he'd had over Declan's new tablet.

"What is Katya asking for?"

"Numbers, mainly." He spread his hands. "Access to the humans you have here, and safe passage for Lucian's crew while they're working. We know you have a dedicated medical facility for infected humans, which is the other reason Lucien wants to test here. The trial kits will be yours, and you'll receive discounted pricing once the tests go to market if they prove to be successful. All we need is your permission."

Anne took his hand and squeezed it. Murphy nodded. There was nothing to lose, and only knowledge to gain.

"You can tell Katya permission has been granted. You're familiar with Brigid?"

"I am."

"Coordinate with her and my first lieutenant, Tom Dargin, when the time comes. They'll be able to work out the details with you."

"I'll make sure to meet with them tomorrow evening if that works with their schedule. I have a call with Katya and Lucien before then."

Murphy nodded, still staring at the tiny kit.

It could change everything.

Anne leaned forward and touched the edge of the table.

"He's isolated the protein," Anne said. "Does that mean... Is he close to a cure?"

Baojia said nothing at first, but Murphy could see the barely contained excitement in the black eyes of their visitor.

"Officially? We're still researching all avenues of study in human and vampire Elixir infection."

Murphy said, "And unofficially?"

"He's close."

MURPHY lay in bed that night with Anne at his side and the water of the Liffey River close enough to lull him to sleep.

"*A chuisle mo chroí,*" he heard his mate whisper. "You are the pulse of my heart, Patrick Murphy."

He rolled toward her, eyes half-closed. "Does that mean my restriction is lifted?"

"Not... yet. But maybe soon."

Anne was still wary about Murphy taking her vein. In the six months since she'd been infected, she'd shied away every time he came close. It had frustrated him at first. Then it had angered him, and they'd had more than a few vicious fights.

But then Murphy realized that Anne was petrified at the thought of any lingering Elixir in her system affecting him. She feared harm coming to him more than she feared his anger.

So Murphy had taken a deep, unnecessary breath and decided to let it go.

She would give him her vein when she was ready. He was no more or less her mate because her blood no longer lived in him. His blood lived in her, and even if it hadn't, it wouldn't change their devotion. They were tied on so many other planes than just the physical.

Murphy cupped her cheek, brushing his thumb over the swell of it, glad of her. So very glad to be sharing his life with her again.

"If I am your pulse, Anne O'Dea, then you are my heart. You move me. You center me. You make me a better man."

She curled into his side and held him as he drifted toward sleep.

"Are you trying to make me fall in love with you again, Patrick?"

"Every night, love. Every single night."

The End

Continue reading for an exclusive preview of
A Very Proper Monster
the next novella in the Elemental World

ELIZABETH HUNTER

Available Fall 2015 as part of
Beneath a Waning Moon:
A Duo of Fantasy Novellas
By Elizabeth Hunter and Grace Draven

Dublin, 1886

My dearest Miss Tetley,

Enclosed you will find the final draft of Viviana Dioli's "The Countess's Dark Lover," a story within which you will no doubt find numerous additional faults. Signorina Dioli turns an indifferent profile to you, her harsh editor. I'm afraid she simply cannot find it in her cold heart to remove the balcony scene and subsequent mortal fall. Gothic romance so rarely comes to a happy end. And after all, what would your actions be when pursued by the grim monster Warwick was revealed to be?

As for your other inquiries, rest assured I am no better or worse than last I wrote. If I am completely honest, Sarah, I seem to be in some terrible stasis. The physicians know I am not so foolish as to hope for a cure, nor am I morbid enough to welcome my inevitable end peacefully. So I trudge on, writing my stories, traveling to visit sea air when possible, and worrying about Father. No doubt, you've heard of his own failing health. I know he wrote to your dear parents only last week, and I do hope he was frank. He is not well.

I have no worries about his businesses, for he has spent the last few years affixing the most competent men in positions of authority. But my own failing health, combined with his inevitable retirement, means that he does worry about the continuance of his legacy. Shaw Mills have employed hundreds, but the boat works are poised to be entirely more impressive than the mills. And you know, for your father has the same honorable bent, how much the well-being of those many men and women weighs on his mind.

Would that I were a healthy son!

But alas, then I would have been forced to turn my head to business instead of literature of questionable moral value, and the world would have been robbed of Miss Dioli's and Mister Doyle's brilliance. (You know, of course, that I speak in false pride, for my own wit does amuse me too much.)

While I wish that my cousin were of a mind to manage the businesses in good temper, I fear he is not. Neville eyes my every discreet cough with a kind of manic glee. Or is it my own morbid fascination that finds his expression so? I confess, I am not impartial, having never liked the boy. I like even less the man he has become.

I do believe that Father will seek to sell if his health shows no sign of improving. There are more than a few eager speculators, but he will sell only to someone who sees the boat works as he does. Not only industry, but the realization of a dream. If he could find an honorable man to carry on that legacy, I believe he would happily sell.

For now, my dear Sarah, think of me and the dark depths of madness I must plumb to write this next horrible tale. I do say that living in Miss Dioli's fanciful (if morbid) mind makes your friend a far pleasanter companion for poor Mrs. Porter. While Mister Doyle's terrible imagination provides more pennies per word, he does take a terrible toll on the household staff. There will be no living with me, I am afraid, until this next monster has been exorcized on the page.

Wish me happy ink stains, Miss Tetley. No doubt you will see the beginnings of horror, though not the ghastly results, within the next fortnight.

Yours always,
Josephine Shaw

TOM DARGIN WATCHED MURPHY reading the report Declan had drafted. Tom didn't want to rely on the numbers alone, but the report, combined with his own discreet inquiries about how Shaw ran his businesses led him to believe his sire was making the right move pursuing Shaw's boat works.

"I like all of this," Murphy said, raising his head. "The mills and the boat works are both profitable. Tom's reported that the whole lot is well run and his workers even like the man. Foremen have naught to say against him. So why are there rumors he's looking to sell?"

"Health," Tom said. "That's what some are speculating. He's gettin' on and his health isn't what it was. That's the rumor, anyway."

Murphy frowned. "And no children?"

"A daughter," Declan said. "Josephine Shaw. But she's consumptive. Rarely seen out in society, not for the last five years. There's a nephew, but they're not close."

"And a sick daughter means that a son-in-law is hardly likely," Murphy mused, rubbing his chin. "Has he said anything publicly?"

"No," Tom said. "Though it seems pretty common knowledge among his foremen. Beecham's sniffing, as are a few human investors."

William Beecham, the vampire lord of Dublin, would be happy to pounce on the struggling company. They'd have to tread very carefully.

"Has Shaw a manager?" Murphy asked.

"He did, but the man was hired away." Tom tried not to let the smile touch his lips. "I believe by one of Hamilton's works in Belfast."

"That bloody woman," Murphy said. "Why am I not surprised? At least it wasn't Beecham. Buying the place with manager in place would be a hell of a lot easier."

"It would," Tom said, "but I can see two or more of the men I inquired about rising to the position if given the proper incentive. Shaw hired lads for brains, not just strong backs."

"Smart," Declan said. "What do you think, boss?"

Murphy tapped his pen for a moment, fiddling with the new watch fob that his mate Anne had given him. Tom wished the woman was there that evening, but she was visiting a friend in Wicklow that week. Murphy always made up his mind quicker when Anne was around.

"He won't be going for money," Murphy said. "Or at least not only money. He has no son. These businesses are his legacy."

"Agreed," Tom said.

His sire could have acquired Shaw's assets through mental manipulation, like many of their kind did. It was a point of honor for Murphy that he didn't, and one of the reasons Tom had been so keen to join his former student in immortality.

It wasn't as if Patrick Murphy needed the old boxer at his side for fighting advice anymore. But Patrick Murphy could be a little too trusting, in Tom's opinion. He needed a bruiser at his back and Tom had been happy to volunteer, even if it did mean having to feed on blood once a week or so. He missed the sun, but if he was honest, he'd been living the last years of his human life at night anyway, hustling through Dublin and even over to London with Murphy, trying to scrounge enough money with fighting to make it worth the blood.

Now, the blood came from donors and Murphy was the one in charge. At least, that's what it looked like to outsiders. For now, Murphy, Tom, and Declan presented themselves as brothers to mortal society. No one questioned their connection. In time, they'd have to adjust.

"If Shaw is truly looking to sell, he will want someone who'll invest more than money," Tom continued. "Someone who cares about the workers. That's my take, anyway."

"Agreed," Declan said.

"No harm in calling on the man," Murphy said. "We've already been introduced. Perhaps I come to him asking about improvements for my own millworks…"

Tom nodded. "Show him you're the kind who cares. A boss willing to invest for the long term."

Declan said, "Plus, he might have something to help with the dust problem in Whitechurch."

"True." Murphy set his pen down. "Declan, write up a letter, will you? Ask Shaw for a meeting next week if he's amenable. Let's see if John Shaw is a man willing to work with creatures of the night."

THE meeting had been six months coming, at least, and Tom had watched Shaw deteriorate in that time. The once-robust man had grown wan and pale as Tom and Murphy's respect for the human grew stronger.

"You know," Shaw said. "I spotted your intentions in our second meeting Mr. Murphy."

Murphy smiled. "And yet you kept meeting me."

"It's the same kind of tactic I would have used when I was young," Shaw said with a drawn smile. "Of course I kept meeting with you."

Shaw was a hell of a businessman, but Tom approved of the core of honor in the man. When he'd been human, he would have felt privileged to work for a man like John Robert Shaw.

"And so," Murphy said more quietly, "we come to the sticking point. I want to buy the factories, John. You know that. What I need you to know is that it's not just about the money to me. I respect what you've done. I'm no Englishman to see only the profit in them. I see what the boat works have the potential to do for Dublin. For the whole of Ireland."

"I know." Shaw took a sip of his whiskey and Tom noticed his hand trembling, just a little. "I've made a study of you, young man. And while there are some... curious things rumored about you, I know a good man when I see one. I like your wife. I like your brothers. You're a man who understands family."

Tom cocked his head. Shaw talked more than a little about family, which made the relative secrecy around his own something of a mystery. It was well-known he had a daughter, but Tom had never seen her. Neither had Murphy. She was a mystery. One that Tom Dargin couldn't help but wonder about.

"Family is very important to me," Murphy said.

"And me." Shaw dabbed at his brow. "I had this all planned and now I find myself nervous to speak of it. Perhaps I'm absorbing some of Jo's fancy after all."

"Jo?" Tom asked from the settee. Shaw has asked both Tom and Declan to join Murphy and him that night for a drink. Tom felt as he always did in company, like the prized ox that had been accidentally let into someone's parlor.

"My daughter, Josephine." Shaw took a deep breath. "As I imagine you have heard, she is not well. She has been unwell for years, despite the efforts of numerous physicians."

Tuberculosis, they called it now. Consumption his mam had said. If the disease had progressed as far as rumors said, there would be no cure for Josephine Shaw, and Tom could see the knowledge in her father's eyes.

"Your own health," Murphy said cautiously. "You fear you are deteriorating."

"I *am* deteriorating. And faster than my daughter. She will be alone."

Tom knew Shaw was worried about his daughter's protection after he died. Those with consumption could linger for years. And while she might not hurt for money, a woman without a family to protect her was still at risk to be taken advantage of.

Murphy said, "Her family—"

"She has little to none. She has friends—good friends—but mostly in England where she went to school. Her cousin should be the one to care for her, but Neville has little interest in anyone but himself, and he will be furious when he learns that I am looking to sell the businesses. He expects to inherit."

Tom's ears perked, and he vowed to keep an eye on Neville Shaw. A disappointed would-be heir was nothing to trifle with. The quicker Shaw sold the whole works to Murphy the better it would be for everyone. Let Neville become accustomed to disappointment while his uncle was alive to manage him.

"Mr. Shaw," Murphy said. "If you are concerned about your daughter, you needn't be. You have met my wife. Mrs. Murphy is a generous woman, both of heart and attention. And I'm sure Miss Shaw has inherited her father's good sense. My family would be happy to count your daughter a friend, as I have come to think of you as a fri—"

"She doesn't need a friend, she needs a husband," Shaw said abruptly.

The whole room fell silent.

Murphy stammered. "John... I say, I'm already married."

"And you've two brothers who aren't."

Tom glanced at Declan, who looked closest in age to Murphy. His eyes were the size of saucers. Declan knew Tom's taciturn demeanor and scarred face, hardly made him husband material, especially for a young woman of not yet thirty. Tom glued his lips shut. Let Murphy talk them out of taking on some consumptive spinster. He was the one with the silver tongue.

"John, wouldn't it be wiser to—"

"She doesn't think she needs a husband," Shaw said. "Has always resisted any attempts at matchmaking. Says she'd only be a burden. Foolish girl." Shaw's whole face softened. "She has been the delight of my heart. She deserves any happiness I can give her."

Tom saw Murphy trying to tread carefully. "If the young woman doesn't wish to be married, then wouldn't it be more prudent to find a reliable companion for her as she declines? Anne's and my offer of friendship remains. We are more than willing—"

"If one of your brothers marries Josephine, then it settles the whole business, don't you see?" Shaw said. "You will be family. There will be no one to contest your purchase. There will be no one to wrest Josephine's fortune from her if she takes a turn. An employee cannot protect her from unscrupulous relations, Mr. Murphy. You know that." Shaw's face grew even paler. "The moment I pass from this world, the vultures will circle, particularly my nephew."

"How sick is she?" Tom asked quietly. "I don't mean to be indelicate, sir, but you may be seeing too dire a circumstance. Your daughter could very well—"

"Her last doctor said that she could expect two years," Shaw said. "At the most."

Shaw looked at Murphy, then at Declan sitting quietly beside him. "Two years, young man. Surely any honorable gentleman understands my concern as her father. It would be nothing to give her two years. She is educated. Independent. And when she passes—"

"Mr. Shaw," Declan interrupted. "While I am sure your daughter is a most pleasant young woman, I do not know her, nor does she know me. Surely she would not consent to this."

"She would if you charmed her," Shaw said. "As if all of Dublin doesn't know of the Murphy brothers' charm! Surely, Mr. Murphy, you could persuade her. I would not try to hide my machinations, of course. But she's a practical girl, my Jo." Shaw grimaced. "When she wants to be."

Tom's mind was racing. Courts could be unpredictable, especially when it came to issues of inheritance. And Beecham was always sniffing around Murphy, watching the younger vampire with jealous eyes. He would use any excuse—manipulate any connection—to thwart Murphy, though he couldn't do it openly.

Shaw was right. If Declan married the Shaw heiress it solved everything. Murphy would buy Shaw's businesses without argument. Shaw would be seen handing over the reins to his daughter's new family. Not even Beecham would be able to manipulate Murphy's claim to the boat works.

And when the girl died... it wasn't as if she didn't have a fortune of her own. In away, marriage to the Shaw spinster would mean they were getting Shaw's businesses for little less than the cost of a wedding and care for a consumptive.

But Declan looked like he was steps away from execution.

Ninny.

Murphy saw the terrified look on Declan's face and leaned forward. "John, as much as I want to buy your factories, I cannot force my brother—"

"I'll do it," Tom said quietly. "If Miss Shaw would consent to marry me, I will marry her."

Every shocked eye turned toward Tom.

"But only if she consents," he said again. "I won't force the girl or put up with having her coerced. From what you've said, Miss Shaw has little enough time left without her being miserable in a marriage she doesn't want."

Murphy's mouth was gaping open. Declan finally took a breath. And John Shaw was smiling.

"Good man," Shaw said.

Tom nodded, uncomfortable being the center of their attention. "Don't be too certain she'll accept me. She's the one who'll have to look at this ugly mug every night."

"Tom," Murphy said. "You don't have to do this. Shaw, I promise we will ensure your daughter—"

"It's little enough, Murphy." Tom glanced at Shaw, interrupting his sire before he could offend their host. "Little enough to ensure the protection of a young woman. I'm no prize. But if she'll have me, I'll have her."

Murphy looked at Tom a long time until Tom looked his sire in the eyes and nodded. Murphy's shoulders relaxed and he turned to Shaw. "John, why don't you talk to your daughter first. We can wait to have my attorney draw up the paperwork. Perhaps you could arrange a dinner sometime this week so my brother and your daughter could meet. I think we'd all like to meet Miss Shaw."

"CHRIST, Tom. Did you have to go and offer for the spinster?" Declan stormed into the room while Murphy and Tom were throwing back a pint of ale. Declan had stayed behind talking to Shaw's family solicitor.

"Did you have to act like marrying the woman was such a torture?" Tom asked. "You'd have thrown the whole deal off with your clumsy excuses, Dec."

His brother pointed at him. "You've no business marrying the girl. Sure, we can fool Shaw and avoid the daylight when we do business with him, but have you thought about the consequences of trying to fool a wife? She'll have a staff. Servants. What the hell do you think you're going to do?"

"Be very careful," Murphy said. "This is Tom, Declan. Who's more careful than Tom?"

Tom didn't feel very careful, and for the first time in thirty years he wished he could taste the sweet oblivion that liquor had once brought him. For the first ten years of immortality, it had haunted him. He still had all the same reasons to drink with none of the relief alcohol once afforded.

When he finally turned his mind to controlling the base urges that had driven him as a human, he found some peace. Now he was voluntarily taking on the care of a wife. A sick wife. He had no business taking care of anyone, much less a sick spinster.

Murphy looked at him with an expression that told him he could hear all of Tom's doubts rising to the surface.

"It'll be fine, Tom," his sire said. "If you need to, you can touch her mind. Or have Anne do it. She has the most control."

"Jayzuz," Declan groaned. "What's Anne going to say? She'll have your head for this, Murphy."

"She'll not," Tom said. "I'm the one that put us all in this by offering. I'll tell Anne."

None of them wanted to anger Murphy's mate. She was the glue that held their small family together. But Tom knew she'd be keen to protect a vulnerable human woman, even if it meant inconvenience for the rest of them for a couple years. Anne had a soft heart.

"I'm going out," Tom said, placing his glass carefully on the bar in Murphy's office.

"I saw some of Beecham's crew on the way here," Declan said. "Be careful. They're sniffing."

Murphy had taken the space near the docks because Beecham never dirtied his fine leather shoes by the waterfront. Their crew could operate with some amount of discretion there, away from the finer eyes of Dublin immortal society and the corruption of its lord.

And Tom's upcoming marriage might blow that all to hell.

"Don't think of it," Murphy said, reading Tom's mind. "We always knew that we'd attract attention with a move to take over Shaw's boat works. There was no avoiding this. Marriage to the Shaw girl won't make that any better or worse."

Declan shrugged. "At least she's not popular in society. She won't have to explain your lack of social graces. I inquired discreetly after you both left. The woman is practically a shut in. Twenty-eight years old, but her health started failing soon after she came out in society. Most of her education was in England. She maintains correspondence, but hardly leaves the grounds unless she's going to their house by the sea for her lungs. Very few callers. No one mentioned her looks, which means she's plain. Probably dim, too. Otherwise, she'd have an offer of marriage, even if she was on the edge of death, solely for her fortune." Declan laughed. "Probably more than one."

"She went to school," Tom said, already feeling protective of the lady. "I highly doubt any daughter of Shaw's is a dullard. Besides that, how do you know she hasn't had an offer? Shaw said she'd never wanted a husband. Said she was 'independent.'"

He found himself admiring her for it, even though independent might have been polite society code for foolish and stubborn. As long as the girl had her wits, Tom wouldn't be miserable. He could respect a stubborn woman. He was no pushover himself.

"Why don't we all withhold judgement until we've met the woman?" Murphy said. "If she's anything like her father, I'd expect her and Tom will get along well. The details can be worked out in time. Tom, take your walk if you've a mind, but keep an eye out for Beecham's lads."

"Will do, boss."

Tom left the warehouse, slipping down the back alleys along the river and heading south toward the Shaw's fine house on Merrion Square. He had a mind to watch it. From what? He didn't know exactly.

He wasn't in any kind of rush, so he stretched the walk out for an hour or so, plenty of time for most of the city to fall asleep. Tom liked the quiet. He was a quiet man, and always had been, even in human life. It was hard enough to avoid gathering notice when you were over six foot tall and built like a brick wall, as his mam had told him. He was only ever going to be a brute with size like that.

It was pure luck that he'd fallen into boxing as a human. More luck that when his own body had started to give out, he'd run into the brash young Traveller who needed coaching and a companion to watch his back. Tom Dargin had thrown in with Murphy within weeks of meeting the young man, seeing in him the kind of luck that Tom had always admired and never captured.

And now he'd be marrying a proper society woman, if that woman would have him.

Wasn't life unexpected?

He lurked across the way from the Shaw house, surprised by the number of lights still on. Comfortable in the shadows, he crossed the main thoroughfare on the north side of the square and walked down a side street, curious to see if the Shaw's garden was accessible. He wanted to know who was awake. Who would be using gas lamps so late at night? Surely not one of the servants. Was it old Mr. Shaw himself, worried about his company and his failing health? Or perhaps it was Miss Shaw unable to sleep or discomfited by her illness.

Either way, Tom was curious. And a curious Tom was a stubborn thing.

He walked across the muddy road behind the house where delivery carts had left deep grooves in the mud. A light mist was falling, and he drank it in, replete with the surge of power it lent his amnis. Unlike Murphy, who preferred fresh water, Tom felt most at home near the sea. But any water would do. He'd never been a particular man.

Following the lights led him past numerous walled gardens until he finally arrived at the back side of the stately red brick Georgian home belonging to John Robert Shaw. It was handsome, but not ostentatious. Respectable, but not ancient. He'd watched Shaw exit the front of the house more than one night, but he'd never investigated the gardens. Declan may have looked through the Shaw books, but it was Tom who gathered information on the ground.

That night, Tom Dargin scaled the garden wall and dropped into another world.

Far from the well-tended, orderly garden he'd imagined from Shaw's tidy appearance, this garden was a wild tangle of trees and flowers. Statuary hid among rocks that were tumbled artfully around the base of trees, giving the dark garden a fantastical appearance. A miniature glass house lit up the center of the lawn, sparkling from the inside with candlelight. Tom felt as if he'd slipped into one of the fairy stories his grandmother had been fond of telling.

And standing in the center of a lush lawn, dressed in a white dressing gown was a tall woman, as willowy as the trees that lined the garden. She stood, swaying a little, her pale skin touched by the moon's silver light as she held a book in her hand and turned in place. Her feet were bare, her dark hair fell past her waist, and her long gown was drenched in the evening mist.

It must have been Miss Shaw. No servant would have taken a book out into the garden in the middle of the night. Certainly not in their dressing gown.

"'But dreams come through stone walls...'" She held up the book to the moon's light and spoke quietly, though his immortal hearing could pick the words. "'...light up dark rooms, or darken light ones, and their persons make their exits and their entrances as they please, and laugh at locksmiths.'"

Then she twirled on the lawn, lifting the book over her head and humming a tune as her hair caught and lifted.

"Dreams come through stone walls..." she whispered into the night as Tom watched from the dark shelter of a drooping willow.

"Oh, feck me," he muttered under his breath, letting out a sigh. "She's mad as a March hare."

For more information about this and other future releases, please visit: ElizabethHunterWrites.com

Acknowledgements

Many thanks to the wonderful professionals who make my books presentable.

Thanks to my lovely and talented developmental editor, Lora Gasway, who has been such a pleasure to work with. I am addicted to your notes. (Though Saulo is cursing you from his dark, watery grave.)

Many thanks to the excellent Anne Victory, a gem among copy-editors, who sticks with me, despite my flagrance disregard for proper comma usage.

A sincere thank you to the wonderful team at Damonza.com, who create such beautiful covers for my books, often with very vague references to work with.

To Jane Dystel and Lauren Abramo, my agents.

To Genevieve Johnson, best assistant in the world and super-organizer extraordinaire.

To my wonderful Irish beta readers who helped me figure out my "arse" from my elbow in this book: Sharon Murphy, Carmel Behan, and Sarah Darcy.

And to my writer friends who make this all so darn fun, Grace Draven, Colleen Vanderlinden, Penny Reid, April White, Killian McRae, Michelle Scott, and more that I'm forgetting I'm sure.

Thank you all so very much.

ELIZABETH HUNTER is a contemporary fantasy, paranormal romance, and contemporary romance writer. She is a graduate of the University of Houston Honors College and a former English teacher. She once substitute taught a kindergarten class but decided that middle school was far less frightening. Thankfully, people now pay her to write books and eighth graders everywhere rejoice.

She currently lives in Central California with her son, two dogs, many plants, and a sadly empty fish tank. She is the author of the Elemental Mysteries and Elemental World series, the Cambio Springs series, the Irin Chronicles, and other works of fiction.

Website: ElizabethHunterWrites.com

E-mail: elizabethhunterwrites@gmail.com.

Twitter: @E__Hunter

Made in the USA
Las Vegas, NV
20 March 2024

87510222R00189